"You tell me the bond madness has begun. You refuse to let me try to heal your soul in order to prolong your life, and less than five chimes later, you're thinking about mating?"

White teeth flashed in a rueful smile. "I am your *shei'tan*. No matter what other thoughts may occupy my mind, the idea of mating with you is always among them."

When she did not respond to his humor in kind, the small smile faded, replaced by sober, unflinching honesty. "There is enough sorrow and danger in our lives. I am the Tairen Soul. Even without the bond madness, how long we will have together in this life has never been certain. Mage Fire or a *sel'dor* bolt could take me in the next battle. Would you have us spend what time we have bewailing our fate or would you rather we drink every drop of happiness we can from each moment we have together?"

Her spine wilted. He was right. Their lives could be cut short at any moment. How could she waste even a moment of the time they had now mourning a future that might never happen? Tears shimmered in her eyes. "Rain . . ."

"Shh. *Nei avi.*" He cupped her face in his hands and kissed her tears away, then took her mouth in a sweet, slow, tender kiss that robbed her of all regrets. When he pulled back, his lips curved in a slow smile, and in ancient, courtly Feyan, he said, "So, *shei'tani* . . . wilt thou swim with thy beloved in a river of dreams?"

C. L. WILSON

QUEEN of SONG And SOULS

TAIREN SOUL

LEISURE BOOKS NEW YORK CITY

A LEISURE BOOK®

November 2009

Published by

Dorchester Publishing Co., Inc.
200 Madison Avenue
New York, NY 10016

Cover art by Judy York
Cover handlettering by Patricia Barrow
Map by C. L. Wilson
Text design by Renee Yewdaev

ISBN 10: 0-8439-6060-4
ISBN 13: 978-0-8439-6060-0
E-ISBN: 978-1-4285-0758-6

The name "Leisure Books" and the stylized "L" with design are
trademarks of Dorchester Publishing Co., Inc.

Printed in the United States of America.

10 9 8 7 6 5 4 3 2 1

Visit us online at www.dorchesterpub.com.

To Alicia Condon. Thank you, from the bottom of my heart, for everything: the late-night phone calls, the brainstorming, the long, tireless hours you spent helping me make this book the best it could be. Most of all, thank you just for being there. I couldn't have done it without you. *Ve sha beilissa te eiri.*

Acknowledgments

As always, thanks to my friends and family who've helped me with this book: Karen Rose, Betina Krahn, my sister Lisette, Elissa Wilds, my mom Lynda Richter, and my daughter Ileah. If I have forgotten anyone, it's leaky memory, not lack of appreciation!

Thank you to all the wonderful readers who submitted poems in my poetry contest. I'm especially grateful to the authors of the poetry included in *Queen of Song and Souls*: Sigrid Robinson, Janet Reeves, Ishshka Rubert, Suhad Saleh, Bridget Clarke, Asia Bey, and Jessica Julian. It is an honor to include your beautiful verse in this book. Thank you so very much for enriching the world of Eloran with your talent.

Thanks to Judy York, the cover artist who brought Eloran to life with her artistic talents. Judy, this cover is the bomb!

Last but not least, thanks to my dad, Ray Richter, the computer programming genius who became an overnight Web site guru on my behalf.

For My Readers

Thank you so much for picking up this book! And thanks to everyone who sent me the wonderful letters of encouragement in what has truly been one of the most stressful and challenging years of my life. Your support means the world to me.

Thank you for your continuing interest in Rain and Ellie's journey. As you know, the Tairen Soul series is now a quintet, so look for the fifth and final book, *Tairen Soul*, coming soon from Leisure Books.

Be sure to visit my Web site, www.clwilson.com to sign up for my private book announcement list, enter my online contests, and scour the site for hidden treasures and magical surprises. I hope you linger a while to learn more about the Fey and the Fading Lands—as well as other Fey tales and C. L. Wilson novels coming soon.

I'd love to hear from you. Please, send me a Spirit weave. Or, if you prefer, you can take the non-magical route and just e-mail me at cheryl@clwilson.com.

QUEEN of SONG and SOULS

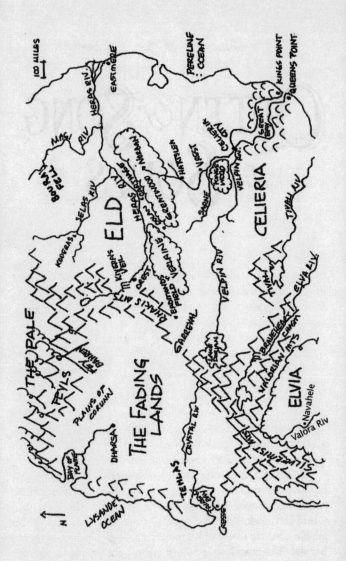

Celieria ~ The Garreval

She was only nine years old, and she was going to die.

Lillis Baristani clung to her beloved friend, Earth master Kieran vel Solande, and showered his throat with frightened tears.

Around them the world had gone mad. Magic, blades, and barbed *sel'dor* arrows filled the air. Blood ran red on the ground. Below, at the base of the Rhakis mountains, dozens of vile, snarling, monstrous wolf-beasts called *darrokken* were charging up the slope towards the small, fleeing party while the creatures' evil masters flung globe after globe of blue-white Mage Fire to cut off all chance of escape.

Whatever the Mage Fire touched disintegrated on contact . . . not dissolved . . . simply disappeared. Entire chunks of the mountain evaporated in an instant. The ground shifted and shook beneath Kieran's feet.

"Kieran!" his friend Kiel shouted, pointing uphill. "The mountain!" Another frightful barrage of Mage Fire had dissolved half the peak above their heads. The remaining rock and stone gave a rumbling shriek and collapsed, sending a wall of dirt, stone, and wood rushing towards them.

"Hold tight, little one," Kieran whispered. Lillis tightened her arms around his neck, pressing so close that her kitten, Snowfoot, mewed a protest and squirmed in the sling tied round her neck. Kieran turned to raise both hands and she felt the electric tingle of his gathering magic. It danced across her skin like crackling sparks of green light. Inside her, Lillis's own magic rose in response.

She squeezed her eyes shut and pressed her face to his throat. *Bright Lord, please help Kieran,* she prayed. *I don't want him to die. Or Papa, Lorelle, Kiel, or me either.*

She felt the vibrations of Kieran's throat against her lips as he shouted defiantly and flung out his weaves. The magic left him—and her, too—in a great rush. *Please, gods, please gods, please, gods.*

Incredibly—or, perhaps, miraculously—the crumbling mountainside froze. Lillis risked a glance up to confirm that they were not about to be crushed flat as a griddle cake, then squeezed her eyes shut again.

"Five-fold weaves, my brothers!" Kieran shouted. "Keep that scorching Mage Fire off us!" Suddenly, he gave a grunt of pain, and Lillis felt him falter. Her head lifted, and though the battle raging all around terrified her, she forced her eyes open.

Kieran was arrow-shot. The sight of the ugly black, barbed metal arrow puncturing his thigh made her belly lurch.

«*Get down, Lillis,*» his voice murmured in her mind. «*Run to your father. Kiel and I will hold them off.*»

«*But what about you?*» It was the first time she'd ever spoken to him mind-to-mind. «*You're coming, too, aren't you?*»

«*In a chime . . . once Kiel and I deal with these Eld rult-sharts.*» From a face too handsome to be mortal, his normally laughing blue eyes regarded her with unsettling solemnity, and then she knew what he would not say. He turned his head to press a kiss to her face, then another to the thin arms wrapped so tight around his neck, and though he did not release his hands from his weave, she felt the tug of Spirit fingers prying her grip loose. She fought to cling, but her childish muscles were no match for his magic. Her hold on him lost, she slid to the ground. «*Go, kitling. Quickly.*» Another nudge from invisible hands shoved her towards Papa.

"Master Baristani," Kieran cried aloud to her father, "take the girls. Go with the *shei'dalins* into the Mists! Run!"

Clutching Snowfoot to her chest, Lillis stumbled across the uneven ground towards Papa's outstretched arms and the small knot of scarlet-gowned healers. Before she reached them, a darting flash of darkness caught her eye and a foul odor filled the air. She turned to find a *darrokken* rushing towards her, its red eyes glowing like the Dark Lord's flames, venomous saliva dripping from its yellowed fangs. All over the foul wolflike creature's scaly back, sores oozed green, odorous slime. She turned to run, but her foot caught between two rocks and she went down. Snowfoot still clutched to her chest, she hit the ground hard. Knees and elbows took a nasty crack, and she bit her lip so hard her mouth filled with the salty, metallic tang of blood. She jumped to her feet, but pain shot out from her ankle, radiating halfway up her shin. With a cry, she fell down again just as the *darrokken* lunged.

One of the Fey warriors made a sprinting leap towards her, and scarlet-hilted Fey'cha daggers flew from his hands. The razor-sharp blades cut through the monster's tough, leathery hide, and the *darrokken* dropped dead in its tracks.

"I've got you." The warrior who'd killed the *darrokken* reached for her arm, but before he could grab hold, another of the monstrous beasts was upon him. Its fangs sank into his leg, and the Fey toppled, rolling over as he fell and landing with unsheathed blades in his hands. "Run, child," he cried.

Those were the warrior's last words. He bared his teeth in a snarl and plunged his red Fey'cha into the vulnerable belly of the beast just as the monster snapped its sharp yellow fangs around the warrior's throat and ripped. Blood sprayed across Lillis's face in a hot, red rain. Fey and beast died together, fighting, tearing, and slashing until the last breath of life left their bodies.

"*Lillis! Get up! Run!*" Kiel cried. His blue eyes were filled with fear, his blond hair spattered with dirt and blood. Two black arrows stuck out of his shoulder like grotesque spines. "Run for the Mists. Lorelle, Master Baristani—go!"

One of the *shei'dalins* in their party rushed forward to grab Lillis. A rapid healing weave spun out in golden-tinted waves of color, and the pain in her ankle subsided. The woman helped Lillis to her feet while another took Lorelle's hand and began to run towards the shifting, sparkling clouds that guarded the Fading Lands. More *darrokken* rushed up the mountainside and dove into the middle of the small group. Lillis shrieked as the monstrous wolf-beasts slaughtered half a dozen more Fey and drove three of the *shei'dalins* back down the mountain towards the waiting Eld.

When she reached the edge of the Mists, Lillis turned back to watch the battle below. The remaining warriors guarding their escape were falling fast to the ferocious maws of the *darrokken*, while the Mages continued bombarding the mountainside with their devastating magic. A tide of Fey warriors burst from the Mists-filled pass of the Garreval and raced across the ground at lightning speed, swords flashing silvery bright in the sunlight.

Black Eld arrows turned day to night, and hundreds of Fey went down. Kieran fell with them.

"Kieran!" Lillis shrieked as she watched him fall. "*Kieran!*" She started to rush towards him, but the *shei'dalin* grabbed her and held her fast.

"*Nei*," the veiled woman whispered. "You cannot go to him. He would not want it. He dies so you may live."

With unexpected strength, the *shei'dalin* shoved Lillis towards the shifting radiance of the Faering Mists. "Quickly, into the Mists. It's our only chance."

Lillis struggled against her hold, squirming and flailing as the tears poured down her face. She screamed Kieran's name again and again as the *shei'dalin* dragged her away. Before they'd gone more than a few steps, the mountain gave a groaning rumble that escalated to a deafening roar.

Kieran's Earth weave collapsed and the entire mountaintop caved in, sending shards of shattered rocks, splintered trees, and a wave of earth crashing towards the valley below. The ground beneath Lillis's feet fell away, and with a wail she toppled back into the shining white abyss of the Faering Mists.

Her last sight was of Kieran, screaming defiance as the avalanche enveloped him.

CHAPTER ONE

Fading Lands, Faering Mists.
Fey warrior, champion of Light.
Fading Lands, Faering Mists.
Leading a never-ending Fight.

Tairen Soul: Singing, soaring high.
Tairen Soul: Thundering, roaring cry.

Fading Lands, Faering Mists.
Fey warrior, fiercest of Fey.
Fading Lands, Faering Mists.
Alone, leading the way.
                    Fiercest of Fey, by Corvan Lief, Celierian Poet

Celieria ~ Orest
Two Weeks Later

Ellysetta Baristani plunged her hands into the gaping cavity of the dying boy's chest. Her fingers closed around his heart, pumping the still chambers with desperate force as a blaze of powerful, golden-white magic poured from her soul into his.

The fading brightness of his life force tasted warm and tart on her tongue, like a sun-ripened peach plucked too soon from the tree. So young. So innocent. He couldn't have been more than fourteen. Too young for this. Too young for war. Too young to die.

Just like her sisters, Lillis and Lorelle, who'd been lost in the Faering Mists during the battle of Teleon.

"Please, my lady. Save him. Please, save my Aartys. He's all I've got left." The mother of the dying child stood sobbing beside the table, her eyes swollen and red rimmed, chapped hands twisting the hem of the blood-soaked apron tied around her waist. Her desperation and grief-induced terror pounded at Ellysetta's empathic senses like hammer blows.

Not that a few more hammer blows made much difference in the emotional din swirling around the scarlet healing tents that had been erected on the mist- and rainbow-filled plazas of Upper Orest. As always when a battle raged nearby, the sheer numbers of wounded and dying warriors made it impossible for the dozen scarlet-veiled *shei'dalin* healers to weave peace upon them all. Not even the roar of the great Kiyera's Veil waterfalls could drown out the screams of pain and pleas for mercy.

"I'll do my best, Jonna," Ellysetta vowed. She wanted to promise to save Aartys, but the last weeks here on Celieria's war-torn northern border had taught her too well. Death, once a stranger, had become an all-too-familiar acquaintance.

Ellysetta looked up and met Jonna's eyes over the boy's limp body. The weeping mortal woman was one of the hearth witches who tended the wounded and dying. She knew death as intimately as Ellysetta now did, but that didn't stop her from fighting against it with every ounce of strength she possessed—or from begging for a salvation she knew was beyond the capabilities of all mortal healers . . . and all but one of the Fey *shei'dalins*.

Ellysetta bit her lip. Aartys shouldn't be here on her table—and she couldn't help feeling partly to blame. After all, if not for her, the Fey might never have engaged their ancient enemy in this new Mage War. If not for Ellysetta, her truemate, Rainier vel'En Daris, would never have blown his golden horn this morning to call his Fey warriors and the mortal men of Orest to battle. And if he'd never blown that blast, the sound would never have spurred Jonna's young son to snatch up his dead father's sword and rush to fight alongside the men of Orest and his heroes, the immortal Shining Folk of the Fading Lands.

Yet those things *had* happened. And now, here they were, a child maimed and dying, his mother weeping and pleading for his life, both utterly dependent on Ellysetta and her magic to snatch his life from the jaws of death.

"Hold his hand, Jonna," Ellysetta commanded. "Feed him your strength. Call to him. Don't stop until I tell you." And then, though she shouldn't have vowed it, she did: "If there's any way to save Aartys, I will."

"Oh, my lady." Jonna's lips trembled and tears flooded her eyes. "Oh, thank you, my lady. *Thank you.*"

She started to come around the table, but Ellysetta stopped her. "Hold his hand, Jonna." The command came out more curtly than usual. She didn't want this woman kneeling at her feet, kissing her hem as other Celierians had done when pleading for her to save a loved one. She wasn't a goddess to be worshiped.

"*Teska,* Jonna. Please," she urged more gently. "Hold your son's hand. There isn't much time." And because there truly wasn't, she infused the words with a spider-silk-thin filament of compulsion, woven from shining lavender Spirit magic.

Jonna instantly snatched up her son's hand.

"And pray, my friend," Ellysetta said, adding silently, *For all our sakes.*

The words to the Bright Lord's devotion tumbled from the mortal healer's lips.

Ellysetta flicked a glance at the tall, grim Fey warrior standing near the corner of her healing table.

Without a word, Gaelen vel Serranis stepped forward to lay a hand upon her shoulder. Crackling energy flooded her veins as the most infamous of the five bloodsworn warriors of her quintet surrendered his immense power for her use. The sort of healing she was about to do would take more than her own vast stores of power, and though usually a *shei'dalin* would rely on her truemate to supplement her strength, Rain was on the battlefield, where the king of the Fey belonged, rather than at her side.

Ellysetta closed her eyes, shut out the world, and gathered her magic. Power came to her call, a dazzling golden-white brightness the Fey called *shei'dalin's* love, a healing gift Ellysetta Baristani wielded with a strength the world had not seen since the dawn of the First Age.

Against her closed lids, the pulsating vibrancy of Fey vision replaced physical sight, darkness teeming with the glowing threads of energy that made up all life and substance. Her consciousness traveled down the blinding-bright conduits of her arms, into Aartys's dying body, then sank deeper. Moving with swift purpose, she followed the threads of her healing weave and descended into the Well of Souls, the blackness that lay beyond and beneath the physical world, the home of demons and the unborn and the dead waiting for passage into their next life.

There, she could see the fading light of Aartys's soul as he sank into the long, silent dark of the Well. When his light disappeared, he would be lost. Determined not to let that happen, she plunged after him, her presence a dazzling incandescence that lit the shadowy world of the Well like a golden-white sun.

«*Aartys.*» She wove Spirit, the mystic magic of thought and illusion, hoping to make him feel his mother's grief and fill him with an urgent need to return to her. «*Fight, Aartys. Fight to live.*» Death, ultimately, was like drowning. Once the initial terror passed, the dying embraced the numbness and simply let themselves fall, like wrecked ships sinking to the bottom of the sea. «*Do not surrender. Reach for my Light. Let me bring you back to your mother. She needs you. She will be lost without you.*»

Her weave was strong, her command of Spirit as exceptional as her command of the potent healing magic of the Fey. Yet still he fell.

So tired, his fading spirit whispered. *Tell Mam I* . . . His voice trailed off and the pale light of his soul began to sputter.

«*Aartys!*» Ellysetta dove after him. The threads of her weave stretched to the breaking point as she followed him deep into the Well, deeper than any other healer dared to go, deeper than she should have gone without Rain to anchor her.

«*Take my magic, kem'falla,*» Gaelen said. «*Use what you need, and quickly. You have been gone from yourself too long.*»

«*Aiyah.*» She seized the magic Gaelen had offered for her use—the dark black threads of magic that throbbed with red sparks. Azrahn, the forbidden soul magic.

Ellysetta worked quickly, reluctant to put Gaelen at risk by making him hold his weave for more than a chime or two. Though Gaelen considered the chance to save Fey lives well worth the risk of wielding Azrahn, they both knew how dangerous the magic was. She plaited the cool, dark threads of his Azrahn into her flows of *shei'dalin's* love, weaving the strands of icy shadow and warm, healing light together.

The new weave—amplified by her powers as well as Gaelen's own—let her descend much farther into the Well. But as deep as she went, Aartys remained out of reach.

«*Enough, kem'falla,*» Gaelen said. «*We're out of time.*»

«*Just a little farther.*»

«*Nei. You've been gone from yourself too long. If you cannot save the boy now, you must let him go. Your life is too important to risk so needlessly.*»

Anger bubbled up inside her. «*Needlessly?*»

«*You know what I mean.*»

«*Every life is precious, Gaelen.*» She'd held too many dying men in her arms, comforted too many stricken loved ones, seen her own mother beheaded by the Eld. She could not bear the thought of one more lost, wasted life—especially not this beautiful boy, whose bright eyes and sunny smile reminded her of her own young sisters.

Nei, she could not—*would not*—lose another soul today. Not to magic, not to war, and not to the thrice-flamed Well of Souls!

Cold whispered through her veins. Azrahn surged up from the great, deep source inside her, summoned by her anger. An almost sentient eagerness pressed against her will, as if the Azrahn inside her *wanted* her to weave it, *wanted* her to embrace its dark, forbidden power.

For her, giving in to that temptation would come with a terrible price. She bore four Mage Marks, placed upon her by the High Mage of Eld, and each time she spun Azrahn, she risked receiving another one. Two more and her soul, her consciousness, her entire being, would be his to command.

Still, the lure was tremendous. Gaelen's threads didn't contain a fraction of the power her own did. She could weave just a little . . . just enough to save the boy. Perhaps she could even spin it quickly enough that the High Mage wouldn't have time to sense it and Mark her again.

Yes . . . yes, just a little, and quickly. Such a small thing. Surely he would miss it.

The siren's call whispered in her ear. Dimly, she heard someone say her name, as if calling from far away, but the voice was soon silenced. Forbidden power throbbed in her veins, and all around her, the darkness of the Well of Souls pulsed to the same beat. Her ears filled with muted susurrations, a rhythmic ebbing and flowing, as if she were a child in the womb, listening to the blood rushing through her mother's veins. The sound was hypnotic . . . entrancing. . . .

She reached for her Azrahn, let its cold sweetness fill her.

«Ellysetta!» A furious and all-too-familiar voice roared her name. Power rushed into her body, and deep within the Well, her Light flared like an exploding sun.

The jolt sent her weave spearing wildly into the Well, so deep it passed the fading light that was Aartys's soul. Stunned, she had just enough time and presence of mind to close her weave around Aartys and cling tight before her soul was yanked from the Well and slammed back into her own body.

The shining brilliance of Fey vision faded to darkness. The tranquillity of the Well gave way to a murmur of voices, muted screams of men in pain, the smells of blood and sweat and suffering. Her eyes fluttered as her senses gradually returned to her body.

She was clutched in a hot, hard, golden embrace, but neither that nor the blazing heat of two burning purple suns glaring down upon her could stop the icy shivers racking her frame. She blinked up into the achingly beautiful, utterly furious face of her truemate.

"Rain, I—"

His eyes flared tairen-bright. Pupils and whites disappeared, leaving only spark-filled whirls of lavender that glowed so bright they could have lit a dark room. "Do. Not. Speak." His nostrils flared, and even the long, inky black strands of his hair crackled with scarcely contained energy. "Just . . . be silent." He was so angry, his temper bordered on Rage, the wild, ferociously lethal fury of the Fey.

A choked sound snagged her attention. "Aartys!" she cried.

Powerful arms encased in heavy, golden, tairen-forged steel tightened their grip around her and held her fast. "Is alive and does not need your help."

She turned her head, but she couldn't see the boy. Scarlet-veiled *shei'dalins* surrounded the table where he lay, and the glow of concentrated healing magic shone so bright even mortal eyes could see it.

"*Beylah sallan*," she breathed.

That remark was the feather that broke the tairen's back. Rain plunked her on her feet, gripped her arms, and gave her a shake strong enough to rattle her teeth. "Thank the gods? *Thank the gods?*" His Rage blazed so hot, flames nearly shot from his head. "Thank Gaelen for having the belated sense to call me when he realized what was happening." He shook her again. "Idiot! Ninnywit! Reckless, rock-headed dim-skull! How many times are you going to put yourself in such danger?"

Her brows snapped together. "Me?" she shot back. "That's a bit of the sword calling the dagger sharp, don't you think?" She yanked herself out of his grasp and returned his glare with her own. "Do I berate you for all the risks you take in battle?"

He drew himself up to his full height, and with his golden war steel adding significant breadth to his already broad shoulders, he loomed over her. "Don't try to turn this on me. I am the Defender of the Fey, and we are at war. It is my duty to lead our warriors in battle."

"And I am a *shei'dalin*," she retorted. "The most powerful healer we have. It is my duty to save every life I can!"

"Not at the risk of your own! You were about to weave Azrahn, Ellysetta! Despite the danger—despite your sworn oath never to weave it again unless we both agreed."

The pain in his voice—even more than the frightening truth of his words—deflated her defensive ire. She had made a vow and nearly betrayed it—nearly betrayed him. Her shoulders slumped and she lifted a shaking hand to her face.

He was right, but before she could admit it and apologize, Jonna gave a short cry. Rain and Ellysetta both turned to the table where Aartys lay. The *shei'dalins* had extinguished their weaves and were already departing. The boy was sitting up, the gaping wound in his chest gone without a trace, even the dried blood and grime of war washed away by *shei'dalin* magic. His mother had her arms wrapped tight around him, and her shoulders heaved with sobs of relief and joy.

"Thank you." Jonna wept, tears raining from her eyes. "Thank you for my son. Light's blessings upon you!"

Ellysetta found Rain's hand. He'd removed his gauntlets, and her fingers curled into the broad, warm strength of his.

His eyes flashed a warning at her, but to Jonna he offered only gentle understanding. "*Sha vel'mei*, Jonna," he said, his voice a deep, rough velvet purr. "You are both welcome. And you, Aartys . . ." He leveled a stern look on the boy. "I do not want to see you on the battlefield again. Your sword is sharp and your soul is brave, but I need you most here, guarding your mother and the Feyreisa." He clapped a hand on the child's shoulder. "There is no more honorable duty for a warrior of the Fey than to protect our women. Do you accept this great honor?"

"You want me to help guard the Feyreisa?" The boy's eyes went big as coins. He cast a dazed glance at Ellysetta before turning back to Rain. "Aye, My Lord Feyreisen," he agreed. "I do accept."

"*Kabei.*" Good. "Then it is decided. Sers vel Jelani and vel Tibboreh"—he tilted his head towards two of the grim-eyed Fey posted at the corners of Ellysetta's healing tent—"will explain your duties to you. For now, go with your mother and get some rest and a change of clothes."

"But the Feyreisa—" Aartys began.

"—will not need your protection at the moment, as she will be coming with me."

Eld ~ Boura Fell

Vadim Maur, the High Mage of Eld, shook off the flicker of awareness that had brushed across his senses and withdrew the part of his consciousness he'd sent into the Well. If the brief touch had been the girl, she was gone now, and the protections that barred him from her mind were firmly back in place. He could still sense her existence, but that was all.

"Master?" The timid, subservient voice near his left shoulder broke the silence. "What should I do with him?"

Vadim tightened his lips in irritation, then just as quickly relaxed the pressure when he felt the flesh split and warm liquid ooze down his shrouded chin. Wordless, he dabbed the edge of his deep purple hood against his mouth. His body had grown fragile these past weeks. The Rot had him firmly in its grip, and not even the ministrations of his powerful *shei'dalin* captives could hold it back any longer. Soon, the truth already suspected by most of his council would be impossible to hide.

His time was running out.

He gazed through the observation portal into the *sel'dor* cage with its wild-eyed inhabitant: a young man, the last of the four magically gifted infants to whom he'd tied the souls of unborn tairen seventeen years ago. The boy had shown full mastery in four of the five Fey magics, but only a middling level three in Spirit, so there'd never been any possibility of his becoming a Tairen Soul capable of summoning the Change. But his bloodlines were strong, and he'd proven quite adept at wielding Azrahn even in early childhood.

Vadim had been using him as a breeder, but recently, with the Rot advancing through Vadim's flesh and Ellysetta Baristani still so stubbornly elusive, he had seriously considered using the boy as the vessel to house the next incarnation of his soul. At least as a stopgap until the much more powerful Ellysetta finally found her way back into his keeping.

That plan was scuttled now. The boy had gone mad, just like the thousands of others to whom Vadim had grafted tairens' souls over the centuries. The madness usually began after adolescence, starting with voices only the afflicted could hear, then progressing to bouts of Rage, and finally complete savagery and destructive madness and death.

Of all the children to whom he'd bound the soul of a tairen, only Ellysetta had survived twenty-four years without a hint of insanity. That made her an invaluable prize, not only as a powerful vessel to hold Vadim's incarnated soul, but as the key to his long centuries of experimentation.

In the cell, the boy put his hands to his head. Shrieking unintelligible gibberish, he pulled great tufts of hair out by the roots and spun around the room, slamming his body against the wall and ripping at his own flesh.

Vadim's fingers curled in a fist. "Restrain him before he

damages himself more. Continue to breed him as long as you can." Too many centuries had gone into the crossbreeding of magical bloodlines to throw the boy away without squeezing as much benefit from his existence as possible. "If he endangers the females, send him to Fezai Madia." The leader of the Feraz witches had been complaining lately over the quality of the slaves he'd been sending for her sacrifices to the demon-god Gamorraz. Insane this boy might be, but there was no denying the strong magic in his blood.

Leaving the observation room, he passed through the nursery and paused to glance into the two cradles resting against the wall. Two infants with bright, shining eyes stared up at him. Both boys, both already showing promise of mastering all Fey magics. Each had the soul of an unborn tairen grafted to his own. Would they go mad, too? Or had Vadim finally discovered the secret to successfully breeding Tairen Souls of his own?

Only time would tell. For now, they represented another generation of possibility, another opportunity to succeed in case Ellysetta Baristani continued to elude him . . .

. . . or in case she fell prey to the same lethal insanity as her predecessors.

Celieria ~ Orest

"Where are we going?" Ellysetta asked as Rain dragged her away from the healing tents. Her quintet had started to follow, but one hot look from Rain had stopped them in their tracks.

"Someplace I can keep you out of trouble."

There was still a snap in his voice, so she offered a small peace offering. "You were good with Aartys."

He gave her a withering look, and her olive branch went quietly up in flames. "Do not attempt to soothe this tairen, *shei'tani*. You nearly died—or worse—and I will not overlook that."

She bit her lip. He was right. She'd gone too far into the Well, and *something* had been quite successfully pushing her to use her most dangerous magic. Still . . . this double standard her truemate imposed on her had gone on long enough.

"Why do you get to be angry, and I do not?"

He glared. "What do *you* have to be angry about?"

She stopped stock-still and yanked her hand from his grip. "Are you serious? I'm your *shei'tani*—your truemate—and you can actually ask me that?" She didn't wait for him to reply. "How many times have you barely made it back to Orest alive? How many times have you crashed into Veil Lake, bloody and half-dead, limbs broken, flesh shredded, enough *sel'dor* arrows in you to supply an entire company of archers? Yet you expect me to patch you up and send you back to battle time and time again. You and every other warrior who ends up on my table."

"You are a *shei'dalin*. That is what *shei'dalins* do."

"Precisely! You fight out there." She jabbed a finger towards the scorched and still-smoking southwest corner of Eld. "Well, *that* is my battlefield." She turned and jabbed her finger back at the healing tents. "And I'm every bit as determined to win my war as you. If that means I occasionally have to take risks— just like you do—then, by the gods, that's exactly what I'll do!"

"Over. My. Rotting. Corpse." His teeth snapped together with an audible click. He grabbed her wrist again and put on a burst of speed that forced her to jog to keep up with him.

The collection of bloodsworn black Fey'cha daggers strapped across her chest and around her hips slapped against her steel-embroidered scarlet robes as she ran, and the feeling of being a chastised child dragged along behind an irate parent only chafed her more.

"You're being unfair!" she exclaimed. "I may not have my wings yet, but I'm a Tairen Soul, too, Rain. I feel the same need to defend our people as you do. Just because the only enemy I can defend them against at the moment is death, that doesn't mean my efforts are any less vital than yours!"

His eyes glowed so bright they nearly shot purple sparks. "Have I ever suggested they were? Have I not let Gaelen weave the forbidden magic for your use so you could save lives that would otherwise be lost? I do not object to your saving lives. But I will not allow you to risk your own in the process!"

"But—"

"*Enough!*" he thundered. "You don't have to like it, Ellysetta, but I am the Feyreisen—both your truemate and your king—*and on this matter, I will be obeyed!*"

Ahead lay the open plaza near Veil Lake that Rain and the tairen used for launching and landing. Four majestic winged cats, each the size of a house, crouched on the manicured grass at the lakeshore. Their heads were extended as they lapped at the cold waters fed from Kiyera's Veil, the gauntlet of three-hundred-foot waterfalls that tumbled down from opposing mountainsides at the lake's western shore.

When they reached the plaza, Rain slowed his pace. Ellysetta yanked her wrist from his grip a second time, marched to the mossy edge of the bricked space, and presented him her back. She pressed her lips in a thin line, angry at his high-handedness. For a woman who'd spent the first twenty-four years of her life as the shy, obedient daughter of a poor woodcarver and his wife, Ellysetta had become mulishly resistant to Voices of Authority. Even when those voices belonged to kings, wedded husbands, and beloved truemates. If Mama were still alive, she would shake her head in despair of her adopted daughter's willful ways.

By the lakeshore, the largest of the tairen, a great white beauty with eyes like glowing blue jewels, lifted her snowy, feline head and turned to pad towards them. Her long tail slapped against several tree trunks as she walked, bringing a shower of leaves raining down in her wake. When she reached the plaza, she spread her wide, clawed wings and reared up on her hind legs to shake the debris from her fur. A deep, throaty purr rumbled in her chest, and she tilted her head down to pin Ellysetta with a whirling, pupil-less blue gaze.

«You worried your mate, kitling,» admonished Steli, *chakai* of the Fey'Bahren pride. The musical tones of the tairen's speech danced in the air like flashes of silver and gold and carried with them feelings of panicked fear and images of Rain whirling in the sky and rocketing towards Upper Orest. *«You should not alarm him so. Tairen frightened for their mates are dangerous—especially to beings as breakable as mortals.»*

"Not you, too, Steli!" Ellysetta crossed her arms, feeling immensely put out. "You think I'm not afraid when he's out there getting maimed by arrows and bowcannon?"

Steli's ears flicked and her tail lashed the earth. *«Ellysetta-kitling would not scorch the world. Rainier-Eras already has. Without you to anchor him, he would again.»*

That simple, inescapable truth deflated Ellysetta's temper as nothing else could. A thousand years ago, after the death of his first mate, Sariel, Rain Tairen Soul had scorched the world in the blaze of tairen flame, killing thousands in mere instants, millions in a handful of days. He'd paid for that act of Rage with seven hundred years of madness and another three centuries spent battling his way back from the abyss.

«Rainier-Eras is proud,» Steli continued, *«and he does not wish to frighten his mate. He does not tell Ellysetta-kitling that each day becomes harder. That each battle weakens what took him so long to rebuild.»*

Ellysetta cast a troubled gaze over her shoulder. Rain stood a short distance away, shoulders hunched, pinching the bridge of his nose as he expended visible effort to calm himself. She'd frightened him badly, and his control hung in tatters. Untruemated Fey warriors absorbed the torment of every life they took—the pain, the darkness, the sorrow of lost dreams hanging like burning stones around their necks—and Rain bore the weight of millions on his soul. Mental and emotional discipline was the only thing standing between him and insanity, and her nearly fatal trip into the Well had stripped those protections threadbare. Shame washed over her.

The tairen bent her head and nudged Ellysetta. «*Go to your mate, kitling. He needs you. Now more than ever.*»

Ellysetta crossed the short distance to Rain's side. Moss grew green and thick along the edges of the plaza's mist-dampened bricks. Winter would be upon them soon, and the spray off the Veil would turn to flurries of ice crystals. The nights would grow longer, the Eld Mages more powerful. Despite the brave efforts of Lord Teleos's soldiers, Celieria stood no chance of surviving the winter as a free land without the help of the Fey. The might of the tairen was the only power Mages truly feared.

Until Ellysetta found her wings, Rain was the only living Tairen Soul capable of Changing to his tairen form and leading the pride into battle. As such, he would have to fight—again and again and again—and the torment of his soul would grow more unbearable with each engagement. Elly-setta hadn't been thinking about that when she'd made her decision to save Aartys. She hadn't been thinking about Rain at all.

"I'm sorry, *shei'tan*," she apologized sincerely. "I should have been more careful—for your sake if not my own."

"That's what you always say," he replied in a low voice, "but it never stops you from doing what you know you should not."

She rubbed her forehead, where a headache had begun to throb. "I never meant to go so deep into the Well, but he was a child, Rain. Not much older than Lillis and Lorelle. I couldn't let him die. Can't you understand that?"

He sighed. "I do understand, *shei'tani*. Better than you think." He turned to face her. "But saving that boy or even a thousand more like him won't bring Lillis and Lorelle back." He took her shoulders in a firm grip. "You've got to stop risking yourself this way, Ellysetta. You're no good to your sisters, or your father, or anyone else for that matter, if you're dead or lose your soul to the Mages."

"I know that. I do. It's just that—" Her voice broke off. She could feel his fear, his love, his guilt for bringing her into the dangers of a Tairen Soul's life, his terror that he might not be strong enough to hold himself in check the next time she came so close to death.

"Oh, Rain." She leaned against him, resting her forehead against the unforgiving golden steel of his tairen-forged war armor and laying the palm of one hand against the smooth warmth of his jaw. Though they could not read each other's thoughts until their bond was complete, they could, when they touched skin-to-skin, feel each other's emotions as clear as day.

Because he was the strongest of the Fey, the most powerful Tairen Soul in living memory, it was so easy to forget how fragile he truly was, how narrow the band that kept him from plunging into madness.

«*Sieks'ta, shei'tan.*» I'm sorry, beloved. She wove the apology into his mind on a thread of Spirit, not reading his thoughts, but offering him one of hers. With her hand against his face, her skin touching his, she knew he could sense her sincerity and the great love she bore him just as she sensed his agitation drain away, replaced by regret and weariness.

He turned his lips into her palm and pressed a kiss there. "As am I," he said. "I know my fear for you is a burden, and it shames me that you must bear it. You are a Tairen Soul, which means you are fierce, born to fight and to defend those in your care; but you are also my *shei'tani*. I thought I would be strong enough to let you embrace the warrior's side of your nature. I know now I'm not. I cannot allow you to be harmed—not even by your own actions."

Ellysetta forced a small smile. "Perhaps when our bond is complete, things will be different."

"Perhaps," he agreed without conviction.

Steli's wings flapped. The white tairen nudged them with her nose. «*Time to fly, Rainier-Eras. The day grows late.*»

"*Aiyah.*"

"Where are we going?" Ellysetta asked.

"Crystal Lake," he admitted.

"The Source in the mountains? But that's bells away—" She broke off and her brows drew together in concern. Every great city in the Fading Lands had a Source at its center, and the Fey drank the water of those Sources to bolster their strength and replenish flagging magical energies. The only Source that existed outside the Fading Lands was Crystal Lake, and its magic-infused waters fed one of the tributaries that flowed into Kiyera's Veil and the Heras River.

If the diluted Source waters of the Veil were no longer powerful enough to replenish Rain's magic or rejuvenate his strength . . .

"It's more precaution than need," Rain reassured her, reading her expression. Fey didn't lie, which meant he was telling the truth—or at least a version of it. "Besides, how long has it been since we've managed to do more than snatch a few bells' sleep together? I thought you might like some time away from the battlefield and the healing tents."

"I would." The other *shei'dalins* slipped back through the Mists every few days to restore themselves in the peace of the Fading Lands. Banished and Mage Marked as she was, Ellysetta didn't have that luxury. "I suppose we could both use a visit to the Source," she said, stepping back to give Rain room for the Change.

He waited for her to get clear before closing his eyes and summoning his magic. Flows of power gathered and swirled around him, darkening to a gray mist that sparkled with rainbow lights. The crackling energy of his magic poured over Ellysetta in hot, electric waves. She gasped and closed her eyes on a shudder of shared pleasure as Rain's Fey body was unmade—his flesh and consciousness flung out into the mist of the Change—then re-formed in a staggering rush into the great, sleek body of his tairen self.

When the magic of the Change cleared, Rain Tairen Soul crouched where Rain the Fey had stood: a magnificent, kingly creature, like one of the sleek black jungle cats Ellysetta had seen in illustrated books of faraway lands, except that his tairen body stood easily half as high as a fully grown fireoak, and great, batlike wings sprouted from his back. Even by tairen standards, Rain was an impressive male, with fur a glossy, unrelieved midnight black, a vast wingspan, and radiant, pupilless eyes that glowed like lavender suns.

He lowered his head to pin Ellysetta with that bright, whirling gaze and rumbled a throaty purr. Her body clenched like a fist, every nerve abruptly sizzling with a rush of pure, primitive heat. She might not yet have found her wings, but the tairen in her soul recognized its mate—and yearned for him with staggering force.

She wet her lips and tried to compose herself while Rain purred deep in his throat and nosed her with unmistakable interest. "Stop that." She laughed, giving him a shove. She summoned an Earth weave that transformed her gown into steel-studded scarlet leathers, with Fey'cha belts crossed over her chest and her quintet's daggers sheathed in the belt slung around her hips. A subsequent weave summoned a burst of powerful silvery Air magic that lifted her body up and deposited her into the cradle of the leather saddle that Rain wove for her on his back. She anchored herself in place with the saddle's leather straps. "I'm ready."

«Then spin the weave, shei'tani. Around Steli as well as us.»

Ellysetta nodded and reached once more into the well of power that lay within her. Lavender Spirit, the mystic magic of consciousness, thought, and illusion, surged up in a rush and she wove the dense threads of energy in a pattern Gaelen vel Serranis had taught the Fey only a few months ago. She flung the weave out like a net, first around Steli—who promptly winked out of sight—then around herself and Rain, rendering them invisible to both mortal and magic eyes.

The other tairen had left the waters of Veil Lake and padded over to the plaza. They leapt into the air seconds before Rain crouched down on his haunches and sprang skyward, and their presence provided cover for the rush of wind that might have betrayed Rain and Steli's otherwise invisible launch.

Ringed by the pride and sheathed by invisibility, Rain, Ellysetta, and Steli soared high over the Rhakis mountaintops into the thin, crisp chill of the autumn sky. A dusting of snow capped the high, jagged peaks to the north. Below, just across the Heras River, the southwest corner of Eld still smoldered from the fiery aftermath of the recent battle. What had two weeks ago been a fortified village was now a scorched plain, razed to the ground, every living and dead thing in a twenty-mile radius reduced to ash. Yet still, the Eld came to battle the legions of Orest with relentless determination, wearing them down bit by bit, then retreating back into the dense forests of Eld, where, thanks to the batteries of bowcannon trained on the skies, not even the tairen could follow.

To the west, the billowing wall of mist that marked the borders of the Fading Lands rose up from the mountaintops. Rain flew close enough that Ellysetta could feel the tingle of magic from the Mists, and her fingers tightened on the pommel.

From the valley floor, the Mists looked like a line of thunderclouds hugging the crests of the Rhakis mountains. From the sky, however, they looked more beautiful than foreboding, like a radiant veil of shifting rainbows that stretched upward as far as the eye could see.

Ominous thunderheads or shimmering veil, Ellysetta recognized the Faering Mists for what they truly were: a deadly magical barrier meant to keep the enemies of the Fey from entering the Fading Lands.

Fey-made, the Mists would never intentionally harm an innocent, and so Celierian lore was filled with tales of those who had wandered by accident into the Mists, only to emerge again, decades later, unharmed, not aged a day, carrying tales of being feted by the Fair Folk in misty forest palaces. To the not-so-innocent, the Mists were far less kind. Entire armies had been swallowed up, never to be seen again.

Ellysetta's body tensed with remembered pain. She knew, firsthand, the torments that lay within those shifting clouds. Thanks to the four Mage Marks she bore, the Mists were now more dangerous to her than the Well of Souls, and the last time she'd entered, she'd very nearly not made it back out again alive.

If it were otherwise, she would not be here in Orest, weaving her magic to save lives. She would be in the Mists, searching every gods-cursed fingerspan of the magical barrier, tearing it apart thread by scorching thread if she had to.

Because somewhere in that veil of shifting mist, the last members of her family had been trapped; and she could not reach them . . . or even tell if they were still alive.

The Faering Mists

"Lorelle! Papa! Can you hear me? Where are you?" Lillis Baristani's voice was hoarse from shouting, and the ocean of tears she'd shed had left her eyes swollen and burning.

She turned in circles and squinted in a vain effort to pierce the suffocating veil of shifting whiteness around her. She'd been in the Mists a long time—bells, certainly, maybe even a day or more, though it was hard to tell time when the vapor was eternally lit by its own magical glow. In any event, she'd not seen or heard another living being since the moment the mountain had shuddered like a wild, angry beast and she'd lost her footing and fallen back into the Faering Mists.

Never in all her life had she been so alone. Always, someone had been with her: Lorelle or Mama or Papa or Ellie.

Alone was frightening. Almost more frightening than the terrible, monstrous *darrokken* or the evil Eld soldiers that had attacked Teleon. Almost more frightening than the sight of Kieran screaming as he disappeared beneath an avalanche of dirt, rock, and toppling trees.

"Kieran?" she cried. "Kiel? Anybody?"

There was still no answer.

Lillis blinked back tears and clutched her small kitten to her chest. "They're not coming, Snowfoot. I don't think anyone's coming." In the sling tied around her neck, her black-

and-white kitten mewed and squirmed and sank its tiny sharp claws into the wool jacket covering Lillis's pinafore.

Papa had always told Lillis, "If ever you get lost, kitling, stay right where you are. Your mama and I will come to find you." But Mama was dead—killed by the same evil people who had attacked Teleon—and Lillis had waited long enough in the white blindness of the Mists to know that either no one was still alive to find her or they were looking in the wrong place.

Either way, she couldn't stay here.

She stroked Snowfoot's soft fur and hummed a little song Ellie had always sung to Lillis and Lorelle when they were frightened or upset. The tune didn't soothe Lillis like it did when Ellie sang it, but Snowfoot stopped his anxious mewing.

"I'll bet you're getting hungry and thirsty, aren't you?" Lillis murmured to the kitten. "I know I am." She wrapped her thin arms around the tiny feline, cuddling it closer and pressing her face to the soft fur at the top of its head. "Come on, Snowfoot," she said. "Let's go find Papa and Lorelle."

CHAPTER TWO

Rhakis Mountains

«*When I find my wings, Rain, I doubt you'll ever get me down from the sky.*»

Ellysetta closed her eyes in bliss as her truemate's sleek tairen form soared into a cloudbank. The wet chill of cloud-mist streamed across her cheeks and dampened her long, spiraling coils of flame-hued hair. She'd dropped the invisibility weave less than a bell's flight north of Orest, and now Rain and Steli soared and swooped side by side through the sky.

Clinging to the saddle on Rain's back, Ellysetta enjoyed the vicarious thrill of tairen flight. She loved flying. She loved the weightless joy of it. She loved the grandeur and the solitude of the heavens. Most of all, she loved the silence—broken only by the whoosh of magnificent wings scooping air from the sky and the rush of the wind passing by.

She hadn't realized how drained she'd become after these last weeks of war—the endless days and nights filled with battle cries and clashing swords and the shrieks of sundered men pleading for her to grant them either healing or a quick end to their suffering. But here, enveloped in the sublime peace of tairen flight, she felt as if a great weight had lifted from her shoulders. She could breathe again.

«*How much farther?*» she asked. The other tairen who'd launched to mask their departure had departed long ago, and Rain and Steli had been flying northward through the icy reaches of snowcapped mountains for several bells now, using the dense, low-hanging clouds that wreathed the peaks for cover.

«*We are here,*» Steli answered. Up ahead, the white tairen's form was nearly invisible against the cloud-covered peak of a snowy mountain. She put on a burst of speed, flying straight for the mountain. Bare instants before crashing into it, her wings angled and she shot suddenly skyward. Up she streaked, arrowing through the clouds and disappearing from view.

«*Hold on,*» Rain warned. A split second later, he mimicked Steli's daring ascent.

Ellysetta gasped as the sudden vertical flight left her stomach several tairen lengths behind. They broke through the clouds and burst into the clear blue sky above, where the tallest peaks rose from a sea of white cloud-mist. Black wings spread wide, gleaming in the late-morning sunlight as Rain glided after the graceful white form of Steli. They soared, weightless, at the apex of their ascent, then folded their wings and plummeted, diving back into the clouds. Ellysetta clung to the saddle and laughed in delight.

The tairen broke through the clouds into a deep, narrow gorge and raced north, following the rushing river at the bottom of the ravine. They zigzagged through the river's bends and curves, then flew up over a series of breathtaking white waterfalls and emerged in a broad basin at the center of five enormous peaks. Crystal Lake dominated the basin, its waters a clear gemstone blue that reflected the five soaring, snow-capped mountains ringing it like a crown.

An abandoned city hewn from the gold-veined gray rock of the mountains rose up on the southwestern shore, seeming to sprout from the mountainside. Clearly Fey but falling to ruin. Beautiful and melancholy in its gilded gray solitude, it stood like a monument to a once great race.

«Dunelan,» Rain said. *«The first lost city of the Fey. Abandoned near the end of the Second Age except as a military outpost. Not because its Source died, like in Lissilin, but because our people were too few to remain. I suppose we should have known then our race was in decline.»*

Rain's and Steli's wings angled to slow their speed and they alit on the rocky shores of the lake just north of the ancient city. Steli padded to the water's edge and stuck her nose near the surface, purring as she inhaled the heady aroma of magic that perfumed the air above the lake. *«Strong Source. Very powerful. Good for Rainier-Eras and Ellysetta-kitling.»*

She stuck a paw in, then gave a squawk of outrage. *«Cold!»* Images of a white tairen encased in icicles accompanied the exclamation.

Ellysetta laughed as she slid off Rain's back. "It's a mountain lake, Steli. What did you expect?"

Steli tossed her head and sniffed. She didn't like being laughed at. A moment later, a calculating gleam entered her bright eyes. She drew a deep breath and breathed tairen fire on the water's surface, holding the flame until the water steamed to near boiling. She padded into the hot water, head held high, tail swishing with feline superiority, and plunked down just off the shore. "Mmmmrrrr," she purred.

A cooked fish, boiled by the sudden heating of the water, bobbed to the surface. Steli's whiskers twitched. She sniffed the floating fish experimentally, then lapped it up with a large pink tongue. Clearly, she liked what she tasted, because she boiled a wider circle of water and paddled around, slurping up the tasty fish treats as they bobbed to the surface.

"Shall we join her?" Rain asked. He'd Changed back to Fey form and summoned an Earth weave to shed his golden war steel. The armor, boots, and blades re-formed in neat piles beside his bare feet, but the magic of the tairen-forged steel left a gleaming aura swirling around him that amplified his natural Fey luminescence. The Fey king's war steel, once donned, could never be returned to the Feyreisen's palace in Dharsa until the Fey were victorious or the wearer of the armor died. Until then, even when Rain removed the armor to sleep or bathe, a part of its magic remained with him.

His lean, well-muscled form glowed with the silvery luminescence that, even unenhanced, had earned the Fey their mortal appellation, the Shining Folk. Black hair, without a hint of curl, hung in fine, silky strands down to his shoulder blades, framing a face of both indomitable strength and breathtaking masculine beauty. Muscles, lean but well-defined and hard as stone, rippled beneath smooth, gleaming flesh. If Lord Brandis, the god of war, ever chose to take physical form, Ellysetta thought he would look like Rain did now, magnificent and male, dazzling and deadly.

She swallowed and tamped down a familiar, visceral surge of lust, quickly directing her attention to her own garb. Time enough for mating *after* they rejuvenated themselves in the Source. She could feel the weariness beating at Rain and the emotions swirling so close to the surface beneath the too-thin layers of his self-control.

"Aiyah," she managed to agree. The word came out throaty, unconsciously seductive. She coughed twice and added with a grin, "But let's keep our distance. I don't fancy swimming in fish stew." Earth came to her call with a green flash. Leathers and steel fell to the ground in haphazard piles.

She glanced up in time to see Rain's eyes rake down her slender body and spark with a hunger as powerful as her own. He took one step towards her, intent stamped on his face. And despite her determination to see to Rain's health first, a thrill of pleasure shot through her. It never ceased to amaze her that all the love, passion, and devotion of this incredible man belonged wholly and eternally to her. Her. Ellysetta Baristani. Who would ever have believed it?

In her mind's eye she still was, and perhaps always would be, that shy, gawky, rather unattractive girl who'd never fit in. Yet even when the glamour set upon her at birth had disguised her true Fey heritage, Rain had always seen beneath the mortal guise. And when he looked at her with such simmering intensity, she felt like a different woman. Not Ellie Baristani, but Ellysetta Feyreisa, a shining Fey queen every bit the equal of her exceptional mate.

"On second thought," Rain growled, taking another step closer, "swimming can wait."

One brow arched. "Who says we have to choose?" Her lips curved in a siren's smile, and with a low, challenging laugh, she bolted. She raced across the stony shore on nimble feet and dove for the lake with an Air-powered leap that sent her soaring gracefully half a tairen length from the shore before she plunged into the Fire-warmed waters.

Magic hit her like a lightning bolt, robbing her of breath. She kicked to the surface, gasping and tingling all over. Rain was on her the instant she came up for air.

"Rain, wait. There's something—"

She didn't get to finish her sentence. His arms wrapped around her, dragging her close. His lips fused to hers. The long, lean lines of his flesh—hotter than the waters Steli had boiled with her tairen flame—pressed against Ellysetta's, burning stone beneath seductive velvet flesh.

Coherent thought evaporated.

Sensation raced through her . . . sizzling, electric. Her flesh was afire. Always when Rain's skin touched hers, she felt his emotions as if they were her own; but now, with the waters of the Source around them, the feeling increased exponentially, instantly forming a harmonic. His desire feeding hers . . . hers feeding his. He breathed, and her lungs expanded as if the breath were her own. She brushed her hand across his skin and her flesh felt the caress. She dragged her nails across his nipple and her own sprang instantly erect.

"Oh, dear gods." She gasped. Her womb clenched. In an instant, her flesh grew swollen, burning and aching . . . needing.

Ellysetta couldn't tell which feelings were Rain's and which her own, and she didn't care. Her arms wrapped around his neck; her legs locked around his waist. Her muscles contracted, dragging him so tightly against her it was as if some part of her mind thought she could physically fuse their bodies together through the sheer strength of her embrace.

«*Ke vo san . . . ke vo lanis . . . ke vo arris. . . .* » I love you . . . I want you . . . I need you. The words chanted in her head with the beat of her pulse, repeating over and over. His voice—or was it hers?—grew more insistent with each utterance. «*Veli ti'ku . . . Vo'shani ti'ku.*» Come to me. Give yourself to me.

The connections of their still uncompleted truemate bond flared with the same rhythmic pulse until she could almost see the threads and their intricate, tightly woven pattern, until she could almost see what was missing and how to spin it. Her dazed mind tried to grasp the image, process it, but sensation overwhelmed her senses. Concentration dissolved, thoughts scattered. The image of their bond flared with sudden brightness, and its pattern merged into a single blinding light.

She could hardly breathe. Then his body surged up, plunging deep into hers, and all she could think was, *Breathe? Who needs to breathe?* They flung back their heads on a mutual shout of pleasure as her body shattered and his followed.

"What in the Haven's name just happened?"

Dazed and still trembling from the overload to her senses, Ellysetta floated in Rain's arms, her limp body draped across his, incapable of autonomous movement. She could barely think straight, let alone summon the strength to actually *move.*

Rain's chest rippled as he dragged in a shuddering breath. "I don't know." His voice came out hoarse, raspy. He swallowed, then tilted his chin against his chest to glance at her. A grin twitched at the corners of his mouth. "But I hope it happens again."

She started to shove his shoulder, decided it was too much effort, and settled for a scowl instead. "Be serious. That was *not* normal."

She'd drunk *faerilas*—the waters of a Source—before. She'd swum in Veil Lake numerous times during these last weeks. But she'd never had a reaction like the one that had just occurred.

«Fine, fierce mating. Rainier-Eras and Ellysetta-kitling will make many strong kitlings for the pride.» Steli, who had given up boiling fish and begun to amuse herself chasing them under the water, surfaced without warning nearby. She shook her soggy head, showering Rain and Ellysetta.

"Ah!" Ellysetta gave a shout of surprise at both Steli's sudden arrival and the distinct chill of the droplets. The tairen had been chasing fish in water much cooler than the surface. With a blush rising to her cheeks, she slapped an arm over her breasts and scolded, "Steli!"

Blue eyes blinked with complete innocence. *«Sorry, sorry. Steli forgot knocking.»*

Ellysetta blushed brighter. She had chided Steli once before about forgetting to knock before interrupting her and Rain in a private moment, but considering the way she and Rain had jumped on each other without a care for Steli's proximity, she could hardly cry foul this time.

"*Nei*, it's all right," she began. She didn't recognize the mischievous light in the great cat's eyes.

At least, not until the white tairen reared up, raised both giant paws high, and brought them slamming back down towards the water's surface.

"Steli!" Ellysetta shrieked when she realized the tairen's intent. "Don't you da—"

Whack! Enormous splashes of water heaved up in twin geysers and engulfed Rain and Ellysetta, sending them tumbling in the resultant wave.

"You wicked cat!" Ellysetta accused when she came back up for air.

Huah. Huah. Huah. Steli chuffed with tairen laughter, infinitely amused with herself. Her wings spread wide and she pumped them in victory, accompanying the gesture with a triumphant roar.

Treading water beside Ellysetta, Rain was laughing, too, quietly, at first, but when Ellysetta turned on him in mock outrage, his smothered snickers turned to open guffaws. "You still have much to learn about tairen, *shei'tani*." He flashed a dazzling grin at the white cat. "Well played, Steli-*chakai*."

"Ha. Ha." Ellysetta crossed her arms and pretended to glare, though, secretly, she was glad to hear Rain laugh with such abandon. "That water was *cold!*"

«*Sorry, sorry. Steli will fix.*» The white tairen rose up again, opened her massive jaws, and blasted an area around Rain and Ellysetta with a sizzling jet of tairen flame.

The water's temperature shot up instantly—and so did the potency of the Source's magic. Ellysetta saw Rain's eyes widen a bare moment before the amplified power of Crystal Lake roared through her veins, once again electrifying her senses, stealing the air from her lungs, and leaving her shuddering in a state of hyperawareness.

"Dear gods. What *is* that?" She lifted trembling hands. Her skin's faint Fey luminescence had become as radiant as the moon.

She looked up at Rain and found him shining bright as a god come to earth. "Rain . . . Steli's tairen flame amplifies the effects of the *faerilas*." Her voice throbbed with throaty, seductive tones of *shei'dalin* compulsion that she hadn't meant to employ.

Rain's eyes flared brighter in an involuntary response to her power. "So it seems."

Ellysetta closed her eyes on a groan. The aural seduction clearly worked both ways, because each deep, velvety word he spoke brushed across her skin like a heated caress. It was as if, by breathing her flame upon the waters of the Source, Steli had spawned a carnal weave like the one Ellysetta had inadvertently spun on all the heads of Celieria's noble Houses several months ago.

Rain moved closer, glowing eyes fixed upon her face. "Are you complaining?"

Her breasts and groin throbbed with each syllable that passed his lips. "*N-nei*." Dear gods. If he said another word . . .

"Then come here."

Lightning ripped through her. Ellysetta gave a gasping cry and her body began to quake. For the second time in a bare handful of chimes, she fell into Rain's arms and locked her shaking legs around his hips, as helpless to resist the seductive enchantment of the Source as Celieria's nobles had been to resist the compulsion of her accidental carnal weave.

"I *like* this new use for tairen fire." Cradling Ellysetta in his arms, Rain floated on a cushion of warm water and smiled up at bright tracts of cerulean blue sky peeking through the thinning cloud cover overhead.

Steli, who was floating on her back nearby, snorted and blew a short burst of fire into the sky. «*Males.*»

Rain grinned. Earlier, citing the need for more definitive

proof of the effect of tairen flame on Source waters, he'd insisted Steli breathe fire upon the lake no less than eight times in a span of three bells. Each time the *faerilas* magic roared to life, so had Rain. And he'd discovered that one of the most beneficial aspects of mating in a tairen-fired Source pool was the near-instant rejuvenation of energy and . . . er . . . interest.

Ellysetta laid a hand over his heart. "You feel better, *shei'tan*. Calmer."

"Three bells of Source-enhanced mating will apparently do that to a Fey," he teased. But it was more than that. The pleasure had gone much deeper than mere physical fulfillment. Several times during their mating, he'd felt closer to Ellysetta than ever before. As if the secret to completing their bond were within reach, if only they could figure out how to grasp it.

Inexplicably, he'd also felt a strange, tingling awareness, like a memory long forgotten, as if there were more at work than just the restorative powers of a potent Source—more even than an irresistible (and thoroughly enjoyable) compulsion to mate.

His brow furrowed. There was something special about this Source. Something important. Why did it thrive so far from the Fading Lands when so many Sources inside the Fey kingdom had grown weak or lost their magic entirely?

"Steli . . . did the tairen often visit Crystal Lake before the Mage Wars?"

Steli's whiskers twitched. «*Too near Eld. And too cold. Tairen's Bay is better for swimming. Warrrrm. Steli likes warm.*» The tairen extended her long, curving claws, then began to groom between her toes with leisurely licks of her pink tongue.

Ellysetta shifted, pulling away to tread water in the cooling lake beside him. "What are you thinking, Rain?"

He righted himself and frowned. "I'm thinking there's a mystery here. You're right that there's something different about this Source, but I can't put my finger on it."

"You mean tairen flame doesn't have the same effect on all Sources?"

"I don't know that anyone has ever tried it. Except for Dharsa and here, most Sources don't empty into a large body of water." Most fed straight into a city fountain, to be used for drinking. "I'll have Marissya ask Tealah to see if she can find anything about Crystal Lake in the Hall of Scrolls. For now, we should be getting back."

They swam to the shore and spun light Fire weaves to warm and dry themselves before Ellysetta donned her leathers and Rain his steel.

"Rain." The light touch of Ellysetta's slender hand upon his carried with it a swell of warming love and troubled regret. "About earlier . . . when I went into the Well after Aartys . . ." The delicate copper arches of her brows drew together over shadowed leaf-green eyes. "You were right to be angry with me. I went too deep. I nearly lost myself—and I did nearly weave Azrahn, but honestly, Rain, I didn't mean to." She blew out a breath. "I only meant to use Gaelen's power, as I've been doing."

Rain hadn't liked that either, but since the practice saved precious Fey lives, he had grudgingly allowed it. After all, a Fey king banished from his own country for weaving the forbidden magic himself to save his mate could hardly protest the use of the same magic to save someone else.

"So what happened?"

"I couldn't reach Aartys. He'd fallen too far into the Well. I was going to lose him. Gaelen's magic wasn't enough. And then . . ." Her voice trailed off.

"Then what?"

She wet her lips and pushed spiraling coils of flame red hair behind her ears. "Then something started . . . pushing me to weave my own Azrahn."

He didn't like the sound of that. "The Mage? He sensed you in the Well?"

"*Nei*, I don't think it was him. I think it was me. Some part of *me* wanted to weave Azrahn, Rain, even knowing what would happen if I did."

She lifted a troubled gaze to his face, and he knew she was searching for the horror she feared would be there. Months ago, she would have found it. Months ago, he'd believed Azrahn could never be woven for good. But he'd watched her save four tairen kitlings trapped in the Well of Souls by spinning that forbidden magic. He'd spun it himself to save her. Most of all, he'd seen the dazzling blaze of her unshielded Light.

"If you hadn't come," she admitted, "I would have spun it."

"But you didn't, Ellysetta."

"But I would have, Rain. *I would have.*"

He gripped her slender shoulders and held her gaze with unwavering confidence. "But you didn't."

She was still so afraid of herself, so afraid that the dark taint she sensed within wasn't just the shadow of the High Mage but proof that some part of her own soul—a part unrelated to the High Mage's Marks—was evil, just as her mother had once feared.

"When we get back to Orest, we'll talk to Gaelen," Rain said. "He was there in the Well with you. Maybe he sensed something you didn't. Or maybe he can explain what happened and help keep it from happening again." Vel Serranis was more familiar with Azrahn and Mage Marks than any other Fey. The infamous former *dahl'reisen* had spent a thousand years outcast from the Fading Lands, living on the borders between Celieria and Eld, secretly fighting the Mages to protect the homeland that had banished him. And though he'd broken more Fey laws than Rain cared to count, the skills and knowledge he'd acquired while living his lawless existence had already proven invaluable to the Fey.

Ellysetta smiled crookedly. "So stop worrying until Gaelen says I should?"

He feathered a thumb across her lower lip. "Something like

that." He dropped a kiss on her lips, then stepped away before the kiss turned into something more. "We should go. I don't want to fly you over Elden land after dark."

He summoned the Change, tossing back his head as the familiar blast of energy shot through his veins, searing and sundering him. His body was unmade, his consciousness flung out into the rainbow-shot gray mist of the Change; then both body and mind gathered back together in his other form . . . his stronger, more savage form.

The black tairen, Rainier-Eras, flexed the hands that had become paws large and strong enough to pluck fully grown cattle from a field. Long, razor-sharp claws curved out and dug deep into the rock and shale of the lakeshore. Whiskers twitched and the nostrils of his sensitive nose flared as he scented both the warm, Fey sweetness of Ellysetta and the deeper, richer presence of the as-yet-unseen tairen that dwelled within her soul, the mate to the tairen he was now. The Source must have brought that powerful magic much closer to the surface. He had never sensed her tairen so clearly.

His chest filled with a low, rumbling growl, the need to claim and dominate rising swiftly. Tairen were intelligent creatures, but they embraced their most primitive instincts, living by the laws of the pride, not the civilized world. They claimed their mates, defended their pride, protected their young, and slaughtered their enemies without regret.

And right at this moment, Rain's tairen was very much aware of the mate he recognized but could not yet claim. His tail thumped the ground and he couldn't stop himself from leaning in and dipping his head down to sniff Ellysetta, nudging her with his nose while the growl kept rumbling softly in his chest.

The light, silky-soft fur on the membranes of his wings registered the shifting of the winds mere instants before a new scent reached his nose. Faint. Very faint. But the scent was familiar and made his hackles rise. The claiming growl vibrating in his throat became the louder, more threatening growl of a tairen preparing to attack. Tairen lips pulled back, baring his deadly fangs, each easily as long as a man's leg. Venom gathered in the hollow tips.

"Rain? What is it?" Ellysetta took a step closer to him, unafraid of the aggression coiling within him.

«Get in the saddle,» he commanded. «Now.» He didn't wait for her to spin the weave. Instead, he spun it himself, whisking her off her feet on a gust of forceful Air and depositing her in the saddle strapped to the juncture of his neck and shoulders. «Steli-chakai . . . » He started to sing his discovery in tairen song, but there was no need.

The white tairen was growling with as much menace as he. Her fur was ruffled, her venomous tail spikes fully extended. «Steli smells the poison on the wind, Rainier-Eras.»

"What is it, Rain?" Ellysetta asked again. "What poison?"

«From Eld.» The autumn winds had shifted westward, and they carried the tang of smoke and the distinctive odor of sel'dor—the foul black metal of the Eld—being smelted in white-hot fires.

He gave a roar and spewed a jet of fire into the sky. His hind legs bent as he crouched, energy gathering in the great ropes of powerful muscle. With a scream of fury, he launched himself into the air. His wings snapped taut, extending forward and drawing back in mighty, sweeping strokes that propelled him high into the now-cloudless blue autumn sky.

Behind him, with a roar and a blast of her own fire, Steli followed. Together, they cleared the mountaintops and soared higher, speeding east, towards the borders of Eld.

As the tairen disappeared over the mountains, still silence fell once more over the basin of Crystal Lake. In one of the narrow passes leading between the surrounding mountains, a small party cautiously rose from the cover of the rocks. Following the gestured commands of their leader, the men made their way down the narrow path to the shores of the lake.

They walked single file, each careful to place his feet in the steps of the man before him, and their boots, wrapped in thick swaths of wool, made no sound even on the loose shale and rock of the shore. They skirted the north end of the lake and continued westward into the Feyls, the formidable volcanic range that formed the Fading Lands' northern border. A gust of wind made the edges of their thick gray and brown woolen coats flutter against the dull, black sheen of *sel'dor* armor.

CHAPTER THREE

Rhakis Mountains, near Eld

Less than a hundred miles of mountainous terrain separated Crystal Lake from Eld. Rain and Steli flew it in a single bell. As they neared the final row of ragged peaks that gave way to the deep, dense, forested land of his enemies, Rain's heart sank.

All of Eld lay under a blanket of fog too thick to be the country's natural autumn cloud cover. The Mages had enhanced the mist—no doubt to prevent Fey and Celierian scouts from detecting what Rain could now see: dark haze on the northern horizon, like a shadowy veil hanging over the countryside.

He was still too far away to see the glow of the foul, ancient forges, but he didn't need to. The bubbling cauldron of black smoke that cast its sooty shadow across the sky was proof enough.

«*Rain?*» Ellysetta's voice sounded in his mind. «*Talk to me. What do you see?*»

«*Koderas.*» Even in Spirit, the word was all but spat from him. «*The fires of Koderas are lit.*»

«*What does that mean?*»

«*It means we haven't yet faced anything close to the worst this new High Mage of Eld has to offer.*» He dipped a wing and banked, circling at the edge of the Rhakis, peering east through the haze of smoke. «*Koderas is the location of the great sel'dor foundries of Eld. That much smoke means all the fires are lit, and that hasn't happened since the Mage Wars. The Eld have just been buying time and testing our defenses these last weeks while they amass a much larger army.*»

The news couldn't be worse. The initial attacks on Teleon and Orest had dealt the Fey and Lord Teleos's forces a brutal blow. If the Eld struck again with an army large enough to require all of Koderas to equip . . . well . . . «*We must get back to Orest and send word to Dorian and the Fading Lands. We're going to need a great many more warriors.*»

He roared a command to Steli. They both wheeled sharply in the sky and shot southwards, hugging the mountains as they raced back towards Celieria.

Eld ~ Koderas

Clad in the purple robes of his office, Vadim Maur, the High Mage of Eld, walked along the *sel'dor*-railed observation balcony that circled the perimeters of the deep, fiery pits of Koderas. His robe's deep cowl shrouded his face, and supple leather gloves, dyed purple to match his robes, covered his hands. He grasped the metal railing, and the rings of power decorating each of his fingers and thumbs glinted in the red-orange glow of the furnaces below.

Along one section of the great pit, slave-powered conveyor belts leading from the nearby mines fed raw ore and *magus*, the black powder that gave *sel'dor* its strength and enhanced its magical properties, into six great smelting furnaces. Two of the furnaces pumped out glowing rods of hot *sel'dor* ready for forging. A dozen workers wielding sharp pincers cut off lengths of the hot metal and passed them on to the hundreds of smiths who pounded, shaped, and forged the *sel'dor* into swords and armor for the High Mage's Black Guard and the other elite troops of his Elden armies. The remaining four furnaces poured continuous streams of liquid *sel'dor* into casting molds for mass-produced armaments. Cast *sel'dor* wasn't as strong as forged, but the frontline troops for whom the weaker armaments were intended wouldn't live long enough to appreciate the difference. There was no sense in wasting quality to outfit a corpse.

"You will have what I need by the end of the month?" Vadim asked Primage Grule, the Mage responsible for managing all activity in Koderas.

"I will, Most High."

"And the rest?"

"Coming along exactly as planned, Most High. I think you will be pleased."

Grule gestured for the High Mage to precede him, but before Vadim could continue with his inspection of Koderas, hurried footsteps beat a rapid tattoo down the walkway. The High Mage turned his shrouded head to see a green-robed novice, his pale face flushed with exertion, running towards them.

"Master." The novice bowed to the Primage. "Most High." He bowed again, much more deeply, to the High Mage. "You asked to be notified, Great One, if there was news."

One purple-gloved hand shot out, gripping the side of the young man's face, fingers pressing against his temple. "Tell me," the High Mage commanded, and the flood of information in the novice's brain poured forth.

Scouts in the Rhakis had spotted two tairen in the skies west of Koderas. The small team heading into the Feyls had confirmed it: the Tairen Soul, his mate, and the white tairen had spent the day at Crystal Lake before flying east, towards Eld and Koderas. They most certainly had seen the smoke, and the Tairen Soul would remember what it meant.

In the shadow of his hood, the seeping flesh that was Vadim's mouth pressed flat. "It seems our secret is out."

Celieria ~ Orest

By the time Rain, Ellysetta, and Steli neared Orest, night had fallen. Pinpoints of flickering light from campfires burning beneath the trees dotted the southwest corner of Eld, and the nightly mortar barrage had already begun. Fiery mortars exploded against the great gray walls of Lower Orest and split the darkness like flashes of lightning. Flames spat from the gaping jaws of tairen diving to scorch the siege weapons, but a rain of black arrows and bowcannon bolts kept the tairen at bay and the Eld trebuchet firing.

Catapults on the walls of Orest sent answering volleys— great, fiery blobs of burning pitch that exploded on impact and stuck like fiery glue to whatever they hit. The added height of the wall-mounted siege gave the Celierian weapons greater distance, and the audible screams of Eld soldiers wreathed in flames and running in wild circles mingled with Celierian cheers when a direct hit toppled one of the Eld trebuchets and sent it up in flames.

Rain flew well out of reach of the missile attacks, and Ellysetta kept the invisibility weave wrapped securely about them until he and Steli dove down into the large, scooped-out hollow that housed Veil Lake and Upper Orest.

Ellysetta's booted feet hit the ground running while Rain Changed and landed only a few steps behind her. Together, they jogged the short distance to the edge of the plaza where Great Lord Devron Teleos and the five warriors of Ellysetta's bloodsworn quintet were waiting to greet them.

"Koderas is lit." Rain delivered the news without preamble. "Every furnace, by the look of it."

Dev's Fey eyes flared with a sudden surge of latent magic. Though he was Celierian born and bred, Lord Teleos's bright eyes and the silvery luminescence of his skin betrayed the strong Fey heritage of his family's House. Long before King Dorian I had wed his Fey bride ten centuries ago, the lords of House Teleos had intermarried with the Fey and guarded the gateways to the Fading Lands—first at the Garreval, and more recently here in Orest as well.

"I suppose I should feel more surprised," Dev said, "but I've been waiting for that blade to drop for months now."

"As have I." Rain had suspected the truth even before the first attack on Orest. "If you'll ready a rider, I'll write a letter to the king. Dorian needs to start calling in favors from his allies immediately. If this Mage attacks with even half of what we faced in the Mage Wars, every man, woman, and child in Celieria could stand before the Eld and still be overrun."

"The last three couriers never made it to their destination."

Rain processed the news without blinking. "Then I'll have a Spirit master send the weave."

"Only if he can send it on a private weave. The Warriors' Path has been compromised."

"What do you mean?"

"I mean we had some unexpected visitors while you were gone." The flash of an illumination mortar lit up the plaza bright as day. "There's news you need to hear, but let's get inside first. No sense giving the Eld a clear target while we talk."

«*Steli . . .* » Rain turned to the white tairen, who had padded to the edge of Veil Lake to slake her thirst.

The white tairen lifted her regal head. «*Go with the Fey-kin, Rainier-Eras. Steli will join the pride and scorch the Eld.*» She crouched on her hind legs and leapt into the sky with a roar. «*Time to run, foolish Eld-prey,*» she sang. «*Steli-chakai is here, and she is hungry.*»

Leaving Steli and the pride to subdue the Eld, Rain and Dev flanked Ellysetta, and her quintet ringed protectively around the three of them as they made their way off the plaza.

"So what's this about the Warriors' Path being compromised?" Rain asked as they walked down the torchlit brick path. The mist off the waterfalls of Kiyera's Vei̇̃l

Gate hung in the air, dampening their hair and making small halos of rainbow-kissed light around each of the torches. "What happened while we were away?"

"We intercepted a raiding party shortly after nightfall." The tall trees lining the walk gave way to neatly trimmed shrubs, topiaries, and flower boxes edging the pearl gray buildings of Upper Orest. "They made it through the outer gates undetected. If not for the wards on the inner walls, we never would have discovered them." Dev pushed open the leaded glass door of the conservatory that served as his command post. "Three Mages, twenty Black Guard . . . and six *dahl'reisen*."

Rain stopped in his tracks and turned to Gaelen. "Yours?" The infamous former *dahl'reisen* had spent most of the last thousand years leading a band of banished Fey he called the Brotherhood of Shadows. He'd be leading them still if Ellysetta hadn't restored his soul.

Faint color bloomed in Gaelen's cheeks, but he held Rain's hard stare without wavering. "Four of them were at one time," he admitted. "They disappeared on reconnaissance missions into Eld. The other two weren't familiar to me."

Instinct pushed Rain closer to Ellysetta. The thought of *dahl'reisen* coming within ten miles of her made his hands ache for the weight of his steel. "So it seems not all in your Brotherhood are as committed to protecting the Fading Lands as you thought them to be."

«*Rain*,» Ellysetta chided softly. Her fingers brushed the back of his wrist.

Gaelen's ice blue gaze flickered briefly as he noted the gesture. "*Nei, kem'falla*, it's all right. The Feyreisen is right to doubt." He lifted his chin, and his eyes narrowed. "Those in the Brotherhood *are* committed, Tairen Soul, but they are still *dahl'reisen*. Even when I was one of them, I never forgot that."

"Meaning you can't trust them." That remark came from Tajik vel Sibboreh, the red-haired former general of the eastern Fey armies who now served as the Water master of Ellysetta's bloodsworn quintet. Tajik had survived a millennium as a *rasa*, one of the haunted, soul-burdened Fey on the cusp of turning *dahl'reisen*, tormented by the lives he'd taken but desperately clinging to honor by a thread, refusing to take that last step that would tip his soul into Shadow. Because of that, Tajik had little liking or sympathy for Gaelen—he certainly didn't trust him—and he rarely missed an opportunity to get in a dig.

"Meaning trust, but not blindly," Gaelen countered. "I knew when I formed the Brotherhood that some would go astray, but I thought it better to save nineteen and lose one than see the full score slip down the Dark Path."

"So were these *dahl'reisen* Mage-claimed, or were they serving the Eld willingly?" Rain asked. Tightness crept over Gaelen's features, and Rain had his answer. "I see—"

"Not every *dahl'reisen* who joins us chooses to stay. And before you ask, *nei*, we don't open our doors to every dishonored blade cast out of the Fading Lands. *Dahl'reisen* we may be, but warriors truly bereft of honor were never welcome in our company."

"Says the *dahl'reisen* who slaughtered every man, woman, and child in an entire Eld clan," Tajik muttered.

"As if you would not have done the same had you seen your sister slain before your eyes. Oh, but I forgot. When your sister disappeared in the Wars, you did nothing."

Color flamed in Tajik's face. "You *grot-jaffing*, *krekk*-eating *rultshart*." He lunged for Gaelen, and only Rijonn and Gil— the Earth and Air masters of the quintet—managed to hold him back. Bel and Rain caught Gaelen's arms.

"Stop it. Both of you." Ellysetta stepped between the two warriors. "What is wrong with you? The enemy is out there." She pointed northward, towards Eld. "Save your anger for them."

Gaelen tugged free of Bel's and Rain's grip. "*Sieks'ta*. I know better than to give in to vel Sibboreh's taunting . . . and I shouldn't have pricked him about his sister. *Sieks'ta*, Tajik."

He held out his right hand in a gesture of peace, but Tajik only glared, yanked himself out of Rijonn and Gil's tight hold, and stalked to the glass wall overlooking the river. The fingers of Gaelen's extended hand curled in a loose fist, and raw emotion shone from his eyes for an instant before a shutter fell over his face.

He smoothed the bunched creases in his black leather tunic and swept the ruffled strands of ebony hair back out of his face. "As I was saying, Tairen Soul, not all *dahl'reisen* join the Brotherhood. Nor do all who join the Brotherhood stay. Many do, but when hope fades, the call of the Dark Path is hard to resist."

"So now the *dahl'reisen*—at least some of them—are in league with the Eld," Rain summarized. "Which means the Warriors' Path and every nonprivate Spirit weave are compromised."

"And the *dahl'reisen* from the Brotherhood are spinning Gaelen's invisibility weave on behalf of the Eld," Bel added. The black-haired, cobalt-eyed Spirit master of Ellysetta's quintet made the announcement with none of the implied accusation that had been in Tajik's voice earlier. Bel had been the first warrior to welcome Gaelen back into the fold, and he was still the only Fey Gaelen truly considered a friend. "It won't take the Eld long to figure out how to penetrate it, if they haven't already."

Some found it odd that Bel, a warrior widely regarded in the Fading Lands as the living essence of Fey honor, could befriend the *dahl'reisen* whose infamous deeds were legend and whose name had become synonymous with the Dark Lord's, but Rain knew that Bel's unswerving sense of honor was exceeded only by the greatness of his heart. Belliard vel Jelani was a warrior who embodied the best of the Fey. He could plan the systematic and merciless destruction of an enemy army, kill with breathtaking skill, and make decisions that would break lesser men—but even when he'd clung to the pained, gray existence of the *rasa*, he never abandoned either honor or compassion. That nobility of spirit, an intrinsic goodness that suffused his every action and yet never blinded him to the harsh realities and demands of a Fey warrior's life, was one of the qualities Rain admired—and envied—most about his oldest and most trusted friend.

It was in part *because* Bel found Gaelen a worthy friend that Rain had abandoned the old prejudices that still kept Tajik and vel Serranis at odds.

"You say you discovered the Eld before they could make it past the inner gates. Was there any indication of what their mission was?"

"I can think of any number of reasons a general would send such a small party into an enemy fortress, and even more reasons why the Eld would do so." Bel glanced at Ellysetta.

"There's more," Lord Teleos said. "The *dahl'reisen* and the Black Guard are dead, but we managed to take one of the Primages alive. The others killed themselves so they couldn't be questioned, but we're keeping this one unconscious and restrained by a twenty-five-fold weave. If we can Truthspeak him before he has time to invoke his death spell, we might learn something."

Rain frowned. "The *shei'dalins* haven't already done so?" It was rare to capture a Mage alive, even rarer to keep him that way for any length of time.

"Once they sensed *dahl'reisen* in the city, their quintets insisted on taking them through the Mists. They won't be back until morning at the earliest."

"What about the wounded?" Ellysetta asked.

"The hearth witches have the situation well in hand, *kem'falla*," Bel said. "This attack looks much worse than it really is. I suspect the whole effort is a diversion meant to hold our attention while the raiding party we intercepted snuck through our defenses."

"So you're saying the only one here to Truthspeak the Mage is me."

Aggression slammed through Rain's body. "That's out of

the question!" He lunged into the space between Ellysetta and her quintet, thrusting her behind him in a Fey male's instinctive gesture of protection. "*Nei*, I forbid it," he reiterated when it looked like Gaelen or Bel might object. "She bears Mage Marks. We have no idea what touching a Primage of Eld—let alone trying to Truthspeak him—would do to her, what doors it might open. Better we get nothing at all from this Mage than risk Ellysetta."

Bel and Gaelen looked away. Even Teleos couldn't hold his gaze. They'd really considered it. They'd really thought Ellysetta might—

"Rain, if there's a chance we can find out what the Eld are planning, isn't it worth the risk?" Ellysetta spoke in a low voice, pitched for his ears only. "Think of the lives we could save. Koderas is lit. You said yourself that means Celieria is in grave danger. If I can Truthspeak this Mage, I might discover something that will help us prepare our defenses."

He spun to face her and gripped her arms. "I know you want to help, but this is not the way, Ellysetta. Be sensible. You've never Truthspoken anyone before in your life. A Primage is hardly an appropriate test subject." He shook his head. "*Nei*. It's far too dangerous in every possible way. Put the idea out of your mind, because it isn't going to happen."

"We could send word to the other side of the Mists." Gillandaris vel Jendahr, Ellysetta's Air master, made the suggestion. Gil's black eyes sparkled with silvery lights like stars shining in a night sky, contrasting vividly with the alabaster paleness of his Fey skin and the even paler hair that he wore bound at his nape with a simple, unadorned tie and left to fall to his waist in a shower of snowy whiteness. His expression was serious—almost grim. He was a blade's blade, hard edged and dangerous. The kind of warrior more likely to slit throats than laugh at jokes, though with his friends he did on occasion display a wit every bit as sharp as his blades.

"The *shei'dalins* who left Orest are still in the Mists," Gil was saying, "but there are others camped just on the other side. They might be able to get here soon enough to Truth-speak this Mage before he fights off the sleep spell and suicides like the others."

"Summon them," Rain commanded.

"Already done," Bel answered. The hazy lavender glow of his Spirit weave still lit his eyes. "Two *shei'dalins* and their quintets are on the way. They should arrive in a few bells." Revan-Oreth, the Mist-shrouded pass guarded by Kiyera's Veil, wasn't particularly long in miles, but it was a steep, winding, treacherous mountain path. Even before the Mists were raised, Revan-Oreth had been a slow road to travel.

"Which *shei'dalins* are coming?"

"Narena and Faerah vol Oros."

Rain took a breath. The women were two of the Fading Lands' most powerful *shei'dalins*, and he knew exactly why they were coming. "Call fifty of our strongest warriors. I want those two guarded at all times." The vol Oros line was one of the most powerful surviving families of the Fey. One of Faerah and Narena's two brothers—both now dead—had been a Tairen Soul, and their eldest sister, Nicolene, had been captured by the Eld during the battle of Teleon. Rain would bet every blade he owned that Faerah and Narena's offer to Truthspeak the captured Mage had more to do with their hope of discovering what had happened to their sister than any desire to find useful military intelligence.

Eld ~ Boura Fell

"You're late, *umagi*." A cuff from one meaty paw accompanied the Eld guard's irritable growl.

The small, ragged, dark-haired girl who'd received both the greeting and the blow stifled a hiss of pain and skittered to one side to avoid the following kick. She was usually more adept at dodging Turog's fists, but she'd been distracted by the battered woman strapped to the table in the center of the room.

When she'd entered the mating cell and caught sight of the

masses of tangled black hair and the faint silvery glow of the woman on the table, the girl had frozen in her steps. For a few, dizzying instants, she'd thought it was Shia, the pretty, black-haired, blue-eyed woman who'd loved to brush the girl's hair and sing her sweet songs. Shia, who'd given the worthless *umagi* girl the name she now called herself: Melliandra.

But Shia had been ripped apart in childbirth, her lifeless body thrown down the refuse chute to be eaten by the savage *darrokken* that lived in the den caves at the bottom of the pit. And when the woman on the table opened her eyes, Melliandra's impossible hope faded. Black eyes, not blue. Dull and dazed from the effects of the drugs and Mage spells used to make her docile and receptive to mating. Just as well, Melliandra thought with an unexpected surge of pity. The stud set upon the woman had clearly been one of the wild ones . . . the kind who sank his teeth and nails into a woman as well as his mating organ.

"What the jaffing hells are you waiting for, *skrant*? Get to work." Turog swung his massive paw again, but this time Melliandra was quick enough to duck.

She dragged her cart of cleaning supplies into the room and suppressed her unexpected surge of emotions with ruthless determination. Emotion was a sign of weakness in Boura Fell. Blank, unseeing eyes, ears deaf to the screams of the suffering, and a heart devoid of caring were the only ways to survive here.

Still, she couldn't keep from watching out of the corner of her eye as the black-garbed *umagi* attendants released the heavy leather straps binding the woman's wrists and ankles and helped her to her feet. The woman's knees gave way, and she would have tumbled to the floor if one of the attendants hadn't caught her beneath her arms and held her upright. The other *umagi* draped a blanket around her—which Melliandra knew was more to keep one of the High Mage's precious female breeders from catching a chill than any attempt to preserve her modesty—and led her out the door.

Melliandra listened to the sound of their departing footsteps, counting the steps and calculating the distance before the slight muffling indicated a turn down another corridor. The new woman was being taken to the garden, the deceptively beautiful chamber that looked like a natural paradise but was, in fact, the prison where the High Mage kept his most valuable and magically gifted female breeders.

A prickle at the back of her neck warned her that Turog was watching, and she promptly snapped her attention back to her chores, dunking a clean cloth into the bucket of warm, soapy water and attacking the mating table with it. Though Turog behaved like every other lumbering, thick-necked bully who guarded the lower levels of Boura Fell, he was more observant than most. And meaner. The High Mage chose the men who guarded his breeders very carefully.

Despite the bruises and bite marks on the woman's body, her mating hadn't been one of the most violent ones Melliandra had been summoned to clean up after. There were only a few smears of blood on the table and almost none on the floor. Within ten chimes, the room was spotless and ready for the next unfortunate participant in the Mage's breeding program.

Melliandra gathered her supplies, loaded them on the cart, and exited. As she passed the corridor leading to the garden prison, her veins hummed with the desire to make the turn. The woman who'd just been taken there was one of the new prisoners, someone whose skin shone with the same silvery luminescence as Lord Death and his mate.

Someone new enough and magical enough to perhaps still retain memory of her life outside Boura Fell, perhaps even information Melliandra could use to her advantage.

The desire to head down that corridor was so strong, she fought to keep her body from making the turn. It was as if something or someone in that room were compelling her with a power almost as strong as the one the High Mage of Eld used when he took command of her body and bent her to his will.

But she knew the compulsion didn't come from someone else. It came from within. *She* wanted to go down that corridor. *She* wanted to visit the newcomer, interrogate her, discover everything she knew about the world above.

Melliandra's muscles clenched in protest as will overrode want. She couldn't go. Not now. Her earlier reaction when she'd entered the mating chamber had roused Turog's suspicions, and she could feel his gaze boring into the back of her head.

She pushed the cart a little faster, forcing herself to walk past the corridor. The High Mage was gone for at least two days, and Turog would head back to the barracks hall when his shift ended in four bells. She would come back then and sneak into the garden room to visit not just the new breeder but all the women held there. She hadn't seen them since Shia's death.

Losing the first person ever to treat her with kindness had left an ache Melliandra had never known before and couldn't seem to quell. She'd shed the first tears of her life over Shia, felt the first consuming burn of rage.

Nothing had been the same since then. There was a hole in her, a yawning, painful emptiness she couldn't seem to fill.

Every night, she dreamed. Not the dull, spiritless gray dreams of an *umagi*, but dreams filled with vibrant color and emotion. Dreams that made her wake each morning with her hands curled into determined fists and the ragged square of folded cloth beneath her head soaked with her own tears.

She dreamed of Shia singing softly as she brushed Melliandra's hair . . . of Shia's torn, lifeless body tumbling out of the refuse cart into the pit of slavering *darrokken* . . . of Shia's child, the tiny, bright-eyed infant in whom a piece of Shia still lived.

Most of all, she dreamed of watching the High Mage die in torment . . . and of the day when she, Melliandra—with Shia's son cradled in her arms and the Mage Marks that made her a slave completely erased from her soul—would step out of the cruel, sunless gloom of Boura Fell into the glorious freedom of the world above.

"Get out of my way, *umagi*."

The curt snap of a masculine voice shattered her unintended reverie, and a swirl of blue silk filled her vision. Primage! Realization splashed over her like a bucket of icy water.

Horrified to be caught daydreaming—and by a Primage, no less—Melliandra gasped. "Forgive this worthless *umagi*, master." She scuttled out of the way, dragging her cart with her. All the while her mind worked at a frantic pace to gather every fragment of dream and whisper of thought that belonged to Melliandra and shove them securely back into the tiny private space she'd somehow managed to create in her mind to hide the time she'd spent with Shia.

That tiny space had grown over the last few months and more thoughts had crowded into it. Hopes had blossomed, and her first timid wish for freedom had evolved into dreams so vivid she could not help pursuing them.

A nameless, worthless *umagi* had no thought, took no breath, envisioned no future that was not allowed by her Mage master . . . but Melliandra did.

Within the body of a slave, the dreams of a free soul had taken root. One day, she would make those dreams come true.

CHAPTER FOUR

Shadow Man
Magic Mages
Lift your hand
Weave your spells

Rising Darkness
Evil Rages
Throughout the land
Azrahn dwells

Shadow Magic, a Fey child's poem of Eld

Celieria ~ Orest

"He doesn't look anything like I imagined."

Ellysetta stared at the blue-robed man lying unconscious on the floor in the center of a large, windowless room carved into the mountain. The Fey had brought their prisoner to Upper Orest to await the arrival of the *shei'dalins*, and they were taking no chances that he might escape. In addition to the chains that bound his hands and ankles, a ring of grim-eyed Fey surrounded the Mage, feeding power into the blazing twenty-five-fold weave that secured him, while another twenty-five Fey had spun a protection weave around the room.

Looking at the Mage, Ellysetta couldn't help thinking that

she had expected a Primage of Eld to look more sinister . . . more openly evil and depraved. The Fey warriors guarding him looked more dangerous than he. This Mage had the face of a handsome young man in his early twenties. "He looks so . . . innocent."

"Don't believe it for an instant," Rain growled. "The boy born into that body might have been innocent, but the Mage that boy has become is anything but. Come away. It's against my better judgment that you're even close enough to look upon him." Despite the twenty-five-fold weave around the Mage, the twenty-five grim-eyed Fey holding the weaves, and the added protection of her own bloodsworn quintet hovering nearby, Rain was clearly on edge at having Ellysetta in such close proximity to a Mage.

Flashing sparks of unsettled magic swirled around Rain like agitated fairy flies. He hadn't wanted to bring her here—he'd even suggested she leave the city entirely—but she had insisted on coming. She'd wanted to put a face to the evil that had haunted her entire life.

Was it odd to feel so . . . disappointed? She'd prepared herself for horror, for a monstrous face from her worst nightmares. Not a handsome youth who would make girls sigh as he walked by. Maybe the twenty-five-fold shields were to blame, but she couldn't sense the slightest hint of danger about him. Nothing. If she'd met him on the street, she would have smiled and offered him greeting. Upon better acquaintance, she might even have welcomed him into her home.

"Do you think Mages ever regret what they are?"

Rain turned to her in surprise—and no little concern. "*Nei*," he said flatly, his tone certain and unyielding. "Regret requires a conscience, and Mages have none."

"But—"

"*Nei*. But nothing." His eyes narrowed. "I know what you're thinking. You look at this Mage and you see a young boy, and you want to save him. Put that thought out of your head this instant. This Mage is no boy. He's probably older than I am.

In fact, he's probably destroyed more lives than I have—yet given none of them a second thought."

"Why would anyone ever choose to live such an evil life?"

Rain put a hand on her back, guiding her away from the Mage. "Who knows, Ellysetta? Lust for power. Something broken in the soul. Or perhaps all it takes is being born into a culture that celebrates death and the enslavement of the soul over life and freedom." Shadows darkened his eyes, turning lavender to moody violet. "Does it matter? The Eld have always served the Dark, and we have always been their enemy."

"But . . . don't you think if we killed the Mages, the Eld from non-Mage families would want to be free?" She thought of her best childhood friend, Selianne, and Selianne's mother, who had been born in Eld and soul-claimed by the Mages. They'd both been loving, caring people. And they'd both died at Mage hands.

"If that was their desire, they had their chance to take it after the Mage Wars. They chose not to."

The sound of many booted feet coming down the adjoining corridor made Ellysetta swallow her next remark and turn towards the door. A score of warriors—*lu'tans* who had bloodsworn themselves to protecting her—entered the room. Behind them, garbed from head to toe in brilliant scarlet and surrounded by ten unfamiliar warriors, two Fey *shei'dalins* followed, while another score of *lu'tans* brought up the rear. The large room seemed suddenly much smaller with close to ninety Fey crowded around its perimeter.

The *shei'dalins* walked towards the Mage without fear or hesitation, throwing back the veils covering their faces.

Narena and Faerah vol Oros were stunning even by Fey standards, with clouds of thick, curling black hair framing alabaster faces dominated by full red lips and large, thickly lashed black eyes.

But it was the look in those eyes—a pitiless, unyielding purpose—that made Ellysetta catch her breath and move instinctively closer to Rain. The vol Oros sisters were not gentle empaths suffused with the customary warmth of *shei'dalin* kindness and compassion. The expression in those searing eyes made it clear they were powerful, confident immortals come to rip truth from an enemy's mind.

Ellysetta's hand crept into Rain's and squeezed tight. The vol Oros sisters reminded her all too vividly of her first passage through the Faering Mists, when a band of ghostly, Mist-spawned *shei'dalins* had trapped and forcibly Truthspoken her, diving into her mind, ripping at the protective barriers that had shielded her all her life, nearly unleashing the wild, violent thing that lived inside her.

«*Las, shei'tani.*» Rain whispered on the private path they had forged between themselves. «*Narena and Faerah mean you no harm.*»

His voice rang with certainty, but Ellysetta still flinched as the *shei'dalins* drew close and gathered their considerable power. No matter how warmly the *shei'dalins* would have welcomed any other mate of their king, Ellysetta bore four Mage Marks. That changed everything.

But the vol Oros sisters barely even flicked a glance in her direction. Their attention was entirely focused on the Mage.

"We need to know what the Eld are planning and where they will strike next," Rain told the *shei'dalins*. "And get the size of their forces, too, if he knows it."

One of the two nodded curtly, and without a word, they walked around the Mage and knelt on the ground near his head, their eyes never leaving his face. The two quintets who had accompanied them from the Fading Lands knelt around the Mage's body. Each of the warriors pulled razor-sharp red Fey'cha from their sheaths and held them over the Mage's body. Twenty blades were poised over vital arteries and organs: neck, heart, belly, thighs, arms. If the Mage so much as lifted a finger against the *shei'dalins*, he would be dead in an instant. Ellysetta shivered at the thought.

"Let's go, *shei'tani*," Rain whispered. "There's no need for you to be here."

"There's every need," she said. "I've never seen anyone Truthspeak a Mage. It's a talent that could come in handy, don't you think?"

He scowled. "Not for you. If you think I'd ever let you put your hands on a Mage . . ."

"Once our bond is complete, no Mage can soul-claim me," she reminded him. "Let me stay, Rain. Let me watch . . . and learn."

He surrendered with ill grace, but insisted she remain securely at his side. On that, he would not budge.

When the vol Oros sisters were ready to begin, they nodded to the warriors holding the twenty-five-fold weave around the Mage. Ellysetta expected the warriors to disperse their weave slowly, cautiously, but instead, one of the Fey cried, "Now!" and each Fey dissolved his thread in the weave.

The instant the weave vanished, the two sisters leaned in and gripped the Mage's head in their hands. Power exploded in a bright, golden-white light around them.

Ellysetta's belly coiled tight as she watched the *shei'dalins* spin their weaves. She'd seen Truthspeaking before . . . but never like this. The threads were sun-bright, blazing with such concentrated power she could taste the snap of it in her mouth, feel the shocking tingle race over her skin. It reminded her of the burst of power that billowed around Rain every time he summoned the Change.

She kept her eyes on the *shei'dalins*, summoning Fey vision in an attempt to see the patterns of their weave. The threads were so bright, they would have blinded a lesser *shei'dalin*, but Ellysetta saw the pattern—or, rather, sensed it somehow—and her mind worked to commit it to memory. Spirit and *shei'dalin's* love . . . not soft, not soothing, but hard and sharp as a knife. It stabbed deep into the mind of the unconscious Mage.

His eyes flew open, filled with shock. His lips parted in a soundless gasp. No other part of his body so much as twitched, because the Fey had spun a paralysis weave on him as soon as the shield weave had dissolved.

Ellysetta heard a voice—a wail. The Mage's wail. His mind rejecting the invasion of his thoughts. On the heels of his cry came a powerful intonation, two female voices, each vibrating with compulsion so strong, a chill shuddered up Ellysetta's spine.

«*Open your mind, son of Eld. Let us in. We can feel how it hurts you to keep secrets from us. Don't torment yourself this way. The knowledge you hold is a knife in your belly, twisting deeper with every moment you delay. Let go of the pain, son of Eld. Open your mind, set free your burdens, and let us bring you peace.*»

Ellysetta's nails dug into Rain's wrist. The Mage was screaming now—a silent scream that ripped through his soul. The *shei'dalins* were not spinning pain upon him; he was doing it himself, thanks to the compulsion woven into their voices. Still, he fought to hold his barriers in place and resist the invasion of his mind. He wanted to whisper the death spell, the one that would free him from this torment and keep what he knew safe, but he couldn't remember the word, and his tongue couldn't move to form it.

«*Torvan . . .* » The *shei'dalins* had pierced the outer layer of his mind and discovered the Mage's name and a memory from his childhood—a memory of a time when he'd been young and still innocent, a powerful child already slated for greatness. He had a mother, a Primage's favored concubine, a beauty with brown eyes and raven hair. She had loved him—at least as much as a woman of Eld dared to love her child.

«*Torvan.*» Narena and Faerah had now tapped the memories of that mother, the feelings the boy Mage had reciprocated until he grew old enough to know that one day he would be her master. Using those memories, the *shei'dalins* spun a vivid illusion of the boy's mother, the sound of her voice, the sweet smell of her skin, the soft warmth of her embrace in those too-brief moments when she was allowed to hold her child. «*Torvan, dear one,*» the boy's mother pleaded. «*Please tell us what we need to know. Please, my son. Trust us.*»

Ellysetta swayed. It was almost as if she were there in the

weave with the *shei'dalins* and the Mage and the Mage's memories. She knew the instant the crack into the Mage's mind opened a little further, gasped as the *shei'dalins* plunged deeper.

«*Tell us what you know, Torvan. Tell us. You cannot hold back. You don't want to hold back. The need to speak, to confess what you know, is too strong to resist.*»

The *shei'dalins'* fingers tightened on the Mage's face, and another wail was wrung from his soul as a surge of fresh power bolstered their weave.

They had tapped other memories of his youth. Rain was wrong: Mages weren't born evil. They weren't born without a conscience. They were a product of their upbringing and the dark weaves of Azrahn that they were taught to spin when they were too young to know the danger. That sort of power was a heady drug for anyone, let alone a child.

Once Torvan donned the green robes of a novice Mage, earning the approval of his teachers and masters became the goal of his daily existence. That desire soon grew into a personal need to excel . . . to be better, stronger, more capable than his fellow novices. But it was only at age ten, when he watched his master force an *umagi* to commit unspeakable acts, that the true hunger for power over others blossomed in his Azrahn-darkened heart.

Cruelty came soon after, born from a mix of boredom and a driving urge to destroy every hint of weakness and emotion in his soul. Weak souls were slaves. Strong souls were masters. And it was much, much better to be a master than a slave.

Soon he moved from novice green to apprentice yellow, then Sulimage red. His rapid rise in rank and exponentially increasing talents caught the eye of a daring young Primage who had just ascended to the blue. Together with a handful of like-thinking Mages, they spoke in hushed whispers and thoughts stored in the small, private area of their minds that every Mage learned to create—the area that, in fact, separated Mages from *umagi*, though only a truly powerful Mage could keep even a small portion of his mind secure against the master who had claimed his soul as a child.

Torvan and his mentor talked about the rule of Demyan Raz, and the hidebound traditions of the Mage Council. They shared treasonous, revolutionary thoughts and plotted ways to increase their own powers by supplanting older but less talented Mages. They even conceived the idea of breeding stronger, more powerful *umagi* by crossing magical bloodlines.

And then the Mage Wars began. Gaelen vel Serranis slaughtered Demyan Raz and every last member of his clan—erasing the most powerful Mage family in Eld and upsetting the balance of power. As the Wars raged, Primages fought like vicious dogs to ascend to the dark throne of Eld. Intrigue, betrayal, even murder became commonplace in the great Mage Halls scattered across the land.

It was Torvan's mentor who finally succeeded where all the others had failed. Torvan's mentor whose revolutionary ideas and forethought had led him to build the first underground stronghold, into which his trusted inner circle and a few thousand Mages and *umagi* fled when Rain Tairen Soul scorched the world. It was Torvan's mentor who assumed the mantle of power and claimed the purple robes of the High Mage of Eld.

And soon, very soon, it would be that same mentor who would lead Eld back to greatness. Then all the world would tremble and fall prostrate before them. And all the world would venerate the name of Torvan's mentor, the High Mage Vadim Maur.

Vadim Maur. The mere mention of that hated name sent a bolt of fear shooting through Ellysetta's veins.

As if alerted by her fear, a familiar sentience suddenly turned its dagger-sharp attention in her direction. Ellysetta gave a choked scream and flung herself backward. She yanked her consciousness back into herself and raised her mental barriers in a flash. Her hands clutched Rain's arm so tightly, her nails broke against the unyielding surface of his golden war steel.

"Fey!" he cried.

A six-fold weave sprang up around her the same instant twenty red Fey'cha daggers sank into Eld flesh. The Mage died. Ellysetta's knees gave out and she collapsed in Rain's arms.

Still kneeling by the dead Mage, the vol Oros sisters continued to hold his head and spin their Truthspeaking weave. Several concerned warriors tried to pull them away, but they resisted until another group of Fey yanked the body of the Mage out of their grip.

"What just happened?" Rain demanded. "Ellysetta?"

Still trembling, her throat too tight to speak, she shook her head and tried to swallow. "The High Mage . . . he was there. While they were Truthspeaking that Mage, he was there."

Rain's head snapped up. His gaze pinned the vol Oros sisters. "Narena? Faerah? Did either of you sense anything?"

"*Aiyah*, but it wasn't *our* Truthspeaking that drew him." The pair turned their piercing eyes on Ellysetta.

"I wasn't Truthspeaking. How could I be, when I've never done it before?" Ellysetta paced the confines of Lord Teleos's private audience chamber. The Fey had Fired the body of the Mage and dispersed the ash into the winds, and Lord Teleos had offered his personal chambers for the use of Rain, Ellysetta, and the vol Oros sisters.

Gaelen, who stood at the perimeter of the room along with the other members of the three *shei'dalins'* respective quintets, gave a humorless laugh. "When has lack of experience ever stopped you from weaving great magic, *kem'falla*?"

"But wouldn't I have known? Wouldn't you"—she glanced at Rain and her quintet—"have known? That weave they spun took no small amount of magic."

"When several *shei'dalins* spin, Feyreisa, even strong threads can hide among the others." Narena, the elder of the two sisters, offered the possibility. "You must have analyzed our pattern and added your own threads to our weave shortly after we began. It is a common way to learn a new weave."

If she had, she'd done it purely without conscious thought.

"May I ask what made you search the Mage's mind for memories of his mother?" she asked the vol Oros sisters. "Is that something you usually do when you Truthspeak a Mage—tap into the emotions he felt as a child in order to enter his mind?"

Surprise flickered in dark eyes. The sisters exchanged a look. "We made no such search, Feyreisa," Narena said slowly.

Ellysetta frowned. "But you did. You discovered his name, and his memories of his mother, and used those to probe deeper into his thoughts."

The sisters continued to look at her as if she were some unexpected—and disconcerting—surprise discovered beneath a scientist's close-viewing glass. Ellysetta's hand rose to her throat. "But surely you heard him? Surely I wasn't the only one to see the memories of his childhood? How he became a Mage . . . how he rose in rank and came to know the High Mage"—she swallowed and forced herself to say the name—"Vadim Maur?"

Faerah moistened her lips. "Did he . . . tell *you* all that, Feyreisa?" Horror and curiosity mingled in equal parts on her lovely face.

"I . . ." Ellysetta's cheeks began to burn and her hands went clammy. She hated when she did things like this. Hated when her gift—or curse, as often seemed more the case—made her seem such a strange, odd misfit of a person. She hated the way it made people look at her—as if they couldn't decide whether she was Fey or foe, magic or monster.

Most of all, she hated how it made her wonder the same thing.

Rain's hand closed around hers, the broad strength of his fingers squeezing gently, and with that simple handclasp came the rush of emotion she needed most: love. Utter devotion and unswerving acceptance. He was the unyielding haven in the center of her storm. «*Breathe, shei'tani. It's all right. Everything will be all right.*»

She took a shuddering breath and nodded as she fought to control her racing heart. So long as Rain was at her side, she could get through all of the oddities of her existence, even the parts that shot terror through her soul.

"What did the Mage tell you, Feyreisa?" Narena echoed her younger sister's query.

"He told me about his life . . . well, 'told' isn't exactly the right word. It was more like he let me live his memories with him. . . ." She glanced at Rain. "Almost the way tairen do when they sing."

"You mean you heard his *song*?"

"Yes." His horrified expression made her flush and begin to stammer. "No. Oh, I don't know, Rain. I don't know what I did, or how he shared what he shared. I only know it was the truth." She squeezed his hands. "I *know* it was the truth. His name was Torvan Zon. His father was a Primage, and his mother was an *umagi* concubine."

She also knew that Torvan Zon had loved his mother. Even after he'd woven so much dark magic that he was no longer capable of love, he couldn't erase the part of him that belonged to her before it belonged to the Mages. By then, however, he had learned to consider love—or any form of emotional attachment—a weakness, and so he had hidden it away deep inside his mind, a shameful secret never to be revealed.

"Rain, Zon knew Vadim Maur—before he was the High Mage. He was Vadim's . . ." She hesitated. "Friend" wasn't the right word. Mages didn't have friends. They reviled all emotional attachments. She finally settled on: "He was one of Vadim Maur's inner circle."

She pressed her hands to her temples as she paced the room. She could still remember everything so vividly . . . as if some part of the Mage had become part of her . . . or rather as if his memories had become her own. She remembered the slow decline, from the child warm in his mother's arms to the Mage who had, without a twinge of conscience, enslaved another person's soul for his own use. She *knew* exactly how triumphant—almost godlike—he'd felt when he'd completed the claiming of his first *umagi* and then forced that *umagi* to do his bidding. She knew the euphoric rush of exultant power that had flooded the Mage's body. That rush—that feeling of greatness and invincible power—was the drug, the addiction, that kept Mages pursuing ever-greater, ever-darker magic. She could still sense it, even now.

And some part of her liked the taste of it.

Her stomach lurched. She stopped pacing and put her head down in an attempt to quell the nausea. Oh, gods. What had she done? Had she opened her soul to Torvan? Had she inadvertently admitted some part of his evil Eld darkness into her own soul—or, worse still, released the darkness that had existed in her own nature all along?

"*Shei'tani?*" Rain was there in an instant, searching her face in concern as he pulled her into his arms. "What is it?"

She leaned against him for a moment, closing her eyes and letting herself shelter in his strength. When he held her like this, when his soul reached for hers as it was doing now, he almost made her fears melt away, almost made her believe that she truly was as bright and shining as he claimed.

If he knew the truth, he would recoil from you in horror.

Ellysetta flinched at the cold whisper that snaked through her mind, taunting her, filling her with doubts. That voice—a voice that sounded more like her own than the High Mage's—was the same that had urged her to weave Azrahn in the Well. Alarmed, she pulled out of Rain's arms.

"Ellysetta?"

"I'm all right," she reassured him, taking a quick step to evade his hands. "It's just that the Mage's memories were so vivid." Not a lie. Not the whole truth either, but she wasn't about to admit the ugliness of her dark thoughts in front of these two *shei'dalins*. "It's unsettling to be that closely connected to evil . . . to know what pleasure the Mage felt when he enslaved a person's soul . . ." Ellysetta's shudder was entirely genuine. That gloating triumph, that thrill of dark joy as a weaker soul succumbed to the Mage's domination, was disturbing in every way . . . but not half so disturbing as her own echo of that thrill.

Gods save her.

She forced her features into a mask of calm and tried to deflect everyone's attention from her. "*Teska*, let's not dwell on this. It doesn't matter, in any case. None of what the Mage showed me shed any light on the High Mage's plans." She infused her voice with a gossamer weave of Spirit to encourage the Fey to turn their attention elsewhere. Spirit was her strongest branch of magic, strong enough that even Rain and Bel admitted she spun a finer weave than they—and they were two of the Fading Lands' most gifted Spirit masters.

Without so much as a blink of suspicion, Rain turned to the vol Oros sisters. "Were you able to learn anything? What were the Mages and *dahl'reisen* doing here in Orest?"

Narena frowned slightly, but if she sensed a compulsion weave, she gave no other sign of it. "As you already suspect, Feyreisen, they came for your mate. The High Mage has not given up his pursuit of her."

A chill raised the hairs on Ellysetta's arms. Though the shields spun around her each night as she slept kept her dreams free of disturbing nightmares, she never deluded herself that the Mage had decided to leave her in peace. He was not the sort to admit defeat.

"Do not fear, *shei'tani*," Rain murmured. "He will never see that aim fulfilled."

"*Nei*, he will not," Bel echoed, his cobalt eyes calm and filled with unwavering certainty.

She turned to the leader of her quintet, who had become her dearest friend over the last months, and for his sake, she forced a smile and pretended a confidence she did not share. Bel meant what he said. He would die to protect her, as would every other *lu'tan* who had bloodsworn himself to her. But that would not stop the Mage from coming after her.

Rain brushed a caress of warm Spirit against her senses, but kept his gaze fixed on Narena. "What of Koderas?" he asked.

The *shei'dalin* nodded and folded her hands in her lap, long fingers twining gracefully. She seemed so calm, so perfectly composed. Serene and queenly. Much more so than Ellysetta, the uncrowned and exiled queen of the Fading Lands.

"The fires are lit, as you surmised," Narena confirmed. "The Eld are preparing their invasion force."

"Where does the High Mage intend to strike?"

"An armada will reach the mouth of Great Bay in five weeks' time and move on to Celieria City once King's Point and Queen's Point are destroyed, but that is not the Eld's primary target. The bulk of the forces from Koderas will attack Kreppes." Kreppes was Great Lord Cannevar Barrial's fortress, located where the Azar River flowed into the Heras. "Once they establish a stronghold there—"

"They can bring the full might of his invasion forces across the Heras to conquer the North." Rain's boots clapped on the hard stone floor as he began to pace. "I thought it would be Moreland, Great Lord Sebourne's keep. It's a straight shot down the Selas River from Koderas. Kreppes is less obvious, but still damaging enough if they capture it."

Narena watched him with a sober gaze. "There is more, *kem'*Feyreisen. This Mage did not know the exact numbers of the Eld army, but every time he thought of it, his mind compared it to the Army of Darkness from the Time Before Memory."

Ellysetta's heart skipped a beat, then resumed at an accelerated pace. Little was known about the Army of Darkness, but all the legends concerning the scouring of the world that had ushered in the dawn of the First Age spoke in awed terms of an army that stretched farther than the eye could see. An army so vast that, even marching nonstop, it would take days to pass through a place. An army that made the earth shake beneath its boots.

An army of millions, filled with dark magic.

Scholars had scoffed at the legends, declaring them a logistical impossibility. The size of the Army of Darkness was a fanciful exaggeration meant to enthrall audiences, they declared. Most credible scholars of the current age even doubted that the cataclysmic battle between the forces of Light and Shadow had ever happened; though they all agreed that some great war had changed the balance of power in the ancient world and ushered in the First Age.

Ellysetta glanced at her *shei'tan*, and her heart dropped into her belly. Celieria's scholars might have scoffed and sneered at the legends, and dismissed any who dared take them seriously as ridiculous flitter-wits, but Rain did not appear so inclined.

If anything, he looked gravely concerned.

"Rain? Surely the legends can't be true." She didn't want to believe it possible. "Millions?"

"The legends are true," Bel answered on behalf of his king, "but I doubt this is. How could the Eld prepare an army of millions with none the wiser? Consider how much food it would take to feed so many. How much cloth to clothe them. How many buildings to house them. Someone, somewhere, would have noticed something—increased farming, increased trade. There would have been some indication long before now."

"Would there?" Rain countered. "They've been using the Well of Souls. Gaelen already told us the Eld have spies in every court in the world. It would be a simple enough matter for those spies to arrange secret transports through the Well."

"And what of their armor? If the Eld had been building such an army, Koderas would have been lit long before now."

"Who's to say it hasn't been?" Rain gripped the hilts of his *meicha* scimitars. "Teleos, how long has Eld been covered in cloud mist?"

The Celierian great lord raised his brows. "Clouds cover Eld every autumn and spring. That's been the way of things ever since the forests grew back after the scorching of the world."

"So six months of every year for the last seven centuries, the skies over Eld have been blanketed with mist . . . which provides excellent cover for a great many things. Including—as I discovered today—smoke from the great forge's fires."

"You don't seriously believe they've been planning this attack for seven centuries?" Gaelen asked.

"All I'm saying is it's possible. The Eld have had plenty of time to build an army in secret—without raising suspicions. Think about it: A Truthspoken Mage has compared this new Elden army to the Army of Darkness. Add that to everything we know—and everything the Eye of Truth has shown us. What choice do we have but to assume the threat is both very great and very real?" He cast a somber gaze around the room, meeting each warrior's eyes. "Koderas is lit. An overwhelming force of Eld will strike Kreppes and Great Bay within a month. King Dorian must be told."

"Agreed," Teleos said. "But how will we get the information to the king when my couriers are disappearing and the Warriors' Path is compromised?"

"Ellysetta and I will deliver the message in person. The Mage came too close to penetrating our defenses for my comfort. Narena and Faerah"—he turned to the *shei'dalins*—"must return to Dharsa and share what you've learned with the Massan. Tenn must set aside his differences with me. War is upon us. All the Fading Lands must fight."

Narena bowed her head. "We will go, as you cannot, my king."

"My thanks." Rain hesitated, then asked, "Did the Mage know anything about your sister?"

The *shei'dalin's* thick lashes fell to cover her eyes. "Our quintets slew him before we could ask about her fate."

Ellysetta's fingers knotted. Guilt weighed heavy on her conscience. The warriors had killed Torvan because her unwitting interference had drawn the attention of the High Mage.

"You have my word, Narena, that if she is alive and we discover where she is being held, I will send warriors into the heart of Eld itself to bring her home."

"*Beylah vo*, Feyreisen.*"

Rain held out an arm. "Come. I will walk with you to the Mists. I also have a message for Loris v'En Mahr, if you would agree to deliver it."

As Rain and the others filed out to escort the *shei'dalins* back to the Mists, Ellysetta turned to Gaelen. "I need a word with you, please." She waited for the rest of her quintet to depart before speaking, and even then she couldn't bring herself to voice the request aloud. On a private Spirit weave spun between his mind and hers, she said, «*I need you to tell me everything you know about Mage Marks and how someone can tell if their mind is being controlled by the Mages.*»

Celieria ~ The Borders, north of the Verlaine Forest

Shadows moved in swift silence, darting across the moonlit ground, keeping to the cover of the trees at the edge of the dark Verlaine, western Celieria's greatest and most haunted and frightening forest.

The shadows moved fast as a pronghorn racing on long, powerful legs, only the shadows ran on two. Slender, black, shrouded in darkness, they ran. Miles swept past beneath their silent footfalls in scant chimes.

A small farming village sat nestled in the bosom of rolling hills. Thatched-roof cottages huddled together as if in camaraderie against the night. The windows were dark, the villagers' lamps blown out for the night.

The shadows left the forest to fly across the cultivated fields like a volley of arrows loosed from archers' bows. Six dozen of them. Three shadows for every thatched cottage.

They circled the village . . . then converged.

They moved with unhesitating precision. Magic glowed in the night. Latches on doors and windows gave way, and the shadows slipped inside.

One farmer woke to find a dark shape standing over his bed. His cry of alarm died with one fierce slash of a blade.

Beside him, his wife's eyes flew open as a second blade drove through her heart.

Within a few chimes, the shadows gathered in the center of the farming village. Fire sparked in pale hands. Pale lips pursed, and with an Air-powered exhalation, blew tiny, glowing red-orange embers into the sky above the village. The shadowy figures then departed as quickly and as silently as they'd come. As they reached the forest's edge, the last one glanced back. Bright moonlight from the Mother shone down upon his pale, faintly luminescent skin and the curve of the scar that marred the beautiful perfection of his face. Bright steel glinted on harnesses that crisscrossed his chest. Glowing eyes whose pupils had lengthened and widened like a hunting cat's quickly scanned the moonlit fields. Finding nothing, he turned and plunged into the concealing darkness of the Verlaine Forest.

Moments later, a cock crowed to announce the coming dawn, but in the village where the shadows had been, the roar of the flames engulfing every thatched cottage drowned out his song.

CHAPTER FIVE

Crouched down beside the waters of Veil Lake, with her ears laid back and wings drooping, Steli-*chakai* was the very picture of an unhappy tairen. Ellysetta and Rain would be gone for more than a week—and she wasn't going with them.

«*Steli should fly with Ellysetta-kitling to the human lair in the east.*»

"We've been over this, Steli," Rain said. "I need you and the tairen here, protecting Orest while I'm away."

Though Rain could have flown to Celieria City in a matter of hours if he used magic to accelerate his flight, he would not risk Ellysetta's safety by taking her there without protection. She'd already been attacked by demons and Mages in Celieria City once before, and since it was clear the High Mage had not given up his pursuit, Rain had insisted the lu'tan—the hundreds bloodsworn to protect Ellysetta—come along to keep her safe from harm.

«Fey-kin not so good at protecting Ellysetta-kitling as Steli.»

"I'll be fine, Steli," Ellysetta assured her.

«Ellysetta-kitling has not yet found her wings or flame or fangs. She is still very . . . » The next part of her mournful tairen song did not translate well, but the rumble of notes conjured images of infant tairen still developing in the egg, utterly vulnerable and greatly in need of their mother to protect them.

"Oh, Steli." Tears sprang to Ellysetta's eyes and she flung her arms around the white tairen's throat. "I will miss you, too, my pride-mother, but Rain and my lu'tan will keep me safe. Besides"—she drew back and forced a smile—"I am not entirely as helpless as you believe, even without my wings."

Discontent rumbled in the tairen's throat. «Maybe, maybe. Steli still does not like.» Her tail twitched and a passing Orestian guard threw himself on the ground to avoid being slashed by the fully extended and very poisonous spikes gleaming amidst the fur at the tip of Steli's tail.

"You would like it even less in Celieria City, Steli. It is filled with only humans—and no mountains."

«There is water . . . and hills. Steli remembers. Water is good. Hills not so good as mountains, but still good. Steli promises to eat no humans. They not so tasty anyway.»

"Well . . ." Ellysetta blinked. "That's good to know. King Dorian would not be happy if Steli-chakai ate his subjects."

Rain stifled a laugh and turned to Steli. "Thank you, Steli-chakai, for agreeing to stay and lead the tairen in defense of Orest." He gestured for Lord Teleos to come forward. "Lord Teleos is Fey-kin. His family descends from the vel Celay line.

This city is his to hold, and he is responsible for her defense. Ellysetta and I ask that you accept him as pride-friend while we are away—and speak to him in Feyan so he can understand you."

«*Mmmrrr. Vel Celay blood very strong. Many pride-kin from that line.*» Steli lowered her head and sniffed Dev Teleos. To his credit, the Celierian didn't twitch a muscle. After a moment, Steli drew back and snorted. «*Agreed.*» She fixed a glowing, pupil-less blue gaze on Dev's face and in perfectly accented Feyan said, «*Steli-chakai accepts you as pride-friend while Rainier-Eras and Ellysetta-kitling are away and will speak to you in your tongue so you may understand.*»

"Steli-*chakai* offers you a great honor, Dev," Rain murmured to his friend. "Tairen rarely speak to those outside the pride."

Dev bowed to the white tairen as deeply as if she were the emissary of a foreign king. "*Beylah vo*, Steli-*chakai*. This Feykin thanks you for the great honor you bestow upon him and the great service you give to his city. I stand forever in your debt."

Steli's ears twitched. «*Well-spoken, Fey-kin.*» With a final growl and twitch of her tail, Steli sang to Ellysetta and Rain, «*Very well. Steli will stay and lead the tairen to defend the Feykin's city.*» She bent low to pin Rain with a whirling gaze. «*Bring Ellysetta-kitling safely back to the pride, Rainier-Eras.*»

"On my life, I do so vow, Steli-*chakai*."

Rain, Ellysetta and the *lu'tan* departed Orest just as the Great Sun began to lighten the eastern horizon. They traveled on foot and under a cloak of invisibility, heading south through the swath of rolling farmland that stretched between the Rhakis mountains and the gnarled, gloomy impenetrability of the Verlaine Forest.

They ran at a grueling pace, using magic to speed their steps. Ellysetta's presence slowed the warriors down a bit—as did maintaining the invisibility weave—but Rain would not take to the sky or allow the Fey to drop their invisibility until they were more than two hundred miles from Orest. Something had slain every messenger dispatched from Teleos's holding, and Rain would take no chance that same something might be lying in wait for them.

Finally, just after dusk, he called a halt, and they made camp in a farmer's recently harvested wheat field. Fire masters roasted field rabbit with weaves of flameless heat while groups of *lu'tan* spun a dome of twenty-five-fold magic over the encampment and posted sentries every tairen length.

"Do you think the king will believe us?" Ellysetta asked as she, Rain, and her quintet sat and ate together at the center of the camp.

"Can he afford not to?"

"I suppose not."

"Then he will believe us." White teeth stripped meat from a slender bone in four bites.

Gaelen snorted. "That's optimism for you."

"Pragmatism," Rain retorted. "The consequences of not believing us—then being proved wrong—are too severe an alternative to risk. He knows Fey do not lie, so believing us will be the only rational choice he can make."

"Since when have mortals ever been rational?" Tajik muttered.

"Dorian is Gaelen's *jita'taikonos*—the descendant of his sister's son. He is not purely mortal."

"He's not purely Fey either." Gil pulled a black Fey'cha from his chest harnesses and sliced a leg from the last of the rabbits. "Not even mostly Fey."

"He's Fey enough."

Gil's dark brows lifted over starry black eyes. "If you believed that, Adrial and Rowan wouldn't still be hiding their presence in Celieria City from him. Bel could have spun the Mage's news to one of them on a private weave and we would never have left Orest." He flung a swath of moon-white hair over his shoulder with a toss of his head and sank his teeth into the rabbit leg.

Ellysetta watched the shutter fall over Rain's face. Like Rain, Adrial vel Arquinas, the Air master of Ellysetta's first Fey quintet, had discovered his truemate in Celieria. Unfortunately for Adrial, his truemate had not merely been betrothed to a Celierian, as Ellysetta had—she'd been wed to one. The heir of a Great Lord, no less, and though Talisa's father, Great Lord Barrial, was friendly to the Fey, her husband's family was not. Great Lord Sebourne had, in fact, been Rain's fiercest foe in Celieria's Council of Lords, and he had fought vigorously to discredit the Fey, pushing to open the borders and allow free trade between Eld and Celieria.

"Dorian is Celieria's king," Rain replied to Gil. "He is bound by Celierian law, not Feyan. If he knew Adrial was still there—in direct violation of his earlier decree upholding Talisa's marriage—he would have no choice but to imprison him."

"It's so cruel that something as joyful as *shei'tanitsa* should be cause for such despair," Ellysetta remarked. "Is there nothing we can do to help Adrial?"

"Short of killing diSebourne?" Rain asked. "*Nei.*"

"DiSebourne's death can be arranged." Gaelen tossed out the offer in a flat voice. Silence fell as unease rippled around the circle.

"As tempting as the idea may be, Gaelen," Rain replied, "honorable Fey do not murder innocent mortals."

"DiSebourne is no innocent. He has refused to free a woman who bears no love for him, and by that willful choice he destroys not one but two lives. Three if Rowan must be the one to end his brother's life."

Ellysetta saw the flicker of remorse cross Rain's face. Adrial was going to die. They all knew that. Though Talisa's soul could never have called Adrial's if her heart were bound elsewhere, duty and honor kept her tied to her mortal husband. As long as she did not consider herself free to accept Adrial, there was little hope she could summon the unequivocal love and trust necessary to complete the *shei'tanitsa* bond. The madness of an unfulfilled matebond would ultimately send Adrial to his death—either an honor death executed by his own hand or a merciful end on the point of his brother's red Fey'cha.

"Even so," Rain said, "diSebourne's choice is no crime. He may be acting selfishly, but by his country's customs, he has every right to do so."

"Then his country's customs are wrong."

"We cannot simply slaughter mortals because we don't like their decisions. If Talisa leaves her husband, every Fey warrior in Celieria will defend her. But while she chooses to stay with him, we will not interfere. The Fey will not kill diSebourne so Adrial can have his wife." His gaze hardened to cold command. "And neither will your *dahl'reisen* friends."

After a brief visual skirmish, Gaelen bowed his head. "*La ve shalah*, Feyreisen." As you command.

Rain pinned him with a penetrating gaze before nodding curtly. "*Kabei*. Then it is settled. We carry the news to Dorian. He will react however he will react. That doesn't change what we must do. We face the Eld and champion the Light, as we always have."

"We need more allies," Bel said. "Even before the Mage Wars, we could not have hoped to face the Army of Darkness with only Celieria at our side. We need the Elves."

Rain grimaced. "You heard the same report as I did when Loris returned from Elvia. Hawksheart and his Elves will not join this fight."

"He also told Loris he wanted to see you and Ellysetta."

"He wants to probe Ellysetta's mind because she calls a Song in their Dance." The Dance was an ancient Elvish prophecy said to reveal all the secrets of the world, past, present, and future. "Well, to the Seven Hells with what he wants. The pointy-eared *rultshart* knows we're facing the greatest threat to the world since the Mage Wars—possibly even since the dawn of the First Age—and still he will not help. Yet he thinks we will take weeks away from preparations for war to come running when he calls? *Nei*, we will go to Dorian, and then to the Danae."

Gil's brows rose. "The Danae? They care even less about the world beyond their borders than the Elves."

"They came to Johr's aid in the Mage Wars. With what we now know, surely they will come to ours."

"The Elves fought in the Mage Wars, too," Bel reminded him. "It makes no sense that they would refuse us now."

Tajik coughed a curse word into his fist and spat on the ground. "Best for all of us, if you ask me. Elves care for nothing except that gods-cursed Dance of theirs."

Bel arched a brow. "That's a harsh remark, coming from you, Tajik. I seem to recall some mention of an Elf or two in your family line."

"Which is why you should believe me when I say we're better off without them." The red-haired general tore the remaining leg from the spitted rabbit and warmed it with a Fire-red glow in the palm of his hand. The silence that ensued made him glance up, and he scowled when he found Rain, Ellysetta, and the rest of the quintet looking at him. "What?"

"Nothing," Rain answered for them. "It's late. We should all get some sleep."

A few chimes later, the remains of their dinner vanished in a flash of Earth and Fire. As Rain spun a cushioned pallet from the wheat chaff and covered it with a scarlet Fey travel cloak, Ellysetta felt eyes upon her, and she glanced up to see Gaelen watching her. He didn't say anything, but then he hadn't said anything all day either. He was waiting, patiently, for her to do the right thing.

"Come, *shei'tani*." Rain grasped her shoulders and bent to press a kiss on the side of her neck. "Your bower awaits." He smiled and led her to the camp bed.

When she glanced back over her shoulder, Gaelen was busy working with the quintet to spin a five-fold weave around

Rain and Ellysetta. His eyes met hers once more, briefly, before he turned away.

"What is it?"

She looked at Rain and forced a smile. "I'm just a little tired."

"The weaves should protect you from Mage dreams, and the *lu'tan* will alert us at the first hint of danger."

She covered his hands with hers. "I know." Stretching up, she pressed her lips to his and let him bear her back into the soft comfort of their bed. He pulled her close against him, his body spooned against hers, wrapping her in a cocoon of warm protection.

The quintet stretched out in the wheat straw nearby. Each warrior slept with one hand on the hilt of a red Fey'cha. Around the camp, all the *lu'tan* not standing first watch did the same, and their bodies formed ring after concentric ring around the *shei'dalin* they'd bloodsworn their souls to protect.

That *shei'dalin* lay awake long after the warriors had gone to sleep, worried not half so much about what dangers lurked outside the *lu'tan's* powerful protective shields as the ones that lurked within. The dangers that lived inside her.

Eld ~ Boura Fell

Melliandra's visit to the High Mage's breeding females wasn't as great a pleasure as she'd hoped, nor particularly informative. She felt Shia's absence too strongly, and the new women—three shining folk, and one mortal—had shied away from her when she'd approached. She'd tried to speak with them, but either their memories had been completely wiped or they simply had not trusted her enough to converse.

A disappointing half a bell after her arrival, she departed again, but instead of heading to her next workstation, she stopped by the door to Master Maur's nursery and examined the glowing threads of the ward spells protecting the locked door against intruders. The wards allowed only Master Maur's most trusted *umagi* through, and even then only once per week at a time known to no one but Master Maur.

The key to the door Melliandra could likely get, but getting past the wards was a different matter. For that, she needed magical help.

The next morning, when the call came to tend the High Mage's prisoners on the lowest level of Boura Fell, it was all she could do to conceal her eagerness behind a mask of sullen apathy. A bell later, she was standing, tray in hand, before the shadow-cloaked last door on the lowest level of Boura Fell.

"Food for the prisoner." Melliandra kept her gaze fixed on the timeworn smoothness of the black stone floor as the guards standing watch outside the cell inspected the unappealing tray of congealed fat and cooked grain.

"Fit for maggots, that is," one of the guards muttered. His ring of keys rattled and clanked as he unlocked the door and shoved it open. "Go on. Deliver that slop and be quick about it."

She ducked through the doorway and hurried across the dank, unlit room. The shaft of light from the open doorway illuminated a portion of the seemingly empty barbed *sel'dor* cage built into the far wall.

"Back again?" a voice, pitched so low as to be barely audible, growled from the shadows.

She turned her head in the direction of the voice and squinted as her eyes adjusted to the darkness. There. Now she could see the faint, almost imperceptible glow of the prisoner sprawled on the floor in the corner.

"Can you feed yourself?" Shannisorran v'En Celay's silvery light was so dim, she knew the Mage's brutes had been at him again, and sometimes, after they finished, nearly every bone in his body was shattered.

"*Aiyah*. Can't walk or sit, but they left me my arms this time."

She reached into the pocket sewn within the folds of her ragged skirt and pulled out a small cloth bundle. "Good."

With swift furtiveness, she unwrapped the cloth and dropped its contents into the bowl of gruel before pushing the food through the barbed bars of the cell. "There's a little cold meat and cheese, wrapped in bread. Take it quickly, before the guards see."

"Why do you bother? As soon as I heal, they just break me again." Even as he asked, his fingers reached for the bowl of food and closed around the plump wad of meat, cheese, and bread. He tore off a small bite with his teeth and chewed.

"I bother because I need you to fulfill our bargain, and when the chance comes, you must be ready." Not long after the High Mage had begun torturing Lord Death's mate, the Fey warrior had agreed to do what neither she nor any other *umagi* could: kill the High Mage of Eld. That was the only way she and Shia's child could ever be free, so she needed to keep Lord Death alive and as healthy as possible until he had the opportunity to prove worthy of his name. She glanced over her shoulder to check on the guards by the door, then lowered her voice even further. "Do you have a hiding spot in there?"

"What would be the point?" His tone was flat. "It's not as if Maur ever leaves me anything to hide."

Her eyes narrowed. It was said Fey could not lie, but he hadn't said no. And he'd been in this same cell for a thousand years. "I was hoping to bring a few things you might find useful. But if you have no place to hide them . . ." She let her voice trail off.

"What sort of things?" Wariness had crept into his voice. Oh, yes, he had managed to carve out some sort of hiding place in his cell.

"Things you will require to fulfill your bargain. A blade. A Fey crystal." She knew from eavesdropping on conversations between novice and apprentice Mages that the Fey crystals contained powerful magic. Lord Death would need every advantage if he were to succeed.

Pale hands shot out to grab the cell bars, despite the barbs that dug into his palms, and Lord Death dragged himself over to her. Matted black hair fell into eyes that had begun to glow green as his magic rose. "My *sorreisu kiyr*? You know where it is?"

"A . . . *sorai zukeer*? Is that what you call the Fey crystals?" She filed the piece of information away. "No, not yours. Everything of yours the Mage keeps close to him or locked away in a place only he knows. But you are not the only Fey warrior ever to be a guest in this place, and some of the other Mages are not as careful with their secrets." She frowned. "You can still use it even though it belonged to another, can't you?"

"*Aiyah*, but my own would be better."

"I can't get yours. You'll have to make do with what I can bring," she told him. No matter how much better his own crystal might be, stealing from the High Mage was suicide. Only a fool would even attempt it, and Melliandra was no fool. Laying hands on one of the other Mages' crystals was already risky enough. "There's something else I need you to do as well."

"What?"

She took a breath, then plunged onward. "If I showed you one of the Mage's wards . . . could you figure out how to undo it?"

"It wouldn't do you any good. It takes magic to undo magic."

"But could you?"

He shrugged. "Perhaps. I'd have to see the weave first to know."

"Hurry up in there!" one of the guards called from the door. "What's taking so long?"

Melliandra turned halfway towards the door. "He's weak. I practically have to feed him myself." To the Fey, she hissed, "Save the bread and meat, but eat the rest quickly. If you don't, they'll be suspicious." She waited for him to scoop the cold, fatted porridge from the bowl with his fingers and force it down. When he was done, she snatched the bowl back and clambered to her feet. "I've got to go. I'll be back when I can."

Celieria

With all the shields around her, Ellysetta should not have dreamed of darkness. But she did.

She did not dream her usual nightmares of war and destruction or of herself, pitiless and damned, leading the Army of Darkness to destroy the earth. *Nei*, this time she dreamed of something smaller, more personal, and therefore infinitely more terrifying.

She dreamed of Lillis and Lorelle, huddled together in the dim filth of a black pit, sobbing her name, pleading for her to save them.

Above, standing on a viewing platform two levels above, a shrouded figure in purple robes watched their torment. At his side, Ellysetta saw herself, clad incongruously in a boatnecked gown of rich forest green velvet, her hair unbound and spilling across her shoulders like a fall of flame. She looked more pampered guest than prisoner, except for the chains fastened to the sel'dor bindings locked tight around her neck and wrists. Two large guards stood behind her, holding her chains in their meaty fists.

Hovering overhead, like a soul cast out of its body, she watched the scene unfold. She was an observer, distant and disconnected, yet some part of her remained intimately linked to the people in her dream. She felt each emotion, each terror, each gloating triumph, as if it were her own.

The robed Mage raised an arm, and the sound of rattling chains and cogs welled up from the darkness of the pit. Then came the howling and the rasping scrabble of claw on rock, as slavering darrokken with eyes like red flames rushed towards Lillis and Lorelle.

The girls shrieked in terror and shrank back against the slimy wall of the pit, clutching each other and crying her name. "Ellie! Ellie, help us! Help us!"

Ellysetta lunged against her bonds, crying, "Parei! Stop! I beg you, stop!"

The Mage, his face hidden by the folds of his purple shroud, remained unmoved. "There is only one way to stop this. You know what that is."

"Please." Weeping, she fell to her knees. "I beg you. I'll do whatever you want, only stop this. Let them live. Please let them live."

Helplessly watching from above, Ellysetta cried a warning to herself: "*Nei! Do not!*" But the weeping Ellysetta did not hear her.

The Mage's hands shot out. A sharp blade sliced across the captive Ellysetta's wrist, and the Mage pressed the wound to his pale, bloodless lips. A hand splayed across her left breast. She threw back her head on a silent wail of despair. Slowly, beneath the Mage's hand, a sixth black shadow appeared on the skin over her heart and her eyes turned from Fey green to pits of darkness that flickered with red lights.

Ellysetta wept in horror as freezing ice penetrated her soul, robbing her of hope, of Light, of all will to resist.

Darkness fell. She floated there, alone, cold, her senses void.

When light returned, it was a dim red-orange flame that slowly drove back the gloom to reveal a different shadowy cave. Lillis and Lorelle were gone. In the flickering light, she saw Rain, bloodied and broken, his body wrapped in heavy sel'dor chains and pinned to a rough-hewn wall. A man in executioner's garb stood before him, a sel'dor sword gripped in one gauntleted fist. The purple-shrouded Mage stood in the shadows off to one side. Of herself, there was no sign.

Rain. She whispered his name, and though neither the executioner nor the Mage gave any indication of having heard her, Rain lifted his head. His gaze swept around the cell, eyes narrowed as if to pierce the impenetrable darkness in search of her. *I am here! Rain, I am here!* For a moment, she thought he could hear her, but then his eyes closed and his head dropped to his chest in weary defeat. He did not look up again, no matter how she called to him.

The Mage lifted his hand in command, and with an abrupt savagery that made her gasp in horror, the executioner drove his sword into Rain's heart. His beautiful eyes opened wide on a breathless gasp and his body sagged against his chains, head lolling forward against his chest.

The Mage pushed back the robe's deep cowl, baring hair the color of tairen flame and monstrous black eyes that observed Rain's death with pitiless detachment.

Nei! Ellysetta screamed a denial. The face beneath that purple cowl was her own, but the heart that beat inside the slender chest was a cold, unfeeling thing, barren of remorse or grief, void of even the tiniest flicker of remembered love.

The executioner yanked his bloody blade from Rain's chest and raised it high, then glanced at the Mage who wore Ellysetta's face. At her nod, he brought the sword slashing down against the back of Rain's exposed neck. Flesh split. Bone severed. Blood sprayed in a scarlet fountain.

She felt the sword as if it fell upon her own neck, and she knew the instant Rain's soul fled his body, because her own was ripped asunder. Invisible, unheard, Ellysetta screamed and screamed until her voice shattered and the edges of her vision went dim.

The last thing she saw before the world went dark was two small figures darting from the shadows. Lillis and Lorelle, their eyes turned black as death, danced in the shower of blood as if it were a warm summer rain. They opened their mouths to catch scarlet droplets and laughed with chilling childish glee. The air filled with the baying howls of the darrokken *and a chorus of voices calling her name.*

"Ellysetta! Ellysetta, wake up! Wake up, *shei'tani.*"

Her eyes flew open, and for a moment she was still locked inside the nightmare, her ears filled with the baying of the Mage's monstrous hounds, her vision dark and blank. Then the blackness lightened to a starry night sky, and a familiar face, beautiful and beloved, hovered over her, his features drawn with worry.

Rain! Air-starved lungs expanded on a sudden, desperate gasp. With a sob, she sat up and flung trembling arms around him, clutching him tight. She cried his name, but the only sound that passed her lips was a harsh, painful whisper. Her throat felt so raw she couldn't talk. She babbled on a weave of Spirit, instead. «*Shei'tan, shei'tan! You're alive! It was just a dream. Please, gods, let it just have been a dream.*» She pulled back and ran frantic hands across his beloved face, his neck, his chest, searching for wounds, but thankfully—blessedly—finding none. She flung herself back into his arms, clinging to his strength, dragging the warm, sweet, reassuring scent of him into her lungs. «*You're real. You're unharmed. Tell me you're real!*» She had felt him die, felt it so keenly her soul still ached like an open wound.

Strong arms closed around her. "I am real, *shei'tani*, alive and unharmed. Whatever you saw was just a dream. I am with you." Again and again, he murmured reassurances, both aloud and across the threads of their bond, while his broad hands stroked her hair and down her back in a steady rhythm until she calmed.

When finally her shivering stopped and her heart slowed to its normal rhythm, he pulled back enough to look into her eyes. He smoothed the wild curls off her face and stroked her cheek tenderly with his thumb. "Talk to me, *shei'tani*," he said. "What happened? What did you dream of that frightened you so badly?"

"I—" She tried to speak, but her voice was ruined. «*Rain, my throat . . . I can't talk.*»

Gentle, worried lavender eyes searched her face. "You screamed, *shei'tani*. A scream like I've never heard before. Your skin went cold as ice and I thought—" He broke off and closed his eyes against a sudden well of emotion. «*I thought I'd lost you. You were here in my arms, but I couldn't feel you. It was as if your soul had fled, and all I held was an empty shell.*» Even his Spirit voice broke on that memory, and his arms clenched tight around her. «*You frightened me,*» he rasped. «*You frightened me as I never want to be frightened again.*»

There were tears in his eyes, and the sight nearly broke her heart. «*Oh, Rain, I'm sorry.*»

"Shh." He put a finger to her lips, then replaced it quickly with a fierce, deep kiss. «*Las, shei'tani. You've nothing to be sorry for. It is I who should be sorry. I see your torment, and I don't know what to do. I'm failing you.*»

Tears sprang to her eyes. «*Nei, Rain. Don't even think it. You've done everything any shei'tan possibly could—and more. I am the one who cannot find a way to complete our bond. I'm the one who's failing you—failing us.*»

«*Never.*» He tracked kisses from her lips to her ear. «*So long as we're together, there is hope.*»

The sound of a clearing throat made her glance up and around, and a blush rose to her cheeks. Her quintet and all the *lu'tan* were ringed around her and Rain, their eyes fixed upon her. Rain glanced up, too, and promptly spun a quick weave to dry her tears as they got to their feet.

"She's fine," he told them. "It was just a bad dream."

"Bad?" Gil repeated with patent disbelief. "That scream pierced our shields and probably woke every creature from here to Orest."

"*Aiyah*, well, she's had bad ones before," Rain assured him.

Ellysetta almost told him then. Because he was wrong; this dream was nothing like the others. She'd dreamed of battles and death gruesome and violent enough to make a hardened warrior quail, but never had one of those nightmares disturbed her on such a visceral level. She hadn't just witnessed her submission to the Mage and Rain's death—she'd *lived* them. Every unspeakable moment had felt as real as this moment did now; as if she'd truly been there, as if she'd truly lost her soul, and Rain had truly died.

That was what had frightened her most. Because if the Mage had sent that dream, his hold on her had become dangerously strong.

Ellysetta glanced up and found Gaelen watching her. For a moment, she thought he might betray the conversation they'd had back in Orest, but all he said was, "We should get moving. That scream lit our position like a beacon. If the Eld *are* following us, they know exactly where we are now."

CHAPTER SIX

The Fey continued south at a rapid pace. Rain ran at Ellysetta's side, and the quintet formed a tight circle around them.

Gaelen ran at Ellysetta's left, his long legs crossing the ground in an easy, tireless lope. He didn't say anything and he didn't look her way, but his silence was reproach enough.

When Rain ran ahead to confer with one of the scouts, she sent a private weave to Gaelen. «*I can sense your disapproval. You think I should tell him.*»

He didn't miss a stride. «*You said you would.*»

«*We're not even halfway to Celieria City. You agreed to give me until then.*»

«*That was before last night.*» Ice blue eyes met hers in a brief, piercing look. «*Ellysetta, you must tell him. Nothing should have gotten through our shields, but that was no ordinary nightmare and you know it. If it came from the Mage—and, unless you have another explanation, we must assume it did—then our time has run out.*»

She set her eyes on the horizon. «*You're right. I know you're right.*» She should have told Rain the instant she and Gaelen had finished their conversation in Orest, but she'd kept silent for a variety of reasons. She hadn't wanted to add another burden to the staggering weight of troubles Rain already carried. She hadn't wanted anything to distract him from reaching

Celieria City and warning King Dorian of the impending attacks. And, selfishly, she hadn't wanted to see the devotion in Rain's eyes turn to horror, as it surely would.

She'd been hoping she'd misread the signs, hoping Gaelen was wrong, but after her nightmare, she couldn't wait any longer. Rain had to know, as did all her *lu'tan*. The threat was too grave, too dangerous for them all.

She drew a deep breath and set her jaw. «*I'll tell him today, before we make camp for the night.*»

Shortly after daybreak, they reached the southern edge of the Verlaine Forest and stopped to rest and break their fast. They spread out in the tall, waving grass of an untilled field, keeping low so that only a bird flying overhead would see them. Some merely sat or knelt to rest their legs; some lay down and closed their eyes to catch a few chimes of sleep. All took the time to eat and sip the rejuvenating waters of Orest's Sourcefed lake from their water flasks.

Ellysetta was tired, but fear of sleep kept her eyes open. Gaelen's words had left such a churning in her belly, she had no desire to eat the Fey journeycake Rain offered her.

"You need to eat, *shei'tani*," he insisted.

"I'm not very hungry."

"Eat anyway. At least a little. You aren't accustomed to so much running. And you didn't get enough sleep last night." Rain pressed the cake into her hands.

For his sake, she broke off a corner and put it in her mouth. Like all Fey food, it was delicious, tasting of sugared lemons and buttery cream, light yet surprisingly filling, but it could have been sawdust for all she cared.

She cast a brooding gaze westward towards the Rhakis mountains. From this distance, the Faering Mists looked like nothing more than a line of clouds hugging the jagged peaks. But somewhere in those Mists, her family was trapped. Papa. Lillis and Lorelle. At the thought of them, her mind filled with a horrible scene from her nightmare. The twins, black fire pits for eyes, their doll-smooth faces streaked with scarlet ribbons of Rain's blood.

The journeycake crumbled in her hands. She glanced down in dull dismay at the mess in her lap.

Rain spun a quick weave of Earth that gathered up the crumbs and formed them back into a solid cake. He set the food aside and took her hands. "What is it, Ellysetta?" He searched her face in concern. "Talk to me."

"I'm just thinking of my family." The evasion slipped from her lips with shameful ease.

"You will see them again, *kem'san*." His expression softened with sympathy. "In fact, there's probably not a safer place in the world for them to be at the moment. Your father and sisters are innocents. The Mists might hold them for a while, but provided they're unharmed, they'll eventually find their way out. I wouldn't be surprised if that was the gods' intention all along."

"I hadn't thought of that."

The corner of his mouth lifted. "When our bond is complete and your Marks are gone, I promise I will take you into the Mists myself, and we will scour every fingerspan of what lies within until we find your father and sisters and return them to the world."

She looked up. "You would do that for me?"

Sadness darkened his lavender eyes to purple. "Of course I would. It pains me you would think otherwise."

She winced. "I didn't mean it like that, Rain." She pulled her hands from his and twisted them together, fixing her gaze on her tightly clenched fingers. "Forgive me. I'm very tired. I didn't sleep well last night even before that dream."

He put a hand under her chin and lifted her face with gentle insistence. "Ellysetta, you've been troubled since we left Orest. But I can't help you if you won't tell me what is wrong."

"I know. And I mean to tell you. I just need a little time." She glanced at Gaelen, who sat nearby, sharpening his blades.

Rain saw the look and his spine went stiff. He withdrew his hands from hers. "You need time before telling me, but you've already discussed your troubles with vel Serranis?" The rise of his tairen rumbled in his voice.

Ellysetta bit her lip. "It's not like that. I went to Gaelen in confidence, *aiyah*, but to ask him for information, not to share it."

"What concerns do you have that you cannot share with me?"

Her shoulders slumped. It was no use. She had to tell him now, whether she was ready or not. "I went to Gaelen yesterday morning for information about my Marks."

"What sort of information?"

She sighed. "We're outside the Fading Lands, outside whatever protection the Mists might have offered me. I bear four Mage Marks. Two more and the Mage will own my soul."

"That won't happen." He looked up, his eyes fierce. "I won't let it."

She laid her palm on the side of his face and smiled sadly. "Beloved, if we can't complete our bond, how could you possibly stop it?" He would die to protect her. Of that, she had no doubt, but it wouldn't be enough. "The risk is there, whether we want to admit it or not. So I went to Gaelen to ask what I should expect, and what sort of danger I would pose to the rest of you."

She motioned Gaelen over, then called the rest of her quintet as well. "Bel, Tajik, Gil, Rijonn, come closer. You four need to hear this, too."

When the warriors had gathered, she nodded to Gaelen. "Tell Rain and my *cha'kor* what happens to people with each successive Mage Mark. Tell them what you told me yesterday."

The former *dahl'reisen* lifted his chin. "As I told the Feyreisa, the first three Marks give the Mage access to the soul only during times of weakness. After that, the fourth and fifth Marks break down the victim's will and the barriers to his"—Gaelen paused, and a small tic near the spot where his *dahl'reisen* scar had once edged the corner of his eye made his lashes twitch—"or her—soul and mind."

"Tell Rain what will happen to me."

Gaelen held Rain's gaze and revealed the truth with blunt honesty. "With four Marks, she will begin to have thoughts and reactions that are not her own. She must learn to guard her mind because the Mage will be able to sense strong emotions and use them against her. He will use that power to sow doubt and fear, to isolate her from you and all others who would protect her. He will coax her into weaving Azrahn again so he can place more Marks upon her. After the fifth Mark, it will not be safe to have her witness military planning or be privy to any information we do not want the Mage to know. He will be able to pull it from her and use what she knows to his advantage."

With each word that fell from Gaelen's lips, Ellysetta felt Rain's temper rise, born of fear for his mate. "There won't be a fifth Mark," he interrupted. His eyes had begun to glow, the elongated pupils narrowing to catlike slits.

Ellysetta laid a hand on his arm. "Let him finish, Rain."

"At five Marks," Gaelen continued, "the Mage will be able to use her senses as extensions of his own. His hold on her is strongest at night and especially in her dreams. That is when Ellysetta will be both the most dangerous and in the most danger, because at those times he will be able to exercise a portion of his power over her. If he gains access to her mind while she is dreaming, he will be able to control her actions. He could command her to come to him, to lay a trap for any of us, even to kill."

"When you were with the *dahl'reisen*, did you ever see that happen?" Ellysetta asked.

"Only at the beginning. And only a handful of times. We quickly learned how many Marks a *dahl'reisen* could bear before he became a danger to the rest of us."

"How many was that?" Gil asked, his starry black eyes merciless and intent.

Gaelen glanced at Ellysetta. "Three."

Rain's spine went stiff. "Ellysetta is no danger to us. You will not even let the thought enter your mind. She is the Feyreisa. She was sent here to save the tairen and the Fey. She has sacrificed much to do just that."

She put a hand over his. "*Las*, Rain. Truth doesn't change just because we don't like it. It's better to know the worst that can happen so we can prepare for it." Even though Gaelen was only repeating what he'd told her yesterday, her heart was fluttering in her chest like a trapped bird, and her palms had gone clammy. "Gaelen, did some of those *dahl'reisen* become dangerous after the fourth Mark?"

Gaelen waged a silent, icy battle of wills with Rain before nodding. "*Aiyah*. After that, we took no chances. Anyone with four Marks died on his own blade—or ours."

Rain growled and leapt to his feet. He dragged Ellysetta up with him and shoved her behind him, putting his body and his blades between her and the rest of the quintet. "Try it, vel Serranis, and you will be the one to die. I promise you."

"*Las*, Rain." Ellysetta tried to spin a soothing weave on him, but he would not be calmed.

"*Nei las*," he snapped. "I scorched the world once to avenge Sariel's death. I'll scorch it again before I allow anyone to harm you."

"*Parei!* Stop!" Unmindful of the danger, she grabbed his arm and spun him around to face her. "Don't even think such a thing. You saw the same vision in the Eye that I did. And that was bad enough . . . but Rain, when I was in that Mage's mind yesterday morning, I learned something else. Something worse. The High Mage doesn't just want to enslave my soul and force me to do his bidding. He means to take over my body."

His spine stiffened. "What do you mean?"

"I mean he intends to live inside me. To become me—or rather, to wear my body and use my magic as his own."

"I don't understand."

"The Mages manipulate souls, Rain. They aren't immortal like the Fey. They're long-lived, but their bodies age and die. So they find a new body—someone young, someone with powerful magical gifts—and then they transfer their soul into that body. They call it 'incarnating.' And that's why the High Mage is so desperate to capture me—he wants to incarnate into my body. That's why he made me. He doesn't want to command Tairen Souls to do his bidding—he wants to *be* a Tairen Soul."

Rain reeled back in horror. "The Mage in Orest—you learned all this from him?"

"Aiyah. And it can't be allowed to happen. You saw the same vision in the Eye that I did. You know what will happen if the Mage soul-claims me. Death would be by far the kinder end—for all of us." She met Rain's gaze. «*Steli has already sworn to do it, so you need not.*»

His face crumpled.

She laid a palm over his heart and sent him all the love in hers. Her lips trembled when his eyes filled with a shimmer of tears. When first he'd flown into her life, he'd been so wounded by loss and full of despair, he had lost the ability to cry. As his *shei'tani*, she was supposed to bring him joy, but so far it seemed all she'd done was melt his heart enough so he could hurt again.

«*It's the only way, shei'tan.*» She lifted her hands to cup his face, thumbing away his tears. «*If we cannot complete our bond, I must die before the Mage completes his claiming. I saw in my nightmare what would happen if we don't. I saw your death. Felt your soul severed for all eternity from mine. I won't let that happen. I can't. Death offers us hope, at least. Not for this life, but for another.*»

«*Ellysetta . . .*»

«*Shh. My soul has found yours now. It will not forget. As long as the Mage does not complete his claiming, I will find you again. Whether it takes one lifetime or a thousand, we will be together, just as the gods intended.*»

He bent his head. His arms crushed her to him while his

lips touched hers with exquisite tenderness. «*Ver reisa ku'chae, Ellysetta. Kem surah, shei'tani. In this life and in every life yet to come.*»

She filled her hands with the silk of his hair and her lungs with the warmth of his breath. «*I will hold you to that, shei'tan. Even if I never come to trust myself enough to complete the bond, you I trust without question . . . and I love you even more than that.*» Her mental voice hitched. «*But you and I both know, we must prepare for the worst.*»

His forehead touched hers in surrender. «*I know. Though every spark of my being cries out against it, I know.*»

When Rain released her, he stepped to the side so she could see Gaelen and the others once more. "The tairen have already promised to ensure I never become that monster the Eye of Truth showed us," she told them. "But now I need your promises as well. If for some reason, Steli and the tairen cannot see it done, I want your Fey oath that you will. Rain cannot, so the duty falls to you. You will not be breaking your *lute'asheiva* vow. You will not be harming me. You will be saving me."

"We cannot, Ellysetta," Bel said. "Our souls are bloodsworn to yours. If you died by our hands, we would become Mharog—evil beings so foul even the Mages fear them. We cannot do this. Not even to honor your command."

She glanced around the circle at each member of her bloodsworn quintet. One by one, they dropped their eyes until only Bel and Gaelen held her gaze.

"Vel Jelani is right," Gaelen said. "No *lu'tan* can harm you. Not even to save the world."

Her shoulders slumped. "Then we must find someone who can—or I must do it myself. I don't know how much time I have left."

Rain's brows drew together. "What do you mean?"

"I mean I think the Mage has already begun to influence my thoughts. First with Aartys, then again yesterday with the Mage, and this morning with that nightmare. Gaelen says he should not have been able to reach me through all those shields, but I can't think of what else could have caused that dream. I think part of him is in me, Rain, whispering to me, just as Gaelen said."

Rain went still as stone. He searched her face intently, as if looking for some hint of the Mage's presence, then said, "The Elves. We will go to the Elves. Hawksheart can see everything that was, is, or ever will be through that infernal Dance of his. If there's a way for us to complete our bond or rid you of the Mage's Marks, he'll know it."

"I thought you didn't trust him."

Rain gave a short, bitter laugh. "I don't, but what choice do we have? You're already willing to sacrifice your life to save your soul. What greater price could the Elf king demand than that?" He shook his head. "Much as I dislike them, Elves are no friends of the Dark. Celieria will have to wait. We head south, to Navahele."

"Rain, *nei*." This was exactly what she'd been afraid he'd say. "It will take more than a week to get to Elvia and back. Celieria doesn't have that much time. We must go to Celieria City first to warn King Dorian about the High Mage's impending attack, then to Danael to ask for their help. After that's done, we can go to Elvia."

His brows climbed up to his hairline. "Are you mad? Ellysetta, you've just convinced me I must accept your murder rather than risk your getting a sixth Mark. We go to Elvia first, and that's the end of it."

Ellysetta scowled. "We've been over this a hundred times. If Celieria falls, we've already lost. We can't hold out against the Eld alone. We need Celieria and the Danae."

"And if you fall to the Mage, you think there will be a different outcome?"

"You're being impossible!"

"And you're a raving crack-skull if you think for one instant that we're going to run around the countryside seeking allies while the High Mage freely torments you in your dreams!"

They glared at each other, sweet murmurs of love and devotion replaced by fiery temper and stubbornness.

Gaelen cleared his throat. "There is a way to help buffer her from the Mage. Something we have not tried yet."

"And what is that?" Rain snapped.

"Let me add Azrahn to her shields. It isn't a permanent solution, but it should buy us enough time to take our news to Celieria and still reach Navahele before the worst comes to pass."

Rain's teeth came together with an audible click. His jaw worked, as if the mere thought left a foul taste in his mouth. "Spit and scorch me." He threw up his hands. "Fine. Do it. I've already blackened my honor beyond repair. What's one more stain upon it?" He glared at Ellysetta and thrust a finger in her face. "One day, Ellysetta. One day in Celieria City. Then we leave for Elvia, no matter what."

"Danael first, then Elvia. There's no sense crossing the entire continent three times," she pointed out when Rain opened his mouth to object. "Besides, if we go to Elvia first, the Danae will be too late to help even if they do agree to fight."

Rain ground his teeth. "Fine. One day in Celieria City. Then we head straight to Danael and Elvia."

"Agreed."

Ten chimes later, Rain took to the air with his Azrahn-shielded truemate on his back and the Fey began to run, heading east towards Celieria City.

Ellysetta turned for one final look at the Mists-enveloped mountains that marked the borders of the Fading Lands, wondering if she would ever see those Mists again—or the beloved family trapped within.

She closed her eyes briefly and sent up a silent prayer. *Adelis, Bright One, Lord of Light, no matter what happens to me, please, watch over the ones I love. Shine your Light upon their Path and keep them safe from harm.*

* * *

The Faering Mists

Lillis sat up with a groan and lifted a shaky hand to her pounding head. Perhaps she shouldn't have left the place where she'd first woken up after all.

Wandering blind on a shattered mountain came with many a deadly peril—including roots and stones to trip small feet, razor-sharp rocks, abrupt dropoffs, and trails so steep a billy goat wouldn't tread them. Even so, she'd managed to survive most of the dangers with only a few minor bumps, bruises and cuts . . . until the ground disappeared beneath her feet.

One moment, she was climbing down a steep, rock-strewn slope; the next, she was tumbling down the mountainside, cradling Snowfoot protectively in her arms as she fell.

The last thing she remembered was the big bump that sent her flying through the air, the sudden, painful jolt of landing, then nothing until she woke again just now.

She was surrounded by a mist so thick and white she couldn't even see her own hands when she raised them to her face. For one terrified instant, she thought maybe she had died and gone to the Haven of Light, but then the mist began to thin. Within a few chimes, she could see her own badly skinned arms and legs and a small circle of the steep, rubble-strewn mountainside at her feet. Grit-filled wounds on her knees and palms throbbed with a dull pain. There was a long slash down her left thigh and a terrible lump on her head just above her left eye. Her head hurt. Her brain hurt. Everything hurt.

And that proved she wasn't dead.

At least, she thought it did.

Lillis put her face in her hands and started to cry. She wanted Papa. She wanted Kieran. She wanted them to hold her in their arms and tell her everything would be all right.

A weak mew emerged from the sling around her neck.

"Snowfoot!" Frantic, she fumbled to open the sides of the pouch to reach her pet. The instant he was free, the kitten clambered into her lap, mewing and rubbing against her the way he did when he was hungry. If she were on her own, she would probably just sit here and cry, but Snowfoot was depending on her. She couldn't let him down.

"All right." She sniffled and wiped her eyes. "All right, we'll keep going." She took off her pinafore and tied it around the wound on her leg. Then she settled Snowfoot back in his sling and hauled herself to her feet.

Carefully, each step slow and deliberate, Lillis began once more to hobble her way down the mountainside. This time, she tested her footing first before shifting her weight. More than once, the ground crumbled beneath her feet, leaving her scrambling for safe purchase, but she didn't stop. After a while, the crumbling ground grew firmer. Shifting, treacherous rubble gave way to grassy mountain meadows dotted with shrubs and fragrant fir trees. The mist began to thin until Lillis could see several tairen lengths around her. Just up ahead, a footpath led through the grass towards the crest of a mountain pass flanked on both sides by dense stands of fir trees.

Lillis started towards the path, then froze in sudden fear as a shadow moved in the stand of trees on the right. Someone—or something—was hiding there. Watching her.

She clutched Snowfoot to her chest and took a nervous step back. "Who's there?"

The shadow moved again. Lillis's heart rose up in her throat. Her shaking hands squeezed Snowfoot so tightly the little cat screeched a protest.

"*Las, ajiana. Nei siad. Ke nei vu'odahira.*" The voice whispered on the breeze, soft and compelling.

Lillis swayed. The tension in her muscles melted away along with her terror. Except for the phrase "*las, ajiana,*" meaning peace, sweet one, which Kieran often said to her, she did not know what the words meant, but the moment she heard them, she felt calm.

The shadow stepped closer, and Lillis couldn't bring herself to run. Closer still the shadow came, and now Lillis could make out a tall, slender figure emerging from the mist. A woman, dressed in gleaming white leathers, with hair the color of golden oak spilling down in thick waves past her hips. She was as beautiful as a Lightmaiden of Adelis, her pale skin shining with a familiar, silvery luminescence. Her amber eyes were bright, yet full of peace and a welcome so loving, Lillis felt her chin begin to tremble.

"*Veli, ajiana.*" The woman stretched out her arms, beckoning. Wounds and tears forgotten, Lillis went.

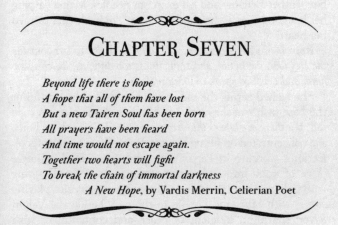

CHAPTER SEVEN

Beyond life there is hope
A hope that all of them have lost
But a new Tairen Soul has been born
All prayers have been heard
And time would not escape again.
Together two hearts will fight
To break the chain of immortal darkness
        A New Hope, by Vardis Merrin, Celierian Poet

Celieria City

With Ellysetta flying overhead on Rain's back, the warriors ran flat-out. They crossed the remaining thousand miles of Celierian farmland in three days and reached the edge of King's Wood at dawn of the fourth. Beyond the wood lay the creamy walls and tiled rooftops of Celieria City, gleaming against a backdrop of blue sky and forested hills cloaked in vivid autumn hues.

Having lived in this city for most of her life, Ellysetta

should have felt a sense of homecoming, but instead, as the signal pennants unfurled on the tower ramparts to alert all the city guard to the Fey's approach and crowds began to gather and stare up at the tairen in the sky, she felt more like a visitor than a daughter of Celieria.

The feeling grew stronger as each beat of Rain's wings brought them closer to her former home, and a strange heaviness fell over her. Too many bad memories, she supposed. The bright-eyed Fey Dajan dying from demon-touch in her family's home. Selianne disappearing in a blaze of blue-white Mage Fire. Father Bellamy and his exorcism needles. Mama gasping her last good-byes as she clutched the *sel'dor* blade that pierced her heart.

Rain sensed her distress. «*Would you prefer to stay outside the city with the lu'tan, shei'tani? If it is too difficult, we can stop here, and I will go speak to Dorian alone.*»

She leaned across the saddle front to stroke the soft fur at the base of his neck. «*Nei. I will be fine. Some memories are sad, but there are others that bring me joy.*» To ease them both, she concentrated on filling her mind with those happier recollections: working in Papa's shop while he turned a simple piece of wood into a gleaming masterpiece of art; laughing with Selianne over Kelissande Minset's pompous airs; playing stones with Lillis and Lorelle in the park beside the Velpin River; sharing a moment of peace and contentment with Mama as they recited their devotions to the Bright Lord.

Rain flew over the west wall as the Fey passed through the West Gate's portcullis and loped down the broad, cobbled avenue that ran east-to-west across the city. They turned north, following the city's main thoroughfare to the elegant square of shops and craftsmasters' workrooms crowded in the shadow of the royal palace. Street urchins chased in the footsteps of the Fey, and curious passersby gathered on the sides of the road, reminding Ellysetta of the day she'd first met Rain. Had that really only been a few short months ago? It seemed like entire lifetimes had passed since the day a woodcarver's shy and awkward adopted daughter had called a Tairen Soul from the sky.

Her hands clutched the raised front of the saddle as Rain tucked his wings and dove towards the royal palace. He Changed in middive, and she slid effortlessly down a draft of Air. Earth magic swirled about her during the descent, transforming her studded red leathers into a silken scarlet gown and silver steel underdress. She landed lightly at the base of the palace steps, surrounded by the ring of her quintet and *lu'tan*. The bloodsworn Fey'cha of her quintet hung in a silver girdle at her hips; a single purple silk belt affixed with sheathed Fey'cha crossed over her chest; and the slight, humming weight of a crown fashioned from whorls of silver studded with Tairen's Eye crystals nestled in her unbound hair.

In a final burst of magic, Rain re-formed at her side, tall and majestic, clad from head to toe in the golden war steel of the Fey king.

Several of the courtiers regarded her with dazed eyes and open mouths, dazzled by the unveiled power of her *shei'dalin* magic. Several others, however, kept their eyes averted, and their cold, suspicious thoughts sliced at her like knives.

Fey witch. How dare she spin her wiles so openly on the lords of Celieria?

Look at her. Look how shamelessly she ensorcels those weak-minded fools.

These Fey are not to be trusted. If we do not resist them, they will use their magic to enslave us all.

She reached for Rain instinctively, and the horrible thoughts she'd inadvertently picked up from the courtiers flowed from her mind to his. The trouble that had been brewing in Celieria City when Rain last visited had clearly not dissipated in the ensuing months. If anything, the air of discontent seemed more obvious, but she wasn't sure if that meant the sentiment was stronger or merely that she'd become adept at perceiving it.

«*Perhaps I should veil myself. The last thing I want to do is cause more trouble between Celieria and the Fey.*» Ellysetta had refused to don the traditional scarlet veil that *shei'dalins* wore outside the Fading Lands. After a lifetime of having her true nature repressed by a powerful glamour, she was through hiding who and what she was.

Rain's glittering lavender eyes fixed on the averted faces of the courtiers whose thoughts had disturbed her. «*You should do no such thing. Certainly not just to put these foul-minded rultsharts at ease.*»

If the ugliness of the Celierians' thoughts weren't so unpleasant, she would have laughed. Back in Orest, he'd practically begged her to veil herself whenever Lord Teleos's men gazed upon her with Light-drunk devotion. But now that she faced unkindness rather than dazzled adoration, tairen possessiveness had darkened to something much more dangerous.

«*They wound your heart.*» The telltale growl was back in his Spirit voice. If he were still in tairen form, he would be spouting flame. «*It is unacceptable.*»

«*You cannot punish them for thoughts, Rain. Nor stop them from thinking what they like.*» She knew it was foolish to give these strangers—arrogant courtiers, no less—the power to hurt her. There would always be those among them eager to find fault with her. And perhaps if she'd lived a life filled with self-confidence, she would not care what they thought. «*They are afraid. Magic can be too easily misused.*»

That was the crux of the matter. These nobles' suspicions struck her most vulnerable spot, and she could not so easily dismiss them. All her life, people had eyed her askance, waiting for the Shadow inside her to spring free. Now these mortal nobles reviled her because they suspected her Light hid a darker Shadow.

And no matter how badly she wanted to deny it, she feared they were right.

Some part of her self-doubt must have shown on her face or touched his senses, because Rain's voice snapped in her mind like a whip. *«You are bright and shining. The darkness you sense is the Eld, not you. You must never think otherwise.»*

His arm snapped up, and he wordlessly offered her his wrist. He fixed an unflinching gaze on King Dorian X, who stood at the top of the palace steps, Great Lords and councilmen by his side. Together, she and Rain mounted the steps, and as they drew closer to the king, a new concern set her senses tingling.

The king did not look well. She remembered him as a pleasant man with warm eyes and a friendly smile, but the last months had aged him. His skin was pale beneath its Celierian summer bronzing, silver liberally threaded the hair at his temples, and circles dark as bruises lay beneath his eyes. Deep lines were etched from the corners of his nose to his mouth.

More disturbing than his wan appearance, however, was the gray shadow that lay over him, dimming his Light. Her first thought was that the Mages had done something to him, perhaps even Marked him. Little could usher in the destruction of Celieria more surely than if the king became a puppet of the Mages.

«Shei'tani?» Rain nudged her with a gentle swell of Air. They had reached the top of the stairs and were now standing before the king. All eyes were on them, and she was staring at the king like a ninnywit.

«Sieks'ta.» She bent quickly to match Rain's half bow in a ruler's courteous acknowledgment of another's sovereignty. When she straightened again, the shadow over Dorian had disappeared. He still looked tired and worn, but otherwise perfectly normal—and even when she dared to open her empathic senses and probe him gently, she discovered nothing more than weariness and deep concern over the troubles facing his country.

"Greetings, Dorian, King of Celieria," Rain said when they straightened. "With joy, my queen and I return to the city she called home for many years. We thank you for greeting us so warmly despite our unannounced visit."

"My Lord Feyreisen, you need no announcement." With grave sincerity, Dorian returned the half bow. "The king of the Fey and his queen will always be welcome as long as a descendant of King Dorian I and Marikah vol Serranis Torreval sits on Celieria's throne." Though he did not take his gaze from Rain's face, Dorian raised his voice enough so that all the courtiers gathered on the palace steps could hear him clearly, and Ellysetta saw several of them stiffen at the reminder of their king's own Fey blood.

Rain stepped forward and lowered his voice. "We bring important news. Is there a place we can speak in private?"

Without hesitation, Dorian said, "Of course. Please follow me."

"Your Majesty." A spare, thin-lipped man in fussy silks and satins stepped forward, disapproval stamped on his features.

Dorian shot the man a single, cold look, silencing whatever objection he'd been about to make and freezing him in his tracks. When the man bowed and retreated, the king turned back to Rain and Ellysetta and swept an arm towards the palace doors. "Please, My Lord Feyreisen, My Lady Feyreisa, after you." Irritation vibrated in every word, and Dorian's normally warm eyes glittered like stones.

Ellysetta's heart thumped. The shadow shrouding Celieria's king might have been a trick of light, but the undercurrents of hostile emotion emanating from the courtiers weren't imaginary. Neither was it merely an increase in her perceptive ability that allowed her to sense them so strongly.

Something—or someone—had been fomenting anti-Fey sentiment since last she and Rain had been here.

And Dorian was aware of it.

The tang of magic filled the wide, gilded hallways of Celieria's royal palace as Ellysetta's *lu'tan* fanned out to search for potential threats to their queen and take up protective stations. As they followed Dorian to his private offices, Rain stayed close to her side, his fingers never far from his Fey'cha.

"Your queen did not join you this morning," Rain commented casually as they walked, careful to keep his tone neutral. Annoura had made her dislike of the Fey clear on more than one occasion. She'd even actively worked against them three months ago. He wouldn't be surprised if the courtiers' hostility was a reflection of hers. "She is otherwise engaged?"

"I received word shortly before your arrival that she wasn't feeling well," Dorian replied.

Rain almost stopped walking. No Fey worthy of his steel would leave his mate's side if she were in poor health, and Dorian was Fey enough that care for his wife should have been a preeminent concern. Brows bunching in a frown, he started to say something to that effect, when Ellysetta's nails dug into his wrist in silent warning.

«*Do not chastise him, Rain. You know mortal ways are different from Fey. He is the king and Celieria is at war. His people expect him to put them first.*»

For Ellysetta's sake, he kept the censure from his voice when he said, "I hope the illness is nothing serious."

They had reached a sprawling marble stair that led to the upper levels of the palace. As they climbed, Dorian slanted Rain a glance that said he knew exactly what Rain thought of his husbandly neglect. "Several members of the court have fallen ill the last few days with a stomach complaint. The physician assures me it isn't particularly harmful—just unpleasant for the afflicted."

"I would be happy to weave healing on them," Ellysetta volunteered. "Or you, for that matter. I can sense your weariness." She gave a crooked smile. "And don't fear; I have become much more adept since the last time we met."

The king gave a quiet chuckle. He had been on the receiving end of her magic before, as one of the unwitting participants in the weave that had plunged the heads of Celieria's noble Houses into seven bells of unrelenting, magic-driven mating. "I would be honored to accept your offer of healing once we're through." His humor faded as he added, "Though the same cannot be said for all the members of my court. I'm sure you noticed the tension outside when you arrived."

They had reached the king's private offices. Guards liveried in hues of Celierian blue and gold pushed open the tall, gilded double doors to admit them into the spacious room. Rain waited for the doors to close and Ellysetta's quintet to spin a five-fold privacy weave before he said, "I take it your troubles with those who would discredit the Fey have not ended?"

"Would that they had." Dorian sighed and paced across the room to the windows overlooking the palace gardens, with their array of spectacular fountains. "Once we began building up our military presence along the borders, the murmurs began. First it was the cost, then the loss of commerce when we ceased trade with merchants known to service the Eld; then the conspiracy rumors began, whispering about how the attack on the cathedral this summer was staged by the Fey to draw us into an unprovoked war against their old enemies, the Eld."

"And when the news came about Teleon and Orest?"

Dorian turned back from the window, his eyes weary. "You mean when the news came that the Fey armies massing in Orest and Teleon forced the Eld to launch a preemptive strike out of self-defense?" He grimaced. "The Eld have been wily; you must give them that. Not once have they attacked a target unrelated to the Fey. That has not escaped the notice of the lords who supported the Eld Trade Agreement this summer. Now they claim the attacks on Orest and Teleon merely prove this is a dispute between the Eld and the Fey—and that we should not allow ourselves to be drawn into your war. They remain convinced that once the Eld are no longer threatened by Fey aggression, there will be peace."

"Peace." Rain gave a harsh laugh. "Oh, *aiyah*, there will be peace. The cost will be misery and enslavement, but your subjects will get their peace." He spun on a booted heel and stalked to the opposite side of the room.

Ellysetta's silk skirts rustled as she took a step towards

Dorian. "Forgive me, Your Majesty, but have you considered the possibility that one or more of the lords leading the opposition might be Mage-claimed?"

Dorian's mouth set in grim lines. "I have considered the possibility, yes. And I pray daily that it is not so." He turned a bleak gaze towards the portrait of his beautiful, silver-blond wife, Annoura, which dominated the wall across from his desk. His shoulders slumped in weary despair. "Because one of the strongest voices against this war belongs to my queen."

"Merciful gods!" Queen Annoura of Celieria groaned in misery as the painful clench of her belly sent her racing to the garderobe for the third time in the last bell. She reached it just as the contents of her stomach spewed out in a series of racking heaves. She retched again and again until nothing came up but bile, and even then the nausea lay upon her like a foul blanket. Her arms and legs trembled as she dragged herself up to her feet and stood there on the cold stone tile floor, swaying and feeling faint.

Whatever illness was sweeping through her court seemed to have found its way to her. A full score of the court's highest-ranked ladies had fallen ill in the last two days, and now she could count herself among them. She'd been retching since before daybreak and showed no signs of stopping anytime soon.

Poison was the first thought that had sprung to her mind. But what miserable excuse for a poisons master would leave dozens of women ill and none dead? Besides, Annoura's food taster hadn't fallen ill, and she used his services religiously. She had too much wily, suspicious Capellan in her ever to give up that protection.

"Your Majesty?" The timid voice of one of Annoura's newest young Dazzles—a sixteen-year-old featherhead with more breasts than brains—called from outside the garderobe door. "Are you all right?"

"Oh, yes, I couldn't be better," Annoura snapped. She

snatched open the door and stalked into her bedroom, ruining the effect of her regal ire when her knees gave out and she nearly tumbled face-first onto the floor.

The Dazzle—Mairi? Miranda? What the Darkness did Annoura care what the little slut's name was?—caught and steadied her. Annoura checked the urge to smack the girl's cheek for witnessing her queen's near-humiliation.

"Help me to my bed, then get out," she snapped. "And find out what in the name of the Seven flaming Hells is taking the physician so long."

The girl helped Annoura back into bed before tucking the covers around her. "Are you sure I can't get you something, Your Majesty? Maybe a nice porridge?"

Porridge? Annoura's eyes bulged. Just the sound of the word made her stomach clench. She leapt from the bed and raced for the garderobe yet again.

This time, when she was finished, the little Dazzle stood there with eyes as big as dinner plates.

Now Annoura did smack her. "I heave my insides out and you ask me if I want *porridge?* Idiot! Ninnywit! Would you offer fire to a burning man? Get out!" She flung a hand towards the door and glared at the other Dazzles gathered in the suite. "All of you, get out now. And the next person to walk through that door had best have a brain between her ears."

The buxom Dazzle burst into tears and fled out the door. The rest of the morning attendants scuttled after her.

Annoura staggered back to her bed and lowered herself gingerly to the mattress. Good, sweet Lord of Light, she felt terrible. She hadn't felt this bad since . . . well, she couldn't remember.

She put a hand over her eyes to block the weak sunlight streaming in from the draped windows. Gods. Even that made her feel like retching. She flopped back into her mountain of pillows, scowling and feeling frighteningly close to tears.

Where was Dorian? Why wasn't he here? The few times in their married life that she'd been ill, he'd always come to her bedside and stayed there, holding her hand, stroking her brow, weaving cool webs of Spirit to soothe her discomfort until the physician's remedies took effect. Where was he? Surely by now one of the yammer-mouths who called themselves her ladies-in-waiting would have whispered the news of his wife's illness into his ear.

Surely he would not be so coldhearted as to continue their estrangement when she was in ill health?

A knock sounded, and the heavy door to her bedroom swung inward. Annoura looked up, a surge of hope lifting her spirits. "Dorian?"

But the feet that stepped over the threshold did not belong to her husband. Annoura sank against her pillows, blinking back tears. Well, at least it wasn't that useless Dazzle or another idiot just like her. The woman walking through the bedroom door did indeed have a brain between her ears—and a face nearly as pale as Annoura's own.

Jiarine Montevero dropped a graceful curtsy to her sovereign as she entered, then approached the bed. "Mirianna said you were taken ill, Your Majesty."

Mirianna. That was the dim-skull Dazzle's name.

"If by ill you mean that I've been retching until my intestines nearly saw daylight, then yes, I suppose I am," Annoura snapped. She hated being sick. The loss of control that came with illness was an agony to her, and she had never borne it graciously or well. "Fetch a cold compress at once."

"Of course, Your Majesty." Without the tiniest blink of hesitation, Jiarine made her way to the nearby nightstand, where a bowl, a stack of scented towels, and a ewer of fresh water had been laid out earlier. Moments later, she laid a damp cloth over Annoura's forehead and eyes.

Annoura sighed as the cool darkness soothed the frayed edges of her temper. Calm, efficient Jiarine. She'd been such a help these last weeks. For all that Annoura had never been keen on keeping female confidantes, she'd come to rely rather a lot on Jiarine recently. Especially after the queen's Favorite,

Ser Vale, had disappeared from court with nary a word save some useless, impersonal scrap of a note claiming a dire emergency on his family estate.

Lady Montevero and Ser Vale had been good friends. She had, in fact, been the one to initially sponsor Ser Vale at court and introduce him to the queen's circle. Now, with Vale gone and no word from him in months, Annoura had found herself talking more and more to Jiarine, hoping Jiarine might have news about the handsome Dazzle who had so quickly become Annoura's indispensible confidant and Favorite. Alas, the lady had received no word from their mutual friend either.

Annoura plucked at the coverlet with restless irritability. "Where is the king? Has he been told of my illness?"

Silence. Then, "I delivered the message myself, Your Majesty. Half a bell ago."

Half a bell.

Half a bell and still Dorian had not come. Time was he would have been at her side in mere chimes, breathless from having run through the palace to reach her. But now, even with half the court afflicted by this mysterious stomach illness, he'd not roused enough concern to visit her?

"I'm sure he will come to see you soon, Your Majesty," Jiarine soothed, "but the Tairen Soul and his mate arrived this morning."

Annoura's fists clenched around the comforter, pulling until the satin was taut. "The Fey . . . are *here?*"

No wonder Dorian wasn't by her side. The Fey. It was always the Fey. They—not she—would always be first in his heart. She could be on her deathbed, and if a single flaming Fey crooked a finger, Dorian would abandon her without a qualm and go running to his magical master's side like the obedient lapdog he had become.

"They arrived unexpectedly this morning," Jiarine said. "I'm sure the king would not otherwise have stayed away."

"Oh, of course he wouldn't."

If Jiarine heard the heavy irony in Annoura's voice, she gave no sign of it. "Your Majesty, I've sent for the physician, but he left the palace a bell ago to attend Lady Verakis. I don't know how long it will take him to arrive." Skirts rustled as Jiarine moved closer to the bed. "Lord Bolor is outside, Your Majesty. He's no physician, but he has a tonic that worked wonders for me earlier this morning."

Annoura grimaced. "No."

"But, Your Majesty—"

She lifted one corner of the compress long enough to fix Jiarine with a withering look. "Have your ears failed you? I said no." Then, because Jiarine had been such a boon companion to her these last weeks, Annoura sighed. "Jiarine, I know you've taken to him. He's handsome enough, I'll grant you, and he has a sharp wit." *Too sharp at times.* "But there's just something about him that rubs me the wrong way. I don't trust him."

Not that she truly trusted anyone except Dorian—and even that was questionable these days—but with most courtiers, Annoura knew what they were thinking even before they did. She could read them. She had a very good idea of how they would react in most important situations, and she knew how to keep one step ahead of them and manipulate them to achieve her own aims.

But this Bolor fellow . . . Annoura didn't know what he was thinking or how to control him. And that bothered her beyond measure. No matter how much Jiarine seemed to like him, Annoura had no intention of granting Bolor entrée to her inner circle.

And she certainly wasn't going to quaff down some potion the man had brewed up just because Jiarine—clearly addled by the man's virile good looks—vouched for it.

"Your Majesty—"

"The answer is no. And if he's waiting outside my door, you can just send him away. Except for the king or the physician, no one sets foot in this room but you. Is that clear?"

Jiarine bobbed a brief, stiff curtsy. "Of course, Your Majesty. As you wish."

"Good. Go sit there, in that chair. There's a book on the stand beside it. You may read to me." Annoura dropped the compress back over her eyes. She heard Jiarine cross the room to the door, whisper something unintelligible to someone outside, then return and take a seat.

The lady's acquiescence pleased Annoura. Ill she might be, but some things the queen of Celieria could still control.

"If there's even a possibility the Mages have claimed your queen's soul, we need to know it," Rain declared after King Dorian spent several chimes detailing the troubled political situation in Celieria City.

Dorian flinched, and Ellysetta's heart ached for him. His deep and genuine love for his beautiful queen was well-known throughout Celieria—even a celebrated point of pride to its citizens—and fear for his wife must be eating at him night and day. «Oh, Rain, no wonder he looks so weary.» His country was at war, his nobles were infighting over the Fey, and now his wife might possibly have been corrupted by the Mages. Those were burdens enough to bring the strongest of men to his knees.

«He'll be ten times worse off if his wife truly is in the service of the Mages.» Rain glanced at Gaelen, who gave a slight nod. "As you know, we now have a way to detect Mage Marks. Gaelen showed us the weave this summer. While Ellysetta spins healing on the queen, Gaelen can check her for Mage Marks. Unless she possesses magic herself, she will not sense his weave."

Dorian looked up from his desk, his hands knotted before him. "You're asking me to let you spin forbidden black magic on my queen."

Rain's eyes narrowed. "I'm asking you to let us check your queen for Mage Marks. If she is Mage-claimed, you need to know. If she's not, it will set your mind at ease. If she bears only a few Marks, you need to know that, too, so you can take precautions to prevent further Marks."

As he spoke, an urgent thread of Spirit stabbed into Ellysetta's mind across the private communication pathway forged by their partially completed *shei'tanitsa* bond. *«Ellysetta, open your senses to Dorian and tell me what you find. Quickly.»*

«What's wrong?» It was a measure of her trust in him that she didn't wait for his answer before tearing down the barriers that kept human thoughts and emotions from battering her empathic senses. With swift delicacy, she sent gossamer-fine threads of Spirit and *shei'dalin*'s love spinning out towards Dorian.

«I told Dorian this summer that the Fey had learned how to detect Mage Marks, but I never told him it required spinning Azrahn. So how did he find out?»

«You think the Mage has gotten to him?»

«I don't know, but he found out from somewhere. And it wasn't from us.»

Her threads reached Dorian, only to encounter a powerful barrier that blocked her attempted probe. *«He has shielded himself from me.»* She tested the perimeters of the shield lightly, not daring to press with any substantive power for fear that he would sense her presence. Celierian king or not, he was a descendant of the vol Serranis line, and not without magic of his own. When he frowned and waved a hand near his face as if to shoo away a buzzfly, she yanked her weave back. *«Sieks'ta, Rain. I can't get past his shields. If I try, he'll know.»*

Abruptly, Dorian pushed his chair away from the desk and stood. "Let us be frank, My Lord Feyreisen. I know about your banishment from the Fading Lands and the reason for it. A messenger arrived not three days ago from Tenn v'En Eilan, the leader of the Massan. He wrote to inform me that he is now the acting ruler of the Fading Lands and to warn me that you and the Feyreisa had been stripped of your crowns and banished for spinning Azrahn."

Ellysetta gasped. The faces of her quintet turned to stone.

Beside her, Rain curled his fingers around the hilts of the *meicha* scimitars sheathed at his hips. "Is that so?"

The shutters on the windows overlooking the gardens trembled and the curtains flanking them fluttered as if from a breeze. Dorian's gaze flicked in that direction before returning to Rain, whose eyes had begun to glow as his tairen rose.

«*Three days. The messenger arrived three days ago.*» Anger vibrated in every shining thread of his Spirit voice. «*It takes only a week at most for a runner to reach Celieria City from Dharsa.*»

Ellysetta processed the calculations quickly. The messenger had left Dharsa ten days ago, which meant—

«*Tenn sent his message after he received the battle reports from Teleon and Orest—and after the tairen declared you the rightful Defender of the Fey. Oh, Rain.*»

"What else did Tenn's note say?" Rain's voice lowered to a throaty growl.

Another man might well have fled in fear of Rain Tairen Soul's infamous Rage, but Dorian stood his ground with admirable calm. "Among other things, he warned me that your mate was Mage Marked and that your bond to her had clouded your judgment. And he vowed I'd receive no more support from the Fey as long as I continued to count you among my allies. Here." He pulled open his desk drawer and withdrew a scroll encased in a gilded wooden scroll cover. "Read it for yourself."

Rain snatched the scroll from Dorian's grip, removed the protective cover, and unfurled the parchment. Ellysetta looked over his arm as he scanned Tenn's message, and the vile, damning words, written in an elegant golden script, jumped out at her.

> *To the Most Honorable and Beloved Fey-kin, His Majesty Dorian vol Serranis Torreval, Dorian X, King of Celieria,*
> *It is with heavy heart and deep concern that I write....*

...Rainier Feyreisen has broken his honor...confessed under Truthspeaking...both he and his mate did with knowing and willful deliberation weave the forbidden magic, Azreisenahn, also called Azrahn, the soul magic....The Massan had no choice but to declare them dahl'reisen *and cast them out of the Fading Lands....*

...Ellysetta Baristani's soul is tainted with Shadow....Elden Mages have begun the possession of her soul....How deeply she is tainted, we do not know, but the danger cannot be ignored.... Already the insidious effects of her presence have divided the Fading Lands...honorable Fey have discarded their honor to follow her into Shadow...her influence drove our king to dishonor....

...The Eye of Truth has foretold a grim future for Ellysetta Baristani, one that honor and duty to the Fading Lands will not allow the Massan to overlook....She will bring destruction....

...If Celieria continues to consort with the dahl'reisen *Rain Tairen Soul and his Shadow-tainted mate, you may expect no further aid from the Fading Lands....*

Each damning declaration drove a spike into her heart. «*Dear gods, Rain,*» she breathed in horror. «*Why would he send this?*»

Rain tossed the scroll on Dorian's desk as if it were a polluted thing. His eyes had gone pure tairen, pupil-less and whirling with purple radiance. A muscle jumped in his tightly clenched jaw. "So you received this ... *message* three days ago, and yet still you greeted us with open arms rather than drawn swords. Why?"

Dorian arched his brows. "You forget, My Lord Feyreisen, I am a king, born and raised. I don't take kindly to veiled threats from foreign powers." He picked up the scroll, glanced at it briefly, then rolled the parchment back onto the scroll rods and slid the cover into place. "Nor does the idea that a usurper could strip a sovereign of his crown sit well with me, for obvious reasons."

He placed the scroll back into his desk drawer and closed it away. "Tenn v'En Eilan is a stranger to me. I know nothing of him. But I have spent time with you, and with your Celierian-born truemate. Given the long history between our two countries, and my aunt's personal regard and affection for you, I thought it best to withhold judgment until I heard the truth from your own lips."

Rain's expression seemed carved from diamondine granite. "I wish I could tell you that what is written there is false, but Fey do not lie. Not even Tenn." He reached for Ellysetta's hand. "Ellysetta and I did both spin Azrahn. Tenn and three other members of the Massan declared us *dahl'reisen* and banished us from the Fading Lands because of it."

Ellysetta sensed Dorian's instinctive recoil and hurried to reassure him. "What we did wasn't as evil as Tenn's message makes it seem. I wove Azrahn to save four tairen kitlings from death, and Rain spun it to save me. The High Mage of Eld was stealing the souls of unborn tairen, and we had to stop him." Quickly, she told him about how the High Mage had been working to breed his own Tairen Soul.

"If Rain and I had not acted, the tairen would have perished with this generation. Tenn knows that, but it doesn't matter to him that we saved the tairen, or that Rain led Lord Teleos's forces to defeat the Eld at Orest, or even that the tairen brought Rain the golden war steel of the Fey king and declared him the rightful ruler of the Fading Lands. All Tenn sees are my Mage Marks, the vision in the Eye of Truth, and the admission that Rain and I wove Azrahn."

"Which facts, you must admit, are troubling," Dorian replied.

Rain took a half step forward, only to freeze when Ellysetta caught his wrist. "We do not deny it. The path the gods have laid out before us is by no means an easy one." Her eyes flashed as she lifted her chin and fixed an unwavering gaze upon the king. "But make no mistake, King Dorian: Azrahn or not, banished or not, Rain is the true king of the Fading Lands and Defender of the Fey. The tairen follow him, as do all Fey who remember that they were born to champion the Light."

Dorian regarded her in silent contemplation for several long moments. "You have changed a great deal from that shy young woman I first met three months ago."

"For the better, I hope."

"That remains to be seen."

"Enough." Rain crossed his arms. "We're wasting time. We came with important news, Dorian, and delayed an even more important visit of our own to do so. But given the unrest in your court and your concerns about your mate, it seems prudent that we share what we know only with those free of Mage Marks. Starting with you."

"*What?*" Dorian regarded him with fresh affront. "You're saying you want to weave the forbidden magic on *me* now?"

"*Aiyah,*" Rain confirmed. "On you and everyone else who will be privy to the information we bring. We cannot risk revealing what we know to anyone who might be Mage-claimed, lest word get back to the Eld. That is why we came in person to deliver our news."

"I am not Mage-claimed, I can assure you."

"No disrespect, but your assurances aren't enough. You could bear Marks and not know it, just as Ellysetta did. Gaelen's Azrahn weave is the only way to be sure."

«*Rain, please.*» Ellysetta laid a hand on his arm. His brusqueness was only making Dorian dig in his heels. Kings didn't take commands from others well. Aloud, to Dorian, she said, "Your Majesty, my best friend's mother sent her daughter and bond son to their deaths because the Mages owned her soul. *Teska,* please, the weave won't harm you, but not knowing could kill us all. I'll even have Gaelen spin the weave on me, so you can see for yourself." She turned to motion the former *dahl'reisen* to her side.

"With your permission, *kem'jita'taikonos?*" Gaelen said with a bow to his twin sister Marikah's royal descendant.

"Either you trust us or you don't," Rain snapped when Dorian didn't respond. "Make up your mind."

The king closed his eyes and splayed one hand across his forehead in a gesture of weary despair. A moment later, he muttered, "Gods save us all," then opened his eyes and nodded. "Fine. Do it. If you've fallen to Darkness, the rest of us are as good as dead anyway."

Rain gestured and the quintet leapt into action, spinning a ten-fold weave around the room to keep the distinctive magical signature of Azrahn from escaping the room. No need to either alarm Adrial and Rowan, who were still hiding in the city, or tip their hand to any Mages who might be nearby.

"Mage Marks are invisible and undetectable except in the presence of Azrahn," Gaelen explained. "Then they appear as a pattern of shadows over the heart of the Marked person." He lifted a hand and summoned a small, spiraling swirl of the forbidden magic into his cupped palm.

Ellysetta shivered as Gaelen's eyes went black and the icy, too-sweet taste of Azrahn filled her mouth. The skin over her heart began to throb. She tossed her hair over her shoulder and tugged at the neckline of her gown to reveal the four Marks lying like a ring of bruises on the shining white skin of her left breast.

"Sweet Lord of Light," Dorian breathed.

Gaelen's weave winked out.

"How badly are you compromised?"

"It is manageable for now," she assured him, "but just to be safe, I will not be joining you when you discuss matters of military importance."

"King Dorian," Rain said, "you have seen what the weave entails. Will you allow us to check you for Mage Marks?"

"Yes, of course," the king agreed. His hands went to his neatly tied neckcloth. He bared his chest to Gaelen's weave, and was soon discovered free of Marks.

"Your Majesty," Ellysetta said, "I will take my leave of you now. Though we will not be here long, may I trouble you for the use of a suite during our stay?"

"Of course." Dorian tugged on a bellpull by his desk, and a moment later the office door opened to reveal his Steward of Affairs. "Davris, please show the Feyreisa to the blue suite."

"Of course, Your Majesty." The steward executed a deep court bow. "My Lady Feyreisa, if you would please follow me?"

Leaving Gaelen to continue checking Celierian nobles for Mage Marks, Ellysetta quit the room. The rest of her quintet and the Fire master selected to take Gaelen's place went with her.

As the door closed behind her, she heard Rain say, "Call your Great Lords, King Dorian . . . starting with whomever you trust most from holdings here, and here, and here."

CHAPTER EIGHT

Surrounded by her quintet and two dozen *lu'tan*, Ellysetta followed the king's steward from one opulent, gilded corridor to another until they reached the palace wing reserved for visiting dignitaries. The carved double doors opened to a richly appointed three-room suite decorated in Celierian blue, creamy white, and lustrous gold.

The quintet made short work of inspecting the suite and

weaving privacy and protection upon all three rooms before rejoining Ellysetta in the main salon.

"You should rest," Bel told Ellysetta. "This business with King Dorian will probably take most of the day."

She gave him a wan smile. "I'll sleep later, when we leave Celieria City." She was tired. Even with Gaelen's addition to the protection weaves, she'd been too afraid to sleep deeply for fear of dreaming some new horror, but she wasn't about to sleep here. An unsettling undercurrent in the palace set her nerves on edge.

Ellysetta leaned back against a pile of plump pillows, closed her eyes, and tried to relax, but her rest was soon interrupted by an unexpected visitor.

The suite doors opened to admit a familiar, dapper little man, and Ellysetta leaped up, lips curved in a smile of sincere happiness.

"Master Fellows! What a pleasure to see you again."

Queen Annoura's Master of Graces, who had tutored Ellysetta in the courtly arts, was dressed to perfection in exquisitely tailored sapphire silk with an elegant rose brocade waistcoat. A mint-green-lined satin demicape was draped across his shoulders. He executed a graceful, flourishing court bow before her—which was quite a feat, considering the snow-white kitten perched on one shoulder.

"My Lady Feyreisa." Master Fellows straightened and pressed his steepled fingers to his lips in a prayerful gesture. "Dear lady, I can scarce believe my eyes. You have exceeded my greatest expectations. Ah." He sniffed and his thick, curling lashes fluttered as if he were fighting back tears of joy. "To think this vision of queenly grace and beauty is the same young woman I tutored three months past."

Standing in the far corner of the room, Bel rolled his eyes, but she laughed in delight. Master Fellows had a warm Light. Fussy and critical and pretentious he might be, but he was also intrinsically honest and well-intentioned and bright of heart.

"With joy, this Fey greets her friend and teacher." She held out her hands and clasped his. The instant their skin touched, she opened her senses. A wave of warm greeting showered over him to mask the probing weave that scoured him for the slightest hint of Darkness. Relieved to find none, she said, "You are looking well. And little Love has never looked finer." She smiled at the blue-eyed kitten that had once belonged to Lillis and Lorelle. "She's gotten so big." Much larger than the little white fluff ball who had adored perching on Kieran's shoulder and flicking his ear with her stubby little tail. But larger or not, Love clearly still believed a shoulder was the perfect perch for her.

Master Fellows smiled with indulgent affection and scratched the kitten under her chin. "She is a fine lady of the court now, very fond of her satin and jewels." A large blue satin bow set with a diamond heart was tied around Love's throat. "And she has become quite the arbiter of fashion. No less than a dozen young ladies and Sers have begun wearing kittens of their own on their shoulders."

Ellysetta laughed. "Really? None so beautiful as Love, though, I am sure." She stepped back and gestured to the upholstered settee. "*Teska*, Master Fellows, have a seat. Shall I ring for refreshments?"

As she spoke, an exquisite china keflee service appeared on the low table beside the settee. Love screeched in surprise and arched her back, hissing it the tea service. "Or would you prefer to simply enjoy the ones we now have?" Ellysetta muttered with a chiding glance at Tajik and Rijonn. The warriors clearly had no use for bellpulls. They had simply spun weaves of Earth and Fire to prepare hot keflee and a tray of sandwiches and sweetmeats from the palace stores.

"How have you been, Master Fellows?" she asked as she poured a stream of fragrant, steaming brown keflee into an eggshell-thin porcelain cup.

"Very well, Lady Ellysetta. The very pink of health."

"Really? And the rest of the court?" She poured honeyed

cream into the cup, stirring twice, gently, before offering it to him. "I couldn't help but notice a disturbing hostility in the air when we arrived. I thought those troubles had been resolved before the Feyreisen and I departed this summer."

"Ah . . . well, I don't think the troubles were ever resolved, merely silenced by circumstance. But once the shock of the attack and Greatfather Tivrest's death faded, the usual dissonance returned. Such strong feelings can rarely be held at bay for long." He blew across his keflee and took a sip.

Ellysetta poured a second cup for herself and added enough honeyed cream to turn the dark, aromatic brew a milky shade of deep amber. She curled her hands around the cup and lifted it to her nose, her lashes dropping in bliss as she breathed in the rich scent.

She'd not had a decent cup of keflee since leaving the Fading Lands. Lord Teleos, whom she held in great regard in most other ways, drank a pallid brew scarcely worthy of the name. The rich drink she held now, however, came direct from Queen Annoura's palace stores. No matter what other faults she might have, the queen knew her keflee and stocked only the finest.

She raised her cup to her lips and braced herself in anticipation of the rush of exquisite pleasure, the thrill of keflee's complex flavors tumbling across her tongue. She tilted the cup and drew the first, hot sip into her mouth. Magic flared the same instant, and her eyes opened in surprise as the sharp bitterness of gallberry tea spilled past her lips.

Outraged, she spat the mouthful back out and set the cup in its saucer with a clatter that sent tea sloshing precariously close to the rim. She turned to glare at Rijonn. The enormous Fey Earth master gave her a look of wide-eyed innocence and pointed one long, large finger of blame at the opposite side of the room. «He made me do it.»

She swiveled in her seat and narrowed her eyes on Bel. Noble, honorable, serious Bel—General of the Fey armies and deadly First Blade of the Fading Lands—was fighting so hard to control his laughter his shoulders were quaking.

"Is something wrong with the keflee, Lady Ellysetta?" Master Fellows inquired in concern.

She turned back around in her seat and forced the scowl off her face. "Not at all, Master Fellows. The keflee"—she emphasized the word and sent another darkling glance Bel's way—"is as exquisite as any I've ever tasted, I'm sure." «*Or would be if some ninnywit would actually let me taste it. Honestly, Bel. Gallberry?*»

Bel made a strange choking noise and pivoted abruptly on one heel. He strode to the window, pulled back the lacy curtains, and stood there looking out, his face turned away from the room, his shoulders shaking.

Master Fellows frowned in puzzlement over Bel's behavior. With a wary glance at his own cup, he set the saucer back on the table.

Ellysetta reached for one of the sweetmeats on the tray, needing something—anything—to take the horrid taste of gallberry out of her mouth. As she did, she noticed a soft rumble coming from the kitten perched on Master Fellows's shoulder. At first, it sounded like a purr, but Ellysetta had spent enough time around the tairen to realize the sound was actually a faint growl. She glanced up and saw that the pupils of Love's blue eyes had widened and tension had gathered in her small body. Even as she watched, however, the signs of aggression faded, and Love went back to purring and tickling Master Fellows's neck with the tip of her tail.

Ellysetta sat back. «*Tajik, say something to me in Spirit.*»

«*Like what?*»

Love's ears flicked back and she began growling again. Ellysetta nearly crowed in triumph. «*Never mind.*» How could she have forgotten Love's special gift?

Scarcely able to hide her eagerness, Ellysetta leaned forward. "Master Fellows, may I ask you something in confidence?"

The slender man raised his brows. "You may ask me anything. Provided it is something I am at liberty to discuss, I will do my best to answer."

"Actually, it's a question about little Love here."

"Love?" Master Fellows tilted his head to look down at the white kitten on his shoulder. Her slender tail was wrapped as far around his neck as it would go. Her claws dug deep, through the material of his demicape into what was apparently a thick pad fixed on his right shoulder.

"Have you ever noticed her acting strangely since you brought her here to the palace?"

"Strangely?" The Master of Graces regarded Ellysetta with a furrowed brow. "How do you mean?"

"Taking an inexplicable fright, for instance? Hissing regularly at particular people in the palace?" At the corners of the room, Tajik, Rijonn, Gil, and the *lu'tan* who'd taken Gaelen's place all emanated a mild sense of curiosity and confusion over her question. Bel, however, suddenly went still and intent. He had been in Celieria this summer and witnessed Love's unique talent firsthand.

"Well, there are a number of courtiers she's never taken a particular liking to, though I simply put that down to discriminating taste. Most of them I don't care for myself."

"Which courtiers? Can you tell me their names?"

"Oh, dear, you want names?" Master Fellows tapped his lip. "Several of the new Dazzles. Ser Egol, Sera Tyrene, Ser Sonneval and his new bride, Lady Giamet, Lord Bolor, Great Lord Ponsonney, Lady Thane, Lord Tufton. Those are just the few I can think of at the moment. And, of course, there's Great Lord Barrial and his sons—and regrettably, on more than one occasion, even the king."

Ellysetta exchanged a look with Bel.

"What is it?" Master Fellows asked.

"I don't know that Love's reaction to the courtiers is so much a matter of discriminating taste as it is a reflection of her rather acute sensitivity."

"Sensitivity?"

"To magic." Ellysetta clasped her hands at her waist. "Love senses when people weave magic. The closer and more powerful the magic, the stronger and more violent her reaction to it."

"Oh." He drew back in surprise.

"So, the likelihood is that all or most of those people were either weaving magic, or present when magic was being woven near them. I know Lord Barrial and the king both possess magic. They each descend from the vel Serranis line of the Fey. The others you mentioned may have inherited magic from their forebears as well, but . . ." She paused. For an instant, she considered holding her silence. What she was about to propose would put Master Fellows—an innocent man and a friend—in danger. And yet no one was better situated to be of help. "Master Fellows . . . Rain and I believe there are Elden Mages at work here in the city . . . perhaps even in the palace itself."

The master of graces blinked. "Here?"

"*Aiyah*. We don't believe this increasing disaffection for the Fey is entirely natural in its origin."

"You think the Mages are deliberately turning people against the Fey?"

"What better way to win a war than to divide your enemy so that they spend more time fighting themselves than you? I know the Mages were here this summer." She lowered her gaze to her clasped hands. "One of them murdered my best friend and her husband and led the attack at the cathedral that killed my mother. It's possible they are still here, working to defeat Celieria from the inside."

Master Fellows didn't hesitate. "What can I do to help?"

He looked so earnest. And so slight to her eyes after her months in the Fading Lands. The Mages would snap him like a twig. What was she even thinking to consider asking him to risk his life? She rose to her feet and paced a short distance away. "I thought . . . but *nei*. It is too much to ask. The risk too great. You could be killed, and I would never forgive myself."

Master Fellows rose as well. "My Lady Feyreisa, for the last months, the men of Celieria—including boys half my age—have been preparing to risk their lives for Celieria's sake. Though I long ago accepted that my talents were more suited to the drawing rooms of noble society than to battlefields, I have always been a patriot. If there is any way I may be of service to my king in the coming war, I should like to hear of it."

"Do you think it wise to enlist the Queen's Master of Graces in spying on the court when we have yet to determine whether the queen herself has been compromised?" Tajik asked after Master Fellows took his leave. "What if he tells her what you've asked him to do?"

Ellysetta stared at the gilded doors through which Master Fellows had just exited. "I don't think he will," she said. "While he listens to every whisper of gossip of the court, he's quite discreet himself." She turned to face the redheaded Fey general. "Besides, there is no one better suited to spy on the court than Master Fellows. He has entrée into every level of court society. He is a fixture in the palace. And since he has taken to carrying Love with him everywhere, no one will be suspicious."

"Do you think Dorian will approve of your enlisting his subjects as spies without his consent?"

Heat warmed her cheeks. Impulsivity was her downfall. "Once I explain the situation, I am certain King Dorian will see the benefits of my idea." When Tajik arched a single red brow, she lifted her chin. "And since I asked Master Fellows to report his findings directly to the king, I cannot see why he would object."

She sank back down onto the settee's blue brocade cushion and reached for the keflee pot. She started to pour a fresh cup of the still-steaming aromatic brew, then paused to give each member of her quintet a warning glare. "And don't any of you dare to turn this cup of keflee into anything else, do you hear me?" She fixed her baleful glare longest on the cobalt-eyed leader of her quintet.

Bel held up his hands. "I swear to you, all I said was, 'Change it,' and that only because I remembered what happened the last time you drank keflee in this place." He attempted to look innocent, but the effect was ruined by the laughter he was fighting to keep in check. "I was looking out for your best interests."

"Clearly you have spent too much time around Gaelen." She sniffed. "*Gallberry*? It's a wonder I didn't spew the entire mouthful directly into Master Fellows's face."

Bel's mouth twitched.

"Oh . . . er . . . that was my fault," Rijonn admitted. "*Sieks'ta*. I am not familiar with Celierian beverages. I thought it was sweet hazel."

A sudden fit of coughing overtook both Bel and, a moment later, Tajik. Gil suddenly found the plaster moldings on the ceiling utterly absorbing. Ellysetta regarded the three of them with a jaundiced eye, but when she lifted her freshly prepared cup of keflee to her lips and found Rijonn watching her with mournful brown eyes and an expression as woeful and penitent as a puppy's . . . she couldn't suppress a snort of laughter. "Sweet hazel, 'Jonn? How in the Haven's name could you mistake gallberry for *sweet hazel*?" Her choked laugh turned into a fit of giggles.

With that, Bel lost his fight and burst into open laughter. "If only you could have seen your face! Gallberry! Sweet brightness! 'Jonn, you're a dim-skull, but flame me if that wasn't the funniest thing I've seen in a tairen's age."

First Tajik, then Gil, then Rijonn and the *lu'tan* joined in the laughter until the room rang with the sounds of unrestrained mirth. They laughed and laughed until tears streamed from the corners of their eyes. After the last weeks of battle, grief, and struggling just to survive from one day to the next, nothing could have felt better or more right.

* * *

Rain found himself reassured in King Dorian's measure of men when the nobles he summoned turned out to be many of the same lords and Great Lords Dev Teleos had once invited to his home to rally support for the Fey and prepare Celieria for an Elden invasion.

Among them was a familiar face that made Rain smile in surprised welcome. "Lord Barrial . . . Cann." He offered his arm in friendship and warrior's greeting to the border lord who had only this summer discovered he was descended from the cousin of Gaelen vel Serranis. "I confess I am surprised to see you still here in the city. I thought you would have left weeks ago."

Cannevar Barrial clasped Rain's arm in a firm grip. "The king asked a few of the Twenty and the border lords to stay for military planning. My eldest, Tarrent, returned to oversee our defenses in my stead. His wife, Anessa, took their children south, to her father's estate. The rest of my boys are here with me."

«And your daughter?» Rain asked privately.

Cann's mouth went grim about the edges. Though he possessed no mastery of Spirit, he still sent his thoughts across clearly. «Talisa is as well as can be expected. She and Colum are still here in the city, residing with me and my younger sons at our house in Tellsnor Square. Sebourne wasn't pleased, you can be sure, but I wasn't about to send my only daughter off alone with an angry, jealous husband and no father or brothers to keep him in check.» He took a deep breath and visibly relaxed. «Once vel Arquinas left, Colum started to settle down, but I'm keeping Talisa close as long as I can.»

Guilt pricked Rain's conscience. He liked Cann. The border lord would not be pleased to find out Adrial had never left his truemate's side and had, in fact, been hiding beneath Cann's nose the entire time.

To change the subject, Rain turned to the former *dahl'reisen* at his side. "You remember Gaelen."

"Of course." Lord Barrial nodded to the Fey whose cousin

Dural had sired Cann's family line. "You are looking well, Ser vel Serranis. Your return to honor seems to agree with you."

Gaelen returned the nod. "What the Feyreisa did was a miracle, and one that I will spend the rest of my life striving to deserve."

"I wish the same could be said of the other *dahl'reisen* on the borders."

Rain's ears perked up. "There is trouble?"

"Not on my land—yet—but Tarrent sent word that an entire village on Great Lord Darramon's land was burned to the ground, every man, woman, and child found dead in their beds. A farmer from a neighboring village saw smoke and went to investigate. No telling exactly when it happened or what killed them, but 'tis middling strange that not a single villager roused from bed or sounded the alarm while the village burned around them. The new Lord Darramon fears dark magic."

"Did your son speak to the *dahl'reisen* on your land?" Gaelen asked. "What did they say?"

"Tarrent hasn't seen our *dahl'reisen* since the Fey arrived."

"My lords." King Dorian rang the Bell of Order, and Lord Barrial broke off his conversation to face his liege.

As Dorian explained his purpose in summoning the nobles, Rain glanced at Gaelen. «*What are your thoughts on that attack?*»

«*Either the whole village was Mage-claimed and the Brotherhood executed them, or this was Mage work.*»

«*Your Brotherhood would murder infants?*»

Ice blue eyes met Rain's with grim frankness. «*If they bore more than three Marks? Without hesitation.*»

"You expect us to submit ourselves to magic spun by Gaelen vel Serranis?" A raised voice made them both turn towards the gathered Celierian lords. "Sire, you cannot be serious."

"Ser vel Serranis's weave is the only way to detect Mage Marks, and the news the Tairen Soul has brought is grave enough that we dare not share it with anyone who has been compromised by the Mages." When no one stepped forward, the king gestured impatiently. "Come now. I've submitted to the procedure myself, and am none the worse for it."

Cannevar Barrial stepped forward, his fingers already tugging at his neck cloth. "I'll be the first. I've no fear of Fey magic." He glanced at Rain and Gaelen, and the corner of his mouth pulled down in a grimace. "It's the Eld kind I worry about."

Despite Annoura's continuing nausea, weariness crept over her. Her vile sickness had left her drained and lethargic. She never slept in the day—kingdoms didn't rule themselves—but right now, if she were any other woman, she would happily let herself drift off to the sound of Jiarine's low-pitched, pleasant reading voice.

Instead, a lifetime of stern discipline kept her anchored to consciousness, and when the soft knock sounded on her bedroom door, she snapped to instant alertness. Whipping the compress off her face, she wriggled into an upright position as Jiarine set her book aside and crossed the room.

A second series of knocks rapped out before Jiarine reached the door, and a thin, quavering voice called, "It's Mirianna, Your Majesty. The doctor is here."

Jiarine threw open the door, using her body to block any curious eyes from peering in at the queen in her bed. "Idiot girl. What are you thinking to keep the doctor waiting outside when the queen is ill? Show him in this instant."

A moment later, Jiarine stepped aside to admit the flushed and harried-looking royal physician, Lord Hewen. His robes were mussed and long strands of his graying hair hung free of his usually tidy queue. He placed a small brown leather satchel on the exquisitely carved table beside the bed and opened the bag's hinged mouth to reveal an impressive collection of powders, vials, and physician's implements.

"You are not going to prod me with those," Annoura said, eyeing several of the torturous-looking devices.

"Unless your symptoms are any different from those of the twenty other ladies I've seen in the last two days, there will be no need, Your Majesty," Lord Hewen replied. He placed a hand on the side of her neck to feel the temperature of her skin, then placed a metal cone shaped like a hollowed cow's horn on her heart and put his ear to the small, pointed end.

"Why? What have they got? It's not poison, is it?" Another thought occurred to her. "Or some new variation of the Great Plague?"

"Shh. No talking, please, until I've had a good listen." He moved the horn to her belly and listened again.

Her lips pressed tight but her eyes flashed with irritation. She let him command her in this one instance because he had been her physician since Dori's birth and was frankly better at healing than anyone except a Fey *shei'dalin*. But she didn't like it.

The moment the horn lifted from her belly, she asked, "Well?"

"Your heartbeat is fine and strong."

"I have always found it works best that way," she snapped. "Now, answer my question. What's wrong with the other ladies? What's wrong with me?"

"Calm yourself, Your Majesty. The other ladies have neither been poisoned nor Plagued, I assure you. In fact, nothing's wrong with them that a little rest, pampering, and time won't cure. As I was saying, your heartbeat is fine and strong, as is the child's."

"The child's . . ." Her voice trailed off. Her brows drew together, then flew upward. "You're not suggesting . . ."

A shocked gasp from behind Lord Hewen made both Annoura and the physician turn. Jiarine stood there, clutching her belly, a look of horror on her face. "You mean she's . . ." A shaking finger pointed at Annoura. "And they're . . ." The arm attached to the finger swung in a tremulous arc to point its accusatory digit at the door behind them, then slowly dragged back around until her finger was pressed against her own well-endowed chest. "And I'm . . . ?"

"Pregnant." King Dorian leaned against the closed door of the private room located at the rear of the council chamber and regarded the royal physician, Lord Hewen, with dazed eyes. "But . . . the queen cannot be pregnant. You yourself claimed her past that age two years ago."

"Yes . . . well . . ." Lord Hewen scratched his head. "I would say I must have been mistaken, except that the Lady of every noble House—at least, all the ones I've seen here in the city—appears to be in the same condition . . . including grand-mothers much advanced into their elder years." The physician held out his palms in a bewildered gesture. "It's the oddest case I've ever seen, Sire. Inexplicable, really. As if the gods themselves decided to waive the laws of mortal reproduction so that the head of every noble House in Celieria could have a child."

Dorian groped for the back of the chair behind him to steady his wobbling legs. "How far along is she—are they?"

"Well, that's rather odd, as well, Sire. I can't really be completely certain, of course, with ladies who have passed beyond their . . . er . . . female times . . . but as far as I can ascertain, they are all about as far along as the younger ladies who discovered their own good news last month."

"I see." Last month, every noble lady of childbearing years who had attended a certain infamous dinner at the royal palace had been discovered pregnant. Glowingly so, in fact. Though considering the seven bells of weave-driven mating that had followed that dinner, the resulting pregnancies had come as no surprise.

These, however, did.

"Thank you, Lord Hewen." Dorian managed to speak with some semblance of normalcy. "I appreciate your taking the time to deliver these welcome tidings in person."

"It is my greatest pleasure, Sire." The doctor bowed. "This

is nothing short of a miracle, Sire. A miracle straight from the hands of the gods."

"Straight from the hands of someone, that's certain," Dorian muttered beneath his breath.

The physician frowned. "I beg your pardon, Your Majesty?"

"Nothing, Lord Hewen. Would you please instruct Davris to tell the queen I will see her soon? Thank you." Not waiting for the physician to depart, Dorian slipped back into the adjoining room where Rain Tairen Soul was just informing the gathered lords about the Mage's Army of Darkness and the planned targets of their main attacks.

"The army that reshaped the world?" one of the lords repeated in a disbelieving tone. "But Celieria's greatest historians and military experts have long dismissed those accounts as myth."

"Then Celieria's greatest historians and military experts were wrong," Rain replied bluntly. "Too many ancient Fey scrolls speak of the Hand of Shadow who created the Army of Darkness and nearly destroyed the world. Many of the details have been lost over the millennia, but we know his defeat ushered in the First Age. Apparently, this new High Mage intends to bring those ancient legends back to life."

"The Army of Darkness was said to be hundreds of thousands strong."

"Millions."

Lord Barrial's expression went grim and hard as stone. "Even if we put a sword in the hand of every Celierian from boy to elder, the entire kingdom doesn't hold enough men to face such numbers."

"No one kingdom does, nor ever has," Rain agreed. "Not even the Fading Lands. Which means we need allies— including as many of the magical races as we can convince to join us. That is why the Feyreisa and I will be traveling to Danael and Elvia once we're done here. Hawksheart rebuffed our last request for aid, but we'll do everything in our power to change his mind."

Dorian stepped farther into the room and cleared his throat. "I dispatched ambassadors to the mortal kings weeks ago. They are already in negotiations with twelve potential allies."

"Time is of the essence," Rain said. "According to the information we obtained, the Eld strike Celieria on the first day of Seledos—by land at Kreppes and by sea here in Celieria City."

"Seledos!" Lord Swan exclaimed. "But that's less than a month from now! I doubt half the kingdoms could send their armies in time."

"That is why a dozen fast ships will set sail within the bell carrying Fey Water and Air masters who can help speed the arrival of all allied troops," Dorian said. "And that is why I have summoned you, my lords. You either have estates directly in the path of the anticipated Eld invasion routes, or you have military expertise that is essential to planning the best defense against this invasion."

"This is a matter that requires the attention of as many of the council as are still present in the city," one of the lords said. "Certainly all of the Twenty. Where are Great Lords Sebourne and Ponsonney?"

"Excluding them was my decision," Dorian admitted. "I doubted Sebourne or Ponsonney would have submitted to a test for Mage Marks, which means they would not have been privy to the information the Tairen Soul just shared with you. Nor should you share what you now know with them. We will come up with our plan. We will deploy troops according to that plan. But the intelligence we have and where it came from are secrets that cannot leave this room. Is that understood? Nor shall any details of our plan be discussed with anyone who has not been verified clean of Mage Marks—not even members of your own family. Not for any reason."

He let his gaze move slowly from lord to lord, hoping to impress upon them his sincerity while also looking for signs of dissent. Finding none of the latter, he said, "Very good. My lords, we are at war. We must accept the possibility that some of our own nobles may have been compromised by the Eld, and we must guard sensitive intelligence against all possible leaks. Do not even discuss it with your wives."

He drew a breath. "And speaking of wives, the earlier interruption was Lord Hewen, bringing me news of the queen. I'm afraid I must call a brief recess so that I may attend her. Those of you whose wives have also been ill this week might wish to do the same. We meet back here within the bell to plan the defense of Celieria against impending attack."

"King Dorian?" As the other lords filed out of the main chamber door, the Tairen Soul followed him to his private exit at the back. "Nothing amiss, I hope? The queen—"

"Is fine," Dorian assured him. "In excellent health, as a matter of fact." He spread his hands. "It seems the sickness sweeping through the courts is not a contagion, but rather a harbinger of good tidings. The queen is with child."

The Tairen Soul smiled, and the expression changed him from dangerous warrior to approachable friend in an instant. "*Mioralas,*" he said, and there was no doubting his sincere joy. "Blessings of the Fey upon your wife and child."

"Yes . . . well . . . I believe those blessings have already borne fruit for the queen and me—and for every other head of a noble Celierian House who attended that memorable banquet three months ago."

The Tairen Soul's smile froze on his face.

"Yes," Dorian said. "It seems your truemate spun much more than seven bells of inescapable desire in that weave of hers. Every woman who attended that dinner—from blushing young brides to grandmothers whose wombs long ago lost their fruitfulness—is now with child."

"Pregnant." Primage Gethen Nour, known to the Celierian court as the newly invested Lord Bolor, stared at Jiarine Montevero in disbelief, then began to pace the luxurious confines of her palace suite. "The queen is pregnant?"

"As are all the ladies who have fallen ill this last week, master," Jiarine confirmed.

His cold brown eyes pierced her. "Including you."

Jiarine's skin went pale. Her lashes dropped to shutter her eyes, a gesture of subservience that was more a matter of self-preservation. "*Ta*, including me, though it should not have been possible." A visit to a butcher of a hearth witch after an ill-conceived childhood dalliance had seen to that. And years of bastard-free mating with Master Manza—the handsome Elden Sulimage to whom she'd traded her soul—had confirmed it.

"Well."

She hazarded a glance up, to find Master Nour tapping his lip with his forefinger and watching her with a calculating gleam in his eye.

"Well," he said again, "this does bear some thought." Then he turned on his heel and began pacing again. "I am disappointed that you were not able to get the queen to drink my potion. Now more than ever."

"Forgive my failure, master," Jiarine murmured. A quick stab of vengeful satisfaction flashed before she could squelch it. Master Manza wouldn't have failed. Master Manza had earned Queen Annoura's trust in a way Nour never would. Master Manza had not turned the queen quickly enough, and the High Mage of Eld had sent Nour to replace him. Jiarine wondered how long it would be before Nour found himself replaced as well. Not too much longer, she hoped. Nour was a sick, sadistic *rultshart*, and had he been the Mage who approached her in her youth, she would never have surrendered her soul.

Nour's eyes narrowed. "Your thoughts betray you, *umagi*. I see another lesson in obedience is in order."

Jiarine broke into a clammy sweat as the blood drained from her face.

At the sight of her distress, Nour's lips curled in a cruel smile. "Never fear, my dear. Sadistic *rultshart* I may be, but I promise none of what I have in mind will damage your child."

* * *

"Pregnant?" Ellysetta stared at Rain in stunned disbelief. "All of them?"

"Every last one, *shei'tani*. From young wives to women well past their childbearing years. You spun fertility even where it no longer existed."

"Bright Lord save me."

The corner of his mouth lifted, lavender eyes warm as he brushed a curling strand of hair back from her temple. "I think it's clear he sent *you* to save *us*, *kem'san*. The Fey prayed for fertility and the gods sent us a *shei'dalin* who can spin life into even a barren womb." He stepped back and drew her with him. "Come. The king has gone to see his queen, and he's asked us to visit her and offer healing."

She hung back. "Do you think that's wise? The queen has never been fond of the Fey—or of me—and to intrude upon her now, when she has just discovered what I did to her . . ."

"What you did was a blessing, not harm, whether she sees it that way now or not. And it is because of the child that Dorian is now so determined to have Gaelen test her before we leave. The possibility of a Mage's puppet sitting on the throne of Celieria . . ."

Ellysetta shuddered. When Rain started for the door, she followed without protest, but as they waited for the quintet to precede them out of the suite, she asked, "What will we do, Rain, if the queen is already fully claimed?"

Rain's mouth went grim and his eyes met hers with stony resolve. Ellysetta swallowed and pressed a hand against her chest to still the sudden pounding of her heart.

Dorian was standing at his wife's bedside when the Fey entered the queen's apartments, and the tension between them charged the atmosphere like an electric storm. Pale and wan, Queen Annoura sat against a wall of pillows like a brittle doll, her lips pressed tightly together as if it were all she could do to hold back a torrent of angry words. Beside her, Dorian exuded an unhappy mix of vexation, disappointment, and dogged determination.

Theirs was not the reaction of a happy couple overjoyed to discover they were having a child.

Guilt stabbed Ellysetta hard, and she hung back in the doorway. «*Oh, Rain, this is not how things should be. A baby should be cause for joy, not anger. How can I make this right?*»

«*There is nothing for you to put right, shei'tani. You gave them the greatest gift of all—the gift of new life. How Annoura chooses to receive that gift is her decision, not yours. You are not to blame for her unhappiness.*»

Ellysetta doubted Annoura would agree with him. Animosity emanated from her like an acid fog, searing Ellysetta's empathic senses with such bitter resentment it made her skin ache.

"My Lord Feyreisen, My Lady Feyreisa, please, come in." With a determined smile that looked more like a grimace pasted on his face, Dorian waved for them to approach the queen's bed. "I was just telling the queen how much better she will feel once your healing weave calms her stomach."

Rain approached the bed, leaving Ellysetta little choice but to follow. She fought to keep her fingers flat against Rain's wrist when what she truly wanted was to grab his hand and squeeze tight. "Your Majesties." She forced herself to smile at Annoura with as much warmth as she could muster. "The Feyreisen and I offer you the felicitations of the Fey and congratulate you on your wonderful news. May your coming child be a radiant Light in your life and bring you both much joy."

The queen turned her head away as if Ellysetta had not spoken. Dorian's lips tightened, but his voice was smooth as silk when he said, "Thank you, Lady Ellysetta. My queen and I long since gave up hope of having a second child. This pregnancy is a blessing indeed, as I'm sure the queen will agree when she is feeling more herself."

Ellysetta moistened her lips and took a hesitant step towards the bed. "Queen Annoura, I do regret intruding upon your privacy when you are not feeling your best, but the weave the king asked me to spin should set you back to rights immediately. I promise there will be no adverse effects to the child."

Annoura made a rude noise and slanted a sour look in Ellysetta's direction. "Considering the unnatural way this child was conceived, it's rather pointless to worry what effect magic might have now, don't you think?"

"Annoura." King Dorian's hands knotted.

"What?" the queen spat. "I agreed to let her heal me as you commanded, but that doesn't mean I must pretend to like it." She turned to sneer at Ellysetta and Rain. "You Fey. You act so righteous, so noble. But you're no better than the Eld. You manipulate our minds, our bodies, just as you claim they do. You spin your weaves, and we dance to your commands like puppets on strings."

"*Annoura!*" Dorian roared. "That's enough!"

The queen clamped her lips in a tight line, crossed her arms, and subsided into glaring silence while her husband struggled visibly to control his temper.

"Spin your weave, Lady Ellysetta," he commanded in a clipped voice.

Annoura's vitriol left Ellysetta shaken, especially because of the uncomfortable thread of truth in her accusations. Ellysetta *had* controlled the queen's mind and the queen's body with magic. She hadn't meant to do it, but she'd done it nonetheless.

«Shei'tani.» Rain's soft murmur prodded her to action.

Ellysetta flicked a glance at Gaelen as she summoned her power. Green Earth came to her call in a generous swell, shimmering with the rich golden radiance of *shei'dalin*'s love. She guided the threads into a now-familiar healing pattern and held her hands over Annoura's body. As the fine web of healing spun out from her palms, she added a puff of Air that blew the hair back off Annoura's face and made the filmy edges of her wrap flutter back to bare the skin over her heart. A familiar, sickly sweet chill bloomed behind her, making her back teeth ache and the hairs rise on the back of her neck. Gaelen was spinning his Azrahn.

As quickly as the unpleasant sensation came, it faded. She finished her own weave, erasing Annoura's nausea and fatigue and replenishing her flagging strength. As her weave sank into Annoura's body, a sudden reactive spark of power made her jump in surprise. She sent a flickering tendril of Spirit into Annoura's womb and smiled at the sudden flood of wordless images and sensations that flowed into her. No matter how antagonistic Annoura was, her baby responded to Ellysetta's presence with instinctive welcome, squirming with happiness and soaking up the warmth of her magic with innocent joy . . . returning bright little sparks of its own nascent power.

The child possessed magic, and not some weak, watered-down version of it either. Strong magic . . . already well developed: green Earth, red Fire, lavender Spirit . . . and a distinct cool black thread of shadowy Azrahn. Ellysetta flinched away from the dark magic, only to freeze in guilt when the baby's joy turned to fright and forlorn confusion at her sudden abandonment. The baby was not to blame for what magic it possessed. «*Las, kaidin, las. Peace, little one.*» She soothed the child with flows of warmth and love and spun a small weave of comfort before withdrawing again.

«*The queen is unMarked,*» Gaelen announced on a private weave. The sudden, relieved slump of Dorian's shoulders told Ellysetta that he'd spun the same information to the king.

"*Mioralas*, Your Majesties," Ellysetta said. "Your son is healthy and strong. May he bring you much joy."

"A son." Dorian took Annoura's hand and smiled with genuine happiness. "Another son. Thank you, Lady Ellysetta. For everything."

"*Sha vel'mei*, King Dorian." Ellysetta glanced at the queen, but Annoura pressed her lips into a tight line and turned her head to stare pointedly at the far wall. With determined graciousness, Ellysetta said, "Blessing of the Light upon you, Queen Annoura. I wish you and your family much joy." She touched her fingers to Rain's wrist.

Rain inclined his head. "We will take our leave of you now. I am sure there is much for you to discuss. *Miora felah ti'vos.*"

Leaving the king and his wife to their privacy, the Fey departed. Ellysetta waited until the door of Annoura's suite closed behind them before saying, "Annoura is right, Rain. If we use our magic to get what we want, how are we any different from the Eld?"

Rain looked taken aback. "*Nei*, she isn't right at all," he answered quickly. "She's angry and out of sorts and looking for someone to blame. We Fey live by a strict code of honor precisely because we don't want to end up like the Eld. We don't use our magic to conquer and enslave as they do."

"And yet Fey think nothing of spinning Spirit to send mortals on their way, or hide amongst them undetected, or read their minds and emotions to better control them."

"We aren't using our magic to manipulate Celierians. We're using it to protect them."

She gave a humorless laugh. "Have you ever stopped to ask if they *wanted* that protection? Mortals aren't children, Rain. They may not live thousands of years or wield magic, but they still have a right to decide their own lives."

"And Fey do not lie, yet mortals do at will," he countered. "Does that make them evil because they use a talent we do not possess in order to manipulate and control us? Do not be foolish, Ellysetta. They are neither so innocent nor such victims as you are making them out to be." He regarded her with a mix of exasperation and concern. "I thought you'd gotten past your fear and distrust of magic, Ellysetta. I thought you had accepted it."

"I have, but that doesn't negate my concern about the ways magic can be misused."

"*Aiyah*, it can be misused, but do not forget all the many ways it can be used to help people as well. Such as the healing you just did. And the way you saved that boy Aartys's life in Orest."

Ellysetta's gaze fell to the floor. He was right, of course, but Queen Annoura's accusation had hit a nerve, and what Ellysetta had discovered about the queen's unborn child had only increased her guilt. "The child wields magic, Rain. A very strong gift, if I'm not mistaken."

"Is that what this is about?" Her *shei'tan* didn't look as shocked or as worried as she was. "Ellysetta, King Dorian has magic, and so does the prince. They are descended from the vol Serranis line, after all."

"He possesses Azrahn," she clarified. "The queen couldn't have children, but my weave made her pregnant, and now she's carrying a child gifted in Azrahn."

"I doubt there is cause for alarm. You've seen Gaelen wield Azrahn. It stands to reason descendants of his sister's line might also possess at least some small degree of it."

She frowned. She couldn't believe he was taking this so calmly. "I don't think what I sensed was a low-level talent. It felt very strong to come from such a tiny baby."

"Rain is right to tell you not to be alarmed," Gaelen interjected. "Much as some Fey would like to believe otherwise, Azrahn is not inherently evil. It's just a Mystic, like Spirit. In fact, I believe many of our most magically gifted warriors also possess a strong talent in Azrahn. It's certainly the case among the *dahl'reisen*."

"Which may explain why they're *dahl'reisen*," Tajik muttered, ostensibly to Gil but loud enough for the rest of them to hear.

Gaelen narrowed his eyes at the red-haired Fire master. "And where do you think *dahl'reisen* come from, vel Sibboreh? You think they pop up like mushballs in a fellroot bog? *Nei*, they were born Fey, which means more than a few Fey possess strong talent in Azrahn. Just because the *chatok* refuse to test for it doesn't mean it isn't there."

"*Setah*," Rain rumbled. "Dorian's lords will reconvene soon. Bel and Tajik, I want you to join us. There are no military minds I trust more than yours. With Gaelen's knowledge of the north, and yours of battle tactics, we can at least give these Celierians a fighting chance until the allies arrive. Call the warriors from Ellysetta's secondary quintet to replace you while you are away." He leveled a commanding eye on Ellysetta. "And you, *shei'tani*, stop worrying. Annoura's child is a miracle, not a monster. Training will teach him to control whatever gifts he has. You should go back to the suite and try to rest."

She gave him a wan smile. "I would be afraid to close my eyes without you there. I think I'll visit the other ladies who are ill, and offer healing. It's the least I can do," she added to forestall his objection, "since I am responsible for their condition." And it would give her the opportunity to see how many other children conceived through her weave also possessed Azrahn.

Rain didn't like it, but in the end Ellysetta had her way. He, Tajik, Bel, and Gaelen went to meet with Dorian's war council while Ellysetta and her *lu'tan* paid a call on the sick noblewomen.

Several of the ladies turned them away on the doorstep, but quite a few did not. For those who received her, Ellysetta spun healing weaves to calm their stomachs and did what she could to bolster the strength and health of the more elderly among them.

But rather than putting her mind at ease, the visits only increased her concern. Because every pregnant woman's unborn child was a son gifted with powerful magic—including a distinct and potent spark of Azrahn.

The proof was irrefutable, the evidence too overwhelming

to be mere coincidence. She, Ellysetta Baristani, had done far more than merely cause barren wombs to bear fruit once more.

She had created magical children and given each of them the ability to spin Azrahn.

Just as the High Mage of Eld had done when he had created her.

CHAPTER NINE

"Well, something must have happened during our break," Cannevar Barrial murmured in a quiet aside to Rain. "I've never seen Lord Harrod so distracted." The war council had reconvened. Prince Dorian was reviewing the defenses of Celieria City, and more than once he had to call a dazed older Lord back to attention.

Rain glanced across the room at the elderly Great Lord Harrod, a former admiral of the king's navy and lord of King's Point. He was clearly suffering from the same shock as his fellow lords who had just discovered their impending fatherhood. "I suppose learning your sixty-year-old wife is with child can do that to even the most focused of mortals."

Cann's jaw dropped. "Learning *what?*"

"Ah, that's right. You came in after I did." The shocked announcements and congratulations had already ended before Lord Barrial returned from the war council's break. "Lady Harrod is pregnant." Rain nodded at the assembled lords. "All their wives are—as is any woman who was at that dinner when Ellysetta spun her weave." He gave Lord Barrial a rueful smile. "It seems my *shei'tani's* weave was more potent than we realized."

"*All* of the ladies are—" Lord Barrial's voice broke off and his face turned to stone. "Will you excuse me?" Not waiting for an answer, he strode out of the council chamber.

As the door closed, Rain winced in sudden understanding. Barrial's wife had died years ago, but he hadn't escaped Ellysetta's weave. Nor had Thea Trubol, the unmarried noblewoman who'd been partnered with him for dinner that night. And apparently Lady Thea either didn't yet know or hadn't yet broken the news of her condition to Lord Barrial.

Poor Cann. First his daughter Talisa had recognized Adrial as her truemate scarcely a month after her marriage to Lord Sebourne's heir, and now this. His friendship with the Fey had not served his family kindly of late.

Two familiar warriors were waiting in the palace suite when Ellysetta returned from her visits with the noble ladies of Celieria. Dark haired, dark eyed, and so alike in appearance they could be twins, they turned to face the opening door when she entered, and the sight of them—unexpected and dearer than she'd known until this moment—shoved her troubled thoughts to the back of her mind.

"Rowan! Adrial!" Joy burst from her heart, and she ran across the room to fling herself into first one pair of arms, then another. "Oh, my friends! *Mioralas, kem'mareskia.* I am so very glad to see you both." She pulled back, then laughed, and hugged and kissed them both again.

"If I didn't know better, 'Jonn," Gil quipped dryly, "I'd say she was happy to see them."

"Only a little." Rijonn gave a laugh that sounded more like the rumble of shifting earth.

Ellysetta beamed. "I refuse to pretend any joy less than I feel. These two lived with my family for weeks before Rain and I married. They are beloved friends, and I have missed them greatly." Emotion misted her eyes. Rowan and Adrial had been with her when she still had a family, and seeing them was like having a little piece of Mama, Papa, Lillis, and Lorelle back in her life. Smiling through the tears, she cradled their faces in her hands and kissed them both again until even brash Rowan's ears turned pink.

"No offense, Ellysetta," Rowan muttered, "but please stop that before Rain arrives. I'm only eleven hundred. Far too young to die."

She laughed and relented, settling for dragging them both towards the cushioned settee. "Come. Sit. Tell me everything. How have you been? How is Talisa? How are you both holding up? Oh, and have you met Gil and Rijonn?"

The brothers shared a dazed look as she bombarded them with her questions, but when she mentioned Gil and Rijonn, Rowan and Adrial glanced in their direction, then suddenly jumped to their feet and stood with spines stiff as pikes.

"*Chakai* vel Jendahr, *Chakai* vel Ahrimor." Rowan executed a shallow bow with crisp military precision. "It is an honor to meet you both." Beside him, Adrial bowed with equal precision.

"So you do know each other," Ellysetta said.

"We have never met," Gil said.

"Only by reputation," Rowan said at the same time. "These are the heroes of Mowbren Glarn, one of the fiercest battles of the Mage Wars."

"All were heroes that day," Gil said, and the silver stars in his eyes dimmed until his irises were almost pure black. "We just happened to be among the few to survive it."

"The few who did survive owe their lives to you. Your weaves from that day have been taught at the academy ever since." Rowan frowned. "But I thought you were both *rasa. . . .*"

"We were," Rijonn said.

"Then how—" Rowan broke off. Both he and Adrial turned to look at Ellysetta. "Ah."

"She restored the souls of three hundred *rasa* at the warcastle of *chakai*," Gil said. "We were among them and serve her now as *lu'tan* and masters in her primary quintet."

"*Aiyah*, well . . ." Ellysetta cleared her throat and quickly introduced the other *lu'tan* in the room.

"Where are Rain and Bel?" Rowan asked. "Is vel Serranis still with you?"

"Rain and Bel are with the king, discussing the defense of Celieria. And, *aiyah*, Gaelen is with them." She leaned over to take Adrial's hand. "How are you, really, Adrial?" Even as she asked, she spun a weave of healing and strength to bolster his flagging spirits. The last months had taken a toll on him.

He smiled, but his eyes remained dark, melancholy brown pools. "As well as a Fey can be, under the circumstances. Rowan has been my rock."

"There is no hope of Talisa leaving her husband?"

Adrial's gaze dropped.

"It does not appear so," Rowan answered for his younger brother. "But then, she thinks Adrial left her months ago to return to the Fading Lands. As Rain commanded, we have kept our presence a secret. She does not know Adrial is here. No one does."

"Poor Talisa." Ellysetta clasped her hands. What would she have done if she'd dreamed of Rain all her life as Talisa had dreamed of Adrial . . . if she'd waited for him, year after year, refusing all proposals of marriage until the day of her twenty-fifth birthday . . . wedding to spare her family the shame and taint of a spinster daughter . . . only then to have her love arrive scant weeks after her wedding? Even now, Ellysetta could remember the soaring joy and drowning despair that had consumed Talisa when she'd realized her love had come—and she could not have him.

And then to be led to believe Adrial had simply . . . walked away.

The breathtaking cruelty of it ripped at her heart.

"How can either of you bear it?" She didn't realize she'd spoken aloud until Adrial made a choked sound and his flare of pain scorched her senses. "Adrial! *Sieks'ta!* Forgive me." She laid her hands upon his, spinning what love and peace she could to soothe his tormented soul.

"We don't bear it. We die a little more each day." He buried his face in his hands, shoulders heaving. "She cries herself to sleep each night and there is n-nothing I can d-do." His voice cracked.

"Adrial." She went to sit beside him and gathered him in her arms the way Mama had so often gathered her. Silky black hair fell across her bodice as she pressed his head to the hollow of her throat and held him close while he wept. Tears blurred her vision. She blinked them away and felt the hot fall of teardrops track down her cheeks as she met Rowan's bleak gaze over Adrial's head.

"What do you mean, there's nothing to be done?" Ellysetta whirled away from the curtained windows to face her truemate, who had returned to the suite at her request when the war council broke for a short recess. "There must be something! Rain! We can't just leave them like this. They're suffering!"

Beneath the dictates of a powerful Spirit weave, Adrial lay sleeping in one of the suite's attached bedrooms. An exhausted Rowan napped in a chair by his side. Ellysetta's quintet had gathered in the sitting room, their expressions blank and stony as they watched their king and his mate argue over Adrial's fate.

"Do you think I don't know that? Do you think I didn't realize when we left Talisa in her husband's care that I was condemning Adrial to death? Celieria is at war, and Dorian is barely holding together the opposing factions of his court. If his control snaps, there is no hope these people can defeat the Eld. No hope for any of us. No matter how my heart aches for Adrial and Talisa, I can't allow that to happen." Rain spread his hands. "I'm sorry, Ellysetta, but my answer must be the same as it was before. In this matter, my hands are tied."

"Then what about Lord Barrial? Talisa is his daughter. Why can he not appeal to the king on her behalf? Then the Fey would not be involved and our enemies could not use this against us."

"Ellysetta, Lord Barrial has enough on his plate. The Eld

are coming—and his lands are directly in their path. He knows he's likely to lose his entire estate—his whole family–before this war is through."

"All the more reason for him to save Talisa now, while he still can."

"At what cost? The Sebournes are his closest neighbor, and the largest military force in the area besides his own. If he alienates them, he runs the risk of losing their aid when he needs it most." Rain sighed and ran a hand through his hair, ruffling the long dark strands into tousled disarray. "Bitter though the situation may be, Talisa made her choice when she wed diSebourne."

"But—"

"But nothing. The joy of a *shei'tanitsa* bond is a treasured gift, not a right. Many Fey die without ever hearing their true-mate's call. Many others die without completing their bond. Adrial and Talisa have found each other in this lifetime. Gods willing, they will find each other again in the next . . . and with a happier outcome."

She took a half step forward. Why was it everyone around her had to suffer? Mama and Selianne dead, her family lost in the Mists, Rain banished. Could no one she loved find happiness? "Rain, please . . ."

He turned away. "There is nothing I can do, Ellysetta."

"The Feyreisen is right, Ellsyetta."

She looked up to find Rowan standing in the doorway, his face drawn with fatigue and sorrow, his dark eyes filled with grieved acceptance.

Rain turned to face him and squared his shoulders. "Rowan. *Sieks'ta.* You know this is not what I would choose."

"I know," Adrial's older brother said softly.

"The best I can give him—could ever give him once Dorian upheld Talisa's marriage—is this time to watch over and protect her until . . ."

Rain's voice trailed off, but Ellysetta knew what he'd left unspoken. The madness caused by an unfulfilled matebond would eventually take hold of Adrial's mind, as it did all Fey males who found their truemates but could not complete their bond. When that happened, Adrial would either commit *sheisan'dahlein*, the honor death, or Rowan would have to kill his brother—at the cost of his own soul.

"We are grateful for that much," Rowan said. "Even though he cannot let her know he's here, at least he can watch over her when she sleeps at night and keep her safe from harm. That brings him a measure of peace."

Ellysetta's heart ached. Rowan, the laughing prankster of her first quintet, had been drained of all humor and happiness. He was watching his brother die a slow and painful death, and she knew each terrible day killed a piece of his own soul.

"We must get back to the king," Rain said. "Before we go, Rowan, you should know we think there are Mages at work in the city, possibly even inside the palace. Have you seen or heard anything suspicious since you've been here?"

"No hint of Azrahn, if that's what you mean."

"Do you know who is fostering the increased hostility towards the Fey?"

Rowan shrugged. "Talisa doesn't come to the palace much. She spends most of her days in her father's house in the company of her brothers, and we stay with her. From what little we've seen, most of the public discord comes from the same group as last time. Sebourne and his cronies. The queen. A few of the lesser lords looking to gain power."

"Keep your eyes and ears open, and not just for that." Rain told him quickly about Truthspeaking the Mage and what they'd learned. "Stay alert. If you see or hear anything suspicious, send a private weave to Bel straightaway. Don't use the Warriors' Path. In fact, you shouldn't even use it amongst yourselves."

"Understood." Rowan bowed his head in acknowledgment of the command.

Rain glanced at the closed door to the bedroom where

Adrial lay in his weave-induced sleep. "Tell Adrial I am sorry I did not have a chance to speak with him. As soon as we finish with the king, Ellysetta and I head for Danael and Elvia."

"I will tell him."

Rain held out a hand. "May we meet again in happier times, *kem'chajeto*."

Rowan clasped his forearm. "Gods will it so, Rain."

Bel and Gaelen bade Rowan their own farewells; then they and Rain exited the room. Rowan's spine remained straight, his shoulders squared, as they filed out the door, and when they were gone, he drew a shaky breath and returned to the bedroom where his brother lay. "We should go, too."

Ellysetta followed him. "*Teska*, let him sleep." She stood with Rowan at the bedside, looked down at his sleeping brother. Adrial's lashes lay thick and dark on his pale cheeks, and his hair spilled like a skein of black silk across the pillows. The tension had faded from his face, leaving tender, youthful beauty in place of his hard warrior's mask. His hands lay across the chest that her *lu'tans* had stripped of steel. "He looks so peaceful."

Rowan murmured a wordless agreement. "It's a shame he can't just sleep like this until Talisa is free to complete their bond."

The moment he spoke, it was as if a great Light suddenly burst forth from the darkness. Ellysetta looked up at Rowan, hope sparking in her eyes. "Why couldn't he?"

"Why couldn't he what?"

"Sleep like this until she is free to come to him?" Excitement shot through her. "Rowan, that's it!" She grabbed his arms. "Just like the Fey tale of the sleeping princess."

"What Fey tale? What are you talking about?"

"Have you never heard the Fey tale about the sleeping princess? An evil witch spurned by a handsome king took her revenge on him by cursing his firstborn child to prick her finger on a rose and— Oh, never mind about the Fey tale." She waved her hand dismissively. "Why can't we put Adrial in a weave that keeps him sleeping peacefully until Talisa lives out her life with Lord diSebourne? Then when Lord diSebourne dies, she will be free to go to Adrial."

"But that could be decades from now."

She laughed. "What's a little time to the immortal Fey? Rowan, don't you see? She could go to the Fading Lands as a ninety-year-old crone and the *shei'dalins* could heal her back to youth. Her age would make no difference. Keeping Adrial safe from the bond madness is all that matters."

"You're assuming the bond madness won't afflict him if he's sleeping."

She nodded. "Yes, I am. But it's a chance, at least. All he faces now is certain death."

Rowan frowned down at his sleeping brother. "I don't know. Nothing like this has ever been done."

"There has to be some sort of weave the *shei'dalins* could spin on him. The Fey made the Faering Mists, and that takes people out of time. If they could spin a similar weave on Adrial—or even put him to sleep and take him into the Mists to wait for Talisa. Then Talisa's quintet could continue to watch over her and bring her to the Fading Lands when she's free."

"The Mists do take people out of time," Rowan agreed. "It's possible whatever weaves the Fey spun to create the Mists are still recorded somewhere in the Hall of Scrolls."

"We can ask Tealah to look into it. She's the Keeper of the Hall of Scrolls now."

"Do you really think this could work?"

"*Aiyah*," she said. "I do."

For the first time since he'd stepped into the suite, she felt hope flicker inside him.

Unfortunately, when Adrial awoke a bell later, he didn't share his brother's interest. Instead of embracing the idea—or even considering it—he shook his head.

"I will not leave Talisa."

"But, Adrial," Ellysetta protested, "if you stay, you'll die.

This gives you a chance, at least—hope that you can still find joy together in this lifetime."

Adrial smiled gently. "I know you mean well, Feyreisa. And I appreciate the idea—truly, I do. But my place is at my *shei'tani's* side. I cannot leave her." He rose to his feet and adjusted the straps of the Fey'cha belts crisscrossed over his chest. "We should go now, Rowan. We've been away long enough."

Rowan's eyes fell, but without a word, he followed his younger brother to the door.

"Adrial . . ." Ellysetta followed them. "Please. Stay with her if you must for as long as you can, but before the bond madness has you in its grip, before you take your own life or force Rowan to slay you, please reconsider. The Fey are too few. Every life is precious. We can't afford to lose you—or Talisa, for that matter."

Adrial hesitated, then nodded before he stepped out the door.

The war council continued past the first silver bells of night. Together, and with the aid of Bel's Spirit weaves, they examined scenario after scenario for the coming battle of Kreppes and the naval invasion of Great Bay.

"There's one last possibility we must consider," Rain told the assembly. "Celieria City." He paced over to the wall of maps and pulled out the map of Celieria City and Great Bay. "We must assume the Eld are here in the city, and we must assume they can simply open gateways inside the city and release their armies directly. We cannot leave the city unprotected. When Prince Dorian goes to King's Point, we must leave an experienced commander with enough forces to ensure the safety of the city."

"The queen will be here," said Dorian. "She will oversee the defenses of the city."

Rain's expression turned to stony blankness. A glance at Bel, Gaelen, and Tajik showed similar reactions. Queen Annoura's blatant distrust of the Fey would make her an uneasy ally at best. He didn't trust her to put her people's safety above her own animosity towards the Fey.

Reading their doubts, Dorian bristled. "Ser vel Serranis has already checked the queen for Mage Marks. She bears none. I can think of no reason why I should not entrust the safety of the city to her, as I always have in my absence. Lord Corrias will be at her disposal, as will Lord General Voth. Both of them have ample experience in military matters."

Rain exchanged a brief glance with Bel. What choice did they have? Despite their concerns, she was Dorian's queen and the ruler of Celieria in her own right. Reluctantly, Rain inclined his head. "If that is your will, *doreh shabeila de*. I suggest, however, that we leave a contingent of Fey here in the city to aid her in the event that the Mages do open a portal within the gates."

«*The regiments remaining in the city should be checked weekly for Mage Marks,*» Gaelen remarked on a private weave. «*And we should check all other troops before they depart. No sense in leaving a fangtooth in the woodpile.*»

«*If there were time, I would agree,*» Rain replied, «*but we cannot delay our departure to Elvia.*»

«*I could send for the dahl'reisen.*»

Rain's muscles clenched in instant protest. «*Out of the question.*» No matter how much he might trust Gaelen now— no matter even that Rain was technically *dahl'reisen* himself— putting his faith in warriors who walked the Shadowed Path was an altogether different matter. «*Even if Dorian would approve it, I would not. I could never trust them. You saw the same thing I did in Orest.*»

«*I cannot deny some dahl'reisen have chosen to serve the Eld; but the dahl'reisen who serve the Brotherhood are not so devoid of honor. They remember what it was to be Fey, and they fight each day against the Dark.*»

«*Do you believe in their honor so deeply you would risk your life to prove it?*»

«*Aiyah,*» Gaelen answered without hesitation.

«*And do you trust them so completely you would also risk Elly-setta's life?*»

Thick black lashes shuttered the piercing ice blue of Gaelen's eyes for a brief moment as he cast his gaze downward. «*Perhaps not,*» he admitted.

«*Neither would I,*» Rain agreed. «*So do not speak of it again. The Fey have survived and fought the Eld for millennia without knowing who was Mage-claimed. Tempting as it may be to know which mortals have been turned, I will not fight off the wolves by inviting a lyrant into our midst.*» He straightened from the table and directed his attention to King Dorian. "The day grows late. We have accomplished much today, but now Ellysetta and I must depart."

"Will you not stay the night, at least?" the king asked.

"There is no time. We must travel swiftly if we are to have any chance of reaching Danael and Elvia in time. I must take my leave of you. My lords." He nodded to the assembled war council. "Cann." To the brown-eyed border lord, he offered a warmer smile of friendship and a handclasp. "Be well, my friend. And good luck . . . with everything." He let his eyes say the words his lips did not.

"Same to you, Rain."

"We'll join you as quickly as we can. Until then, keep your blade sharp and at the ready."

Cann gave his trademark wolfish smile. "Always."

King Dorian walked Rain to the council room doors. Bel, Gaelen, and Tajik followed close behind. "Assembling the armies and preparing the supply wagons will take a few days, but we should begin the march to Kreppes by the end of the week."

"*Kabei.* I will leave one hundred warriors behind to aid your fleet and protect the Points and Celieria City. The Fey already stationed on Lord Barrial's lands will do what they can to speed the preparations in Kreppes. Ellysetta and I will meet you there as soon as our business with the Danae and Elves is completed. I pray we will not come alone."

They had reached the entrance to the council room. As Dorian released the privacy seal on the chamber and started to open the doors, the sound of a voice raised in anger made him pause.

"What do you mean, I can't go in there?" a deep, familiar voice demanded in outrage. "I am a Great Lord of Celieria and one of the Twenty! You dare deny me entry?"

"I'm sorry, Great Lord Sebourne. King's orders," a thinner, less bellicose voice replied, but a thread of steel underlay the polite response. "The king has convened a special council, my lord. The chamber is closed to all others."

Great Lord Dervas Sebourne, the border lord whose son Colum was wed to Cann Barrial's daughter Talisa, gave a rude snort. "Council? What council? There are no special councils convened without the knowledge of the Twenty!"

"I am sorry, my lord. I am not at liberty to say."

"Why, you little—"

"Sebourne!" King Dorian shoved open the council room doors and strode out into the chamber where guests scheduled to testify before the council gathered before their appearances.

The Clerk of the Council was normally seated at a gleaming hardwood desk near the front of the chamber, working quietly and guarding the entrance to the council room. At the moment, however, he was pressed against a wall, standing on his toes, his neck cloth clutched in Great Lord Sebourne's very large fist.

"Release him at once! What is the meaning of this?"

Sebourne shoved the clerk to one side, sending the thin young man staggering into a nearby bank of files. His gaze shot to the king. "'What is the meaning of this' is precisely the question I have for you, Sire. Is it true you have called a council without notifying the Twenty?"

"You forget yourself, sir," Dorian exclaimed. "The king of Celieria is not the servant of the Twenty, nor must he beg permission to see to the duties of the monarchy."

"What duties could include a select handful of lords and yet be of no concern to the Twenty?" Sebourne shot back. His scathing gaze raked past Dorian and shot towards the open doors, only to freeze at the sight of the Fey. "Ah, I see." His brows rose with mockery and a sneer pulled back the corner of his mouth. "I should have known. For whom would you subvert the lawful ruling order of this country except the Fey?"

"Sebourne!" Dorian exclaimed. "You will beg my pardon this instant and apologize to the Feyreisen for your rash remarks."

Sebourne drew himself up to his full height. The rich velvet of his fur-lined robes swirled about him. "The Hells I will. Those immortal *rultsharts* can go flame themselves before they hear a word of apology from me. What are you up to now, Tairen Soul? Come to enslave more weak Celierian minds?"

«You sure you don't want me to kill diSebourne after all?» Gaelen muttered on a private weave as Great Lord Sebourne continued his bombastic tirade. *«I could do the father, too, while I'm at it. I'll wager plenty would thank me besides the vel Arquinas brothers.»* The lethal tonelessness of his Spirit voice made it clear he was not joking.

For one fraction of a moment, Rain savored the suggestion. To be honest, the idea of cutting off the air to Sebourne's lungs and watching his face turn purple *did* harbor a certain savage appeal. The arrogant *rultshart* was the kind of man who made Rain grateful mortals were short-lived. Then honor reared its head, and with a sigh, he declined. *«Not without cause, Gaelen. Besides, it looks like Dorian has reached the end of his patience this time.»* He flicked a glance at the Celierian king, whose fists were clenched as tightly as his square jaw.

Dorian's chest expanded on a deep breath. His spine straightened, and his shoulders seemed to broaden nearly half again their width.

"Apparently, Lord Sebourne, you have misinterpreted my tolerance these last months, mistaking my compassion for the emotional distress your family suffered this summer as a sign of weakness. Because clearly you have forgotten who is the Great Lord and who is the king." Dorian leaned forward, faint green sparks of Earth magic flashing in his eyes. "How dare you insult your king, question his motives, and bark at him like an unruly dog because he did not beg your permission to call a meeting of his lords?"

Surprise and the first hint of wariness flickered across Sebourne's face, but prideful temper soon eclipsed it. "An unruly dog, am I? Because I dare to speak my mind? Because I dare object to my king being led about by the Fey like a trained monkey on a leash?"

"Enough!" Dorian smacked a palm on the desk. Green sparks shot out from the point where palm hit wood, and the desk shuddered. The inkwell and lamp rattled across several fingerspans of desktop, and a stack of papers toppled off the edge onto the floor. "Guards!"

Boot heels clattered against marble floor as the King's Guards standing outside the gathering chamber rushed to their sovereign's call.

"Escort Great Lord Sebourne to Old Castle and secure him in the west tower." To Sebourne, Dorian said stiffly, "Perhaps a few days of solitude will cure whatever maggot has possessed your brain before you bring your entire House to ruin."

Sebourne's eyes narrowed, glittering like shards of glass. "You will regret this," he hissed between clenched teeth. When one of the guards stepped closer and reached out as if to take his arm, the border lord froze him with a glare. "Lay that hand on me and you will lose it." With brittle pride, he adjusted his clothing and smoothed back his hair. After one final glare for Rain and the Fey, he marched away in the center of a half dozen King's Guards.

When the Great Lord disappeared from view, the king's

shoulders slumped and he pinched the bridge of his nose in a weary gesture. "He is right. I will regret that. He has been waiting for any excuse to divide the lords and set his followers against me."

"He gave you little choice," Rain said. "Your ancestor Dorian the Second would have tried and executed him for sedition."

"Perhaps, but I blame myself for his insolence." Dorian grimaced. "I've let Sebourne and his cronies grow too bold. I should have reined them in months ago."

"Perhaps boldness alone is not the only reason for his behavior, *kem' jita'taikonos*," Gaelen suggested. "You should let me check him for Mage Marks before we leave."

"To what end?" Dorian crossed his arms. "If he is unMarked, it doesn't make him any less of a challenge to my rule. If he is Marked, who among his followers would believe it? They'd just say it was Fey illusion spun on their weak-minded fool of a king, my kingdom would split in two, and the Mages would simply find some other lord to use against me." He expelled a weary breath. "No, I'm better off to continue as we did today— trust the war council you cleared this morning, and consider all others potential agents of Eld."

"And Sebourne?" Rain asked.

"Once he has time to cool off and come to his senses, I'm sure he will beg my forgiveness. I'll keep him under watch. He will not catch me off guard." Forcing a smile, Dorian held out a hand. "*Beylah vo* for everything, Rainier Feyreisen. I am indebted to you."

Rain clasped Dorian's arm, feeling for the first time a genuine affinity for the mortal king. Perhaps he had judged the man too harshly in the past. They were both kings leading countries divided in a time of war, struggling to do what was right for their people. Neither had an easy road before him.

"If it is within my power to convince Hawksheart and the Danae to aid us," he vowed, "you have my oath I will. Farewell,

Dorian vol Serranis Torreval. Until we meet again, may the gods Light your Path and keep you safe from harm."

As night fell over the city, the Fey who had arrived without announcement left in secret. Impenetrable invisibility weaves surrounded all but the one hundred *lu'tan* left behind to aid in the defense of Celieria.

In the queen's apartment, Annoura stood at the open glass doors that led to her private balcony. A strong downdraft from the palace roof gusted through the door, setting rich draperies swirling and carrying with it the rich, earthy aroma of tairen. Her fingers tightened on the door frame, and her free hand splayed across her belly.

So, the Tairen Soul and his witch queen had left. She should have felt a measure of relief, but all she felt was agitation and a disturbing sour note of fear. She and Dorian had been happy until Rain Tairen Soul and that girl had entered their lives. And now here she was, her husband's kingdom at war, pregnant with a child conceived through Fey magic—gods only knew what sort of monster it might turn out to be—and a husband who seemed determined to distance himself from her even when she needed him most.

A husband who'd suspected she might be in the service of the Mages.

After the Fey departed, Dorian had come to tell her about their suspicions of Mage-claiming in the palace. He'd shared what they'd learned from the Elden Mage, and informed her she would govern Celieria City in his absence. He'd also said she should trust only himself, Dori, and the lords of his war council, because only they had been checked and verified clear of Mage Marks.

The chime he'd said that, of course, she'd suspected the truth.

"My gods," she'd breathed. "You had them check me, didn't you?"

The guilt on his face gave her all the answer she required,

and they'd had a row to end all rows. She'd screamed like a fishwife. He'd roared back like a surly bear. They'd said bitter things, angry things, ugly, hateful things. And he'd stormed out, slamming the door behind him.

He'd not come to visit her since. Not to apologize. Not to set things right between them. Not even just to sit beside her in silence and wait for her to unbend, as he often did after one of their arguments.

Three times, she'd started to send him a note, and three times pride kept her from it. He would come on his own, or not at all.

And so far, he'd chosen not at all.

Her hands tightened on the frame of the glass-paneled doors. All because of the Fey.

Silk rustled behind her. "You should close the door before you catch a chill, Your Majesty."

Annoura turned to Jiarine Montevero. Dear Jiarine. Dorian had not come, but Jiarine had hardly left her side. "You are a good friend, Jiarine. The kind even a queen can confide in."

Eld ~ Boura Fell

Vadim Maur peered into the shimmering dark red liquid that filled the wide, shallow bowl of a Drogan Blood Lord's chalice. The discarded, bloodless body of an infant lay at the bottom of a small refuse cart nearby, its tiny throat slit from ear to ear, its skin a pallid gray-white. The rings of power on Vadim's hands glittered with red lights as he passed his palms over the chalice and murmured, *"Daggorra droga."* Around the mosaic-tiled confines of his private spell room, the sconces flared, and shadows danced like living silhouettes against the walls.

Within the rune-inscribed cup, the infant's still-warm blood swirled with opalescent hues. Dark red became a shimmering silver. Shimmering silver changed to a shadowy translucence in which the wavering visage of Primage Gethen Nour slowly took shape.

Or, rather, the visage Primage Nour now wore. A mortal's face—weak and without magic.

Oh, by Celierian standards, he looked fine and powerful enough. As the newly invested Lord Bolor, he was the picture of a well-dressed, sharp-eyed nobleman: handsome, fit, and clearly secure in his wealth and power. His brown hair had been powdered a deep, lustrous copper and pulled back in a queue at the nape of his neck, and his pale Mage skin had turned bronze, as if tanned by the sunlight he had rarely seen in all his centuries of life. Though his eyes were the same hard green, they bore no hint of the dark Azrahn that would have alerted the Fey in Celieria City to his presence.

Vadim leaned over the chalice, careful to keep his disfigured face concealed in the shadowy folds of his hooded cloak. "Report," he commanded his former apprentice.

Gethen's image shimmered in the cup of blood. The Primage's lips moved and his voice emerged, liquid and distorted, but still intelligible. "Our plans are progressing as scheduled, Great One. All the pamphleteers belong to us now, as do two of the more respectable news journals. One hundred lords and four of the Twenty belong to us, with another fifty lords and two Great Lords who have allied themselves with the ones we control. My *umagi* in the king's army have assembled their teams and are ready to serve when you give the command."

Vadim nodded. "Excellent. And what progress have you made with the queen?"

A telling silence lasted for several moments before Nour said, "I have made every attempt to ingratiate myself, but she has been difficult to approach. I think her volatile temperament may have something to do with this morning's revelation." Nour's visage shimmered in the Drogan chalice. "Celieria's queen—and every other Lady of a noble House—is with child. Even those who by age or physical infirmity should have been incapable of conception. It seems there was a dinner this summer—"

As the Primage spoke, Vadim recalled Kolis's report of a

palace dinner where Ellysetta Baristani had spun a carnal weave so strong that every man and woman in the banquet hall had fallen upon one another in ravening lust. Apparently, that weave had contained much more than mere Spirit.

"The queen carries in her womb an infant heir to the throne of Celieria, an *umagi* is her closest companion, yet still you have not claimed her?" Irritability made Maur's voice crack like a whip. "Kolis would have had her bound and kneeling in service by now."

Nour's lip curled. "Kolis was the queen's lapdog."

"Then you'd best learn to wag your tail," the High Mage snapped. "I didn't send you to Celieria to bring me excuses. I sent you to bring me results."

The Primage lifted his chin. "And results are what you shall have, Most High," he said, "but as it happens, my delay in Marking the queen may actually have worked in our favor."

"Oh?" Vadim crossed his arms and arched a skeptical brow. "And why is that?"

"Because Manza was right. The Fey have found a way to detect Mage Marks. And the king has allowed them to begin checking his nobles—including the queen."

"The Fey? They are there in the city?"

"The Tairen Soul and his mate arrived this morning," Nour explained. "They were granted a private audience with the king, and shortly after, the king called a select group of lords into council. I regret to say none of my *umagi* were among them, and all have remained tight-lipped. I cannot tell you the specifics of what was discussed, but the king's army is preparing for deployment within the week."

Vadim didn't need specifics. He could well imagine what had been said at that meeting. His enemies knew their messages were being intercepted—both the mortal couriers and the messages sent on the Fey Warriors' Path. No doubt Rain Tairen Soul and his mate had traveled to Celieria City to pass on the information they had extracted from Vadim's old friend Zon.

No matter. When Vadim's Army of Darkness swept across

the land, even the most legendary of Fey warriors would find victory a fleeting dream.

"The Fey checked each member of Dorian's war council for Mage Marks," Nour continued, "and they checked the queen, too . . . without her knowledge. Needless to say, she was not pleased. So, you see, Great One, it's fortunate that I haven't been able to Mark her yet. Our secret is still safe, and we can use the queen's anger to our advantage."

Vadim waved an impatient hand. Celieria's queen could wait. She wasn't half so important to Vadim as Ellysetta Baristani. "How many Fey are guarding the Tairen Soul's mate now?" Pain spiked in his belly. His next incarnation was upon him, and the mere thought of claiming Ellysetta Baristani and her extraordinary gifts made his soul rage for release from the fragile bonds of its current, rotting form. "Is the Tairen Soul with her? How many *chemar* have you managed to place near her?" He calculated rapidly. It would take three hours to get an attack force through the Well of Souls, but if he sent one of the *dahl'reisen* with them to spin that very useful invisibility weave, they might yet achieve what Zon and his men had failed to accomplish in Orest.

Nour's silence made Vadim's eyes narrow. "Nour?"

For the first time in the conversation, Nour looked nervous. "The Tairen Soul and his mate are already gone, Most High. They left the city shortly after dusk."

"Gone." His fingers clenched tight around the stone altar top. "They were there, in the city, and you just let them go? Did you even attempt to capture the girl?"

"There wasn't time, Most High. They were not here for more than a few bells, and they brought several hundred Fey with them. Before I could make arrangements to separate her from her guard, it was too late. They must have used the same invisibility weave as the *dahl'reisen* to leave the city without being detected."

The temperature of his spell room plummeted as Vadim's ire rose. "You haven't Marked the queen and now you tell me you let Ellysetta Baristani come and go without a single attempt to bring her to me?" Vadim's teeth came together with a snap. Ellysetta Baristani should already be his, fully Marked and under his control, not running about the countryside eluding him and his Primages. "You do remember whom you replaced in Celieria and why you replaced him, do you not?"

Nour's throat bobbed as he swallowed. "Yes, Master Maur."

Sulimage Kolis Manza, who had been the High Mage's agent in Celieria before Nour, had done a much better job infiltrating the queen's inner circle and gaining her confidence. He'd done so well, in fact, that he'd turned her against her king and half her lords and used her as one of Vadim's most powerful political pawns in Celieria's royal court. Were it not for the fiasco he'd made of the attempt to capture Ellysetta Baristani, the young Sulimage would still be there.

"I will see to Ellysetta Baristani myself," Vadim bit out. "As for you, I expect significant results with the queen before your next report. Since you can no longer Mark her without running the risk of discovery, you will have to find another way. I will have the hand of Eld guiding the Celierian throne before the month is out, or you will beg me to show you one tenth the mercy you offer your own *umagi*." Even among the Eld, Nour's brutality was legend. To Vadim's grim satisfaction, the Primage went pale as milk beneath his Celierian tan. "We will speak again at this same time seven days hence. I will expect better news."

"Of course, master. It shall be—" Nour's muffled voice died abruptly as Vadim lifted the Drogan chalice and tossed its thickening contents down the spell room's drain hole.

Bah. Sending Nour to Celieria had been a foolish decision. Vadim had hoped a more seasoned Primage would be better equipped to manipulate the mortals and their minds, but despite his substantive magical gifts, Nour lacked finesse. He was a sledgehammer in a situation that clearly required a chisel. Which just went to prove that power alone wasn't the measure of a great Mage.

Well, Nour was one mistake Vadim would soon remedy.

For now, however, he had a Tairen Soul to trap.

After cleansing his spell room of the Drogan blood magic, he sent his consciousness to every *umagi* within four hundred miles of Celieria City. Whichever way the Fey had headed, if they dropped their invisibility weaves, he would know it. Finally, carefully, he sent a subtle seeking thread out into the darkness of night and settled in to wait with all the tireless patience of a spider in its web.

When Ellysetta Baristani lowered her defenses, he would be there.

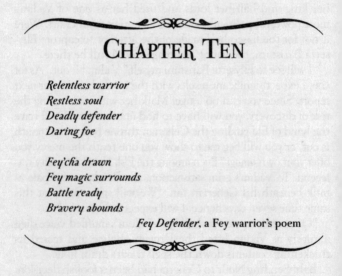

CHAPTER TEN

Relentless warrior
Restless soul
Deadly defender
Daring foe

Fey'cha drawn
Fey magic surrounds
Battle ready
Bravery abounds

Fey Defender, a Fey warrior's poem

Southeast Celieria

The Fey ran hard through the first silver bells of the night, stopping only once to rest, and then but briefly. Rain flew overhead, Ellysetta seated on his back. The stars scattered the sky like plentiful diamonds, shimmering silver-bright against their backdrop of cool, black velvet.

The twin moons of Eloran reached their apex in the sky, the Daughter still nearly full, the larger Mother a waning quarter. Fatigue weighted Ellysetta's eyelids. Her lashes drooped, and she slumped in the saddle. The binding straps held her securely in place as she swayed in a boneless rocking motion to the rhythm of Rain's flight, and her thoughts began to drift like weightless feathers floating upon the cool night wind.

As she drifted, the light of the stars dimmed, and the sparkling night sky became a lightless well, cold and dank and black as pitch. *In the silence came the susurration of fabric dragging across stone, the soft pad of slippered feet. Her right palm twitched from the sensation of cool, damp stone abrading the sensitive pads of her fingertips.*

She was in a dark cavern wandering through corridors carved out of the surrounding stone. Gradually, the darkness began to ease. Light flickered in the distance. The rough corridor opened to a smoother hallway whose walls were tiled in a mosaic pattern that made her bones tingle with recognition. Whatever the pattern was, it was magic, and some part of her knew it. The flickering light came from the sconces installed along the length of the corridor. This was no simple cavern. This was a place of great power and magic. The same part of her that recognized the patterns of the tiles also recognized this place.

She turned down an adjacent hallway and walked to its end, where another two doorways offered the only possible exits. The first, directly in front of her, was a large wooden door with a golden knob. The second, to her right, was a seldor-clad door that shimmered with powerful magic wards. Both doorways drew her, but the pull from the doorway on the right was overwhelming.

She turned and laid her hand upon the tingling veil of magic. Words in a language she did not know spilled from her lips, and power flowed down her arms to her fingertips. The weave of magic protecting the doorway began to unravel. She reached out to turn the knob. The door swung open.

Inside, another well-lit corridor opened to a wide room. Several tables dominated the center of the room, each fitted with leather restraining straps. The tables were currently occupied by women in advanced stages of pregnancy. Their faces were flushed with exertion. Sweat beaded upon their brows, and it was obvious they were giving birth.

As she drew closer, she gasped in shock, recognizing several of the faces.

These were the Celierian noblewomen she had just visited this morning. The women pregnant because of her carnal weave.

Attendants scuttled around the room, moving with swift efficiency as they tended the laboring women. As Ellysetta watched, one of the women strapped to the tables gave a straining grunt that turned into a shrill wail. The attendant waiting between her spread knees lifted a squalling newborn in triumph. Two more attendants hurried over to swiftly cut the cord and carry the baby away to a nearby table, where they washed the child and swaddled it tight in white linen wraps. The woman lying on the table mumbled, "My baby . . ." but one of the attendants was already carrying the infant away to a connecting room. The mother began to weep and struggle weakly against her bonds.

The empathic part of Ellysetta's soul seemed strangely distant, unmoved by the woman's obvious distress. Instead, drawn by the same driving compulsion that had brought her to this room, she followed the attendant carrying the child. A short corridor led from the birthing room to a nursery. Inside, dozens of cradles lined the walls of the room, and in each lay a swaddled infant.

Now a sense of triumph filled the distant hollowness that seemed to have overtaken her senses. She looked about the room and her chest expanded on a swell of pride. She lifted her hands and summoned her power, and the infants burbled unintelligibly in response, waving their tiny fists in the air as if happy to see her. She walked from one cradle to the next, peering in at the tiny occupants. Each infant's eyes shone up at her like gleaming black coins, and on each tiny, pale chest, a dark smudge lay like a spot of ink over the baby's heart.

Without Rain, there would never be a child born of her body. But that did not mean she would be childless. These infants were her offspring, souls summoned from the Well into bodies created by and infused with her magic. They might be flesh of another's flesh, but she was the one who'd breathed life and magic into their bodies.

They were hers, and they were just the beginning.

Ellysetta returned to consciousness with a sudden gasp. Her eyes flashed open, and she straightened in the saddle abruptly. Her hands clutched at the leather pommel as she dragged breath into her lungs and tried to still her pounding heart.

«*Shei'tani.*» Rain's tairen head turned, and one glowing purple eye fixed on her in concern. They were still in the air, and the sky was still dark.

Feeling hazy and disoriented, she peered down at the night-shadowed land below them. «*Where are we?*»

«*About two hundred miles southeast of Celieria City.*»

They'd traveled at least one hundred miles since last she remembered. «*I think we need to stop,*» she said. «*I fell asleep, and I was dreaming again.*» She couldn't keep the tremor out of her Spirit voice. The gloating triumph in her dream had felt all too real, and she knew that if the Mage succeeded in incarnating into her body and claiming her magic for his own, he would use that magic to build an army of Azrahn-gifted children who would be bound to him, serving only him. He and they would rule the world of Eloran like gods.

Without another word, Rain tucked in his wings and dove for the earth, spreading them wide again just in time to break his fall. He landed with smooth grace in a grassy field, back claws digging into the earth for balance as he settled. He set Ellysetta on her feet in the center of her quintet and Changed.

"*Bel, bas paravei taris,*" he told his second in command. We stop here. Ellysetta needs to sleep.

Bel gave a swift nod and gestured to the gathering *lu'tan.* Protective twenty-five-fold shields sprang up in an instant, and the quintet added a smaller six-fold weave around Rain and Ellysetta for added protection.

Rain spun a bower for them from tender grass and divested himself of armor and steel before gathering her in his arms. He didn't ask about her dream. He didn't pry. He simply held her close, resting his head against hers and stroking one hand along her spine. "*Ke sha taris, shei'tani,*" he said. "I am here if you need to talk."

She closed her eyes. She hadn't told him about her visits to the pregnant noblewomen and the magic their children possessed. He was so preoccupied with worries about the war and fear that he wouldn't be able to gather allies powerful or numerous enough to turn back the Eld, she hadn't wanted to add another burden. But now, she could keep silent no longer.

"Annoura's baby isn't the only one with magic," she confessed. "They all have it—and they all wield Azrahn. I'm to blame, Rain. I gave them magic—or the Mage did through me. There's no other possible explanation." Quickly, before she lost her courage, she told him about her dream.

He heard her out, but his only reaction was one of concern, not fear or horror. "I will have Bel contact the *lu'tan* and bid them guard those women. The Mage can't do anything to their children if he can't get his hands on them." He pulled back to look into her eyes. "And you need to stop blaming yourself for everything. You didn't mean to spin that weave. You certainly didn't mean for those women to become pregnant or for their children to be magical."

"But I did . . . and they are."

"You gave them a gift, Ellysetta. A great and wondrous gift. What comes of that has yet to be seen, but I will not be so quick to assume the worst. No matter what the Mage may have done to you before you were born, I will not believe you are anything less than the gods intended you to be."

"But—"

"Shh. You are my *shei'tani* and my truest love, and all that you are is bright and shining. I know this, even if you do not.

And that means whatever gift you gave these children came from the Light, not the Dark." He spun a small Earth weave to free her hair from its plait and ran his fingers through the spiraling curls before nudging her back into his arms with a gentle push of Air. "*Liath dai taris.* Sleep now. And do not fear to dream. I am with you."

She closed her eyes and settled against him. In his arms, protected by the six-fold weave of her quintet, the twenty-five-fold weaves of her *lu'tan*, and the unwavering warmth of Rain's love, she slept.

She woke to the oppressive weight of evil. The night was eerily still. Moonlight shone down upon the encampment, illuminating the forms of Rain and the other warriors lying motionless on the ground around her, and everywhere the bright scarlet of blood lay upon them.

Panic seized her by the throat.

They were dead and she was sitting in a field of corpses.

But then she saw movement out of the corner of her eye and turned to find one of her *lu'tan*, his Fey skin shining faintly silver in the night, walking along the perimeter of the encampment. He paused to speak with another warrior seated on a tree stump and whatever they were saying made them laugh softly.

Ellysetta blinked and the wash of red disappeared. She looked at Rain more closely and noted the faint glow of his skin and the rise and fall of his chest. The air left her lungs on a relieved breath. Not dead, thanks the gods. Only sleeping.

Gods save her. She scrubbed her hands over her face. She'd had so little sleep this last week, her mind was playing tricks on her. She could have sworn that when she first looked at them, she'd seen them all dead. She'd been sure of it.

Even now, she could still smell the bitter stench of death in the air, taste it with each breath she dragged into her lungs. Evil crouched in the darkness, reeking of malevolence. The sensation was so real, so vivid, every muscle in her body drew tight. Her skin throbbed with revulsion and stabbing pain.

Ellysetta drew her hands slowly from her face and strained her eyes to pierce the darkness beyond the borders of the camp. Neither physical eyes nor Fey vision could detect anything amiss, but she knew something was wrong. Something was very wrong, and it wasn't her imagination.

"Rain." She reached for his shoulder, keeping her movements small. «*Shei'tan, wake up. I think we're in trouble.*»

His breathing stilled. He went motionless as stone; then his eyes opened.

«*There's something out there.*» She touched her fingers to the skin of his neck so he could feel the sick horror coiling inside her.

«*Demon.*» His eyes glowed and their focus went slightly hazy. Around them, she sensed as much as saw the change in her quintet as each warrior woke, and their hands crept towards their steel.

A split second later, the two guards laughing softly by the perimeter of the camp fell abruptly silent. She turned to see them fall to the ground, bodies limp, throats gaping. There was no sign of whatever had killed them.

«*Stay close to your quintet.*» That was all Rain said to her before his shout ripped the stillness of the night. "Fey! *Bote cha!*" Blades at the ready! "*Lu'tan, ti'Feyreisa!*"

Warriors leapt to their feet, magic blazing. Fey'cha flew into the darkness. Her quintet closed ranks around her as Rain shot skyward on a jet of Air, summoning the great magic of the Change.

Whatever was out there still did not show itself, but from all around them came a strange whirring thrum, like a thousand cats purring.

"Shields!" Gaelen cried.

"Air masters, deflect missiles!" Bel shouted alongside him.

Bowstrings, Ellysetta realized. The purring sound was bowstrings, hundreds of them, released in near-perfect unison from a close distance. Her quintet ringed close, spinning a canopy of steel and magic over her head. The rest of the *lu'tan* hefted steel war shields high while Air masters spun a whirlwind to disperse the incoming arrows. The *sel'dor* missiles were too numerous. A dozen *lu'tan* fell to the enemy's fire, and scores more flinched as barbed *sel'dor* shafts sank deep in their flesh. Overhead, Rain's vertical ascent ended abruptly as black shafts, far thicker than standard arrows, slammed into his golden war steel, piercing his chest, hip, and thigh.

"Rain!" she cried as he dropped from the sky. Instinctively, she lurched towards him.

«Stay with your quintet!» he commanded. His Spirit voice throbbed with pain.

He landed hard, but leapt to his feet in an instant. With both hands, he griped the thick *sel'dor* shaft protruding from his chest and yanked it free. Ellysetta cried out as pain seared her senses, but Rain just set his jaw and pulled the second missile free from his hip, then the third from his thigh. He dropped them on the ground at his feet and spun a small weave of Earth and Fire to stop his wounds from bleeding.

Ellysetta wept. The need to go to him was overpowering, but he was already wading into battle, blades drawn, teeth bared in a snarl. Red Fey'cha flew from his hands into the darkness.

Something else rained down along with the arrows, and the cold, sickly sweet stench of Azrahn filled the air. Black shadows rose up from within the circle of gathered Fey, as if night itself were attacking. All around, *lu'tan* went gray, their glowing essence siphoned away in an instant. Lifeless, their bodies dropped to the ground without a sound.

"Demons!" Warriors near the fallen men shouted the warning. "Five-fold weaves, Fey!" Powerful weaves flared to life, but between the demons, their invisible attackers, and the hail of *sel'dor* arrows raining down, Fey were dropping at alarming rates.

"Where are they?" someone cried. "Flames scorch it, I can't see anything!"

"They're using the Brotherhood's invisibility weaves, like they did in Orest," Gaelen shouted over the din. "If we can find the ones spinning the weaves, we can bring them down."

"Fat lot of use that is," Tajik snarled. "If we can't find the *rultsharts* shooting those jaffing arrows, how the scorching Hells are we going to find the *bogrots* spinning those weaves?"

"Well, we'd better do something, and fast," Bel snapped in reply. "Because they're slaughtering us like sheep in a pen."

On the west flank, a red Fey'cha struck the holder of one of the invisibility weaves in the throat. A body sprawled in the grass, Fey in appearance, except for the scar that ran from temple to the corner of his mouth.

"*Dahl'reisen!*" the *lu'tan* closest to the body cried. The dead *dahl'reisen's* invisibility weave winked out, revealing a company of Elden archers and three blue-robed Primages. "*Dahl'reisen* are holding the invisibility weaves!"

The warrior who'd slain the *dahl'reisen* fell to his knees, shrieking as if his skin were being peeled off his body. Fey could not kill other Fey—not even *dahl'reisen*—without losing their own soul in the process, but the *lu'tan* had bound their souls in service to Ellysetta. They could not become *dahl'reisen*. Apparently, however, they still felt the agony of taking a life that had once been Fey.

"Blessed gods," Ellysetta wept as an echo of his agony ripped across his *lute'asheiva* bond. Even protected by twenty-five-fold weaves, she could practically feel her soul being ripped asunder. She fell to her knees and pressed her hands to her temples.

"Ellysetta!" Bel cried.

«*Shei'tani!*»

She clenched her jaw and fought to keep from screaming. «*It's not me. It's Lathiel. He's in such pain. Oh, gods, it hurts. It hurts.*»

"Fey!" Rain shouted. "*Sel cha!* Unless you see your target, throw black, not red! They have *dahl'reisen* with them!"

Behind the slain *dahl'reisen*, the now-visible Elden archers fired a barrage of arrows towards the Fey, while two Primages loosed large, blue-white globes of Mage Fire as cover. The third Primage spun Azrahn to open a portal to the Well of Souls. Fey'cha rained down upon the Eld, but the Mages and most of the archers leapt to safety into the Well before the Fey daggers hit their marks.

At the sight of the Mages, hot anger sparked to life deep inside her, and a familiar voice hissed, *Vengeance. Vengeance. Make them pay for what they've done.* She clapped frantic hands over her ears and cried, "Stop it!"

Another demon spawned barely two man lengths from her, and two *lu'tan* died before her quintet vanquished the dark thing with blazing tenfold weaves.

"Flames scorch it," Tajik swore. "If we don't get rid of those archers and the Mages calling those demons, we'll all be dead inside of half a bell."

"If we can get rid of the *dahl'reisen* holding the invisibility weaves, the Eld won't find it so easy to evade our blades." Bel glanced at Ellysetta, then away. His eyes took on the faint lavender glow of Spirit.

A few moments later, Rain's voice sounded urgently on a private Spirit weave. «*Ellysetta. Forgive me, shei'tani, but we need your help to locate the dahl'reisen. None of us can sense them, but you can if we lower your shields. And if you can find them, you can guide our aim so we can take them out and bring down their invisibility weaves.*»

She looked at the fallen *lu'tan* and the desperate battle raging around her. Once more, the familiar terrible rage rose up from within her and clawed for release. *Kill them all. Shred their flesh from their bones.*

Having just felt Lathiel's torment after he'd slain that *dahl'reisen*, she knew what Rain was asking her to do. Simply opening herself up enough to sense the *dahl'reisen* would cause her incredible pain. But that would pale in comparison to the agony the *lu'tan*—and she, through their *lute'asheiva* bond— would feel when they killed the *dahl'reisen* holding the weaves.

But she also knew that if they didn't do something soon, they were all dead. Or worse than dead. What choice was there?

«*Do it,*» she said. And the wild, angry thing inside her hissed its delight.

Rain sent the instruction to Bel on a grim private weave. «*Do it, Bel.*» He stifled his protective *shei'tan*'s instincts and braced himself for a fierce surge of Rage. Once those shields came down and Ellysetta could sense the *dahl'reisen*, her pain would drive him to the edge of madness. He knew it. Bel knew it. He just hoped he had strength enough to keep the tairen in check.

Sel'dor burned in his chest, arm, and thighs where the Eld's foul missiles had struck him, leaving the barbs buried deep in his flesh. His Fey body continually tried to heal the wounds, but the *sel'dor* responded by burning like acid and twisting his magic into pain. There was enough *sel'dor* in him now to make each breath an effort and set his teeth on edge each time he spun a weave, but not enough to stop a tairen in full Rage from changing.

He had been hiding the truth these last weeks from Ellysetta . . . from everyone. Bel suspected, but then, Bel had known him too well for too long. There wasn't much he could hide from his oldest and dearest friend.

The bond madness had begun. The little slips of control were growing more frequent: The times he broadcast thoughts he'd meant to keep private, how quick he was to anger—and how hotly his temper burned when it came. He didn't know how much time he had left, but it wouldn't be long. The war would see to that. Every battle—each life he took in defense of Ellysetta and the Fading Lands—drove him that much closer to the edge of his control and his sanity.

«*Prepare yourself, Rain,*» Bel warned on a private weave. «*We're lowering her shields now.*»

Rain closed his eyes and drew as deep a breath as the throbbing shrapnel in his chest allowed. *Please, gods, whatever happens, don't let me fly. Teska, don't let me fly.* One scorching of the world was enough for any lifetime.

Ellysetta thought she was prepared to open her unshielded senses near *dahl'reisen*. She thought she knew what to expect.

She was wrong.

Dark emotions screamed down her veins, invaded her blood, ate at her body from the inside out. Despair. Rage. Hatred. Vile, virulent emotions. Whatever had once been good and honorable when these *dahl'reisen* were Fey was utterly gone now. What remained in its place was such bitter hate that the briefest touch of her mind against it made her whole body revolt.

The difference between them and what Gaelen had been before she restored his soul was staggering. His torment had defied description, true, but his soul had still stubbornly clung to the Light, to some concept of honor. He'd still retained the memory of love in his heart. The *dahl'reisen* in the service of Eld were well down the Dark Path, beyond redemption. They took savage pleasure in watching the deaths of their former brothers. They hated them for the Light that still shone within them, and they wanted to crush it, to extinguish it.

"Ellysetta." Bel prodded her urgently. "Ellysetta, quickly, show us where they are so we can reweave your shields. Hurry. For all our sakes."

She turned her head in Rain's direction. Across the field of battling *lu'tan*, she could see him clearly, see the fierce determination on his face as he fought not only his enemies but also his response to her pain. She was broadcasting it to him through the threads of their bond. She was broadcasting it to the *lu'tan* as well.

Gods. She pressed the heels of her palms against her temples and tried to slam her barriers back in place, tried to block out the overwhelming flood of tormented emotion.

«*Ellysetta,*» Bel urged again, «*I know it hurts, but we need you to concentrate on finding the dahl'reisen. Find the source of*

*your pain, and you will find them. That's all we need. Teska,
kem'mareska.»*

It wasn't as easy as all that. At the moment, the source of her
pain was all of them. Her pain hurt Rain and the *lu'tan*, and
their pain echoed back at her, each amplifying the other, building a harmonic of agony and despair, until she could hardly
stop herself from screaming and ripping at her own skin.

"*Kem'falla.*" A hand gripped hers. A cool clarity cut through
the layers of pain. She opened her eyes to find Gaelen standing
before her, his ice blue gaze steady and direct. "Give me the
pain. Feed it to me. I've borne it before, and I can bear it again.
You know I can. Let me bear it for you, for all of them."

"Gaelen . . ."

"Give it to me."

She wasn't certain whether she fed him the pain or he just
took it. Either way, the blinding agony began to fade. The
flicker of Gaelen's eyelashes and the tightening of his mouth
were the only outward signs of his suffering.

"*Kabei,*" he said. "Now, forget about the pain. The pain
doesn't exist. Find the hate. Find the bitterness, the blame.
The anger towards the Fey. Find self over sacrifice. That's how
you'll know these *dahl'reisen.*"

She nodded. Concentrating was easier now, without the
debilitating overload to her senses. Slowly, hesitant to open
herself up to agony again, she peeled back the outer layers of
her internal shields and sent a questing thread of empathic
awareness outside herself. As Gaelen instructed, she tried to
filter her senses to detect only the dark, selfish emotions
Gaelen had described, the blame and anger towards the Fey.

There. Her mind zeroed in on a well of bitterness and hate.

"I see it." Gaelen gestured to the others, directing them to
the location in Ellysetta's mind. A moment later, the foul hatred simply . . . disappeared. A sharp pain lanced across her
senses, but it was gone almost instantly. "Well-done, *kem'falla.*"
Gaelen's voice sounded breathless, strained. "That was perfect."

"Gaelen." She started to open her eyes and turn to him. He'd absorbed the pain of the *dahl'reisen's* death.

"*Nei.* I'm fine. *Teska,* find the next. Quickly."

Ellysetta's efforts were working. The invisibility weaves were failing, and now the Fey weren't the only ones dying.

Rain found what hope he could in that and clung to it desperately. His breath came in ragged gasps. Fey'cha flew like lightning from his fingertips, and scores of Eld fell to his blades. Each death was a bitter, searing draft of darkness, another heavy weight slung around his neck until he could scarce move beneath the weight.

Still, he fought grimly. Ellysetta's life was at stake. If he didn't fight, the Eld would take her. There was no choice but to fight. His blades flew and came back with each choked mutter of his return word, to be plucked from their sheaths and sent flying again. His vision went red and blurry as pain battered him and the Rage crowded the edges of his control.

Mage Fire roared towards the Fey. He flung a five-fold weave in its path, and the two magics exploded with concussive force. He heard the Eld scream, "The Tairen Soul! Kill the Tairen Soul! Bring him down now!"

Sel'dor arrows flew towards him. Savage blasts of Air and Fire knocked down and incinerated many, but his body shuddered and fire seared his veins as the longer, more damaging spears pierced his armor and his flesh. He roared and yanked the missiles free. His hand shot up, but the magic he called didn't come. Too much *sel'dor*: burning, twisting acid eating at his flesh as the Rage consumed his brain. He roared again. A bloody red haze covered his vision. There was nothing in his mind now except the need to kill, to slaughter, to destroy.

Screaming a wordless battle cry, he plunged into the midst of the Eld, *meicha* in one hand, red Fey'cha in the other, slashing, gutting, stabbing, rending. Blood bathed him in hot, red death, and he howled with triumph and savage joy.

* * *

"Got him!" Tajik cried. "I think that's the last one." The invisibility weaves were down, the enemy now in full view.

"*Beylah sallan*," Ellysetta wept. She slammed her shields back into place while the warriors around her respun the protective twenty-five-fold weaves. With a ragged moan, Gaelen released her. He managed to add a thread of Azrahn to her shield weaves before he staggered a short distance away, doubled over, and began to vomit helplessly in the blood-soaked grass.

"Gaelen." She started to go to him. He'd suffered far worse than she. He'd taken the brunt of the *dahl'reisen* pain into himself, using his soul's connection with hers to shield her.

"Ellysetta." Bel grabbed her shoulder with sharp urgency. "Gaelen will be fine. You need to call Rain. Call to him now."

She turned, and her heart froze. Rain stood in the middle of an Eld horde, separated from the main force of the Fey, soaked in blood from head to toe, his face a mask of gore. His teeth bared in a snarl of savage, mindless Rage while his blades hacked and slashed without mercy or surcease. An Eld soldier, little more than a boy, fell to his knees before him, clearly pleading for his life. Rain's sword swung and the boy's head flew from his shoulders.

"Rain." Ellysetta gasped in horror. "Oh, dear gods, Rain." Then her eyes caught sight of the three Primages gathered behind him, of the growing ball of Mage Fire gathering above their hands. Horror turned to terror, and she screamed a warning: "Rain! Look out! Fey! *Ti'Feyreisen! Ti'Feyreisen!*"

The Mages prepared to launch their Fire.

A sudden streak of light zipped across Ellysetta's vision. The Mage Fire winked out as the three Primages clutched the blazing arrows embedded in their chests. Their bodies shuddered and began to glow, as if lit from within by the light of the Great Sun. Shrieking, they burst into flames.

More streaks of light flew across the night sky, and more Eld wailed as they lit up like candleshades and burst into flames.

"What is that?"

"Not what. Who." Bel's grim expression lightened with the first signs of genuine hope, and he pointed to a line of warriors who had appeared in the distance, surrounded by a faint golden glow. "The Elves have come."

With their invisibility weaves gone and the sun-bright arrows of the Elves dispatching Primages and Eld soldiers at a swift rate, the Eld fled in full retreat. Azrahn weaves opened portals to the Well of Souls, and those lucky enough to be near one as it opened ran for the relative safety of the Well. The rest of the enemy force died beneath Fey and Elvish firepower.

Even before the enemy was gone, Ellysetta was racing across the field towards Rain. She summoned her full strength of *shei'dalin's* love, gathering as much power as her body could hold and more, spinning it in weaves of peace and love that she flung towards Rain.

«*Shei'tan!*» The first slight touch of his mad, ravaged mind made her weep. There was nothing of her beloved Rain left, nothing of his gentle Fey heart, his guilt and grief, nothing of the Fey who wanted to be better than he was. There was only Rage, a savage bloodlust, a driving need to kill and destroy.

Tears trembled on her lashes and spilled down her cheeks. *Nei*, she wouldn't accept that. She couldn't. «*Rain, shei'tan, ku'ruvelei. Come back to me, beloved.*» Along every thread of their bond she called to him, spinning love and peace and compulsion.

For once, at least, the savage sentience in her own soul was quiet, and though she didn't know why, she was grateful for the small reprieve. She'd reached Rain's side. "*Shei'tan.*"

He spun to face her, blades clutched in his hands and raised in threat. Droplets of the wet blood drenching his steel flew off as he whirled, and splattered across her face and neck.

She flinched but stood her ground. "Rain. It's me. Ellysetta. The battle is over, *shei'tan*. We are safe. The enemy is gone. Sheath your blades, *shei'tan*, and come back to me."

There wasn't an inch of skin or a fingerspan of his steel that wasn't drenched in blood and gore. His hair hung wet, thick with blood. The fierce blaze of his lavender eyes was filled with tairen power and unfocused Rage.

This was the savage side of his tairen that he'd tried so hard never to show her. The side that had no mercy. The side that could kill without remorse. The wildness that lived in every tairen. The same wildness that lived in the tairen part of her.

It frightened her, but she stepped closer to him, her hands outstretched. "*Las*, beloved. *Las*." She sang to him across the threads of their bond, spinning weaves of love and warmth. "Come back to me now. I need you, and so do the Fey." She spun images of the Fading Lands, the tairen kitlings, Amarynth blooming in Dharsa, the pair of them locked in an embrace, everything they stood to lose if they lost the war with Eld.

Gradually, the wild whirl of his eyes began to slow and his breathing grew deeper, less ragged. She reached for his hands, gently pried the blades from his grip and dropped them to the ground at their feet. She raised his bloody hand to her face and pressed it against her cheek, then laid her own against his.

He blinked, and a pinprick of darkness formed in the whirling brightness of his eyes. A pupil that expanded slowly, growing and lengthening as awareness returned and Rage faded. His eyes focused, fixing on the bloody hand cupped against her cheek, the spatter of drying scarlet across her face. "Ellysetta?"

He frowned and pulled his hand from her cheek. He stared at his bloody palms, his armor coated in gore. His lips pressed tight, but even that could not stop their trembling. "*Nei*. Ah, *nei*. Did I . . ." He glanced around, horror stamped on his face.

She caught his hands. "Only Eld, beloved. None other." She knew without words what he feared he had done: that he'd slain Fey again in his madness as he had the day he'd turned Eadmond's Field into the Lake of Glass.

His face crumpled. "Ellysetta." He fell to his knees and the tears he'd once lost the ability to shed poured from his eyes. His body shuddered in an outpouring of grief and shame.

And she did the only thing she could: She held him, and loved him, and crooned songs of peace and forgiveness to his ravaged soul.

Eld ~ Boura Fell

Vadim Maur called the tendrils of his weave back into himself and breathed in short, quick pants. Sitting for bells on end while his consciousness traveled outside his body to coordinate and oversee the attack had drained him.

Tremors shuddered through his frame, and muscles knotted in painful lumps beneath his skin. As he rubbed at the worst of them, something wet trickled down his arm. He opened his eyes and pushed back his sleeve to find that several new, gaping sores had opened in his deteriorating skin.

Vadim grimaced and dabbed at the suppurating skin with his sleeve hem. Such was the price of weaving magic when the Rot had you in its teeth. The stronger the spell a Mage wove, the weaker he became. The weaker he became, the faster the Rot consumed him.

He'd been taking a chance, holding out for the capture of Ellysetta Baristani. But if he didn't incarnate into a new vessel soon, he risked losing the ability to do so altogether. And no matter how much he wanted Ellysetta Baristani's power for his own, that was not a risk the High Mage of Eld was willing to take.

Two bells later, with much of his strength returned after a lengthy visit to the healers, Vadim Maur stood before the thick, reinforced *sel'dor*-and-steel door of the torture chamber he reserved for Mages who displeased him. The hinges groaned as the two guards outside the door pulled the weighty thing open. Light from the passageway torches cast a thin, fragile illumination in the chamber's gloom, revealing the shivering form huddled on the chamber's cold floor.

"Get up, Kolis."

The huddled figure flinched but did not respond.

Vadim gestured, and two of the guards hurried into the chamber to grab the High Mage's apprentice by his arms and drag him out into the warmer, less frightening light of the flame-lit hallway. The stench of sweat and worse rose up from the apprentice's limp body, making Vadim's nose wrinkle in disgust. He uttered a spell that blocked the odors and reached out to lift the apprentice's face. The remnants of mucus, blood, and vomit clung to Manza's skin.

"Kolis." The High Mage snapped his fingers in the younger man's face, but still received no response.

Vadim ground his teeth together and released the younger Mage's chin. Perhaps the tortures he had devised for his apprentice had been a bit more severe than necessary. But then, he'd not expected to need Kolis so soon.

Vadim stared in distaste at the bodily fluids clinging to his hand, then wiped them off on the uniform of the nearest guard. "Clean him up and take him to the healers. I want him fit for use within the week."

Celieria

Except for Bel, who came to cut the *sel'dor* shrapnel from Rain's body, neither Elf nor Fey intruded as Ellysetta spun her healing weaves on Rain and pulled him back from the brink of Rage. Instead, with swift, silent efficiency, the Elves healed the worst of the wounded Fey, while the able-bodied cleared the battlefield. The Fey Fired the bodies of the dead and gathered the *sorreisu kiyr* of the slain *lu'tan*, to be given into Ellysetta's keeping. Forty *lu'tan* had perished in the battle with the Eld.

Several bells later, as dawn broke over southern Celieria, the worst of Rain's Rage had passed. With Ellysetta's help, he had rebuilt the fragile walls of discipline in his mind. Together, they rejoined the others and offered greetings to the Elves.

Tall and slender—clearly not mortal—the Elves shone faintly gold in the pale morning sunlight rather than glowing with silvery luminescence like the Fey. Sleeveless tunics of iridescent bronze scale mail lay over embroidered shirts and leggings in varying woodland hues of green, ecru, and brown. Bows and quivers filled with arrows were slung across their backs. They wore their long, rippling hair pulled back off their faces with a series of small beaded leather ties, baring ears that swept back to a distinctive, tapered point.

Rain cast a narrowed gaze over the Elves' faces. They were strangers. None he had ever met before. Their obvious leader had hair the burnished gold hue of amberleaf trees in the fall. The beaded ties in his hair fluttered with a collection of bird feathers. And his eyes—those distinctive, too-piercing Elvish eyes—were the clear, translucent green of a sunlit forest pond.

Those eyes met Rain's with uncanny directness.

Ellysetta's fingers tightened around his. The Elf's attention switched to her, and she shivered as if she could feel his gaze prying into her soul.

But that was what it always felt like to be Seen by an Elf. As if your skin had been peeled back and your mind and soul had been opened up for inspection. All of the Elves possessed the talent to some degree, but with certain of their number, the effect was decidedly pronounced.

This Elf seemed one of the latter.

"*Las, shei'tani.*" After a grief-racked night of her weaving peace upon him, he was grateful to return the favor. He ran a thumb over the back of her hand in a soothing caress, but with each subtle stroke, he could feel her tension rising higher. She was afraid of the Elf. Or, rather, unnerved by his presence and disturbed by his gaze. "This Elf is a Seer, like Hawksheart. It is his power you feel."

"He is probing me?"

"Not with deliberate force."

Her brows drew together. "It feels deliberate. And very unsettling."

"Build a barrier in your mind. Use the strongest weave of Spirit you can in a pattern like this." He demonstrated a dense, complex pattern of lavender threads. "It won't stop him from Seeing more than you'd like, but it will help you bear his gaze without discomfort."

She did as he suggested and together they approached the blond Elf, who introduced himself as Fanor Farsight of the Deep Woods clan.

The Elf fixed his penetrating gaze on Rain and said, "Galad Hawksheart, Lord of Valorian, Prince of the Deep Woods, King of Elvia and Guardian of the Dance, sends you greetings, Rainier vel'En Daris of the Fey."

Rain inclined his head. "I accept his greetings, and I offer his envoys welcome to our camp and my deepest thanks for your aid last night. Our hospitality is not so fine here as it would be in Dharsa, but we offer you all that we have." Rain waved towards the center of the makeshift camp. "Please join us and refresh yourselves."

"*Alaneth*. With pleasure, we do accept."

Fanor Farsight nodded and he and his Elves followed Rain and Ellysetta into the center of the gathered Fey. Earth masters spun a simple wooden table and stools for their use, and set out a platter of journeycakes while Water masters filled cups with cool water drawn from a nearby stream.

Fanor was the only Elf to take a seat. The others remained standing in a semicircle at his back, but one of them leaned forward to pluck a journeycake and a cup of water from the table. He took a bite of the journeycake and passed it to the Elf beside him, then took a sip from the cup and passed that on, too. The gesture was an Elvish sign of courtesy, a formal acceptance of Feyan hospitality shared by all the members of Farsight's party. The last Elf to eat and drink handed the final bit of the journeycake and the near-empty cup to Fanor, who consumed what was left.

Rain waited for the Elf lord to finish before he leaned forward and put his palms on the table. "I must tell you, Fanor

Farsight, I am as surprised as I am grateful that the Elves have decided to join us in this war after all."

"You misunderstand, Worldscorcher." The Elf's expression did not change. "We know what you wish from us, but that Song ended before it could begin. The aid you seek from the Elves can no longer help you."

Rain's eyes flickered, the only outward hint of the anger coiling in his veins. "If you are not here to join us, then why did you come?"

"Because my king sent me to escort you and your mate safely to Navahele."

"*Keita?* Why?" Rain's shoulders drew back.

"You already know the answer. Your mate calls a Song in the Dance. My king wishes to understand that Song better."

Anger rose, swift and furious, threatening to rip the fragile rebuilt barriers in his mind. Ellysetta laid a hand over his, and that warm touch gave him the strength to stifle his Rage.

He drew a short, hard breath and curled his free hand in a fist. "I do not understand you or your king," he said in a low voice. "The Eld slaughtered thirteen hundred Fey and nearly five thousand Celierians at Orest and Teleon less than a month ago; as you saw yourself last night, the High Mage hunts my mate to claim her soul; we're facing a new Army of Darkness; and still you tell me the Elves will do nothing to help us?" Despite his efforts, anger spiked. He flattened his palms on the wooden surface of the table and half rose from his chair. "What will you do when the Fey are gone from this world and there are none left with the strength or will to champion the Light? What good will your Dance be then?"

Rather than taking offense, the Elf lord crossed his hands over his heart and bowed his head in a polite Elvish gesture. "The Elves have Seen your plight and the dangers that exist for your truemate. Our king understands what hangs in the balance, but the way is not certain. That is why you must come to Navahele." Farsight turned to Ellysetta. "The Song you call is more powerful than any living Elf has ever Seen.

More powerful even than the Worldscorcher's Song. Many will die; that much is certain. How many will live is yet to be Seen."

Ellysetta flinched, and Rain wrapped an arm around her in a protective gesture. "Enough, Elf," he growled. "You will not frighten my mate with Elvish visions of doom."

The Elf looked puzzled. "*Tenala.* Forgive me. But how did I offer fright, when your own Eye of Truth has already shown a much grimmer future in greater detail?"

"The future *Shei'Kess* showed us is only a possibility, not a certainty," Rain replied with an aggressive thrust of his chin.

"*Banas,*" the Elf agreed, "but the possible outcomes of her Song are far fewer than they were when Ambassador Brightwing extended my king's first invitation this summer. Lord Hawksheart regrets you did not come then."

"Well, our apologies for his regret, but tell him we will make our way to Elvia once we've been to Danael. Celieria needs allies willing to fight at her side, and time is of the essence." Navahele was on the other side of the continent. If they traveled there first, there would be little hope of Danae aid reaching Celieria before the Eld attacked.

"We Saw your intent, but Lord Hawksheart bids you come now, without delay. We will escort you safely to Navahele. Lord Hawksheart will summon the Danae to meet you there once his business with you is concluded." Farsight lifted a hand and several hundred more Elves emerged from the surrounding vegetation, bows in hand.

Rain regarded the small army of Elves. Mad though he was becoming, he wasn't a fool. That show of force meant Hawksheart's request was a command, and one he was prepared to enforce. Rain closed his eyes against an instinctive surge of anger. He'd never taken well to commands of that sort, even without Rage and bond madness urging him to rebel. "As you insist," he growled. "We will accompany you to Navahele."

"A wise decision," Farsight agreed. He stood. "If you and

your mate will come with us. The rest of your warriors may await your return here."

His eyes flashed. "Unacceptable." A change of travel plans he might accept, but he would not let the Elves endanger Ellysetta. "The weaves of my *shei'tani*'s *lu'tan* help protect her from the influence of the Mage when she sleeps. Surely you and Hawksheart already know this. We go nowhere without them."

Fanor considered it, then nodded. "Very well. Your mate's dreams will be safe from the Mage once we enter Elvia, but until then, the *lu'tan* may accompany us. Only her quintet may cross our borders, however," he added. "Deep Woods is home to too many wild creatures who would consider the presence of so many unfamiliar Fey warriors an act of aggression. Blood would be shed."

Rain bowed his head. So long as Ellysetta was safe, he wouldn't push his fragile control enough to argue. "*Bas'ka.* We are agreed."

Fanor spread his hands. "Then let us depart."

CHAPTER ELEVEN

Celieria ~ Celieria City

"Why must you go yourself?" Queen Annoura paced the luxurious confines of Dorian's private chambers, glaring at him as his valet strapped and buckled him into the burnished steel plate and mail of his armor in order to check the fit. Dorian had just informed her that he would personally be riding out with his army tomorrow to defend the northern border against

Eld. "What can you do in the north that the border lords cannot?"

Dorian cast her a sharp glance. "I can lead as the monarch of this kingdom. I can defend my people—as every ancestor who ever wore Celieria's crown always has."

"It's ridiculous!" She threw up her hands, then planted them on her hips. "You could be killed! And then where will Celieria be?"

"In good hands. Your son is not incompetent, madam. He is young, but he's been well trained, and my advisers are honorable men who will guide him true."

"Yet he is heading into danger as well—by your command. It's insanity!"

"It is war, Annoura." Dorian closed his eyes and took a deep breath, visibly taming his emotions. "Dori is as safe as I can make him—and I pray the gods will watch over him— but he understands that Celieria needs us now, no matter the cost to ourselves. You should be proud of our son, Annoura. He will make a fine king."

"And what of this son?" Annoura wrapped her arms around her still-flat belly. "Should he grow up an orphan simply because his father abandoned him to chase some fool notion of honor and glory?" She still hadn't forgiven Dorian for once more choosing the Fey over her—or having them check her for Mage Marks without her knowledge. She doubted she ever would.

Dorian lifted his chin while his manservant strapped into place the metal neck guard that would protect his vulnerable throat from enemy blades and arrows. "Defense of those entrusted to my care is not foolish glory-hounding, Annoura."

"Am I not entrusted to your care? Yet you leave me on a whim to fight a senseless war started by your Fey kin." She stamped a foot. "There would be no war if it were not for them!"

Dorian held up a hand. "Marten," he said to his valet, "please excuse us. The queen and I need a few chimes of privacy."

The valet bowed smoothly. "Your Majesty." He turned and bowed just as smoothly to Annoura. "Your Majesty."

When he was gone and the door was closed behind him, Dorian lifted his hand. A faint glow lightened his palms, and Annoura knew he was spinning a privacy weave around the room. Dorian wasn't a master of magic by any means, but the blood of Marikah vol Serranis, his ancestor Dorian I's wife and queen, was strong enough that even after a thousand years, her mortal descendants still possessed third- and fourth-level talents in certain magical branches. Dorian's weave could be pierced by any master of magic, but it was effective enough against the eavesdropping ears of his mortal subjects.

When the glow around Dorian's hand faded, he turned to her. His hazel eyes—which once had regarded her with such dazzling warmth and love that she'd felt like the most cherished woman in the world—now pierced her with cool reserve.

"The Fey did not start this war, Annoura, but Celieria will finish it." He spoke each word in a clipped voice. "The Eld declared war on my kingdom. Without warning—with the ink on their trade agreement offer still damp and their ambassador's heels barely clear of Celierian soil—they invaded my kingdom, slaughtered thousands of my subjects, and laid waste to two of my cities in an unprovoked act of aggression. And now—" He clamped his lips shut, spun abruptly away, and marched to the window.

"And now what?" she pressed.

Dorian shoved aside the delicate lace curtain to gaze out over his kingdom. "And now it is time to show the Eld that Celieria is not so easy a mark. I do not forget their equally outrageous attack on the Grand Cathedral or the murder of Greatfather Tivrest and Father Bellamy. Such treachery will not go unanswered."

Annoura took a breath. Long had it been since she'd seen him looking so fierce, so stern and determined. "Dorian, stop and think this through. Celieria has lived in peace with Eld for the last three hundred years. They wanted to further that peace until Rain Tairen Soul returned to the world. We have no reason to believe the Eld would ever have attacked us if it were not for the Fey. Now, once more, Celieria is caught in the center of a war between magical races. Our best and only hope is to remain neutral—let the Eld and the Fey destroy one another. Celieria's involvement can only end in our destruction."

His brows drew together and his lips compressed in a sure sign of rising temper. "Your senseless dislike of the Fey has impaired your judgment, Annoura. The Eld did not attack the Fading Lands. They attacked Celieria. *My kingdom.* It pains me that you would ever think I should allow their murderous aggression to go unanswered."

Seeing that spark of genuine anger in his eyes, she backtracked quickly. "You're right, Dorian. If the Eld attack Celieria again, they should be met with force. But why must you be the one to lead our armies along the borders? Surely the border lords can see to our northern defenses without you there to guide them." She moved forward, reaching for his arms. Fingertips met hard steel. She reached for his hands, but he stepped back. "I love you. Can you not understand that I don't want to see you hurt—or worse, killed? I want you here, safe, with me. With our baby."

He made a sharp, slashing gesture. "Stop, Annoura. It's not love of me that drives you; it's hatred of the Fey. Do you think I haven't noticed all the little ways you've been testing me these last months? Trying to make me choose between my kin-ties to the Fey and my love of you. I've had enough. The Fey are my blood kin—but more than that, they are this country's staunchest ally. The sooner you accept that, the better for all concerned."

"Dorian—"

"This discussion is over. I leave for the borders at twelve bells tomorrow. I am Dorian the Tenth of Celieria. It's long past time I began to live up to the honorable name of my forebears." He waved his hand to dispel the privacy weave and called, "Marten!"

The door opened, and Dorian's valet stepped inside. "Your Majesty?"

"The queen is leaving. See her out; then come finish getting me strapped into this thing."

Annoura stood there, trembling with a mix of despair, fury, and disbelief over the way Dorian was dismissing her from his presence—as if she were a mere courtier whose company had grown wearisome. She wanted to cry out for him to love her again, but pride wouldn't let her beg—especially not in front of a servant.

She'd loved him more than she'd ever thought herself capable of loving anyone. And for a Capellan princess raised in a lion's den of deceit, intrigue, and political maneuvering, the sheer vulnerability of forming such a strong emotional attachment had been one of the most terrifying—albeit exhilarating—experiences of her life.

And Dorian had betrayed her.

She'd loved him, given him everything, but he'd chosen his Fey kin over her, and now he was cutting her out of his heart.

Annoura drew herself up, locking her emotions—such weak, useless things—behind a curtain of steely self-control. Her expression hardened into the impassively regal mask she had spent a lifetime perfecting.

"Your Majesty," she responded. Her tone was pure silk but without a drop of inflection. She sank into a flawless full court curtsy, so deep her forehead nearly touched the floor, then rose with smooth grace in an elegant rustle of silk and starched lace. "May the gods watch over you in the north and see you safely home again. And may victory be yours, my king."

His eyes flickered then—an awareness that some threshold had been crossed, and that things between them would never be the same. "Annoura . . ."

She waited in silence, cool and composed, her hands clasped lightly at her waist.

His brows furrowed. For a moment, she thought she saw a slight softening in his demeanor, but then his jaw clenched and he looked down on the pretext of adjusting the buckles holding his chest plate in place. "Never mind. I will see you again before I depart."

Annoura's last flicker of hope winked out. Strange how quietly even great love could die.

"Of course, Sire." She inclined her head and turned to leave. Marten started towards the door with her, but she waved him away. "Go to His Majesty, Marten. I'm perfectly capable of seeing myself out."

Head high, emotions trapped in a tight web of discipline and pride, she walked the short distance down the corridors of Celieria's royal palace from Dorian's suite of rooms to her own. Never had the walk seemed longer.

Inside her suite, the Dazzles of her inner court were lounging about, sharing titillating gossip and nibbling on sweetmeats. They all rose and dropped into curtsies and deep bows when she entered, and uttered a chorus of respectful greetings. "Your Majesty."

"Ladies. Sers." Her voice didn't quaver in the least. She took pride in that. The accomplishment was no mean feat. "Please leave me. I am weary and need to rest. I am not to be disturbed. Is that understood?" With the news of her pregnancy, she knew none of them would think her request odd.

"Yes, Your Majesty. Of course, Your Majesty." The ladies and young lordlings of her court bowed and curtsied some more as they exited her rooms.

Jiarine Montevero was the last to leave. "Your Majesty? Shall I call the physician?"

What cure was there for a broken heart? "Thank you, Jiarine, but no. I'll be fine. All I need is a few bells of undisturbed rest. Tomorrow the court sees off His Majesty and our army. I have informed my guards that I am not to be disturbed by anyone for any reason. Is that clear?"

"Yes, Your Majesty."

"Excellent. That will be all." Though she kept her tone gracious, the dismissal was unmistakable.

Jiarine curtsied. "Of course. Rest well, Your Majesty. And please send for me if there is anything at all you need."

"Yes, thank you." Annoura turned on her heel and waved Lady Montevero away. The tears she'd vowed not to shed were burning her eyes, and she wasn't sure how much longer she could hold out. Especially in the face of Jiarine's sincere concern.

She stood stiffly until she heard the click of her parlor door closing, and then the dam burst. The tears of a lifetime came pouring out in great, racking heaves.

Outside the door of the queen's chambers, Jiarine's steps faltered at the anguished sounds filtering through the heavy door. She considered turning back, but the Queen's Guard had already moved to block the door, and their expressions made it clear they intended to enforce the queen's command for privacy.

Awareness tickled the back of her neck like a chill wind, and she turned to find the Primage Gethen Nour—she could never think of him as Lord Bolor—standing in the hallway. He met Jiarine's gaze, then turned and walked with casual purpose down the hall to one of the small parlors where courtiers often gathered while awaiting the queen's pleasure. No sooner had he entered than half a dozen young ladies exited the same room.

Jiarine steeled her nerves and forced herself to walk towards the parlor. Her heels clapped a measured beat on the marble tiles.

The moment she entered the room, Master Nour caught her by the elbow and dragged her into the corner, out of sight of any passersby.

"Well?" he snapped.

"I'm sorry, my lord. I never had the chance to ask her." For days now, he'd been pressing her to arrange a private audience with the queen, but Annoura had rebuffed each of her attempts. "As soon as she returned from the king, she dismissed her entire court. She is crying like I've never heard her cry before." Jiarine marveled at the unexpected surge of sympathy she felt for Annoura, then stifled it quickly and marshaled her thoughts before Master Nour decided to pry into her mind.

He placed a hand on her throat and tightened his fingers ever so slightly. "This does not please me, Jiarine. You've had five days to arrange for the queen to meet me alone, away from her guards, yet at every turn, you have some reason why you cannot give me what I want. I begin to think you are deliberately thwarting my will." His fingers tightened more. "Your time is up, Jiarine. We will give her a bell or two to calm herself; then you will take me to her. You will make up some excuse to get us past the guards."

She bit her lip. She hated him—*hated* him—and though she was too afraid of his wrath to deliberately thwart him, she hadn't pushed as hard as she otherwise might when the queen repeatedly refused to grant him an audience. Still, if he pressed tonight, he would fail—and fail badly—and she would pay the price.

Her voice dropped to an urgent whisper. "Lord Bolor, you do not understand the queen's moods. Believe me when I tell you that would be a mistake. If I defy her command, she will dismiss me from her service."

He moved closer, crowding her back against the wall. He was a tall man, broad shouldered and fit. If it weren't for the calculating look in his eyes and the hint of cruelty in the set of his lips, he would be truly handsome. He stroked a finger gently along her jaw. The tender gesture made her stiffen in fear. His eyes were icy cold, as was the sibilant whisper that sliced across her nerves like a serrated blade.

"If you defy *my* command, I will punish you much more severely than that."

She closed her eyes and swallowed. If she worshiped the gods, she would have prayed to them now, but she had turned her back on them long ago. "My lord, please. I'm not defying you. I'm trying to help you. If you press her now, you will ruin everything. She could well dismiss us both from court in a fit of pique. Tomorrow, when she is calmer, I will arrange for you to meet her—without her guards, and away from the Fey and the palace wards."

Master Nour's eyes narrowed, and she knew her last remark hit its mark. He'd been complaining all week about how the Fey were making a total nuisance of themselves, spinning detection spells upon almost every fingerspan of the palace so that the barest hint of strong magic set off alarms and brought guards running. He had even taken to meeting his *umagi* outside the palace walls to avoid detection when he spun his will upon them.

"Very well. You will bring the queen to me." He leaned closer, crowding her against the wall and pressing his lips to her ear. "Tomorrow, *umagi*, and do not fail me again, or I promise you will spend your last hours of life screaming for mercy." His fingers lightly caressed her jaw.

The pointed clearing of a throat behind them made Nour freeze. He straightened and turned to glare at the small, exquisitely garbed Master of Graces standing in the corridor not half a man length away.

Jiarine could have kissed Gaspare Fellows. Never had she found him so welcome a sight.

The same could not be said of Master Fellows. He was looking at the pair of them as if he'd found Nour's hand on her breast instead of her jaw.

"Lady Montevero. Lord Bolor." Disapproval crackled in each syllable of their names. As the arbiter of all things fashionable and mannerly in the court, Master Fellows held the unique position of being able to dictate propriety to all but the most powerful courtiers. It was a responsibility he took quite to heart.

"Master Fellows." Jiarine forced a smile. "How delightful to see you. And how is your precious Love doing today?"

The Master of Graces was clad in expertly tailored forest green satin breeches and waistcoat with an amber-lined demi-cape slung rakishly across one shoulder. A small, fluffy white cat wearing a matching diamond-studded green satin ribbon sat perched on his other shoulder like a Sorrelian sea captain's talking bird. The feline looked at Master Nour and hissed, her thick fur standing up on end.

"Love!" Master Fellows scolded. "That's quite enough." But the kitten would not be soothed or silenced. She hissed again and swatted extended claws in Nour's direction. Master Fellows apologized. "I do beg your pardon, Lord Bolor, Lady Montevero. I don't know what's gotten into my little Love. She's been quite beside herself lately."

The Primage's eyes narrowed.

Alarmed, Jiarine smoothly inserted herself between the two men. Despite Master Fellows's ofttimes pretentious ways, she'd always held a secret admiration for him. He was a self-made man, and even though she knew he did not approve of her, he nonetheless always treated her with impeccable courtesy.

With a winning smile, she clasped Master Fellows's elbow and steered him out of harm's way. "Master Fellows, I'm actually quite glad to see you. I'm planning a small tea to welcome one of the queen's newest Dazzles to court, and I wanted to ask your opinion on the matter of the table linens. Lady Zillina insists that I must use satin, but that strikes me as entirely too formal for an afternoon tea. Am I in the wrong?"

As she and Master Fellows turned the corner, Jiarine risked a final glance over her shoulder. Master Nour was gone.

Southern Celieria

Elves were exceptional runners by mortal standards, but they didn't hold a candle to the Fey. At a warrior's run, the Fey could have crossed the five hundred miles of southeastern

Celierian farmland in three days. With the Elves slowing them down, it took them the better part of five.

They made camp their last night in Celieria beside a small stream, where the thick, arching branches of a fireoak tree would provide shelter.

"If one of the Fire masters will build a flame," Fanor Farsight said, "there are fish in that stream. I'll sing us up a few for supper." Not waiting for their response, he walked to the mossy edge of the stream and lay on the bank.

"I'll just get that fire, shall I?" Tajik muttered with a scowl as curiosity sent the other Fey wandering over to the stream's edge.

"Watch this," Rain murmured to Ellysetta as they joined the others near the stream.

Fanor put one hand in the cold, clear water and sang a hypnotic Elvish tune. Within a chime, a fat river trout swam into his hands, its sides gleaming with flashes of gold and green scales. Fanor's fingers closed about the fish and flipped it up, out of the stream.

Gaelen caught the airborne fish with swift, instinctive Fey reflexes.

"Still it, but do not kill it," Fanor advised, and Gaelen spun a simple weave to calm the flopping creature.

Fanor sang to the stream four more times, and four more fish swam into his grasp to be flipped up into the waiting hands of the Fey.

Fanor rose to his feet and stood before the Fey. He sang another soft, achingly beautiful song, each note ringing with pure, perfect pitch. Then he closed his eyes, splayed one hand, and tiny globes of white light shot from his fingertips and enveloped each fish. When the light and the last notes of his song faded, it was clear the fish were dead.

"What did you do just then?" Ellysetta asked. The Elves had hunted small game each night when they made camp, but this was the first time she'd watched one actually catch and kill his prey. The others had simply shown up with meat already prepared for roasting.

He smiled at her puzzlement. "We are all connected, Ellysetta Erimea. You and I. Every rock, plant, and animal. We all spring from the same Source, and to that Source we all return. These fish came when I asked, so I thanked them for offering their bodies to nourish ours and sent their Light back to the gods."

He stepped across the springy grass to the fire now blazing in a circle of river rocks at Tajik's feet. The Fey deftly gutted, scaled, and spitted the fish over Tajik's flames, and Fanor disposed of the offal by burying it at the base of a tree and singing another Elvish song. "What part of their bodies we consume will now become part of ours, and what we do not consume will become part of the earth. And so they are not gone. They are merely transformed."

Ellysetta found herself disturbed by the idea that Fanor's fish had willingly delivered themselves up to be slain and eaten. When Bel offered her a chunk of steaming fish on a broad leaf, she thought squeamishness might rob her of her appetite, but the first whiff of hot food made her belly rumble. Hunger overrode any pretense of delicate sensibilities. She tucked a bite into her mouth and closed her eyes in bliss as the succulent, flavorful fish practically dissolved on her tongue. Her eyes flashed open again almost instantly.

Fanor smiled. "Life is meant to be savored, Ellysetta Erimea. And death is not without purpose." His smile faded. "Most of the time, at least. There are some deaths that are simply an end, with no hope of renewal and no return of life to its Source." His glance, gone suddenly shadowed and brooding, shifted to rest on Rain. "Death by tairen flame, for instance," he added in a low voice.

The Fey all went still as stone. Ellysetta saw the grim mask snap into place on Rain's face, hiding the sudden swell of guilt and self-loathing that seared him. His emotions were still so raw, his discipline so fragile, since the night of the Eld attack.

She frowned at Fanor and opened her mouth to defend her truemate, her fingers feathering across the back of his hand in the lightest of touches.

«*Bas'ka, shei'tani,*» Rain said privately. «*It's all right. You don't need to keep protecting me.*»

She bit her lip and fell silent. She had been protecting him since the Eld attack, hovering around him like a mother tairen with one kit. He'd been getting stronger by the day, meditating each time they stopped to rest, using his magic only sparingly, constantly performing mental exercises to restore and strengthen his internal barriers. But she couldn't forget the sight of his face soaked in blood, or his eyes filled with horror and fear that he might once more have committed an unspeakable act.

"*Aiyah,*" Rain told Fanor. "Death by tairen flame is an end from which there is no return. Mage Fire is another."

"Perhaps Tairen Souls and Mages are more alike than the Fey care to consider," Fanor suggested.

Gil reached for his Fey'cha. Tajik grabbed his wrist. "Don't be a fool, Gil." His gaze never left Fanor. "The Elf is merely testing us."

"Elves have their own fair share of blood on their hands," Ellysetta said. They were all on their feet now. "I've read the histories. Elvish armies slaughtered hundreds of thousands in the Feraz and Demon wars."

"*Bayas,* but none who die at Elven hands are truly gone. They all return to the Light, to be born again into this world."

"Then perhaps that is why the gods created Tairen Souls—because some evil is so foul it should be wiped from all existence." She would not let Fanor Farsight impugn Rain even obliquely without challenge.

But Fanor was through with subtleties. "As it was at Eadmond's Field?" His gaze pierced Rain as deeply as an arrow shot from an Elf bow. "Did all the souls who perished there deserve to have their Light extinguished for all time?"

Rain absorbed the blow with only a small flinch, but inside, where Fanor could not see, Ellysetta knew his soul howled in pain. His lashes fell to hide the shame burning in his eyes. "You know they did not. My act was a crime so great, only the gods could grant me forgiveness."

"And is that why you returned to the Lake of Glass to spin memorial weaves for those who died there?"

Rain looked up again in surprise.

"*Bayas*," the Elf confirmed. "I Saw the weaves you spun at Eadmond's Field, so I went there before journeying to meet you." The Elf tilted his head to one side, a quizzical expression on his face, as if he were trying to solve the puzzle that was Rain. "Why did you do it? Did you think a few memories woven in Spirit could atone for the innocent lives lost to your flame? Did you hope such a gesture of compassion would make the gods look more kindly upon you and your mate? Or make the children of those immortals who fell less likely to seek vengeance now that you have returned to the world?"

"I did it because it needed to be done."

Beside Rain, Ellysetta bristled. "He suffered more torment than any one person ever should for what he did," she told the Elf with a scowl. "And he survived, with Light still shining bright in his soul." Her hands curled into fists. Her mate had once shared the merest fraction of his torment with her, and that small taste had nearly shattered her. She would not stand idly by while anyone—let alone this . . . this Elf!—criticized him. "He has already earned his forgiveness. The gods found him worthy, as have the tairen. So you will not judge him, Fanor Farsight. You haven't the right."

"*Las, shei'tani.*" To the Elf, he said, "I cannot undo what was done. That is a torment I will carry with me forever. But what I did at the Lake of Glass, I did because I wanted to make certain those who fell were not forgotten."

Farsight eyed Rain thoughtfully. "Elvish Sight shows events clearly, but emotions are more difficult to ascertain. I did not See your remorse," he admitted. "Nor how bright your mate truly is." He glanced at Ellysetta. "No wonder the Shadow lies so dark upon her. It fights hard to extinguish its greatest foe."

Rain's spine stiffened and sudden aggression emanated from him like waves of heat from a volcano. "Watch your words, Elf," he commanded. "My *shei'tani* is bright and shining and I will not tolerate anyone saying otherwise."

"I meant no insult," Farsight said mildly. "It was a true observation, one that does your mate credit." His golden-brown skin shone with a rich luster in the evening light, making the translucent green of his eyes all the more vivid. "And you, Tairen Soul, are different from what you once were. You have learned humility and regret. You truly are learning to be a king rather than just the madman who scorched the world . . . and slew my father."

"Your father?" Ellysetta repeated. Her brows furrowed as fragments of memory began to piece themselves together. Elves . . . Eadmond's Field . . . Fanor . . . She drew a breath. "You are Fanor . . . son of Pallas Sparhawk." Her hand caught Rain's. «*The Elf bowmaster who fell at Eadmond's Field . . . the one for whom you created that first memorial on the lake . . . Rain, Fanor is the young son who filled his last memories.*»

"Does my mate speak true?" Rain asked.

The Elf inclined his head. "*Bayas*, Pallas Sparhawk was my father. I had seen but three winters when he fell to your flame. I had few memories of him . . . until I visited the Lake of Glass, where I met him again and felt his love for me and for my mother." The Elf's lashes lowered to hide his eyes.

Ellysetta felt the old demons of guilt and remorse that had haunted Rain for centuries rise up and sink their teeth into him once more. She laid a hand on his arm, offering what peace she could, knowing it was nowhere near enough.

"*Sieks'ta*, Fanor, son of Sparhawk," he said in a gravelly voice. "There is nothing I can do to repay your loss. If I could take back that day, I would."

"I think I believe that now." Fanor drew in a deep breath.

"When I touched that weave you spun for my father, I felt his presence in a way I never have before. It was as if you'd spun a bit of his soul into your weave. And perhaps you did." Bittersweet emotion shone in the shadowed depths of his eyes—a sort of melancholy acceptance and a fragile sense of peace, as if some lifelong wound had finally begun to heal. "Perhaps, Rainier Feyreisen, those who perished to your flame did not die so utterly as I have always believed. Their Light did not return to the Source, it's true, but I think perhaps at least some part of it still lives . . . in you."

Rain's gaze fell. "The gods will it should be so," he said in a low voice.

The Elf drew up his knees and rested his arms atop them. "I never wanted to forgive you for what you did—not even after I stood in your weaves at the Lake of Glass and felt my father for the first time in a thousand years—but I should have done so long ago."

"The resentment you harbored is understandable. You were a child who lost his father to my flame."

"And you were a Fey called to do a terrible deed because that was what the Dance required," Fanor countered. "I should not have blamed you for fulfilling the will of the gods. All Elves know those who call a Song in the Dance rarely have a choice of the tune. It's what they do afterward that reveals their true measure." He shook his head. "*Anio*, I clung to my anger out of grief, and I think you cling to your guilt from the same. Perhaps it is time for both of us to forgive what you did."

Rain closed his eyes and leaned his head against the thick, ribbed trunk of the fireoak tree at his back. "Some things are not so easy to forgive."

"Perhaps not, but I do forgive you. If you truly do carry what remains of my father's Light, then I am glad. His was a bright soul, and something of him deserves to live on."

"Something of him already does, Fanor," Ellysetta said softly, her hand resting upon Rain's shoulder. "In you." The moment the Elf had said those three magical words, "I forgive you," she'd felt a portion of Rain's terrible pain ease. For that alone, she felt herself warm to Fanor.

"Of course." The softening of Fanor's expression faded and he was once again all Elf, inscrutable and mysterious. He rose to his feet and dusted off his hands. "We should sleep. Tomorrow will be a long day."

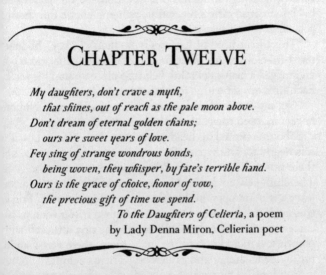

Chapter Twelve

My daughters, don't crave a myth,
*   that shines, out of reach as the pale moon above.*
Don't dream of eternal golden chains;
*   ours are sweet years of love.*
Fey sing of strange wondrous bonds,
*   being woven, they whisper, by fate's terrible hand.*
Ours is the grace of choice, honor of vow,
*   the precious gift of time we spend.*

To the Daughters of Celieria, a poem
by Lady Denna Miron, Celierian poet

Celieria ~ Old Castle Prison

Great Lord Sebourne scowled with bad temper and held out his arms as his valet slipped a sumptuous, gold-embroidered waistcoat over the freshly ironed and perfumed silk tunic. The Great Sun had risen, signaling the end to his five days of incarceration in the west tower of Old Castle Prison. The prison master of Old Castle would arrive soon to set him free, but Lord Sebourne was determined not to set foot outside this cell looking anything less than his most powerful and resplendent self.

No trumped-up incarceration was going to bring *this* Great Lord of Celieria to heel; and, by the gods, that spineless puppet of a king and his cadre of bootlicking Fey lovers would soon know it!

In anticipation of his pending release, his valet had arrived well before sunrise to bathe, shave, oil, and powder the Great Lord to pampered perfection. And now, as the Great Sun began its morning ascent into the sky, Lord Sebourne donned his finest court garb: silks, satins, rich and exotic furs, heavy gold rings set with radiant jewels.

"This Great Lord of Celieria is no man's lackey," he muttered irascibly as his valet finished buttoning the waistcoat and tugged a heavy gold-link belt into place around his waist. Each link was set with a jewel the size of a hen's egg.

"No, my lord," the valet agreed in a placid voice. Nimble fingers snapped the golden belt clasp closed.

Sebourne turned his head to stare out the window. The sun was nearly touching the silhouetted rooftops of the city, but there was a chill in the air. Winter was definitely on its way. The chill grew colder, and he frowned at his valet. "Did you leave a window open in the other room after my bath?" Prison this might be, but even Dorian had known better than to incarcerate a Great Lord of Celieria in some tiny little cell with no privacy. In addition to the main room, there was a small private bedchamber and garderobe. "There's a draft."

"My lord?" The servant glanced up from his work with a puzzled frown. "No, my lord. The windows are all firmly shut and it's warm as springtime in here."

"Nonsense. Springtime? In what country—the ice wastes of the Pale?" Lord Sebourne harrumphed. "Put another log on the fire to cut the chill."

The servant was clearly disbelieving, but nonetheless he murmured, "Yes, my lord. Of course, my lord," and rose to put another log on the fire blazing in the hearth.

Just before the valet reached the fireplace, he stopped in his tracks and stood there, motionless.

"Brom?" Lord Sebourne stared at the valet. "What's the matter with you, man?"

Before he could say another word, he caught a glimpse out of the corner of his eye of something moving to his right. A man. "Ah, come to release me, have you? It's about time." He turned to face the prison master of Old Castle.

But the man who stepped out into the center of the room was not the prison master. A long-bound corner of Lord Sebourne's mind cracked open and spilled a lifetime of suppressed memories into his consciousness. Suddenly Brom's unnatural stillness made perfect sense. Lord Sebourne himself froze as at last he realized it was no draft from the window that had chilled him to his soul.

Lord Bolor—or rather the Elden Mage passing himself off as Lord Bolor—moved towards Great Lord Sebourne with surprising speed. He caught the Great Lord and clamped a hand around his throat before Sebourne could do more than take two steps back and open his mouth in a silent cry.

"Who are you?" Sebourne croaked against the tight hold. "What do you want?"

The Mage leaned close, a cruel curve tilting up one corner of his mouth. "You know who I am—or rather what I am—and you know why I've come. It's time to pay your family's debts, Great Lord Sebourne. Your masters in Eld require your service."

In a narrow alley across from Old Castle Prison, Gaspare Fellows pulled his gray woolen coat close against the morning chill and waited for Lord Bolor to reemerge from within the prison's old stone walls. His breath made little puffs of fog before his face, and he stepped deeper into the shadows to hide the telltale sign from any observer.

What business, he wondered, could Lord Bolor possibly have in Old Castle Prison so early in the morning?

After Lady Ellysetta had taken Gaspare into her confidence to share her concern that Elden Mages were at work in

Celieria City, he had begun looking for suspicious activity. His powers of observation were, in all modesty, considerable—honed by years of noting the smallest details of dress and etiquette exhibited by Celieria's nobles.

So last night, when he'd interrupted Lady Montevero and Lord Bolor in the parlor outside the queen's suites, their behavior had caught his interest. There was something not quite right about the way Lord Bolor and Lady Montevero acted when they were together. Lady Montevero had made a point of squiring the new Lord Bolor about the court, so Gaspare had naturally assumed there was some sort of friendship or other intimacy between them. And at first glance, their meeting in the parlor last night had appeared to be an ordinary romantic tryst. That was until Gaspare glimpsed the fear and loathing in Lady Montevero's lovely blue eyes before she masked her feelings behind a sun-bright smile.

Whatever Lord Bolor was to Lady Montevero, he was neither friend nor lover. On that, Gaspare would wager every last one of his finest silk waistcoats.

Love's reaction to Lord Bolor had only increased Gaspare's suspicions. The kitten didn't like Lord Bolor at all—and never had. She reacted to his presence exactly the way Lady Ellysetta said she reacted to magical weaves.

Of course, a kitten's dislike and a look in a courtier's eyes weren't reason enough for Gaspare to take his suspicions to the king. No untitled man—not even one elevated to the position of Queen's Master of Graces—accused a Lord of Celieria of being an agent of Eld without some sort of proof.

So Gaspare had decided to investigate.

He paid a trusted servant to alert him as to Lord Bolor's movements in the palace, and when word came before sunrise that the lord had departed the palace, Gaspare followed.

"*Mrrow.*" The testy complaint rumbled from beneath his greatcoat.

"Quiet, Love." Gaspare unbuttoned the top buttons of his

coat so the kitten could poke out her head and look around. "Now be still!"

Luckily, whatever business Lord Bolor had in Old Castle Prison was soon concluded. The lord emerged from the ancient stone fortress, paused outside the doors just long enough to sweep a cautious gaze up and down the main street, then pulled up the collar of his cloak and walked briskly south, towards the river.

"Time to go, Love. Back in you get." Gaspare hid the kitten again, refastened the buttons up to his neck, and tugged down the brim of his black hat to hide his face. He hurried into the thoroughfare in pursuit of the nobleman, careful to keep a distance between them so Lord Bolor would not suspect he was being followed.

Lady Talisa Barrial DiSebourne closed the book of poetry and set it on the cushioned seat beside her. She tilted her head back and pressed her cheek to the cold windowpane of the small reading alcove in her father's library.

If only she could have heeded the poet Lady Denna's advice, but it was too late for her. Those eternal golden chains had trapped her long ago, binding her heart, her love, her very soul to the Fey warrior she'd dreamed of her whole life.

She'd waited for him until the day of her twenty-fifth birthday. Had she remained unwed a single day more, she would have brought the shame of spinsterhood to her family. Society would have looked at her and wondered what evil curse had kept any good man from offering the honor of his hand in marriage. Her brothers would have found it difficult to find wives of their own. And so she had wed.

And then, when it was too late, he had come. Adrial vel Arquinas. The man from her dreams. A Fey warrior of such breathtaking beauty and fierceness and gentleness that everything within her, every fiber of her being, had known from the instant she'd first laid eyes upon him that he was the purpose of her existence, the soul she'd been born to make whole.

Talisa pressed a hand to her mouth. Just the memory of his velvet brown eyes, the luminous glow of his pale Fey skin, made her want to weep for the joy that could never be hers.

"Adrial." She spoke his name in a whisper, barely daring to breathe it out loud. His name had become a prayer, a sacrament to her, whispered in the dead of night and times of loneliness as a ward against the gray despair her life had become.

He'd come, the mate predestined by the gods, but mortal laws kept her from him. She was another man's wife, and Adrial could not claim her. Though it had been like ripping her heart from her chest with her own hands, she'd begged him to leave her and find what happiness he could, and he had heeded her pleading. He'd left with his people to return to the Fading Lands, and even though the Fey had returned to Celieria City last week, Adrial was not among them.

It was time—past time—for her to accept that he wasn't coming back. Time for her to make peace with her lost dreams and find what happiness she could in her marriage.

The crack of a slamming door made her jump. She sat up and turned towards the closed library door. She could hear the sound of boot heels beating an angry tattoo against the marble floor as they approached the library.

Talisa swung her legs off the edge of the window seat and rose to her feet. She smoothed a hand over her skirts and hair and pinched her wan cheeks to erase their pallor. The library doors swung inward.

Colum stood framed in the doorway. He'd gone to visit his father after Lord Sebourne's release from Old Castle Prison, and clearly something had happened. His face was flushed, his hair windblown. A wild light glittered in his eyes.

"What is it?" She gasped. "What has happened?" All she could think of was the war threatening Sebourne and Barrial lands. Had their homes been besieged? "Colum . . ." She took several steps towards him.

"Pack your bags, Talisa. We leave for home today—and by home I mean Moreland."

Her jaw dropped. "Leaving? But just last night you said we weren't going to leave the city. You and Da both agreed the borders were too dangerous and that we needed to stay here."

"That was before I knew what you were up to."

She blinked in utter confusion. "What I was *up to*?" she echoed.

His mouth twisted in a bitter sneer. "Don't take me for such a fool, Talisa. My father had a visitor this morning before I arrived at Old Castle. Someone who informed him on good authority that your lover—that wife-stealing *rultshart* of a Fey—didn't go back to the Fading Lands. He didn't even go north to your father's lands, which is where I suspected he'd be waiting for you. The thieving *bogrot* has been here in the city all this time."

Her hand rose to her throat, and the sudden, wild acceleration of her pulse pounded against her fingertips. "Are you talking about . . . Adrial?"

Colum's handsome face contorted with rage. "Don't you dare pretend innocence!"

"It's no pretense!" she shot back. "I haven't seen Adrial since he and his brother left with the Tairen Soul and the rest of the Fey over a month ago."

"Lying *petchka*!" His hand shot out.

Talisa gave a choked cry, but he moved so fast she had no chance to duck his blow. Her eyes squeezed shut in an instinctive reaction and she braced herself for the smack of his hand against her cheek.

The blow never came.

She pried open her eyes to find Colum frozen, his hand a scant breath from her face, his face purple with rage.

"Colum? Oh, gods." Realization sucked the breath from her lungs, and she gave a short gasp. "Oh gods, he was right. You are here." She turned on trembling legs as the air around her began to sparkle with tiny flashes of light.

Seven leather-clad Fey warriors shimmered into visibility, their pale, shining faces grim, their eyes cold and flat and filled with lethal intent.

She barely saw six of the warriors. Her gaze—her entire being—focused on only one: the achingly beautiful face of the man she'd dreamed of all her life, the truemate she'd never thought to see again. Her heart leapt into her throat, and even though Colum was standing frozen a scant arm's length away, her soul soared with dizzying joy.

"Adrial." She took one step towards him, her shaking hands outstretched. He closed the rest of the distance in a flash. His arms wrapped around her, pulling her tight to his chest, pressing her so close she could feel the hard forms of his Fey'cha daggers and hear the beat of his heart in her ear. Abruptly, the tears she'd kept to herself as she cried into her pillow each night burst free, and she began sobbing as though her heart were breaking. "Adrial . . . oh, Adrial . . ."

He bent his head, his black hair spilling over his shoulders to envelop her in fragrant dark silk. He smelled of springtime and warm meadows, of fresh sunlight after a long winter's dark. "*Aiyah*, I am here, *shei'tani*. I never left your side . . . and I never will."

"Oh, Adrial." Talisa nearly wept with regret. "You cannot be here. You can't," she said, no matter how much she wanted him to stay. Her hands traced the soft, fine-grained skin of his face. She couldn't stop gazing at him, touching him. "The reasons you had to leave before haven't changed. I cannot go with you."

"You cannot stay with him." Adrial jerked his chin towards Colum's frozen body. "And you definitely are not going to the borders. It is far too dangerous. The real fighting hasn't yet begun, but it soon will, and I want you nowhere near what's coming."

"What choice do I have? Colum is my husband, and he has said we must return to our home."

"Your home is with me."

Her lips trembled. The fingers stroking his face trembled, too. "No. It isn't. Though I wish with all my heart it were."

He caught her hand and pressed a kiss into her palm. "Say the word, Talisa, and I will make it so. Ramiel—the Fey who serves as Spirit master of your quintet—can spin a weave to change diSebourne's mind so that he will agree to let you go."

"That sort of weave is forbidden. If you were caught, the penalty would be death!"

"Then I would take care they didn't catch me." His grip tightened. "*Teska, shei'tani,* let me set you free."

The lure was so powerful, so tempting. But before she could open her mouth and damn herself, she saw her father's face and heard once more his sober lecture on the inviolability of a Barrial's vow and the dangerous political explosion that would ensue if the wife of Great Lord Sebourne's heir ran off with a Fey warrior. She turned her head away, closing her eyes to block out the sight of Adrial's beloved face. "I can't. He's not just some common man, Adrial. He's the heir of a Great Lord, and his father already hates the Fey. You saw it yourself this summer. If I left with you, Lord Sebourne would plunge this country into civil war. Celieria can't be divided that way right now."

"No one needs to know. If Ramiel spins the weave, they'll all think it's Colum's idea."

"Lord Sebourne would know . . . and so would I." She bowed her head and stared at her tightly clasped hands. "When I married Colum, I swore an oath before the gods that bound my life to his. I cannot forsake my vow."

"He has already forsaken it. Did he not vow to care for you and keep you from harm? Yet he lifted his hand against you. If we had not been here, he would have struck you."

"He was upset."

"He would have struck you," Adrial repeated. The thickly lashed eyes that could be so meltingly warm were hard as polished stones. "If he had, I would have killed him for it."

She pressed her fingers to his lips to silence him. "Don't say such things. Don't even think them."

"There is nothing I would not do to keep you safe, *shei'tani*. No Celierian law I would not break, no enemy I would not kill. Wed to this mortal you may be, but I will not let him touch you. I *cannot*."

With those words, Colum's strangely accommodating behavior these last weeks suddenly made sense. She drew back, covering her mouth with a hand to stifle her shocked gasp. "You're the reason he hasn't pressed me to come to his bed. Oh, Adrial, what have you done?"

"I did what I had to do." Adrial gripped her arms. "You are my mate, my *shei'tani*, and our bond is not complete. If he touched you, I would kill him. Since both you and Rain made me swear not to do so, I had no choice but to make certain he never laid a hand on you."

"Bright Lord save me." Talisa began to pace. "You spun a weave on him." When she drew near Colum, who now lay senseless in a heap on a nearby chaise, she gave a small, choked cry and whirled away to pace in the opposite direction. Around the room, Adrial's brother and the other five Fey watched her in silence. "Oh, gods, if anyone suspects—if they find out—you'll be executed."

Adrial rose to follow her. "Talisa . . ."

"No!" She spun to face him and raised her hand. "I'm his wife, Adrial. His *wife*!"

"And you're my truemate!" he retorted. "DiSebourne can get another wife. Mortals often do. There is no other mate for me but you, and never shall be."

"Adrial . . ." A sudden commotion outside the library doors made Talisa break off. She blanched at the sound of familiar male voices calling her name. "Oh, dear gods. My father and brothers are here. Lord Sebourne is with them. Quickly, you've got to leave! They can't find you here!" She whirled and started to race across the room, only to stop in a spurt of panic. "Wait! What about Colum? You can't leave him like this."

Adrial turned his head and rapped out, "Ramiel." The

Spirit master moved to Colum's side, and Talisa saw his hands and eyes begin to glow.

"Talisa?" Her father's voice called just outside the library doors. The crystal doorknobs began to turn.

"Go!" she cried softly. "Hurry!" Tiny sparks of electricity raced across her skin, raising the hairs on her arms. Adrial and the Fey shimmered into invisibility just as the library doors swung inward.

"DiSebourne!" Talisa's father stormed into the room and made a beeline for her husband, who had risen to his feet and was rubbing his temples. "What's this I hear about you planning to take my daughter to the borders? Have you lost what sense the gods gave you? There's a war on, man!"

Colum turned, his brow knit in confusion. "Lord Barrial? Father?"

"Stay out of this, Barrial," Lord Sebourne snapped. "You've done enough interfering as it is. She's a Sebourne now, and Sebourne wives go where their husbands guide them. Colum is going home to our estate to help oversee its defenses—and his bride *will* accompany him!"

Talisa's father whirled on his neighbor. His lips drew back in a snarl, and in that moment, he looked every bit like the wild wolf that dominated the Barrial coat of arms. "You will not endanger my daughter's life just so your son can feel like a man in control of his wife. If he possessed an ounce of regard for her safety, he would insist she remain here, as far away from the conflict as possible."

"Oh, would he?" Lord Sebourne sneered. "You'd like that, wouldn't you? Was arranging for Talisa to be alone here with her lover part of whatever plan you and the Fey were hatching with the king?"

"What in the Seven Hells are you talking about?" Cann exclaimed. "Did a week in Old Castle rot your brain?"

"Don't play the innocent. Colum and I know what's been going on here. Don't we, Colum?"

"I . . ." Colum shook his head and dragged his fingers through his hair.

Lord Sebourne squinted at him and stepped closer. "What's wrong with you, boy?" His brows shot up to his hairline.

Alarmed that Lord Sebourne might discover Adrial had been manipulating Colum's mind, Talisa leapt forward. "Father. Lord Sebourne. Please. There is no need for you to argue." Talisa put her hand on Colum's arm. "Colum has already explained why we must go north with you and the king's army. I was just about to have my maid begin packing when you arrived."

"Talisa!" her father exclaimed. "It's out of the question. War has begun. Every estate on the borders is in danger of being overrun by the Eld. You could be killed."

«*Shei'tani, nei! I've already told you, it is too dangerous.*»

Adrial's voice was so clear in her head, it shocked her that the others could not hear him. The rich tones shivered up and down her spine like a warm caress, the sound so intoxicatingly sensual it was all she could do not to groan aloud and rush towards the spot where she now knew he was standing.

Her reaction solidified her resolve. Adrial and her father were wrong. The most dangerous place for her wasn't in the north near the battlefront. It was right here in Celieria City—especially if Colum went north with his father and left her behind. Talisa harbored no illusions. If she were left alone with Adrial—honor, marital vows, even duty to the Bright Lord be damned—she would not long withstand the lure of his presence. She would throw away everything to follow him. To be with him.

And that meant she could not stay.

"We're borderfolk, Da. We've lived in the jaws of the beast our whole lives, and we don't run from danger. Colum is my husband, and if he is leaving, then I must accompany him."

"Well." Lord Sebourne regarded her with an expression that flickered between surprise, suspicion, and reluctant approval. "I'm glad to see you're thinking like the wife of a Sebourne. It's about time."

Talisa bit her lip. Shame rode her hard. She wasn't any sort of a proper wife for Colum. She never had been. "Yes, my lord."

"Then see to it my son and you are packed and ready to depart within the bell. We ride out with the king. I'll send a carriage at half ten to collect you."

"Yes, my lord." Talisa dipped a brief curtsy. "Colum and I will be ready and waiting. Now if you'll please excuse me, I'll go see to the packing." She turned to exit the room.

At the foot of the stairs, a warm breeze brushed across her face, and Adrial's voice whispered in her ear.

«I won't leave you, shei'tani. No matter your Path, I will walk it beside you.»

Talisa shivered and paused with one foot on the stairs. "You'll do what you must," she whispered in response. "And so will I." And with stoic resolve, she started up the stairs.

Celieria City ~ The Royal Palace

When Jiarine entered the queen's antechambers to prepare Her Majesty for the army's departure celebration, she found Annoura's bedchamber door firmly closed and the space outside filled with Dazzles milling uselessly about.

"What are you doing here?" she cried when she saw them. "Why aren't you helping Her Majesty get dressed?"

"The queen has refused to let anyone enter, my lady," one of the Dazzles explained. "She says she's not coming out. She says she will not watch her husband ride to his death."

Alarmed, Jiarine hurried to the bedchamber door and rapped twice.

"Go away!" a hoarse croak of a voice called from within the room. "I told you, I will not go!"

"Your Majesty, it's Jiarine. Lady Montevero."

Silence. Then she heard the sound of the lock twisting inside. The door swung inward a bare crack. "Only you, Jiarine. No one else."

"Of course, Your Majesty." Jiarine shooed the other courtiers away, then slipped inside. When the door closed behind her and she turned, Jiarine was shocked by the appearance of Celieria's beautiful and rightfully vain queen.

Annoura's face was blotched and swollen from tears, her blue eyes so badly bloodshot her irises stood out in stark relief. With her silvery blond hair hung in a wild tangle around her face, she was the living picture of despair and inconsolable grief.

"Oh, Your Majesty," Jiarine breathed. Never would she have believed that there was anything or anyone in the world Annoura cared for this much.

Once again, an unexpected flash of sympathy for Celieria's queen welled up inside Jiarine. Poor Annoura. She would never know how hard the Mages of Eld had worked to bring her so low. Nor would she ever know how great a role Jiarine had played in bringing this state of affairs about.

Annoura turned away and lifted shaking hands to cover her face. The queen's shoulders quaked and the sound of a shuddering inhalation told Jiarine a fresh torrent of tears was struggling to break free.

"What should I do?" Annoura wailed softly. "The king's departure is in less than a bell, but I can't let anyone see me like this." In a softer voice, she added, "Least of all him."

Oh, yes, there'd been a break between the royal couple. Exactly the devastating chasm Master Manza had worked so hard to orchestrate. And after her years at court, Jiarine knew Queen Annoura well enough to suspect that nothing would ever be the same between the king and queen again.

Jiarine's thoughts churned rapidly. The queen was expected to see her husband and Celieria's armies off to war. Dorian would not want his people to perceive a divided front. But there wasn't enough time, short of healing magic, to repair the queen's swollen face, painfully red eyes, and tear-splotched complexion before she was due to step out into the public eye.

Jiarine snapped her fingers. "Veils."

Annoura lifted her head from her hands. "Veils?"

"Yes." Feeling more confident, Jiarine nodded. "Veils. Your Majesty, it's the perfect solution."

She turned and hurried to the door that led into the queen's extensive personal wardrobe chamber. Struck by the perfect, almost ironic symbolism of her idea, Jiarine went straight to a scarlet gown that Annoura had had made last year but never yet had the occasion to wear. She also fetched a neatly folded stack of sheer scarlet veils.

She brought them back into the main room and brandished them in triumph. "What better solution than to see them off just as the *shei'dalins* of the Fey see off their men to war?"

Annoura recoiled at the sight of all the scarlet cloth filling Jiarine's hands. "You think I want to look like one of . . . them?"

There was no time to argue. "Not red, then, white if you prefer. Blue. The color doesn't matter, Your Majesty, only the fact that you can appear in public without anyone seeing your face and knowing how badly you've been hurt."

"I . . ." The queen hesitated, and Jiarine could see Annoura's pride returning. Her shoulders squared and her spine straightened. She gave her reddened eyes a final swipe and reached for the clothes in Jiarine's hands. "You're right. It's the perfect solution. Come help me put this on. And hurry. We've only half a bell."

Dorian looked shocked when he saw her.

It was the scarlet, Annoura decided. Jiarine had chosen well. Red was the color of the *shei'dalins*, but it was also the color of blood. Like the blood that would soon flow across Celieria's northern borders. Like the blood that gushed from a mortally wounded heart.

His eyes darkened, and his brows drew together in a troubled frown. "Annoura . . ." He reached for her hands.

She drew them back out of his reach and clasped them at her waist. "Our people are waiting, Sire."

His expression went blank. Not quite as stony as the Fey

could manage, but close enough. "Then let us go to them, madam." He turned and held out his arm.

When she laid her hand over his, she was glad for the scarlet satin of the gloves she wore. Dorian was Fey enough to sense her thoughts and sometimes her emotions when she touched him skin-to-skin. In the past, that connection had been a special bond, something that had drawn them closer, until at times they could think and act as one. But now, such insight into her broken heart would only be an unwanted intrusion and a humiliation.

They walked stiffly towards the open doors leading to the grand stair at the front of the palace. And each step that rang out against the polished marble palace floors tolled like a death knell, echoing forlornly in the vast, cold silence of the empty palace.

Outside, the sun shone too bright for a day of such sorrow. The palace courtyard was packed with armored soldiers and cavalry horses. Brilliant blue, white, and gold banners waved in the breeze. Beyond the palace gates, the populace of Celieria City had gathered. The people gave a great roaring cheer when Dorian and Annoura stepped forth.

Dorian did not pause for speeches. He'd already given enough of those to the Council of Lords and to the populace these last days, explaining why it was necessary for the sons, husbands, and fathers of Celieria to march to war—and why even more would be accompanying Prince Dorian when he left for the coast the following week. Now, he and Annoura simply walked down the stone palace steps to their waiting mounts. The lords and ladies of the court followed and mounted their own gaily caparisoned steeds and took up silken banners. The pipers and drummers in the infantry ranks began to play, and with great celebration and pomp, Dorian, Annoura, and the court led the army north through the city to King's Gate and the start of the North Road.

All along the roadside, from the palace to King's Gate, the

inhabitants of Celieria had come to watch their soldiers depart. They waved and cheered and threw small bouquets of flowers in the cobbled street before the procession. From second- and third-story windows lining the thoroughfare, flower petals and scented ribbons showered down.

War was such a great, lovely spectacle.

At least, Annoura thought bitterly, until its dreadful ravages arrived upon one's own doorstep.

«*Annoura* . . . »

Behind her veils, Annoura closed her eyes as Dorian's voice brushed against her mind. He could weave Spirit well enough to speak without words. Before now, every time he'd spun words directly into her mind, it had always seemed like a caress, an intimate secret between them, private and treasured.

Now the trust between them had been broken.

Stop it, Dorian. Get out of my mind. She couldn't weave Spirit, but she knew he would hear her. He was there at the periphery of her mind, listening for her answer.

«*I ride for war, wife. There is a possibility I will not return. I don't want harsh words to be the last between us.*»

Then perhaps you should not have spoken them. Nor dismissed me from your presence like a lackey. I will never forgive you for that. Anger bubbled up, acid and burning.

«*Annoura.*»

We are here at the gates. The party had arrived at the great, majestic arch on the northern side of the city. She pulled on the reins and brought her mount to a halt. *Lead your men. Go to your war. Be with your friends, the Fey. They are the only ones you truly love.*

He leaned across, caught her horse's reins, and brought her up short. "Enough." With a kick of his heels, he brought his horse alongside hers. "I would bid you farewell, wife."

He lifted her veils before she could stop him, and his face froze at the sight of hers. She caught his wrists in a fierce grip. "Haven't you humiliated me enough?" she hissed. "Leave me some shred of dignity." The veils slid from his unresisting fingers and fell back into place.

"Annoura . . ."

Her jaw clenched and she had to force the next declaration out through a tight throat. "You . . . *hurt* me." Her voice cracked, and she had to pause to regain her composure. "You promised me you never would, but you did." She drew a deep breath and pulled icy calm around her like armor. "It will never happen again." The invisible distance between them widened to a chasm.

The softness faded from Dorian's eyes and face. "Very well, madam. Since you are determined to put your pride between us, I take my leave of you. We will speak again when I return from this war. Until then, may the gods keep you and our children safe." With a stiff nod, he clucked to his mount, tugged the reins, and rode away. The army followed him, pipers and drummers still playing their joyous march to war.

Annoura stared blindly forward as the army of Celieria passed by. Her sheer scarlet veils fluttered around her face, casting the world in a wash of blood and catching on the damp tracks of her tears.

CHAPTER THIRTEEN

Celieria City ~ The Royal Palace

"Your Majesty, I've taken the liberty of preparing a little surprise for you." Jiarine Montevero gave Queen Annoura her most charming smile. The court had just returned from seeing the king's army off, and most of the courtiers were partaking of a sumptuous banquet on the terrace.

"I'm very tired, Jiarine," the queen replied, "and I'm not fond of surprises."

"Indulge me, Your Majesty. I promise you will like this one. I thought you might desire some peace and quiet away from the court."

The queen was still heavily veiled, so Jiarine could not see her expression, but her years of dancing attendance on Annoura had not gone to waste. The queen hesitated. "What did you have in mind?"

There was just enough curiosity in Annoura's voice. "I've prepared a private meal for you in the south garden, Your Majesty." The south garden was a walled retreat, well away from the noisier lawns and gardens frequented by the rest of the court. Its use was reserved exclusively for the royal family.

Annoura's veiled figure went stiff. "His Majesty granted you permission to use the south garden?"

"No, ma'am," she answered smoothly. "I didn't ask His Majesty. I asked His Highness, the prince. He thought it was a wonderful idea." When Annoura hesitated a moment more, she added, "I've arranged for your favorite food and music. I could keep you company, if you like, or you could be all alone, uninterrupted, away from the prying eyes of the court."

The queen capitulated. "Oh, very well. I suppose I could use a few bells of peace and solitude."

Gaspare Fellows had lost sight of Lord Bolor.

The nobleman had been here, on the terrace, partaking of the luncheon banquet following the departure of the king's army. Gaspare had turned to answer a question from one of the courtiers, and when he looked back, Lord Bolor was gone.

He hurried to the edge of the terrace and scanned the castle grounds. Though he couldn't see Lord Bolor, a flash of scarlet veils caught his eye. In the distance, he could see Jiarine Montevero leading what looked like a *shei'dalin* away from the palace.

Gaspare's heart began to race. The queen had worn scarlet

and veils this morning. He lurched forward and Love gave a tiny screech of alarm at the sudden movement.

This morning's pursuit of Lord Bolor had resulted in more questions than answers. After leaving Old Castle Prison, Lord Bolor had traveled to a pub located near the main barracks of the king's army. There, he'd met a young man wearing the uniform of a lieutenant.

Gaspare hadn't been able to get close enough to hear what they were saying, but had managed to get a good look at the soldier on his way out: a young brown-haired man with a distinctive, brownish red birthmark on his left cheek—Shadow's brand, superstitious folk would have called it. It was a wonder the man had made it to a lieutenancy with a mark like that on his face.

The soldier had returned to the barracks, and Gaspare had continued to follow Lord Bolor, but the nobleman had returned straightaway to his rooms in the palace, presumably to prepare for the king's departure. The rest of the morning had passed without incident. Lord Bolor had gathered with the rest of the court to cheer the king and his army, and though Gaspare had watched him intently throughout the procession, he'd seen nothing more to rouse his suspicions.

Yet suspicious he still remained.

And now here was Jiarine Montevero leading the queen away from the palace towards the secluded south garden. And Lord Bolor had just disappeared. Presumably into the palace gardens.

Call him a crack-skull, but something about the situation just didn't feel right.

With no thought in his mind but to stop the queen from going wherever Lady Montevero was leading her, Gaspare snatched up a plate of food and a goblet of red wine and hurried across the palace lawn.

He was out of breath, and half the wine in the goblet had left a trail in the grass behind him, but he managed to get ahead of the women and step into their path. "Your Majesty! I spotted you across the garden. Your Majesty, I heard about your distress, and I know you have not eaten this morning. I took the liberty of bringing you a small plate. I thought you might prefer to eat a little something in private, away from the court."

"Very thoughtful, Master Fellows," Jiarine said, "but as a matter of fact—"

"Please, Your Majesty," Gaspare said quickly. "To put my worries to rest, won't you have a little something?" He stepped towards them, and with a sigh of farewell to his impeccable reputation as the man who never put a foot wrong, Gaspare Fellows, the Queen's Master of Graces, tripped on his own feet. The plate of food and red wine went flying.

Directly into Her Majesty.

"You idiot!" Jiarine shrieked. "You fool! Look what you've done!"

"Oh, Your Majesty!" Gaspare all but fell over himself a second time to apologize. "Please forgive me. I'm so sorry! So very, very sorry!" He whipped out a spotless handkerchief to wipe up the mess.

"Master Fellows!" the queen exclaimed. "Enough! That's enough! You're only making it worse!" She batted his hands away.

"Your Majesty—" he began again.

"Not another word, Master Fellows. Not one. I am returning to the palace. Jiarine, you will attend me." Still veiled, but smeared from bodice to hem with red wine and food stains, the queen gathered her royal dignity, lifted her soiled skirts, and marched stiffly back to the palace. With a final hostile look at Master Fellows, Jiarine hurried after her.

Gaspare trailed behind them, trying his best to look inconsolably embarrassed and apologetic. Not that it was difficult. He'd just shattered his reputation and pride for love of queen and country. But the moment Her Majesty and Lady Montevero entered the palace, Gaspare went directly to the first Fey warrior he could find and warned him, "Whatever you do, please make sure someone watches the queen at all times."

Elvia ~ Elfwood

Ellysetta stifled a groan and rubbed her backside, spinning a light healing weave as she hobbled over to the campfire. After they'd crossed the Elva River this morning, Elves had been waiting with *ba'houda* horses to speed the rest of their journey to Navahele. As smooth as the *ba'houdas'* gait had been, Ellysetta wasn't used to riding—let alone riding for bells at a stretch—and she'd developed aches in spots she didn't even know she had.

Rain watched her with a mix of concern and amusement. "If it hurts that badly, you should spin healing on yourself," he suggested. He and her quintet—except for Bel, who'd claimed first watch—were ringed around the fire, preparing for sleep. "Or let me spin a Spirit weave to take away the pain." Though every warrior with the appropriate talents learned emergency battlefield healing weaves—basic patterns used to stanch mortal wounds and keep injured warriors alive long enough to get to a *shei'dalin*—few had ever mastered more than that.

"I'm too tired to weave, and you should still be conserving your strength."

"I can spin a healing weave on you, Ellysetta Erimea," Fanor offered, but before he could get the words out, her pain vanished in a tingling glow of powerful lavender magic.

"Rain," she chided.

His arms tightened around her. "I am not so weak that I cannot spin a simple weave," he said. «*Nor so far gone I would let an Elf provide a shei'tan's service to my mate.*»

She rolled her eyes at his territorialism. To Fanor, she said, "You keep calling me Ellysetta Erimea. What does it mean?"

"Erimea is the Elvish name for the star Celierians call Selena."

Her brows drew together in faint alarm. "Selena?" Selena

was a seasonal star that appeared low on the horizon just before the first day of Seledos, the winter month dedicated to the God of Darkness, and shone in the sky throughtout that ill-favored month when the golden bells of daylight were the shortest of the year. "Why would you call me that?"

"It is what we Elves have always named you. Why does this alarm you?"

"Because Selena is the winter star Celierians call 'Shadows Light,' and they don't mean it kindly. Children born when Selena shines in the sky are considered touched by Shadow. They say those born beneath Selena when the moons are new will be haunted by Darkness all of their lives." Dear gods . . . was it possible she had been born on such a night? Was that why the Elves had named her after such an ill-favored star?

Fanor muttered something in Elvish. She didn't understand the words, but the tone sounded uncomplimentary. "If Celierians believe that, they are fools. Erimea is the brightest light in the winter sky. We Elves call her Hope's Light, the star that shines brightest when the world is at its darkest."

Ellysetta glanced uncertainly at Rain.

He gave her hand a reassuring squeeze. «Las, shei'tani. Nei siad. Don't be afraid. Much as I dislike the Elves, when it comes to matters of omens and stars, I'll take their word over mortal superstition any day.»

When she continued to frown, Rain said, "Enough talking. Time to sleep."

Fanor took the hint. He bowed and rejoined his men on the other side of camp. Rain patted the space beside him. He'd shed the hard plates of his golden war steel and chain mail and lay in the scarlet padded-silk tunic he wore underneath.

With a sigh, Ellysetta knelt beside him and nestled in his arms, resting her head on his chest. The steady beat of his heart sounded softly in her ear. He gestured and the quintet spun their shielding weaves to protect Ellysetta from her

Mage-haunted dreams. Rain added his own five-fold weave to theirs.

"Rain," she scolded again. "You promised you would conserve your strength. Fanor said a single five-fold weave would be enough to shield my dreams in Elvia."

"If one is good, then two are better." He traced the curve of her lips with one finger. "Humor me, Ellysetta. It pains me to see the fear in your eyes when you wake. To know that I cannot protect you from what haunts you."

She pressed a kiss into his palm. "You are with me. That is protection enough."

"I will always be with you." «*Even should I die.*»

Ellysetta frowned at him. "Really, Rain. You need to stop talking that way." She shook her head. "Or, rather, thinking that way. You keep thinking about dying, as if you've already accepted it as your fate, and I don't like it."

A faint flush colored his cheeks. "*Sieks'ta, shei'tani.* I didn't realize I'd said it so you could hear."

"Well, you did, and you shouldn't." She propped herself up on an elbow and regarded him earnestly. "The gods listen, Rain. Put a thought out there often enough, and they'll think it's what you want."

"Death is not what I want, Ellysetta. Believe me, even if that's what the gods have in store for me, I won't go without a fight."

"You won't go at all," she corrected fiercely. "I won't let you. I'll fight every demon in the Well of Souls if I have to."

To that, he merely smiled and said, "Come here, *kem'feyreisa shanis.*"

She resisted his efforts to pull her close. "I mean it, Rain." He could call her his fierce Feyreisa all he wanted, but she wouldn't be diverted.

"I know, *kem'san.* I have seen you do it, remember? Now, come here and let me hold you. It's time to sleep. Tomorrow will be another long day."

With a sigh, she turned on her side, and he spooned his

body around hers. One arm draped across her waist. She snuggled back into his warmth. He'd shed his blades and steel, but the body beneath was nearly as hard as the shell of armor, his long, lean form honed by centuries of training and discipline. Silky, fragrant skin, shining silver in the darkness, was his body's only softness. The realization comforted her. It was almost as if he were her armor, her living shield against the Darkness that hunted her.

She looked into the Elvian night sky, where silvery stars winked and shimmered against the black velvet of night. Soon, for that one month of the year, when the days were their shortest and nights their longest, Selena—Erimea— would appear, a fierce light gleaming low on the horizon, the brightest star in the darkest winter sky.

But which, she wondered, was the true name of that star? Was it Selena, Shadow's Light, a dreaded and fearful harbinger of the Dark, as the Celierians believed? Or was it Erimea, Hope's Light, the Bright Lord's promise that even in a world grown cold and dark, his Light would still shine triumphant?

And which, she wondered, would she be?

CHAPTER FOURTEEN

A flick of wrists, a seldom miss.
A deadly song, the Dance goes on.
So learn it well, this warrior's spell.
    For a killing blade,
    Means many lives saved.

              Dance of Knives, a warrior's poem
              by the *chatok* Remal v'En Alathir

Celieria ~ Celieria City

Lord Bolor was meeting with the young lieutenant again—
the one with the unfortunate birthmark on his face.

Gaspare Fellows hung back in the shadowy corner of the
Spear and Shield pub across from the army barracks and kept
his eye on the two men. He had to admit Bolor was a genius
to arrange his meeting here, in the middle of a bustling pub at
lunchtime. It was so open, so crowded, who would believe a
Mage of Eld would arrange an assignation with one of his
minions in such a public spot?

Assuming, of course, that Lord Bolor actually *was* an Elden
Mage.

For four days, Gaspare had surreptitiously followed Lord
Bolor about the city. He'd watched the nobleman meet with a
variety of individuals, from rabble-rousing pamphleteers and
bully boys to shopkeepers, wealthy merchants, and lords of the

realm, and even on one occasion a priest in the Church of Light. That was the problem: Most of the individuals seemed to be normal, ordinary people going on about their normal, ordinary lives. Several were decidedly unsavory, but then, many a fine lord had been known to utilize the services of such men.

And since most of Lord Bolor's actual meetings had taken place behind closed doors or in locations not conducive to eavesdropping, Gaspare still had no proof that Lord Bolor was anything more than a nobleman with an eclectic collection of acquaintances.

This second meeting with the lieutenant in the king's army was Gaspare's best chance to discover what Lord Bolor was up to. Patting the kitten-size bulge in the leather courier's pouch at his hip, he began to stealthily work his way across the crowded pub. He'd nearly reached the table where Lord Bolor and the lieutenant were sitting when Love let out a terrible screech and began to squirm and claw like a mad thing inside her pouch. Lord Bolor turned so suddenly Gaspare had to dive behind a wooden support beam to avoid being seen.

When he gathered up the nerve to peer around the corner of the beam, Lord Bolor and the lieutenant were heading for the exit. He flipped open the flap of his leather pouch and scowled down at the furry white face of his disgruntled pet. "For shame, Love. You'll get us caught if you keep that up!"

Blue eyes blinked with feline innocence. "Mrowwwr?" Her soft head butted against his hand, begging for a chin scratch. With a sigh, he obliged, then fished a treat from his coat pocket and held it out so she could nibble it from his fingers.

"Spoiled puss," he chided with a fond smile. "Now be good, hmm?" He gave her head a final scratch and closed the pouch flap again.

Lord Bolor and his friend passed through the pub door. Gaspare darted after them. The lieutenant appeared to be heading back to the barracks, while Lord Bolor had turned left and was walking down the cobbled street towards the wharf.

Gaspare waited for him to turn the corner, then followed. He kept his distance, but even so, once or twice when Lord Bolor paused or turned his head, Gaspare had to flatten himself against the side of a building or dodge into an alleyway to avoid being seen. Love, fortunately, kept her silence.

He turned down one of the narrow side streets leading to the wharf, and his steps slowed. He frowned at the empty street. Lord Bolor had turned down this street, he was sure of it, but the narrow, cobbled way was empty. He turned around, searching the dank, shadowy corners of the buildings that lined either side of the street, but there was no sign of Lord Bolor.

Had the man realized he was being followed and sped up in an effort to lose his pursuer?

Gaspare jogged towards the far end of the street, hoping to catch sight of his quarry there, but Love began to hiss and then to screech in protest. The sides of the leather courier's pouch bulged and writhed. Near the end of the street, just a stone's throw from the Velpin River, he paused to flip open the flap of Love's carrying pouch and hissed, "Quiet, Love! He'll hear you!"

A cold, familiar voice said, "Too late," and Gaspare spun around in shock. His eyes went wide. The breath rushed from his lungs in a sudden, painful rush as ice stabbed into his belly and ripped its way up to his chest.

The empty air of the alleyway shimmered with faint sparkles of light, and the figure of Lord Bolor became visible. His eyes were bottomless wells of darkness that glittered with malevolent red lights. The corner of his mouth curled in a sneer. "Did your mother never tell you, Master Fellows, that curiosity killed the cat?"

Impaled to the hilt on a blade clutched in Lord Bolor's hand, Gaspare couldn't twitch a muscle. He could literally feel his blood and his soul being sucked out of him, as if the blade in his belly were some evil, ravenous leech.

Bolor's terrifying eyes flashed, and the hand clutching the

dagger gave a hard thrust, driving the weapon deeper. He lifted his free hand towards Gaspare's face. "Before you die, you're going to tell me everything you've seen and everyone you've told about it."

Magic gathered at his fingertips. Sensing it, Love screeched like the possessed and struggled out of her pouch. Needle-sharp claws dug into Gaspare's side as she scrambled up his torso. When she reached his shoulder, she launched herself, claws bared, fur standing on end, straight into Lord Bolor's face.

Bolor gave a shout of surprise and stumbled back, flailing as the crazed cat clawed at his face.

Gaspare could feel his strength draining away. His hands gripped the hilt of the blade buried in his belly and yanked it free. A dark jewel, glowing deep red, topped the end of the wavy black blade. Clutching the hilt in one hand and his bleeding abdomen with the other, he staggered into the road that ran alongside the river. "Help," he cried weakly. "Help me."

In the alley, Love gave a mighty screech. Gaspare glanced back to see Lord Bolor peel the kitten off his face and fling her to the cobbles. Love landed hard, but on her feet, and arched her back, hissing and spitting. A ball of glowing blue-white light formed in Lord Bolor's palm. Gaspare had never seen Mage Fire, but he'd heard about it and seen depictions of it in the war paintings hanging in the National Museum of Art.

"Run, Love!" he cried as Bolor flung the ball of deadly magic at the kitten. Gaspare still clutched the Mage's knife in his hand. He threw it at Bolor with all of his rapidly dwindling strength. The blade fell short of its mark, but the distraction was enough to jar Bolor's aim. His Mage Fire hit the side of the building, a bare handspan from Love's head. The brick wall of the building simply . . . disappeared.

Love screeched and skittered away, darting around the corner of the building.

The Mage whirled on Gaspare, his snarling face hatched

with bleeding furrows. A fresh ball of Mage Fire gathered in his palm.

Blood poured from Gaspare's wound, soaking the fine wool of his trousers. His mouth had gone dry, his knees weak. He knew he was dying. Even so, when the Mage drew back his hand to launch his lethal magic, Master Fellows knew *that* was not the way he wanted to leave this world.

The ball of blue-white light came roaring towards him. Gaspare did the only thing he could: He turned and dove for the Velpin.

Nour cursed as he watched Gaspare Fellows disappear over the stone embankment lining the river. He dabbed at his bleeding face and hissed at the resulting stab of pain. Darkness take the meddling little *rultshart*—and that demon-spawn cat of his, too.

Celieria's Master of Graces had made a regular nuisance of himself, always showing up at inconvenient times and ruining Nour's plans to ingratiate himself with Celieria's queen. And now this. That Mage Fire would bring every Fey in the city running.

Nour spun swift weaves to erase the signs of his presence, then ran across the road to finish off whatever was left of Fellows, but when he peered over the embankment to the river below, there was no sign of the Master of Graces.

Pounding bootheels on the cobbles and the sound of shouting voices told him it was time to go. Nour snatched up his Mage blade, pulled the hood of his cloak up over his face, and ran into the alley.

He couldn't go back to the palace with his face in shreds, so he headed for the boardinghouse near the wharf district. He would hole up there while he summoned a hearth witch to repair his face, changed out of these blood-soiled clothes, and tried to find a way to turn the murder of Gaspare Fellows to his best advantage.

He hadn't thought to plant a Fey blade at the scene to

throw suspicion on the Fey or *dahl'reisen*, and he couldn't very well go back now to leave one. But perhaps he could still sow the seeds of doubt in Annoura's mind. Perhaps this was just the foothold he needed to gain her trust. After all, when it came to politics, didn't most leaders follow the ancient Merellian maxim: "The enemy of my enemy is my friend"?

The scorched scent of Mage Fire still hung in the air when the Fey arrived at the riverside, but of the Mage who'd spawned that Fire, there was no sign. The warriors searched the roads, alleys, and buildings in a three-block radius, but they couldn't even find a witness who had seen what happened. The Mage had covered his tracks too well.

"Well, my brothers, he was here, without a doubt, but he's gone now." Ilian vel Taranis stood near the top of the stone steps leading to the river landing where boats could moor.

A feline howl rose up from the stairwell, followed by the sound of claws scrabbling on stone. A small white cat shot out of the stairwell like an Elf bolt and raced down the street.

Ilian would have dismissed the animal as one of the many feral cats that prowled the wharf except for the distinctive flash of Celierian blue around its neck. A bow. A blue satin bow, to be precise.

White cat. Blue bow. Bad temper.

What in the Bright Lord's name was Master Fellows's spoiled princess of a cat doing alone by the city wharf?

"Vel Mera, catch that cat!" he cried to the warrior standing in the white kitten's path.

Rorin vel Mera flung a net of Earth magic around the cat, and the kitten went into a frenzy, hissing, spitting, and clawing like a mad thing.

"Scorch me," Rorin muttered. "This little beast can Rage like a tairen."

"You frightened her." Ilian frowned at his blade brother, then knelt beside the terrified cat and attempted to soothe it. "Here, now, kit. Here, now. *Las. Las.* We'll not harm you." He reached for the kitten and got four bleeding furrows across the back of his hand for his trouble. He persisted despite the wounding, and a few chimes later, he rose to his feet, Master Fellows's white kitten clutched to his chest.

"You think Master Fellows could be our Mage?" Rorin asked. The Master of Graces had made a nuisance of himself with stories of Mages attempting to harm the queen, and though the Fey had dutifully investigated his every claim, they'd found nothing to substantiate his fears.

Ilian held up his unscratched hand—the one now smeared with the still-damp blood spattering the white kitten's fur. "I think it's more likely Master Fellows was following his Mage, hoping to find evidence enough that we would believe him. And from the looks of it, he got caught." With a sinking sensation in his stomach, he said, "Let's search the river. If the Mage Fire didn't get him, he might have jumped for it."

They fanned out and began searching, calling more Fey to aid them.

Ten chimes later, they found him, two tairen lengths downstream, tucked into a culvert that fed the runoff from the city's storm drains into the Velpin. He was soaked in his own blood and hovering on the cusp of death.

Elvia ~ Elfwood

The Fey and their Elvian escort stopped to rest and eat at midday. After a quick meal, Ellysetta's quintet gathered off to one side to practice their swordplay. Ellysetta watched them, laughing as Gaelen amused himself by taunting his brothers and trying to goad them into foolish attacks.

"That was so slow, vel Sibboreh, it was nearly decrepit. An old mortal could move faster than that."

Tajik was too smart to take the bait. He just laughed evilly, flipped back his red plaits, and said, "*Aiyah*, and you should know, vel Serranis. You'd already seen well beyond your first five hundred years before I was even a glow in my *gepa's* eye."

"Ha!" *Meicha* scimitars drawn, Gaelen suddenly lunged for Tajik. The former commander of the Fey's eastern army brought his own weapons up to block, and twisted lithely out of the way, then spun around to attack Gaelen's unprotected back. Anticipating the move, Gaelen ducked, rolled, and came up with his blades in a blocking position so that Tajik's swords landed harmlessly on gleaming steel.

"Not bad for an old Fey," Tajik told him with a grin.

"You should know," Gaelen retorted. "As you are one yourself."

Ellysetta laughed at the verbal skirmish. Their taunting exchanges had begun to lose the curt hostility that had marred their relationship. She had started to hope that Tajik's initial distrust of Gaelen might even eventually change from grudging admiration to cautious friendship as Gaelen continued to teach the others the weaves and battle skills he'd perfected during his centuries as a *dahl'reisen*.

A short distance away, Rijonn, Bel, and Gil practiced hitting distant targets with their Fey'cha, striving to achieve the blurring speed with which Gaelen could so effortlessly launch his own daggers.

Ellysetta watched them and within a few chimes found her hands reaching for her own Fey'cha. "Can you teach me how to do that?" she asked.

Gil and Rijonn looked at her in surprise.

"You wish to learn the Dance of Knives? But why?" Surprise and disapproval mingled in Gil's starry eyes. Fey women didn't learn weapons skills. Their empathic sensitivity made them incapable of taking a life without losing their own.

But Ellysetta wasn't like other Fey women. "Because we're going to war, and at the very least, I should learn how to defend myself."

"Defending you is our job," Gil said.

"And if you're wounded—or dead? If I'm *sel'dor*-shot like Rain was and can't call my magic?" She shook her head. "I should at least know how to protect myself."

"Teach her," Fanor said quietly when the Fey hesitated. Everyone turned towards him. "I do not know all the verses of her Song," he told them soberly, "but those I have Seen are fraught with peril. The gods did not intend her for a path of peace. The kindest service you could offer would be to prepare her for that purpose. She will need all her strength and skills to meet what lies ahead."

The quintet looked to Rain for direction. He turned to Ellysetta.

"I need to do this," she told him. "I cannot stay helpless."

"You are far from that."

"You know what I mean."

His sigh spoke of fear and regret mingled with grim acceptance. "Teach her," he said. "Teach her to fight. Teach her to defend herself, and teach her to kill. The five of you must be her *chatoks* in the Dance of Knives. Teach her as you have taught no other. Give her everything. Hold nothing back."

"Rain . . ." Bel murmured, his eyes troubled.

Rain waved off his unspoken objection. "She is a Tairen Soul, and we Tairen Souls were born for war. I may not like this path the gods have set before her, but Farsight is right. I must do everything in my power to ensure she is prepared to walk it."

"Fey'cha," Bel explained, "are weighted in the center to ensure a perfect circular arc as the blades travel through the air. The most basic grip—the first a *chadin* learns in his dance of knives—is the *takaro*, the hammer. . . ." He showed her how to grasp the knife with her fingers and thumb curled around the hilt. "Your stance gives you balance and adds strength to your throw, as does the manner in which you draw back and release your blades."

He demonstrated the slightly crouched stance—right foot forward, left foot back a pace—that would give her arm the most power for the throw. "The first throw all *chadin* learn is an overhanded throw called *Desriel'chata*—Death's Bite. You pull your arm back like so." He bent her arm at the elbow and guided the hand gripping the knife back over her shoulder. "Then, when you are ready to throw, you snap the arm forward and release your grip no later than here in your swing." He raised his forearm to stop the slow downward motion of her arm.

"Watch. See the knot in that silverfir tree there?" He pointed to a tall, broad-trunked fir tree a few man lengths away. "I will use that as my target." Using the same grip and stance he'd just shown her, Bel drew a black-handled Fey'cha from his own chest harness, cocked his arm, then threw it in one smooth whip of motion. The blade flew from his hand in a blur and it thunked home in the tree trunk moments later. "Any questions?"

Ellysetta shook her head.

"*Kabei*, then you try. Take your stance." He nodded approvingly when she positioned her feet and crouched as he'd shown her. "Get a good grip on your blade. *Aiyah*, just like that. Now, draw back your arm. Keep your eye on the target."

Ellysetta drew back her arm and fixed her gaze on the dark knot in the silverfir tree. The world narrowed down to a slender, focused tunnel and she could almost see the line that her blade would need to take to hit the target. The grip didn't feel comfortable in her hand, so she moved her thumb parallel to the knife blade, pressing lightly on the spine.

"And now throw," Bel said.

Her arm snapped forward. The blade left her hand and cartwheeled through the air in perfect silver circles. It thunked into the exact center of the tree . . . several handspans below the knot that had been her target.

The miss surprised Ellysetta more than it should have. Once she'd changed her grip on the blade, she'd been so sure she understood the angle, the throw, the blade's trajectory. As if she'd thrown the same blade a thousand times.

"Don't look so disappointed," Bel said. "The throw itself was well-done. We just need to work on your aim."

Rijonn walked over to the tree to extract the blade. "You had decent strength in your throw, too," he announced. "The blade sank two fingerspans deep into the tree." He pulled the blade from the tree and sent it spinning towards Bel with a flick of his wrist.

Bel snatched the Fey'cha out of the air with casual ease and handed it back to Ellysetta, hilt first. "Try again, *kem'falla*."

She waited for Rijonn to clear out of the way, then sent the next dagger spinning towards the tree. Once again it sank, quivering, into a spot below the knot she'd been aiming for.

"Well, you're consistent, at least," Gil said with a grin.

He tossed back the blade, and Bel handed it to Ellysetta again. "This is why *chadins* practice for so many years. Give it another try."

She threw the blade a third time, and a fourth and fifth. Always, the result was the same: She consistently hit the center of the tree, but below her target.

"Throw again," Gaelen commanded, his eyes narrowed slightly. "But this time, don't aim for the knot; aim for this." His hand flicked out. Green magic swirled from his fingertips, and a red circle appeared on the tree above the knot.

Ellysetta took aim, cocked back her hand, and flung the Fey'cha at the red circle on the tree. The dagger cartwheeled through the air and struck the tree dead center in the middle of the knot she'd missed every other time.

She gave a rueful laugh. "Now I hit it."

"*Kabei*. Now, try this one." Gaelen spun Earth again and another red dot appeared on a tree much, much farther away. "Do you see it?"

"You've got to be joking." The tree was at least two tairen lengths away.

"Can you see it?"

Ellysetta squinted. "Barely." The new target was little more than a pinpoint of scarlet against the distant tree.

"*Kabei*. Now try to hit it."

"Gaelen, don't be a dim-skull." Bel scowled at his friend.

"Shh." Gaelen put a finger to his lips. "*Kem'falla?* Take aim and throw your blade."

"It's too far," Bel protested. "If she can't hit a larger target at a third the distance, how do you expect her to hit a pinpoint at two tairen lengths?"

"Humor me. *Teska*, Ellysetta, take your stance."

Bel rolled his eyes but stepped back so Ellysetta could take clear aim at her target. She set her feet and drew back her throwing arm.

"Concentrate," Gaelen advised. "Calculate the distance, the force you will need to throw so far. See the blade's path in your mind. Do you see it?"

"I think so."

"Then throw."

Her arm whipped forward. The blade whirled through the air in a swift, blurred arc. It hit the target tree dead center . . . but again well below the red dot.

"Well-done, *kem'falla*," Gaelen praised. "Well-done indeed."

She scowled. "Well-done if you want me to hit consistently below my target, you mean."

"*Nei.* Your aim was perfect. You hit a target the size of a sand fly from two tairen lengths away."

Bel gave a disbelieving laugh. "I think you need the Feyreisa to check your eyesight, *kem'maresk*. She missed that tiny little red dot by two handspans, at least."

"The red dot wasn't the target." A slow, satisfied smile spread over Gaelen's face. "'Jonn, go inspect her blade. Tell me what you see."

The Earth master shot forward with a speed that seemed incongruous with his great height, and his exceedingly long legs crossed the distance in no time. "There's a second target," he called, "and she hit it dead-on. Gil, come look at this."

Curious, the black-eyed Fey leapt off the fallen log he'd been sitting on and ran to join his friend. After a brief inspection and an exchange of words Ellysetta couldn't hear, Gil yanked the blade from the tree and he and Rijonn came running back.

"There was a second target." Gil held up the Fey'cha. A small circle of brown leather was pinned to its tip.

Rain, who had hung back with the Elves to observe Ellysetta's lessons, stepped forward. "Let me see." He held out a hand for Ellysetta's Fey'cha. The brown leather circle at its tip had been sliced almost in two—dead center, just as Gaelen had said.

"I wasn't aiming for that," Ellysetta confessed. "I never even saw it."

Gaelen's smile grew wider. "I know, Ellysetta. I made the real target brown specifically so you *wouldn't* see it. But I put it where your blade would hit if your aim at the red circle was true."

"I don't understand." She took back her Fey'cha from Rain and returned it to its sheath. "How can you say my aim was true when I missed what I was aiming at?"

"Because your aim *was* true. It's your reach that is lacking."

"Explain," Rain said.

"It's actually easier to show you than tell you. If you would indulge me?" He waved Rain and the others back. "This will require a little room."

Ellysetta had turned to watch Rain back up a short distance, when suddenly Gaelen called, "Ellysetta, *bote hamanas!*" Hands at the ready!

That was all the warning he gave her before one of his own black-handled blades flew through the air straight towards her.

Her mind froze in surprise, but an instinct she'd never known she possessed took command of her body. Even before she realized what she was doing, she snatched the whirling blade out of the air and sent it flying back towards Gaelen in a single smooth, graceful motion.

He caught the dagger on its return flight with similar ease and launched a second blade immediately. He launched a third before the second even reached her hand, then a fourth and fifth shortly thereafter. She caught and returned each blade until there was a constant stream of Fey'cha arching through the air between them, and her hands moved with a blurring speed that matched Gaelen's own.

He spoke a word, and the Fey'cha disappeared in the blink of an eye, re-forming securely in the sheaths crisscrossing his chest. Silently, he dissolved the barrier of magic he'd erected to keep Rain and the others from rushing to Ellysetta's rescue when the first of his blades had flown.

The moment the weave was down, Rain leapt forward. His hand shot out and a hammer of power exploded from his fingertips. It slammed into Gaelen and knocked the former *dahl'reisen* off his feet, flinging him several man lengths through the air to smack into a tree. Rain snatched Ellysetta up into his arms, his eyes glowing fierce and deadly bright.

"Every time I begin to trust you, *vel Serranis*," he snarled, "you insist on proving me a fool for doing so. You dare throw a blade at my *shei'tani?*"

"She was never in any harm," Gaelen muttered. With a grimace, he peeled himself off the tree trunk and gingerly took two experimental steps.

"You didn't know that. What would have happened if she had not caught your Fey'cha?"

"Don't take me for such a dim-skull," Gaelen snapped. "I am her *lu'tan*. I would die before letting her come to the slightest harm—and you need to begin believing that. I can't have you trying to stop me every time I do something without explaining it to you first."

"And yet you knew I would distrust you. That shield was up even before you threw."

Gaelen grimaced. "I know you, Tairen Soul. But put your mind at ease. Before I threw my Fey'cha I spun a weave on them that would have invoked my return word if her catch were even a fraction off."

That admission mollified Rain. His tight, protective grip on Ellysetta loosened, and she slipped free.

"Next time, give a warning."

"I wanted to see what her instincts were. A warning would have negated the test."

"What sort of test, Gaelen?" Ellysetta asked in a shaken voice. She stared at her hands as if they belonged to someone else, then lifted her gaze to his.

Tajik answered in Gaelen's stead. "You reacted to his throw like a warrior dancing the Cha Baruk. Though how vel Serranis knew you would escapes me."

Cha Baruk, the Dance of Knives, was what the Fey called warfare, but it was also the name of the warriors' dance in which deadly blades were tossed back and forth in a show of power and dexterity. Ellysetta turned to Gaelen in confusion. "How did I manage to do that, when I haven't hit a single target I've aimed at since we began?"

"I spun a weave on the blades to make you see them as if they were a bit higher and farther away from your hand than they truly were."

"Why?" Rain asked, his eyes narrowing.

"For the same reason I drew a red circle on a tree when a brown circle was the real target. I knew where her hands would be when she saw my blades coming."

"And how did you know that?" Bel asked softly, his eyes steady on his friend's face.

"Because everything she has done since she gripped her first blade has been without flaw. Every throw she made, the way she held her blades, the way she released them— everything was exactly as I would have done it. The only difference is that I stand a head taller and my reach is a hand or two longer. No one—no matter how natural a talent—just picks up a blade and executes such perfect form the first time they handle a knife."

Gaelen turned to Ellysetta. "You modified the grip Bel showed you before you threw, to put your thumb on the spine of the blade for better guidance and surer aim. Why did you do that?"

"I . . ." She glanced at her hands in surprise. "I don't know. It just felt . . . *right* that way, more comfortable."

"I throw the *Desriel'chata* the same way. As does Gil. As did our mentor, Shannisoran v'En Celay. It was the grip he taught all his *chadins*."

"What are you getting at, Gaelen?" Rain demanded.

"Do you remember that time in Teleon, before we traveled through the Mists, when the seizure took her and she spoke the Warrior's Creed?"

"Of course. It's not something I would ever forget."

"Well, what if the Mages did more than just tie the soul of a tairen to hers? What if they tied the soul of a Fey warrior to hers as well? It would explain how she can kill without suffering the way our women do. And how she knows the words to the Warrior's Creed and throws *Desriel'chata* and dances the Cha Baruk like a Fey who long ago heard the Warriors' Gate whisper his name in greeting."

"You are suggesting that the soul of my *shei'tani* has been somehow . . . manufactured . . . by the Mages, pieced together from the souls of others. But you forget she is my truemate. That bond only the gods can forge between two souls. *Nei.*" He shook his head. "*Nei*, there must be some other explanation." Rain turned to the Elf in their midst. "You Saw my *shei'tani*'s need to wield steel like a warrior—did you also see this?"

Fanor shook his head. "*Anio*, but you should ask your question of the Elf king. He who is Guardian of the Dance Sees many things lesser Seers do not." The Elf waved a hand towards the crackling fire, where the spitted rabbits had turned golden crisp. "Come and eat. The food is ready, and we must ride again soon."

The Faering Mists

The beautiful Fey lady guided Lillis through the steep cliff paths of the Rhakis. As if in deference to the lady's presence, the Mists thinned while they walked so Lillis could see the tree-filled valley below.

"What is your name?" Lillis asked.

The lady smiled down at her and answered in Celierian. Her voice sounded like music. "You may call me Eiliss, little one."

"That's a pretty name. My name is Lillis. Where are we going?"

"Someplace where you will be safe."

Lillis scrambled over a hillock. "You're speaking Celierian now."

"Because that is the language you speak."

"Oh." Lillis accepted the answer without question. "Have you seen my Papa or my sister, Lorelle?"

Eiliss brushed the backs of her fingers across Lillis's cheek. "I have, *ajiana*. I'm taking you to them now."

"Really?" Tears of relief pooled in Lillis's eyes. "You mean they're safe?"

"They are, and soon you'll all be together. Will you like that?" The trail turned in a steep U and continued on downward another several tairen lengths before reaching the valley floor.

"Oh, yes." Snowfoot was purring quietly against her chest. The comfort of Eiliss's peaceful Fey presence soothed him, too. Lillis stroked the kitten's downy fur and scratched beneath his tiny black chin. His eyes closed in bliss and his purring grew louder. "What about Kieran and Kiel? Are they safe, too?"

"Their fate is not mine to know, but if they entered the Mists, they will find the welcome due all warriors of the Fey."

When Eiliss smiled into Lillis's eyes as she was doing now, Lillis just knew everything would turn out all right. Her concern for Kieran and Kiel melted away like the fingerling curls of mist swirling around them.

CHAPTER FIFTEEN

Elvia ~ Deep Woods

"Do you think Gaelen is right about a warrior's soul being tied to mine?"

Ellysetta and Rain walked along the crystalline banks of an indescribably beautiful Elvish river called the Dreamer, whose bed and banks were lined with sparkling cabochon jewels worn smooth by the river's gentle current.

After their bell's rest at lunchtime, they'd ridden hard and fast throughout the day, stopping only to rest and water their horses. They'd reached the river just before dusk and made camp. Tomorrow, they would cross the Dreamer and enter Deep Woods, the ancient forested heart of Elvia.

"You are a Tairen Soul," Rain replied. "Most of your abilities can be explained by that fact."

"But not the warrior's skills."

Ellysetta hadn't touched another blade since lunchtime, half-afraid of what other deadly skills and disturbing revelations might come if she did. All afternoon, she'd felt the curious and speculative gazes of the Elves—and even her quintet—upon her. Once more, she had become an oddity, a mystery, a puzzle to be solved, and she hated it.

"It occurred to me that the High Mage could be a swordsmaster and that I know how to throw a blade because he does," she confessed, when Rain didn't answer immediately. "But he wouldn't know the Cha Baruk, would he?" The tiny jewels that lined the riverbank like sand crunched beneath their boots as they walked.

"It is unlikely," Rain said. "*Chadin* train for three hundred years before they stand in the Dance as you did with Gaelen this afternoon."

"So then you *do* think Gaelen's right?"

"I don't know what to think." He stopped and turned to take her arms. "*Shei'tani*, I can see this troubles you, and I know my reaction earlier is partly to blame. Believe me when I say that any horror you sensed was not directed at you but rather at the idea that the Mages might have discovered how to manipulate truemating."

"Rain . . ."

"Here, feel for yourself." He took her hands in his, and her acute empathic senses—heightened further by their *shei'tanitsa* bond—could detect his sincerity. "No matter how your soul came into being, it is still the soul—the only soul—that calls to mine. And I would have it no other way." He brushed a curling tendril of hair back behind her ear. "*Ver'reisa ku'chae. Kem surah, shei'tani.*"

She did not doubt him. With his skin touching hers, his emotions as clear as words on a page, she could not. Still . . .

"But what if the next skill I discover isn't something good, Rain? What if it's something horrible?"

He gave her a smile so sad it nearly broke her heart. "You're speaking to the man who scorched the world, Ellysetta. There is little even a Mage could do that is worse than that."

"Rain . . ."

He bowed his head and resumed walking. "I do not pretend to understand how or why you can do most of the things you do. I merely accept all that you are, and wait for the day that you can do the same."

That was the crux of the matter. Rain struggled every day with his guilt at what he'd done, just as she struggled every day with her fear of what she one day *might* do—and not even just what she might do if the Mage claimed her soul. She was beginning to think Mama had been right to fear Ellie's magic and try to rid her of it.

"And if that day never comes, Rain? If I never can accept what I am?"

"You will. You seek answers to the questions you hesitate to voice—even though you fear what those answers might be. I see it each time you discover some new, unexpected talent." He reached up to stroke a hand through the thick, unbound curls spilling down her back. "You insist on thinking yourself a coward, when you are braver than any woman I've ever known. And though I do not much care for the Elves, there is no one better than Hawksheart to unravel the mysteries of your past and reveal the possibilities of your future."

"Our future," she corrected. He'd taken to doing that these last days since the Eld attack . . . talking about events to come as if he wouldn't be there to share them with her.

"Our future," he agreed. *For what little time we have left.*

"'What little time we have left'? Why do you keep saying things like that?" When he didn't answer, she stopped walking. "What's going on, Rain? I know you're not thinking of returning to the war without me, because I won't be left behind. We're stronger together than we are apart. I thought that was already settled."

"Ellysetta . . . *shei'tani* . . ."

He reached for her but she brushed his hand away. "Don't 'Ellysetta *shei'tani*' me. Talk to me. Tell me the truth."

"I always tell you the truth."

"*Nei*, you don't. You never lie, but you don't always tell the whole truth either. You simply don't talk about things you don't want me to know."

He opened his mouth, then wisely shut it again. "I do not want to worry you unnecessarily."

"Silence when I know something's wrong worries me more."

He lowered his eyes. The thick black lashes formed shadows on his cheeks in the moonlight and shielded the lavender glow of his eyes. "We are at war, Ellysetta. Much can happen. I am the Tairen Soul. I will lead each battle, and the Eld will make me their primary target."

"And none of that is any different than it has been since we left the Fading Lands."

He sighed. "Something is different." He gazed out at the river. The crystals lining the riverbed refracted the silvery moonlight, making the water dance with pale rainbows. "I am different."

"How so?"

He bent to pluck an oval crystal from the bank and rolled the stone slowly between his fingers.

"Rain?" she prompted.

With a swift flick of his wrist, he sent the crystal skimming across the river's surface. Each time it touched the water, a splash of bright color lit up and rippled out in concentric rings. When the stone sank, he turned a somber gaze upon her. "The bond madness has begun."

For a moment, her heart stopped beating. Her mind emptied of all thought, leaving only a disorienting buzzing. The world itself seemed to freeze for several long moments. She swallowed and licked suddenly parched lips. "H-how can you be sure?"

"I am sure."

"But how? What makes you think it?"

"The signs are beginning."

"What signs?"

"A moment ago, you heard my thoughts. I did not send them in Spirit, but you heard them nonetheless."

"Perhaps that's a sign of our bond becoming stronger."

"*Nei*. Our bond is strong—stronger now than it ever has been—but you cannot enter my mind at will until the union is complete. You heard my thoughts because I am losing the ability to keep them contained. It is one of the first effects of bond madness."

She frowned. "How can you be so sure that's what it is? Nothing else about me—about us—has followed Fey conventions. Why should this be any different?"

He smiled sadly. "I am sure. Each moment of the day, I make

a conscious effort to keep from broadcasting my thoughts. I have been doing so since the first battle at Orest. If I stop . . ." He closed his eyes. And just like that his thoughts were in her mind. Not on Spirit, not backed by power, and not because she was making the effort to hear them. They were just there, as clearly as if he'd spoken them aloud.

The first sign of bond madness is a Fey's inability to keep his thoughts private. He broadcasts them. First in moments of weariness or vulnerability, but then more frequently, until he cannot stop what is in his mind from spilling out. The next sign is difficulty controlling his temper, so he is swift to Rage. Then comes loss of control over his magic.

She clasped her hands together to stop their shaking. "How long?" She could barely force out the question. "How long do you have?" She loved him. She loved him more than she ever knew she could love someone. More than she loved Mama and Papa and even more than she loved the twins. In their few short months together, he'd become the foundation of her existence, the Great Sun that shone light on her world. She could not even contemplate the thought of a life without him.

"Not long. A few months, if the gods are kind." Swaths of straight, silky black hair brushed his cheek as his head drooped. "The war and all the souls I still bear upon mine will speed the madness. You saw yourself how quick I was to Rage that night the Eld attacked. I've been testing my control of magic since then, too. If I don't focus enough, my weaves don't spin as they should." He looked up. "Bel suspects the truth, but I would rather none of the others know until I can no longer maintain my control."

She tried to assimilate what he was saying, while her mind worked frantically to think of a solution, or at least a way to slow the progression of his madness until they could complete their bond. "I could try to heal you—to heal your soul as I healed the *rasa*."

He shook his head. "*Nei, shei'tani*. My soul is yours to heal, but only through the completion of our bond."

"But Rain—"

He pressed fingers to her lips. "Shh. *Las, shei'tani. Shei'tanitsa* bars you access to my thoughts and to my soul until you accept me into yours. Even if it did not, I know what it cost you to heal the *rasa*. I bear more death on my soul than Gaelen did when he was *dahl'reisen*, and I remember what it did to you when you touched him. Not even to save my own life could I allow you to go through that again."

"So you'd rather *die* than let me try? Rain!"

His jaw clenched in unyielding lines. "I would die a thousand times over before I let you suffer one-tenth of my torment—especially on my behalf."

"And what do you think I'll suffer when you're gone?" she cried. "I *love* you, Rain."

"And I love you, but there is only one cure for the bond madness. Without that, there is nothing to be done." He took her hands. "Let's not waste our time fighting a battle that cannot be won. Instead, let us concentrate on winning the one that can."

Ellysetta wanted to protest. She wanted to force Rain to let her at least try to heal him. But he was so certain it would not work—and so unwilling to risk hurting her—that she knew he would not be budged. She pulled out of his grip and stared blindly at the river.

He regarded his empty hands and sighed.

For several chimes, they stood there in silence, watching the river flow by. A fish leapt into the air, its scales shining like blue jewels in the moonlight. It splashed back into the water, and ripples of purple, green, and pink flowed out in vivid color.

Rain was the first to break the silence. "Farsight told me the Elves call this the river of true dreaming," he said. "Apparently the crystals in the riverbed absorb the light of the moons and the Great Sun and convert it into some sort of magical energy that Seers use to better understand their visions of the Dance. He suggested we might find a swim . . .

nlightening." He offered a coaxing smile. "I'm not at all fond
f Elvish mysticism, but I confess I thoroughly enjoyed the
ast time we swam in magical waters."

She turned to glare at him. "You tell me the bond madness
as begun. You refuse to let me try to heal your soul in order
o prolong your life, and less than five chimes later, you're
hinking about mating?"

White teeth flashed in a rueful smile. "I am your *shei'tan*.
No matter what other thoughts may occupy my mind, the
dea of mating with you is always among them."

When she did not respond to his humor in kind, the small
mile faded, replaced by sober, unflinching honesty. "There is
nough sorrow and danger in our lives. I am the Tairen Soul.
ven without the bond madness, how long we will have to-
ether in this life has never been certain. Mage Fire or a
el'dor bolt could take me in the next battle. Would you have
s spend what time we have bewailing our fate or would you
ather we drink every drop of happiness we can from each
noment we have together?"

He was right. Their lives could be cut short at any moment.
How could she waste even a moment of the time they had
ow mourning a future that might never happen? Tears shim-
nered in her eyes. "Rain . . ."

"Ssh. *Nei avi*." He cupped her face in his hands and kissed
er tears away, then took her mouth in a sweet, slow, tender
iss that robbed her of all regret. When he pulled back, his
ps curved in a slow smile, and in ancient, courtly Feyan, he
aid, "So, *shei'tani* . . . wilt thou swim with thy beloved in a
iver of dreams?"

Her lips trembled. He was dying now because of her, be-
ause she could not complete their bond. And yet, as his skin
ouched hers and his emotions flowed freely into hers, she
ould not detect a single trace of remorse or regret or blame.
He loved her unconditionally, even if that love would lead
im to his death.

She blinked back the tears he would not have her shed. Never could she have loved anyone more. Never had she felt more undeserving of him. "*Aiyah*." She stood up on her toes and found his mouth with hers. "*Kem'san. Kem'reisa. Kem'shei'tan*." She murmured the words against his mouth between kisses and sang them to his soul across the threads of their bond. "*Ke vo san*, Rainier Feyreisen. I love you."

His eyes glowed warm lavender. "*Te ke vo, shei'tani*," he answered. "For the rest of this life and every other life that follows." He kissed her thoroughly. "No matter what happens, never doubt that. No one—mortal or magic—could be happier than I am to be your *shei'tan*."

She managed a slightly watery smile and treasured the small surge of joy it gave him. That reaction gave her the strength to thumb away her tears. "*Veli*, Rain. Let's find out how magical this river really is."

She spun a quick weave of Earth to shed her leathers and steel, and dove into the water. A kaleidoscope of color lit up around her as she cut through the current, and she surfaced in an explosion of shimmering pink and blue light. Her feet settled on the crystal sand of the riverbed, and a tingle rippled through her body. Oh, yes, there was magic here.

She traced her hand through the water, swirling magic in her wake, and a dazzling color lit up the waters in response as the river amplified the glow of magic like a million tiny prisms.

On the shore, Rain shed his war steel and the padded silk tunic he wore beneath, baring the smooth, silky strength of his leanly muscled frame. Tall, unearthly beautiful, Rain shimmered silver in the moonlight as he walked into the river. A small wake trailed out behind him, ripples of scarlet, green, and deep violet.

Droplets of water tracked trails down her skin. The autumn night air kissed her damp breasts with tantalizing coolness and brought her nipples to tight peaks.

His eyes began to glow as he reached for her, but she laughed and danced just out of reach. She cast a teasing look over her shoulder and began to circle him. Ribbons of yellow, pink, and summer blue streamed out behind her.

The colors around him flared with sudden brightness as he spun arms of Spirit that caught her tight and pulled her towards him. "*Veli taris, fellana.*" Come here, woman.

She laughed again and let him pull her close. Her lashes fluttered down as his real hands closed around her, and her laughter changed to a slightly breathless moan. "*Taris ke sha.*" Here I am. Her head tilted back, and her hair fell freely to her waist. She loved the feeling of strength and protectiveness that always came with even the simplest touch of his hands to her skin. Adoration . . . even reverence . . . mingled with the hot stamp of desire. Never had there been a woman born who felt more cherished than she did when Rain Tairen Soul took her in his arms.

"Rain . . ." She murmured his name deep in her throat as the burning heat of his mouth closed around her and his tongue and teeth teased the sensitive skin of her breasts until a mere breath made her tremble. He hadn't summoned his magic, yet he ensorcelled her as surely as if he'd spun a Spirit weave to captivate her mind and set her senses afire. He purred against her skin, and the vibrating hum made her body convulse in pleasure. Her fingers knifed into the thick, inky silk of his hair and clutched his head, holding him to her.

She'd never felt beautiful in her life, until him. Even free of the glamour that had hidden her Fey appearance behind a mask of plain, awkward mortality, she still felt more like Ellie Baristani than Ellysetta Feyreisa. Except when Rain looked at her and touched her the way he was doing now.

She skimmed her nails across the silky skin of his back and gave a throaty growl as his muscles twitched and shuddered in response. Desire roared through her in a fiery rush, his and hers combined, the sensations and emotions so intertwined she could not separate them. Her sex throbbed with a hot, heavy ache, and her hips bucked against his in instinctive, rhythmic demand.

Rain shuddered as heat blasted through his veins. Tender devotion incinerated like thin silk wrapped around a white-hot coal, softness replaced by consuming heat. His teeth grazed her skin, nipping with sharp little bites that made her gasp and arch against him.

His tairen roared inside him, turning blood to fire and flesh to burning stone. *Give us our mate. Take her. Claim her. Make her ours.* The fierce snarl whipped through his mind. His tairen growled and hissed, baring fangs and claws. There was no sweet gentleness when tairen mated. There was only fire and heat, the rush of the wind, the stab of talons gripping tight, the scream of desire and fierce possession that rocked the heavens.

Spirit spun from his fingers in wild waves, and the river around them blazed with fiery lights. Hands, teeth, tongues, lips, wings, talons, his Spirit bodies—both Fey and tairen—caressed and tormented her, claimed and plundered. Gone was the gentle lover. He poured out upon her his magic, his essence, the blazing need of his soul, the primal core of him that existed when all else was stripped away: pure, dominant male energy, unyielding and fierce, aggressor and defender, protector and conqueror, the darkness to her light.

Ours, his tairen hissed. *She is ours. Our mate. Our female. Our pride.*

"*Kem,*" he snarled to Ellysetta, sending the claim in Spirit and across the threads of their bond as well. Magic flowed across her naked flesh, drawing her muscles tight, detonating shuddering bursts of pleasure in her breasts, her loins, her womb. She screamed and his soul flared with triumph as her pleasure fed his own. "*Ve sha kem.* You are mine. Say it."

She clutched at him with greedy, wordless hunger. Her mouth dragged across his skin, trailing fire in its wake. Her legs wrapped around his waist, trying to draw him to her, her own tairen seeking completion without submitting to his claim.

"Say it," he demanded. His hands clutched her hips, fingers

sinking into her flesh as he raised her up. The head of his sex brushed against the soft entrance of her sheath, tempting her, teasing her with the promise of what she desired. Her hips bucked again, and her teeth closed on his neck in a swift, sharp bite, a female tairen's nip of irritation and command. He tossed his head back, shaking his wet hair out to its full length, but he refused to give in.

In the pride, the females were *makai*, those who led the pride. But in mating, it was the male who staked his claim with unyielding dominance. A tairen male pursued his mate with relentless intensity, chasing her through the skies, using his greater speed and endurance to wear down her willful resistance. He herded her where he wished her to go with darting passes and daring swoops. He demonstrated his mastery of the skies by diving towards her on a collision course, only to pull back at the last moment so that he merely brushed her flying form, wingtip to wingtip, fur to fur. And with each brush of tairen bodies, he released the heady mating scent that teased and tormented her, driving her wild until she could do nothing but scream a final roar of defiance and succumb to him.

"Say it," he rumbled again. "*Ve sha kem.*" A bump of his hip brought another tantalizing brush of his sex against hers. "You are mine. Say it."

She clawed at him, snarled at him, twisted and writhed in his grip, but he would not relent until finally, exhausted and aching for him, she growled, "*Aiyah, ke sha ver.* I am yours."

"Forever, *kem'tani.*" And, gripping her hips, he plunged into her core. Their eyes closed and their heads flung back on a mutual cry as he filled her, joining them in body as their magic swirled and twined about them.

When he opened his eyes again, the world around them had changed.

They were not in a magical river in Elvia anymore, but lying together, his body covering hers, on a silken couch in a tent whose purple silk drapes swirled and flapped in a warm night breeze, redolent with the heady scent of tairen. Muted roars rumbled in the night, and flashes of fire lit up the distant sky where tairen played near the snowy peaks of the Feyls. He recognized the place as the shellabah on his ancestral family lands near the Feyls.

He stared down into her face as his body surged into hers, and her gold-kissed hair spilled about her head in a wild tangle. He frowned . . . not gold. Her hair should be . . . ? Thought disintegrated. His back arched, ecstasy splashing across his senses. "Fellana, what you do to me." His hips surged again and he watched her face. Her eyes were closed and her lips parted on a gasp.

"No more than you do to me." Her voice was a husky purr, rich and deep and throaty. It hummed across his skin and vibrated in his soul in a place no other woman had ever touched.

His hands stroked the silky, pale skin, its silvery glow so bright it was as if the Mother Moon herself shone from within. So soft. So sweet. All woman. All his. His own true love. He bent to trail kisses down her arm, her palm, drawing the delicate, slender fingers into his mouth. His tongue slid across the sensitive pads of her fingertips and touched lightly on the delicate edges of her fingernails.

She stretched and purred like a cat, and a smile spread across her face. Such luminous beauty. So unexpected, so perfect in every way. If he had ever dreamed of a truemate, she would have been the woman in his arms. Silken curls like sunlight gleaming on golden seas. A body strong and yet soft beneath his hands. And eyes . . . Her lashes lifted, revealing eyes of purest tairen green, pupil-less and blazing with the magic of her kind. Tairen's eyes. Her eyes. The eyes of the soul that he loved.

Tears sprang up, surprising him, shimmering on his lashes. "How could you do it?" he asked. "How could you give up the sky for me?"

She pulled him down for a kiss, licked at his tears in the way of her kind. She was still, in so many ways, more feline than Fey. "Van, kem'san, kem'Fey, I would give up much more than that to

*spend a lifetime with you. In the pride, love is a choice, and I
chose you."*

"But your wings . . . your beautiful wings . . ."

*She smiled. "How can I miss my wings when you make my
soul fly?" She wrapped her arms and legs around him and purred
against his throat. "Make me fly now, Van. And fly with me." She
gave a smile that was pure woman—nei, pure female, fierce and
free. She was silken heat, hot as tairen flame; and he was burning stone, hard, unyielding, absorbing her heat, amplifying it
and feeding it back to her with each demanding thrust of his body
in hers.*

*Her inner muscles clenched tight around him, making his eyes
close on a sudden gasp and wringing a cry from his lips. "Fellana—"*

Rain's eyes flashed open as Ellysetta's body clenched tight
around him. Her hair shone bright as flame in the moonlight,
and her eyes had gone pure tairen, pupil-less and blazing
bright.

"Make me fly, Rain." Her body surged against his. Her nails
dug into his back like claws. "Fly with me."

"*Aiyah.*" His voice rumbled low and guttural, choked with
emotion and need. His body surged into hers, one powerful,
driving thrust after another, as if through strong merging of
bodies he could also merge their souls. The water around
them whirled with explosions of vivid color as their passions
burned higher and hotter. He could almost see them, two
tairen joined in a fierce dance of mating, soaring and plum-
meting, tails twined together, wings outstretched.

With their bodies united, their emotions so closely en-
twined he could not tell them apart, Rain knew what it was
to be pure Light, untainted and absolute. There was no place
for Shadow, no place for sorrow or guilt, fear or regret, no
place for Rage or remorse. At this moment, he was just Rain,
beloved of Ellysetta, whose passion burned bright as the hot-
test flame and whose soul soared higher than even tairen
dared to fly.

* * *

Celieria City

The prancing little prissypants had survived!

Gethen Nour stormed about the confines of his boarding-house room, heaping curse after curse upon the perfumed head of Gaspare Fellows, Master of Graces. The knife wound should have seen him dead from blood loss within minutes.

He stopped walking. The Velpin. The Light-cursed Velpin. The Fey had put a cleansing weave on the waters a thousand years ago, and one of the side benefits was a mild healing effect. No doubt that had helped keep Fellows alive until the Fey found him, sealed his wound, and took him back to the palace, where one of the local hearth witches had managed to revive him enough for him to give the name of his attacker.

And now the city streets were crawling with King's Guards looking for the missing courtier, Lord Bolor.

He was ruined.

Returning to the palace was out of the question. He'd be imprisoned and held for torture or Truthspeaking. The queen already despised him, so he could expect no aid from that quarter. As his closest companion in the court, Jiarine would likely be questioned and tortured as well, and even if she invoked the spell to wipe her memories, its effects were not indefinite. She'd give him up to save herself.

And returning to Eld was no better option.

The High Mage had already expressed his displeasure with Gethen's performance in Celieria. To return in utter failure—as the Primage who had revealed his presence to the mortals . . .

Gethen shuddered. It didn't bear thinking about.

No, he couldn't stay here, and he couldn't go home. He had to go somewhere else. Merellia, perhaps, or Droga. Or, better yet, someplace no Mage would think to look for him—someplace the long arm of the High Mage hadn't yet reached.

Gethen snatched the small leather case stuffed in the ar-

moire and began throwing into it the cache of magical implements he kept hidden here. *Selkahr* crystals, rings, and bands
of power for the Mage spells he'd thought he might need here
in Celieria, *somulus* powder, other herbs and potions. He had
another such cache at the Inn of the Blue Pony. He'd go there,
collect it, then find some way to smuggle himself out of the
city. He didn't dare use the Well of Souls to travel for fear the
High Mage would detect him.

Throwing on a cloak with a deep hood, he exited the room
and snuck out the back door of the boardinghouse into the
alleyway.

From the darkness, a familiar voice said, "Going somewhere, Nour?"

Gethen spun, magic sparking to his fingertips, but before he
could raise his shield, he felt the prick of a dart stab into his
neck. His vision went dim, and his legs collapsed beneath him.

"Please, I don't know anything." Jiarine Montevero wept as
the guard dragged her down the corridor of Old Castle Prison.
"I've already told you everything! I don't know any more.
Please! You've got to believe me!"

After Master Fellows's revelation that Lord Bolor was the
Mage who had tried to kill him, Prince Dorian had convinced
his mother to let him bring everyone closely related with Lord
Bolor to Old Castle Prison for questioning. Since Jiarine was
Bolor's most constant companion in the court, she had, of
course, been among the courtiers taken and detained.

She'd spent all afternoon being questioned. How well had
she known Lord Bolor? What had they spoken about? Did she
know where he was? Thanks to the memory spells she'd invoked the moment she realized the guards were coming for
her, she'd been able to answer all their questions with bewildered innocence.

Now it was the middle of the night, and the guards had come
to take her from her cell again. She was certain this did not
bode well. Worse, the memory spell had long since worn off.

The guards delivered her into what was clearly a torture chamber: stone walls lit by the flickering orange firelight of bare torches on the walls, a table laid out with all manner of knives and pincers, what looked to be an ancient rack to stretch limbs until bones popped from their sockets. A cloaked figure stood in the shadowy corner of the room.

The guards pressed her into a chair, locked the manacles welded to the armrests into place around her wrists, and left the room.

Alone with the cloaked man in the corner, Jiarine began to shake as genuine terror set in. "P-please. I swear to you, I've told you all I know. Call a *shei'dalin*. Truthspeak me! I've nothing to hide."

"Such a convincing liar. My dear, it really is an exceptional talent. I almost believe you myself."

Jiarine froze. She knew that voice. She knew it as well as she knew her own. "M-master?"

The man in the corner threw back the hood of his cloak to reveal a face she knew. A face she had known and loved and hated since she was a foolish teenage girl who sold her soul to a handsome Mage in exchange for wealth and power.

Kolis Manza cocked his handsome face to one side and gave her the charming, slightly quizzical smile that had won her heart so long ago. "You know, I had almost forgotten how truly beautiful you are."

"Master Manza! Thank the gods you are alive."

His expression hardened instantly. "The gods had nothing to do with it, I promise you." He took a breath and forced another small smile, but this time she realized there was something different about him. A coldness to his eyes that hadn't existed before.

"M-master? Why are you here? Why did you have me brought here?"

"As it so happens, this is one of the few rooms in the prison with privacy wards woven into the stone. With a Mage on the loose, the Fey are scanning every fingerspan of the city, looking for magic that might give away Master Nour's position. But thanks to the construction of this room, any magic woven in here is undetectable outside these walls."

He sighed and walked towards her. "You see, Jiarine, in exposing himself, Nour has cast the light of suspicion upon you as well. Given our past association . . . and my upcoming return to court, this will not do. Your integrity must be beyond reproach so that no hint of suspicion should fall on me. Unfortunately, no matter how skilled a liar you are, there are ways to elicit the truth from you. Which is why, my sweet *umagi*, as much as I regret it, I must permanently erase from your memory every delectable moment we have spent together as our true selves."

"Master?"

He leaned towards her. "Don't worry, Jiarine. This won't hurt." He smiled coldly. "That part comes later."

"Tortured?" Annoura stared in disbelief at the Dazzle kneeling before her. "You expect me to believe that Lady Montevero—a Favorite in my personal court—was *tortured*? You must be mistaken, Ser! She was simply taken for questioning, and to be detained until a Truthspeaker could arrive to verify her word."

The Dazzle bowed deeply and kept his eyes lowered. "I went to visit her this morning, to bring her a few trinkets to help pass the time. There isn't a fingerspan on her poor face that isn't bruised and mottled . . . and her hands, her poor hands. All her fingers were broken. She was barely conscious. All she kept saying was, 'I am innocent. Tell the queen I am innocent.'"

Annoura rose to her feet. She clenched her hands at her waist to keep them from shaking. "Get out. All of you. This instant!"

The courtiers knew that tone of voice. Every last one of them leapt to their feet and beat a hasty retreat.

Annoura began to pace, her mind a whirl. First, Master Fellows's near death, then the revelation about Lord Bolor, then the manhunt across the city that still—even a full day later—had turned up nothing.

All that had been upsetting enough, but this news . . . this defied all belief.

After Master Fellows had named Lord Bolor as his attacker—and an Elden Mage to boot—she had, of course, wondered if Jiarine's fervent attempts to insinuate him into Annoura's presence were part of some plot. That was why she had not objected when Dori insisted on taking Lady Montevero to Old Castle for questioning.

But *torture*! She never would have approved that. Not for Jiarine. At least, not without some sort of proof, beyond baseless supposition and guilt by association! After their last months of friendship, Jiarine deserved that much, at least.

Annoura marched over to the wall and yanked on the bell-pull. Her Master of Chambers arrived a few chimes later, just as she was pressing her royal seal at the bottom of a parchment. "Your Majesty?"

"Summon my son this instant. And send Lord Hewen and a carriage to Old Castle Prison with this." She held out the sealed parchment. The ink was still damp, and the handwriting her own rather than the royal calligrapher's flowing script, but that seal on the bottom made the document as legitimate and binding as any law of Celieria. "Have him deliver this royal writ of release to the prison master. I want Lady Montevero under this roof and in Lord Hewen's care before dinner this evening."

The Master of Chambers bowed. "Of course, Your Majesty. I will see to it personally."

Three bells later, she and half the court stood waiting in the courtyard as the royal carriage carrying Lord Hewen and Lady Montevero rolled across the paving stones and came to a halt at the foot of the stairs.

Her skin mottled, her blue eyes dazed with pain, Jiarine Montevero clung to Lord Hewen's strong arm as she made her trembling descent from the carriage to the courtyard.

"Lady Montevero!" Annoura swept across the remaining distance, her arms outstretched. "You poor dear. I sent the release the moment I heard." She had intended to clasp Jiarine's hand, but seeing the mangled state of her fingers, Annoura chose to grip the lady's face instead and deliver a light kiss upon her cheeks.

"Good gods!" a rich, masculine voice declared. "What's happened to her?"

Annoura's heart stilled for a moment. She turned her head to see the familiar, stunningly handsome nobleman standing beside the open door of a second coach she hadn't noticed coming in after the first. Her eyes drank in the long-missed sight of his face, his eyes, the careless tousle of his hair as it fell across his brow.

"Your Majesty," Lord Hewen murmured, "we need to get Lady Montevero inside. In her current weakened state, she could easily catch her death of cold."

The admonishment snapped her back to her senses. "Of course." Turning to the courtiers, she waved two of her current Favorites to her side. "Come quickly. Help Lady Montevero to her rooms. You there . . ." She caught sight of the dim-skull Dazzle. "Mairi, have the servants stoke the fire. Tell cook to send hot tea and keflee—and something warm and nourishing for the lady to eat. Quickly!"

As the courtiers carried Jiarine Montevero inside, Annoura turned to the unexpected new arrival to court, the handsome, too-long-absent Favorite who had occupied her thoughts far more than was prudent. "Ser Vale." He still had the power to make her pulse pound when he fixed his gaze so intently upon her. He looked at her as if she were the center of his universe.

"Your Majesty." He bowed deeply and lifted his eyes to smile in that slow, seductive way of his that made her heart leap into her throat. "Your beauty, my queen, still shines as brilliant as the sun, and I am but a poor, withered bloom too long absent from your radiance."

From any other courtier, such effusive, overblown compliments would sound ridiculous. But Vale spoke with such a ring of sincerity, the words fell like beautiful poetry from his lips. It was all she could do to maintain her composure and say, "We are glad you are returned to us, Ser," in a modulated voice when what she wanted to do was leap and shout for joy, as giddy as a schoolgirl deep in the throes of her first crush.

Vale was back.

CHAPTER SIXTEEN

Elvia ~ Deep Woods

Six days after leaving the Dreamer River, the Fey approached the heart of Deep Woods. Close-knit stands of trees vying for sunlight and rich soil gave way to fewer, much older trees, massive arboreal giants that soared so high Ellysetta thought their treetops might just pierce the clouds.

She glanced back at Rain as he rode through a shaft of sunlight, and for a moment, she saw him differently, as if a second image were superimposed atop him. Rain, but not Rain. His hair a deep bronze rather than black, his muscular body encased in gleaming silver armor, not golden war steel. The image reminded her of the man she'd seen in that strange vision she'd had in the Dreamer. The vision she and Rain had both shared.

Ellysetta was convinced they'd seen a glimpse of the life of Fellana the Bright—the tairen who had transformed herself into a Fey woman to be with the Fey king she loved. But when she'd asked Fanor about it, all he'd said was that the

Dreamer showed what it liked. The vision could have been the past or the future or possibly a vision born of their own dilemma that had never truly existed, nor ever would. The point was to find meaning in the vision that they could apply to their current situation.

She blinked, and the image of the bronze-haired Fey king disappeared. What meaning was she supposed to have gained? Was she supposed to accept that her tairen would never find its wings? That she and Rain had lived before—or would again? That love was a choice and she just needed to accept it to complete their bond?

Fanor had said the Dreamer River would enlighten them, but all it had done was confuse her more.

Ellysetta ducked her head to miss a low-hanging branch that was as big around as the trunk of a hundred-year-old fire-oak. "These trees are incredible," she said to Rain as they rode past the massive trunk of the colossus. "They remind me of the Sentinels outside of Dharsa, only much, much larger." The Fey and the Elves were riding single file down a narrow trail that wound through the ferns carpeting the forest floor. Beams of sunlight filtered down from the canopy overhead, illuminating the rich, vivid green hues of the undergrowth and the golden tones of the smooth tree trunks so that the forest seemed to glow with radiant light.

"These *are* Sentinels," Rain said. "The ones in Dharsa came from the Elves, a gift long ago, when our two races lived as one. But these are much older even than those." His body swayed to the leisurely walking pace of his *ba'houda* mount.

"They are the watchers of the wood," Fanor said. "Nothing escapes their notice—or their memory—and they live for a very long time."

"How long?" Ellysetta asked.

"Longer than any Elf or Fey." The Elf leaned left in his saddle and patted a nearby tree whose trunk was at least a full tairen length wide. He murmured a stream of lyrical Elvish to it, and the tree's branches fluttered in response. "This Sentinel, for instance, has lived since the dawn of the Third Age. He is a fine young tree."

Ellysetta laughed. "Young? The Third Age began at least a hundred thousand years ago."

Fanor smiled. "It's young for a Sentinel. In Navahele, the oldest of the ancients there put down his roots in the Time Before Memory, before the First Age."

Her jaw dropped. "But that was over a million years ago."

"*Bayas*, so it was. He and the other ancients of Navahele hold in their life rings many memories long since forgotten by the rest of the world."

"Do they share those memories?" Rain asked.

"Not with me." Fanor ducked his head to miss a low-hanging branch. "The ancients speak only to the king and queen of Elvia, Lord Galad and his sister Ilona Brighthand, the Lady of Silvermist."

As they rode up the crest of a hill, Fanor's face brightened. "We are here." He spurred his mount faster, and the *ba'houda* took off. When they reached the top of the crest, Fanor reined his mount to a halt and waited for the others to catch up.

"Behold," he said when they drew near, "Navahele. City of the ancients." A smile of joy and pride spread across his face and made his skin glow with a soft golden aura.

Ellysetta drew back on her mount's reins, pulling the mare to a halt at the top of the hill. She stared down into the valley below with dawning wonder. Whatever she'd been expecting, it wasn't this.

There were no buildings.

Navahele wasn't just a city in the trees; it was a city *of* the trees. Rings of Sentinels nearly twice the size of any they'd seen so far were twined together in overlapping harmony. Their glossy golden trunks and branches had grown into living cathedrals in which the Elves dwelled. Stairs circled massive trunks, and bridges crisscrossed the air above, all formed from branches, vines, and other symbiotic vegetation that grew along the great Sentinels' trunks and branches. Columns and elegant latticework of supporting roots grew in graceful splendor beneath the heaviest branches in a manner similar to bania trees. Leaf- and flower-covered vines hung from the canopy like ribbons around which birds and a dazzling array of butterflies fluttered like flying jewels.

"Come," Fanor said. He touched his heels to his mount's side, spurring the horse down the trail towards the stunning city of trees. "My people are expecting us."

Leaving their mounts at the bottom of the hill, the Fey followed Fanor as he led the way through the central grove of colossal, ancient trees. Thick, spongy moss, soft as eiderdown, carpeted the ground below the great branches. Each step was like walking on clouds.

Ellysetta couldn't stop herself from craning her neck and gawking like an awestruck child as, behind every tree, she found a scene of utter pastoral tranquillity. Clear streams burbled over rounded stones, and lacy waterfalls tumbled in musical white waves down moss-covered boulders. Everywhere, creatures of myth and legend abounded—animals and birds that had long since disappeared from the mortal world.

"Is that a . . . Shadar?" she whispered to Fanor when she caught sight of a trio of Elf maids weaving flower garlands into the long, lustrous mane and tail of an enormous white stallion with a single, spiraling horn sprouting from its forehead. The stallion turned its proud head in Ellysetta's direction, then whickered and pawed the mossy ground with gleaming silver hooves. The soft laughter of the Elf maidens fell silent as they watched Ellysetta and the Fey pass.

"It is," Fanor said.

"I didn't know they still existed—or ever truly did, for that matter."

"Mortals hunted them nearly to extinction for their magic—the Aquilines as well." Aquilines were fierce, winged chargers who were said to spawn thunder with the beat of their wings and lightning with the strike of their golden hooves. "But both still thrive in Elvia."

Just looking at the Shadar made her almost giddy. "Is it true what the legends say about the power of a Shadar's horn being able to nullify any poison and purify any foulness?"

Fanor's white teeth flashed in an indulgent smile. "*Aiyah.* Shadar horn is a curative like no other, which is why mortals hunted them so exhaustively. They could touch Shadar horn to a poisoned well, and the waters would be instantly purified. 'Tis said the touch of a Shadar horn can even save a man poisoned by tairen venom."

Rain snorted. "Now, that *is* myth. Not even our strongest *shei'dalins* can counteract tairen venom."

The Elf shrugged. "Well, that's what Elvish lore claims. I don't know of anyone who's ever tested to see if it's true."

Tajik snorted and cast a speculative look Gaelen's way. "Perhaps vel Serranis could give it a try while we're here. Purely in the interest of science, of course."

Bel rolled his eyes. Gil and Rijonn sniggered. Gaelen just lifted a fist with his thumb tucked between his index and middle finger in a crude gesture. Tajik grinned and smacked a sarcastic kiss in his direction.

They stopped before a beautiful vine-covered arbor that curled up the trunk of one of the great Sentinels. A dozen Elves, golden skinned and beautiful, stood waiting at the base of the tree.

"Go with them, please," Fanor said. "Lord Galad bids you rest and refresh yourselves. At sunset, we hold a dinner to honor your arrival. He will see you after that."

The Elves led the Fey to individual guest chambers formed from spacious hollows that appeared to have been purposely grown into the Sentinel tree's massive trunk. Rain inspected the chamber he and Ellysetta had been escorted to and could find no hint of tool mark on any part of the smooth, seamless golden surface of the floor, walls, or ceiling.

Light inside the chamber was provided by a silver chandelier shaped like drapes of flowing vines, only instead of holding candles, the chandelier was covered in phosphorescent butterflies whose bodies gave off a gentle, silvery blue light as they slowly fanned their jeweled wings.

"When you wish to sleep, simply open the window and the *damia* will leave," said the Elf maiden who had escorted them to their chamber. "To call them back again, pour a few drops of this honeywater into the bellflowers." She held up a crystal flacon and pointed to the upturned tube-shaped silver flowers at the end of each of the chandelier's vines. "Refreshment and a change of clothing have been provided. There is a bathing pool at the base of the tree. The banquet to honor your arrival will be held on the terrace overlooking the pools that surround Grandfather's island. Make yourselves comfortable until then."

"*Talaneth, elfania,*" Rain said with a bow of his head.

The Elf, a beautiful woman with hair like nightfall and eyes as gold as sunrise, returned the bow. "Blessings of the day," she murmured, and departed with silent grace.

"What now?" Ellysetta asked, when they were alone.

"Now we relax as much as we can, and wait for sunset." Rain smiled at Ellysetta's disgruntled expression. After the long days of riding, she'd expected her waiting to be over once they reached Navahele. "In Elvia, all things come in their own time."

They helped themselves to the fruits and delicate pastries provided for them and availed themselves of the bathing pool. When it came time to dress, however, Rain left the Elvish clothing in a neat, untouched pile. As long as the Fading Lands were at war, the golden war steel of the Fey king would be his only garb. He cleansed the dust and grime of travel from the armor with a weave and polished the black and gold plates until they shone.

While Rain dressed, Ellysetta transformed her studded leathers into a silver-and-scarlet gown ornate enough for an introduction to an immortal royal. She left her hair down, flowing in thick ringlets to her waist, and settled a crown made of woven platinum, diamond, and Tairen's Eye crystal on her head.

"Well," she said, when they'd both finished their preparations. "Shall we go?" Her heart was thumping in her chest, and bands of nervous tension were drawing tight around it.

"You shine bright as the Great Sun, *shei'tani*," Rain said with a smile. "*Aiyah*, let us go. And don't worry. Hawksheart is bound by the laws of Elvish hospitality. We are here by his invitation, as his guests. By that law, we're safer here than we would be anywhere else in the world."

"It's not physical danger I fear," she admitted.

"I know. But whatever answers he may have, Ellysetta, we're better off knowing, don't you think?" He held out his wrist.

She grimaced and placed her fingers on it. "That depends on the answers," she muttered.

They met the other Fey at the base of the tree. Like Rain, Ellysetta's quintet had forgone the proffered Elvish attire, and had merely cleaned and buffed their leathers to a glossy black shine and polished their steel until it sparkled diamond-bright. An Elf maiden joined them and, with a smile and a melodic command for them to follow her, she led Ellysetta, Rain, and the warriors down the stair that spiraled around the great Sentinel's trunk.

They walked across the meadow to a vine-bedecked terrace overhanging one of the crystalline pools in the heart of Na-vahele. There a wooden table carved from gleaming Sentinel wood awaited, its glossy surface adorned with glittering crystal plates and goblets and heaping platters of aromatic roasted meats, vegetables, and glistening fruits.

Elf maidens with ribboned garlands in their hair stepped forward to offer goblets of chilled golden Elvian wine that smelled of honeyblossoms. Ellysetta accepted a glass with a murmured word of thanks and took an experimental sip. Delicate flavor burst upon her tongue, lightly sweet and very refreshing.

"*Beylah vo*. It's delicious," she told the Elf maid who had proffered the glass.

"We call it *elethea*, which means sunlight in Elf tongue," Fanor's voice explained from behind.

Ellysetta turned to find that Fanor had joined them on the terrace. He'd traded his hunter's garb for shimmering Elvish splendor: a long tunic that shone alternately moss green and gold when he moved, tied at his waist with a golden belt forged in the shape of leafy vines.

He gestured to the glass of wine in her hand. "It is made of the fruit and blossoms gathered from the highest branches of Navahele's Sentinel trees."

As the sun sank below the horizon, music filled the air. The Elves gathered in the meadows and arboreal balconies throughout the city to greet the twilight with soaring arias sung by voices so pure, the sound of them brought tears to Ellysetta's eyes. The maiden who had led the Fey to the terrace, the Elves waiting to serve them, even the warriors stationed throughout the city: all paused to add their voices to those of their kin and offer up their song to the heavens.

"They sing the *alinar*," Fanor told her, "a hymn of thanksgiving for the blessings of the day."

"It's beautiful." Ellysetta closed her eyes as the sound washed over her. The melody struck a chord deep inside, suffusing her senses with quiet joy and a hushed, reverent peace. To hear the Elves of Navahele sing was to hear everything good and lovely in the world transformed into glorious music.

The sun descended below the horizon and the Elvish song came to its end. With unhurried grace, Galad Hawksheart's people returned to their previous activities.

"That was breathtaking," Ellysetta said in the ensuing silence. "I think if I ever heard the Lightmaidens of Adelis sing their glorias, they would sound just like that."

"No matter what else one may say about the Elves, no one can deny the beauty of their song," Rain agreed.

Fanor bowed. "*Alaneth*. Thank you for your compliments. One of the highest aims of all Elves is to perfect our song."

"And yet you did not sing."

The Elf smiled. "I stand as your host this night. Elvish hospitality forbids me to sing a song you could not also join."

"Lord Hawksheart will not be joining us, then?" she asked.

"He rarely takes time away from studying the Dance. He will meet with you after you dine. For now, he bids you enjoy the peace and splendor of Navahele."

All around the forest city, as the rosy warmth of day faded to the dark of night, the soft lights of the *damia* began to glow, replacing the dying sunlight with a silvery blue beauty, as if the city had been dipped in starlight and moonbeams. Glittering night birds joined a host of smaller, tiny phosphorescent insects that darted amongst the leaves, branches, and vines of the city, until all the city sparkled with magical beauty.

"Come." Fanor gestured for the Fey to take their seats at the table and partake of the feast that had been prepared for them.

Celieria ~ South of Greatwood

Talisa diSebourne stood in the small, cramped, shadow-filled room of a small posting inn built on the southern fringe of Celieria's Greatwood forest and stared in growing horror at the tidy double bed tucked against the wall.

Since leaving Celieria City seven days ago, she'd managed to avoid sharing a marital bed with Colum, claiming first a severe travel sickness, then a mysterious ailment that left her vomiting for several days (if her lady's maid had noted the scent of the gallberry steeped in Talisa's morning tea, she'd kept her silence), then the genuine affliction of her woman's time (thank the Bright Lord for his mercy). But now her excuses had come to an end.

Candle lamps cast a flickering golden glow around the room. The inn's goodwife had rushed to freshen the pillows with a new stuffing of sage and sweet balsam before her noble guests Lord diSebourne and his bride retired for the night.

Upon learning the two were recently wed, the kindly good-wife had done her best to turn the small room into a bridal bower. In addition to the fragrant herbs she'd used to stuff the bed, the well-meaning woman had set out nuptial bouquets of fragrant Brightheart, slender twigs of an evergreen shrub whose soft, pale green needles exuded a divine aroma, mixed with scented wildflowers like the tender Love's Song, pale pink Blushing Bride, and soft blue Evermore. She'd even laid out a plate of sweetmeats and a bottle of her best pinalle, chilling in a small pewter bucket filled with precious ice chips. "To wish the happy couple joy," she'd said with a smile as she'd backed out of the room and left them alone.

Her kindly efforts had only rubbed salt in the open wounds scoring Talisa's heart.

Talisa clasped her hands together at her waist, her fingers surreptitiously clutching the edges of her robe with tense desperation as she turned to the man she'd wed. "Colum, please. I just need a little more time."

He laughed, the sound harsh and bitter. "Time? I doubt there's enough time in all the world to make you want me again instead of *him*. Not that you ever did."

"Colum . . ."

"I'm not a fool, Talisa. You wed me on the day of your twenty-fifth birthday because the one you really wanted never came. And I accepted that, because I knew if you gave me a chance, I could make you happy." His voice cracked on the last word. He caught himself quickly, lips pressing together in a thin, bloodless line.

"Oh, Colum." She stepped towards him, hands outstretched in instinctive sympathy. He'd been her friend long before he'd been her husband, always a tad too prideful and arrogant, thanks to his father's predilection for the trappings of power and nobility, but dear to her nonetheless. He was the boy who'd spent his summers running with her brothers across the rolling hills outside of Kreppes on their families' neighboring country estates. The lad who'd blushingly offered her a bouquet of wilted Evermore by the banks of the Heras River. The man who'd proposed on her seventeenth birthday, then waited patiently another eight years for her acceptance.

Now, he was the husband who flinched from her sympathy and stepped back to avoid her touch. "I love you." The declaration was spat from his lips, more accusation than vow. "Do you know how many women have begged me to say that to them?"

She withdrew her hands. "Then perhaps you should have. Colum, I was never less than honest with you."

He laughed bitterly. "Of course you weren't. You're far too noble to mislead a man with sweet lies. But not too noble to marry a man you don't love to spare your family shame."

It was her turn to flinch. The barb stung because it was so despicably true, but that didn't stop her from exclaiming in outrage, "How dare you throw that in my face, Colum? You not only knew my reasons for accepting your suit, you *counted on* them to convince me to say yes. Don't bemoan the bitterness of the bargain when you set the terms!"

As soon as the sharp words flew off her tongue, she wished she could have called them back. Colum's temper had an ugly edge, and though he was usually careful to hide the worst of it from her, she knew better than to prod him into a rage.

He crossed the room in two strides, grabbing her by the upper arms and shaking her so hard the pins in her hair fell out and her curls tumbled around her shoulders and down her back. "I bargained for a wife, not some Fey's whore who'll take my name and title, then lock her legs against me. You want to talk about bargains?" He shook her again. "You made a bargain, too, Lady diSebourne. Before your family, a priest, and half the nobles of the northern lands, you swore an oath to be my wife, and by the gods you are going to honor your word."

With a snarl of rage, he threw her on the bed. The bed frame knocked the night table and sent the bucket of ice chips and the bottle of pinalle crashing to the floor. Talisa rolled across the bed to the side opposite Colum. He lunged for her, but she evaded him, snatching up the candle lamp and raising it like a weapon as she backed towards the open window.

Her teeth bared in a smaller, more feminine version of her father's wolfish snarl. "Do this and I'll loathe you forever, Colum diSebourne," she hissed. "You'll never have anything of me that you don't take by force. Never!"

For one dreadful moment, she thought he might take what he wanted anyway; but then, with a bitter oath, he spun away and stalked to the opposite side of the room, his chest heaving, his fists clenched.

"Gods, Talisa, you drive me mad." For a moment, the boy who'd been her friend was there in his voice, hurt and lonely, too proud to ask for the kindness his heart ached for. "This isn't what I want between us. I want what we had before *he* came."

When they'd first wed, before Adrial had come into their lives, she'd shared Colum's bed, if not with joy, at least with loving friendship. Now even the thought of that was more than she could bear. "Colum . . . I'm sorry. . . ."

"As am I." He drew a deep breath and his shoulders squared. "But you're my wife, and you're going to honor your vows."

Before he could expand on that, a knock sounded at the door, and the muffled voice of Talisa's brother Luce called, "Is everything all right in there? We heard a crash."

Without taking his eyes from her, Colum called, "We're fine, Luce. Your sister just knocked something over."

"Ah. You all right, Tallie?"

Talisa clutched her robe tight. "I'm fine, Luce," she called, but she didn't lower the candle lamp still clutched like a weapon in her hand. "Colum and I were just . . . roughhousing."

"Ah. Well, keep it down, would you? Parsi, Sev, and I have the room next door, and we're turning in for the night. You know how cranky Sev gets when he doesn't get his beauty sleep."

Clomping boots marched down the hallway, and a door opened and closed. Then the sound of cheerful whistling filtered through the thin walls, accompanied by the voices of each of her brothers calling, "Good night, Colum. Good night, Tallie."

"It seems your brothers are determined to afford you the time you say you need," Colum observed with a bitter sneer. "Very well, then. You shall have it. We reach Kreppes in a week. I suggest you use that time to forget about your Fey lover." Colum's gray eyes, which at times could seem soft as doves, glittered like hot steel coins still glowing from the red-orange flames of the forge. "Because, one way or another, Lady diSebourne, our estrangement ends your first night on Sebourne land."

He stalked from the room. He didn't slam the door behind him. He closed it with very deliberate calm. Somehow, that seemed worse. Talisa sat there in silence, dragging air into her lungs as shock set her body trembling and tears burned her eyes.

She covered her face with shaking hands. A gasping sob burst from her throat and the tears fell from her eyes like hot rain. *Oh, gods, what am I going to do?*

In the woods a mile away from the Celierian inn, Adrial vel Arquinas fought his brother Rowan's hold. "Let me go, scorch you!"

"And let you slit the *rultshart's* throat?" Rowan snarled back. "Flamed if I will!" He shook his brother hard, hoping to shake some sense into the *shei'tanitsa*-crazed madness of his mind. "Don't you remember what Rain said? You can't touch diSebourne. You sure as hell can't kill him. You do, and you start a damned war."

"He's frightening her!" Adrial howled.

And for that Rowan wanted to slit the miserable maggot's throat himself. No warrior worth his steel could watch another Fey's mate suffer abuse without feeling the surge of killing Rage all Fey called the tairen rising in their souls. Though only the rarest and most powerful Fey, masters of all five magics, would ever see his tairen sprout wings and spout flame, that didn't lessen the fierce, predatory killing instincts of the rest of them.

Rowan's jaw clenched tight and only his desperate hold on his brother kept him from reaching for steel himself. Fire, Rowan's own strongest magic, kindled in his eyes. Blessed gods, he ached to teach that spoiled, spineless *rultshart* diSebourne a scorching lesson about respecting women.

"Talisa!" Adrial cried out. Wild, whirling cones of Air spun around him, shredding leaves and branches from the nearby trees, while overhead a strong wind howled across the forest canopy. "She's crying, Rowan." His lips drew back in a snarl, brown eyes flaring bright with deadly magic. "He laid hands on her. If he does it again, I'll kill him. War or no flaming war."

"He's her husband, Adrial," Rowan reminded him. "To his mind, he has the right to lay hands on her." Up until now, they'd been lucky. Talisa had managed to keep her husband at bay, but it was clear that brief blessing had ended. Rowan closed his eyes, offering up a quick plea for strength. Ah, gods, what a tangle.

Adrial's body suddenly went limp and sagged in Rowan's arms. Alarmed, Rowan loosened his tight grip on his brother. "Adrial?"

The blast of Air caught him off balance. He flung his arms out instinctively as his body flew backwards into the trees. As he tumbled, he saw his brother racing towards the Celierian inn.

«*Adrial!*» he cried. "*Krekk!*" He grunted as his body slammed into the trees and slid to the ground. By the time he cleared his head enough to follow, Adrial was gone.

"You shouldn't be here." Talisa turned to face Adrial as he slid his leather-clad legs over the sill of her open bedchamber window.

"Here is the only place in the world I should be." The creaky slats of the inn's wooden floor didn't make a sound as Adrial crossed the room to sit beside her. When he drew her into his arms, she didn't protest, but instead pressed her face into his throat and began weeping softly. For those tears alone, he could kill diSebourne without a qualm. If diSebourne hadn't gone downstairs to cool his temper in a pint of ale . . .

"Oh, Adrial . . . what are we going to do? I don't know how I can bear to let him touch me when the only man I want is you."

He stroked her dark, tumbled hair. "He isn't going to touch you. Not ever again." His lips found the soft skin of her temple, her damp eyelids, the tender fullness of her mouth.

She pulled back. "Adrial . . . no, this is wrong."

"*Nei, shei'tani,* finally, this is right." Holding her gaze, he lowered his lips again and kissed her. Softly at first, delicate brushes of his lips against hers, tiny nibbling kisses, tasting her lips with the tip of his tongue. Soft kisses deepened with increasing ardor as she began to kiss him back. She tasted like light and joy, like hope and peace and happiness and all the sweet, secret dreams of his heart.

And as her arms lifted to wrap around his neck, he knew he would kill any man who tried to keep her from him.

Colum diSebourne clutched the stair rail tight and concentrated on planting his heavy, uncooperative feet squarely in the center of the stair treads. He took pride in being a man who could hold his liquor, but that last round of whiskeyed ales had nearly dropped him.

With the company in the inn's small pub so much warmer than the reception awaiting him upstairs, Colum had not objected when the first celebratory round had turned into another. Somewhere after five, he'd lost the ability to count.

He reached the landing and clutched the wall to keep from

falling back down the stairs he'd just climbed. Five more staggering steps brought him to the door of his room.

He wasn't sure what to expect when he opened the door, but the sight of Talisa sleeping in the flickering candlelight made him squeeze his eyes shut against the sudden burn of tears. She was so beautiful. He'd loved her since he'd first laid eyes upon her as a boy, and his father had always promised she would be his. He'd never wanted anything more than he wanted Talisa, never known a longing so deep. Yet now she was his wife, and his dreams of the life they would have together had turned to bitter gall.

He took a ragged breath and began shrugging out of his clothes. Drink made his hands and legs unsteady and he nearly fell several times, but finally he managed to strip and climb naked into the bed beside his wife.

The sweet, warm scent of her dizzied his inebriated senses, and when he pressed his body against her back and cupped her small, round breast through the thin silk of her nightgown, she awoke with a soft sigh. He held his breath as she turned in his arms, and her lovely eyes, large and dark as a doe's, blinked up at him.

"Colum," she whispered. Her arms slid around his neck, and her petal-soft lips parted for his kiss.

Outside, on the rooftop just above the bedchamber window, a lavender glow of magic swirled as the Fey Spirit master spun his weave, while behind him in the darkness of the forest, Adrial vel Arquinas and his *shei'tani* slipped silently away.

CHAPTER SEVENTEEN

Elvia ~ Navahele

Three bells after sunset, the last of the dinner dishes were finally cleared away and the hauntingly beautiful strains of Elvish night music filled the meadows of Navahele.

Fanor pushed away from the table and rose to his feet. "Come, my friends. It is time. Lord Galad will see you now."

He led the Fey off the terrace and across delicate bridges that spanned the silvery pools ringing the island at the city's heart. There, rising in splendor from a wide, mossy knoll, stood the centermost tree of Navahele, a giant king among Sentinels, with a trunk easily twice the width of any other.

"This is Grandfather," Fanor said. "The ancient I told you about, who was a sapling in the Time Before Memory."

"He is magnificent," Ellysetta breathed. She tilted her head back. Grandfather was so tall she could not see his upper branches. Beside it—him—she felt dwarfed. An ant standing at the foot of a giant. Grandfather's bark was smooth and ageless, shining a silvery gold that shifted color in the glow of the butterflies hanging from the Sentinel's vines and branches.

"*Aiyah*, he is that," a low, musical voice agreed.

Rain put a hand on Ellysetta's shoulder, and together they turned to face the stranger who seemed to materialize from the forest itself. One moment, the stretch of mossy ground to their left was empty; the next, the Elf king stood there.

Galad Hawksheart, a man who'd been a legend before Gaelen was born, needed no introduction. Tall, broad shouldered, and lean hipped, the Elf king was even more breathtakingly beautiful than most of his kind, with strong, masculine features framed by a fall of burnished gold hair threaded with shining beads, aromatic leaves, and fluttering hawk feathers. Except for the golden cast to his skin and his tapered ears, he was almost Fey in appearance.

Until you looked into his eyes.

Hawksheart's eyes were a fathomless emerald, swirling with infinite sparkling lights, as if all the stars in the sky had been cast down a bottomless green well. Those eyes looked so ancient, Ellysetta wouldn't have been surprised to learn they had witnessed the birth and death of worlds or gazed upon the faces of the gods.

Hawksheart studied her with those too-intent eyes, and she could feel him in her mind, probing her thoughts. The tairen shifted inside her, sensing a threat. It gave a warning growl and began to rise. Afraid of what it might do, Ellysetta lowered her lashes to break the Elf king's gaze and bowed her head in greeting.

"My Lord Hawksheart," she murmured. "It is a pleasure to meet you."

"Ellysetta Erimea." The Elf king had a voice like a song, low and musical and enchanting. The accented Feyan rolled off his tongue like water tumbling over the stones in a brook. "Long have I waited for the day you would stand here among the ancients of Navahele."

She raised her eyes in surprise. "Y-you have?"

"*Bayas.* I have lived ten thousand years, Ellysetta Erimea, and I have been waiting for your arrival since I saw my first glimpse of the Dance as a boy." His eyes bored into hers once more. Despite herself, she flinched, and her tairen growled and roared.

"*Parei,*" Rain commanded curtly. "Ellysetta is not used to your Elvish ways. You are unsettling her."

The Elf turned his piercing gaze on Rain, but Rain just narrowed his eyes and stood his ground.

Galad Hawksheart smiled. "We meet again, Worldscorcher."

The Elf turned back to Ellysetta. "Your truemate and I met many years ago in Tehlas when I went there to visit kin of mine." He paused briefly, almost expectantly, before adding, "Though perhaps he does not remember it. He had only just returned from his Soul Quest and was still absorbing the wonder of being a fledgling Tairen Soul."

"I remember," Rain said. "You were there for the bonding ceremony of your cousin Hollen Stagleaper to the niece of Shanisorran v'En Celay. You told my father the next Song of the Dance had begun, and that I was the one who called it. I didn't understand why that left my father so troubled, until I learned that the ones who call the Song always suffer for it. You can imagine my concern when I learned that Ellysetta calls a Song, too."

"Is that why you stayed away? Did you think that by ignoring my summons, you could stop her Song?"

"My only concern was to get her to safety behind the Faering Mists."

"And yet here you stand, and she is less safe now than she was then. The Dance will not be denied, Worldscorcher. Of all people, you should know that."

Rain reached out with Spirit to probe Galad Hawksheart's mind, intending to discover exactly what Hawksheart's intentions were and what he knew of Ellysetta's role in the Elvish prophecy.

Galad brushed aside Rain's weave with a careless wave. "Fey weaves could never hope to enter an Elvian mind, Worldscorcher; nor is there need. I mean your mate no harm. Look to others for that and guard her well. She will need all the protection those of the Light can give her."

"Hundreds have already sworn to guard her, in this life and the death that follows," Tajik growled before Rain could reply.

"Kinsman." Galad turned to Tajik. "So you have returned to Elvia after all."

"As you Saw I would," Tajik said.

"*Bayas.*" The Elf king held out an arm, which, after a brief hesitation, Tajik clasped in greeting. "I am pleased indeed to see your Light shining bright once more."

Tajik dipped his head in Ellysetta's direction. "That is the Feyreisa's doing, cousin, which surely you must already have Seen as well."

"I did, but that does not make me any less glad to know that what I Saw came to pass."

Ellysetta glanced between them. "You and Lord Galad are related, Tajik?"

Tajik shrugged. "His father's sister wed one of my ancestors fifteen thousand years ago, but Elves never forget their family lines. Once Elf blood joins your own, you and your descendants will always be Elf-kin."

"Great Lord Barrial of Celieria is another of your kinsmen, is he not?" Rain asked.

Hawksheart nodded. "Descended from a different cousin. Our line comes directly from the first Elf king, who founded Navahele in the Time Before Memory."

"How many kinsmen do you have?" Ellysetta asked.

Galad turned to her and his mouth curved in a smile that surprised Rain with its warmth. Elves were notoriously aloof with those not of their kind. They lived too long and Saw too much for them to easily form attachments with others.

"Since the dawn of the First Age," Hawksheart said, "this world has greeted nine hundred eighty-nine thousand, two hundred seventy-three of my kin, but fewer than one hundred of us still live."

"How many of those that remain are your direct descendants?"

The Elf king's smile turned pensive. "I have no young; nor does my sister, Ilona. We two are the last Elves born to the direct royal line of the first king. Our remaining kin are cousins."

"The family history lesson is all well and good," Gaelen interrupted, "but surely that is not the reason you summoned Rain and Ellysetta to Navahele."

Now Hawksheart's expression went cool again. He regarded vel Serranis with an unblinking gaze. "*Anio*, it was not. Feyreisen, you and your mate please follow me." He hesitated and gave each Fey a measuring look before adding, "The rest of you must remain here."

"Ellysetta goes nowhere without her quintet." Rain's tone was as hard as stone. "Whatever you have to say to us, you can say before them as well."

"I assure you, your mate is in no danger here."

"All the same, we all go, or none of us do," Rain insisted.

Their gazes battled for a several moments before Hawksheart sighed and conceded. "Very well. You may all come. But none of you will reveal what you see to another—not through any method of communication, spoken or unspoken—and I will have your sworn Fey oaths on that."

"Agreed," Rain said. "I do so swear."

After the others gave their own oaths of secrecy, Hawksheart led them though an archway into the center of the enormous Sentinel tree called Grandfather. The trunk opened up to a soaring, cathedral-like hollow. Stairs twined up the interior of the hollow in helix patterns and joined together the numerous levels of graceful balconies that ringed the throne room.

"Rain," Ellysetta whispered, "look." She pointed to the ceiling high overhead, where glowing lights formed a shifting pattern that looked like clouds moving across a blue sky. As they watched, the lights left the ceiling and flew about in a complex aerial dance. "They're butterflies!" Ellysetta exclaimed. When the butterflies resettled, their pattern had changed to a sun shining over a forest meadow blooming with flowers. "How beautiful."

"The *damia* enjoy your admiration, Ellysetta Erimea," Hawksheart said with a smile as the scene on the ceiling changed again into an image of two tairen flying across blue skies.

the center of the chamber, the Elf king's throne rose up

on a large mound shaped like an exquisitely detailed forest. Aquilines, Shadars, and countless other creatures peeked out between the trunks and leaves of the trees. The entire thing was a solid piece of smooth golden wood that looked as if it had grown in place from the heart of the Sentinel tree.

Expressionless Elvian guards stood at attention at the four corners of the throne, and another two stood beside a small, rune-etched door set into the rear of the throne. The door opened as Hawksheart approached to reveal a long, winding stair that led down below the throne.

As they descended, Rain's nose filled with the aroma of rich, earthy life, redolent with magic. The scent reminded him of the caverns deep in the heart of Fey'Bahren. No sconces burned along the walls, but tiny glowing golden orbs gave off just enough light that the Fey could place their feet without fear of falling. The stair itself seemed hollowed out of the tree, the walls smooth and unmarred. There was no railing to hold on to, but there was no need. The passage was so narrow Rain's armor-clad shoulders nearly rubbed the walls as he walked.

After what seemed an eternity, the stair finally opened to a dark cavern and a pool buried deep in the earth. No flames flickered within, but the pool in the center glowed bright blue from phosphorescent mosses lining it, and the soft light lit the entire chamber.

"This is the great mirror of Navahele," Hawksheart told them when they had all gathered beside the pool. "It is the reason I requested your presence here, and the reason I would accept no ambassador sent by the Fey in your stead."

"Explain," Rain prompted. Already the hairs on the back of his neck were tingling as his tairen senses went on alert. This was Elvish magic—the very root of it—and Hawksheart had something up his sleeve.

«*There is no need for your distrust.*» Hawksheart's voice plunged directly into Rain's mind, calm and commanding. «*I only seek a better understanding of your truemate's Song.*»

Aloud, he said, "When a person calls a Song in the Dance, sometimes the verses of that Song are revealed more clearly when the Caller peers into the mirror. I had hoped, Rainier Feyreisen, that you and your mate would come when I first sent my ambassador to meet you in Celieria City. There were many verses your mate's Song could have played then."

Rain moved closer to Ellysetta. "And now?"

"Fewer. All of them dangerous. Most of them shadowed."

Ellysetta's fingers closed around Rain's wrist, and her sudden rush of fear brought his protective instincts to the fore.

"Are you saying the Mage will succeed in claiming my soul?" she asked.

Hawksheart tilted his head. His eyes fixed on her face unblinkingly as he admitted, "Several possibilities of your Song end on that note."

"Is there no hope?"

"If there were none, I would not have sent Fanor to you except as an assassin."

A warning growl rumbled in Rain's throat, and Ellysetta's quintet instantly closed ranks around her, fingers hovering over red Fey'cha hilts.

Hawksheart held up his hands. "Peace. The laws of Elvish hospitality are inviolable. Once you crossed the river Elva at my invitation, every Elf and forest dweller has ensured your protection."

The assurance didn't settle Ellysetta's quintet. Their hands remained hovering over their steel, and their expressions remained stony, emotionless masks.

A sudden creaking groan broke the tense silence. The satin-smooth, seamless wooden walls of the chamber trembled, and the waters of the glowing blue pool rippled.

Rain dropped to a slight crouch—both to keep his balance and to prepare for an attack. His pupils widened, tairen and Fey vision combining, as he scanned the dim chamber with sudden suspicion, looking for the threat.

"What Elvish trick is this?" he snapped. Around Ellysetta,

the quintet struggled to keep their balance as the wood beneath their feet shifted and bucked like a living creature.

"Grandfather does not like the threat of steel so close to his heartwood," Hawksheart replied. "Put him at ease, my friends. Move your hands away from your blades."

Warily, the quintet pulled their hands away from their blades. A moment later, the groaning tremors ceased and the floor beneath their feet went still and solid once more.

Ellysetta regarded the smooth wood of the tree's interior with wide eyes. "This tree really is alive . . . like a person."

"*Bayas*, Ellysetta Erimea. The Sentinels, especially, are intelligent—and deadly when roused. Grandfather was simply giving your quintet a polite warning. Had they truly threatened him or me, he would have slain everyone in this chamber in a matter of moments."

The warriors tried to hide their unease, but Rain saw several of them flicking suspicious glances at the tree walls. When Rijonn thought no one was looking, he gave the wooden floor a thump with the toe of his boot. The floor thumped him back—hard enough that the great Fey jumped and nearly lost his balance. Gil gave his friend a withering glance.

Hawksheart ignored them both. "Ellysetta Erimea, will you look in my mirror?"

She wet her lips. "What will I see? Because I've looked into oracles before, and they've never shown anything pleasant."

"I doubt that will be any different now." A surprising note of kindness gentled Hawksheart's voice. "You were born to be a world changer. It is not an easy path to walk; nor, as your mate pointed out, is it one without great suffering and sacrifice." He took a step forward, arms outstretched as if he meant to take her hands, but Rain and the quintet closed ranks again. The Elf king stopped in his tracks. "The question, Ellysetta Erimea, is not whether you will change the world, but whether you will change it for the good."

"How can you doubt?" Rain growled. "You have only to look at her to see she is bright and shining."

"Elvish eyes see differently from Fey," Hawksheart answered mildly. "Your truemate's Song is neither simple nor certain. She holds within her the potential for great good as well as for the greatest evil this world has ever seen. She is a vessel of the gods the likes of which has not been seen since the Time Before Memory. Not even Grandfather has ever spoken of her except to say she was coming and that the Lord of Valorian must look for her arrival. Make no mistake, Tairen Soul, the fate of the world lies in the balance, and your mate will determine which way the scales tip."

"I have already said I will choose death before I allow myself to fall to Darkness," Ellysetta told him. "The tairen will see to it. I have their oaths."

"*Bayas.* Those are possible end notes of your Song, and they still shine brightly, which means they may yet come to pass. But there are many different verses that lead to other possibilities, and they are the ones I hope to see more clearly. If you will consent to look in the mirror."

Rain put a hand on Ellysetta's shoulder. "If she consents, will you commit Elvia to join us in our fight against the Eld?"

Gold-tipped lashes shuttered the Elf king's piercing eyes. "I cannot. If Elvia joins you now, the fate you fear most will come to pass."

"All will be lost if you *don't* help us," Rain countered. "We cannot win against the Eld alone."

"I agree you cannot, but if the Elves enter the coming battle, the High Mage will complete his claiming of your *shei'tani*—and that will mean the end of all Light in this world. I have seen this in every variation of her Song. It is a certainty, not a possibility. The Elves must not fight. It would seal the doom of us all."

Ellysetta half turned towards Rain, instinctively seeking the shelter of his arms.

"Explain. How would your aid in this war ensure her Mageclaiming?" Rain persisted. He didn't even ask how the Elf king knew she was Mage Marked. Elves Saw too much—about everything.

"She will not take the journey she must if the Elves come to your aid. That is all I can say. If I reveal more, the outcome might be equally as devastating."

"Do not toy with us." Rain's fingers itched to pull his blades from their sheaths, but he kept his hands firmly at his sides. "Forgive my bluntness, Lord Galad, but if you want Ellysetta to help you better See her Song in the Dance, you need to offer us something in return. And what she needs now is help to rid herself of her Mage Marks and complete our bond. What I need now are swords and bows and warriors to wield them."

"There are only two ways to remove her Marks—either complete your bond or kill the Mage who Marked her. As for military aid, you have already been receiving that, whether you know it or not—or did you think the Feraz were going to sit idle in this new Mage War?"

Rain drew up short. "The Feraz?"

"Have been harrying my southern borders for months now."

"Ambassador Brightwing said nothing of it when we met in Celieria City."

"And I would say nothing now, except you are determined to think the worst of me." Hawksheart pinched the bridge of his nose in a weary gesture. "Believe me, Tairen Soul, I will give what aid I can when I know my interference will not send your mate's Song down the path of destruction. How to help is what I've been trying to See since the day I first Saw her Song as a boy—and lest you forget, I dispatched Brightwing to Celieria City to offer you that help the day I learned that her Song had begun, the day a Celierian maiden called a tairen from the sky."

Rain grew suddenly still. "That day in Tehlas, when you told my father I called a Song in the Dance, did you also know that I would have a truemate—and that she would be the one you'd been waiting for?"

The Elf's expression grew shuttered, but he admitted the truth. "I Saw it before you were born."

"You knew that I would scorch the world."

"I knew. That Song was certain long before you were born."

Anger simmered in his heart. "So you knew Sariel would die?"

"Your truemate could never have called your soul if you were still bound to Sariel."

"And you just stood by and let it all happen?"

"Stood by?" For the first time, anger sparked in the Elf king's eyes. "My people fought beside yours in every battle and died by the tens of thousands—many by your flame—which I and many of those who perished had Seen before it happened. Loved ones I had known for millennia surrendered their immortal lives to help the Fey hold the Shadow at bay, but some things, Rain Worldscorcher, we could not prevent. Some things had to unfold exactly as they did because the gods willed it so."

"The gods," Rain spat. "You mean that flaming Dance of yours."

"Of course I mean the Dance!" Hawksheart exclaimed. "The Dance is the will of the gods, and our ability to See it was the gift entrusted to the first Elf, Taliesin Silvereye, when the gods fashioned our peoples from the stars. You Fey are the champions of Light, the chosen swords of the gods in the fight against the Dark. We Elves are the beacons, born to guide and aid you."

"Guide us? If the Mage Wars were the outcome of your guidance, the Fey can scorching well do without it!"

"And yet, here you are, seeking my help and guidance."

Rain opened his mouth, then snapped it shut. Damn the Elf. "Because I have no choice. Because my *shei'tani* needs answers only you can provide. And because I know we cannot win this war without your help—and you know it, too, yet still you refuse to provide it."

"There is much you do not understand."

"Because you refuse to tell me."

"Because I cannot reveal the future I have Seen without changing what will happen!" Hawksheart snapped. "Too much is at stake, Tairen Soul. More than you can imagine. You distrust me, and I understand that. But I assure you, the Elves are in the service of the Light and always have been. My people left the Fading Lands when the Fey raised the Mists, but the moment you returned to the world, I sent my ambassador to you so that I could offer guidance and counsel as I have to every other Defender of the Fey who has ruled the Fading Lands. Your response," he added pointedly, "was to send one I did not invite in your stead."

Rain scowled. "I needed to get Ellysetta behind the Mists. Keeping her safe from the Mages was my first priority, and that took precedence over any desire of yours, Elf." Violence simmered just beneath the surface of Rain's skin. Already he could feel the tairen raking at its bonds, claws unsheathed and sharp as knives, the hunter's growl rumbling deep within him.

Ellysetta put a hand over his. «*He is not the enemy, shei'tan, and though he is definitely keeping something from us, he is sincere in his desire to help.*» Aloud, to Hawksheart, she said, "Rain did what he thought best, Lord Galad, just as I'm sure you do. I will look into your mirror, but I want three things in return." Her voice throbbed with low, persuasive *shei'dalin* tones.

Whether influenced by her push or not, Hawksheart bowed his head in agreement. "Name your price, Ellysetta Erimea. If I can give you what you request without endangering the outcome of your Song, I will."

"First, I want your oath, sworn on all you hold dear, that you will do everything in your power to stop me from becoming the monster I saw in the Eye of Truth."

The Elf king nodded. "This I am already sworn to do. If you fall to the Mages, Ellysetta, Light falls with you, and the Dance of this world dies. What else?"

"I want to know how to complete my truemate bond with Rain."

Even before she finished speaking, Hawksheart was shaking his head. "*Anio*. That, I am afraid, I cannot tell you. That is a journey you and your mate must take together—without outside aid or interference."

"But—"

"I am sorry," he interrupted, his tone firm and uncompromising. "I cannot guide the journey your souls must take. Only the two of you can do that."

"Will you at least tell us if we will complete our bond?" she persisted.

The Elf king hesitated, clearly reluctant, but after several moments, he admitted, "There are several variations of your Song that contain that verse."

"*Beylah vo*, Lord Galad." She threaded her fingers through Rain's. "That gives me a measure of hope, at least." She took a deep breath. "Then I have one final request."

"Which is?"

"I want to know the truth about myself. I want to know how I know the things I do. Why can I wield Fey'cha like a master when I've never touched one before? Why can I heal souls in ways no other *shei'dalin* can? Where did I come from and what was done to me—and can it be undone? I want to know who my birth parents were and if they're still alive."

Hawksheart bowed his head for a moment, and his eyes closed as if he were suddenly weary. "What was done cannot be undone, my child. The past can only be used to shape the future."

"I understand that. But if I agree to look in your mirror, you must give me the truth about my past." She took a step closer. "You do know it, don't you? If I am the one you've been waiting for, surely you must have Seen it."

He inhaled deeply and exhaled a heavy sigh. "*Bayas*," he admitted. "I know your truth. If you are certain you wish to know it, too, then I will share it with you. You have Seen a part of it yourself already."

"Thank you." Ellysetta drew a deep breath. A sense of fatalistic calm suffused her. Not knowing was far worse than any unpleasant secret Hawksheart might reveal. She couldn't change what she was or where she came from, but she could at least face the truth and find a way to make peace with it. She was tired of jumping at shadows and fearing what she was.

"Then we have a compact?"

Rain's arm tightened around her waist. «*Be very sure this is what you want, shei'tani,*» he whispered. «*Once you strike a bargain with an Elf, he will hold you to your word; and inevitably what you bargained for doesn't turn out the way you expected.*»

She patted the golden steel brace covering his forearm. «*I need to do this, Rain. Mama always used to say it's better to choke on a bitter truth than savor a honeycake lie. He has the answers I need, and this may be my only chance to discover them.*» She stroked his hand, each touch a caress filled with love and understanding and pleading. After a few moments, his arm fell reluctantly away from her waist.

"Well?" Hawksheart prompted. "Do we have an agreement?" His piercing Elvish eyes never left her face.

Ellysetta swallowed a sudden stab of fear and nodded. "*Aiyah.*"

"The offer has been made and accepted. The bargain is Elf-struck." He clapped his hands and sparks shot out in a blossom of gold and green fire to swirl in the air between them. A sudden electric tingle raced through her veins. When the sparks faded, the Elf king waved an arm towards the shining blue pool. "Kneel beside the mirror. I would first See your Song, and then I will give you the truth of your past."

As Ellysetta moved towards the pool and knelt on the spongy moss at its bank, Hawksheart walked towards the edge of the dim chamber. He laid his hands upon the inner tree wall and murmured something in lyrical Elvish. A moment later, the chamber was flooded with a pleasant but rather overpowering woodsy aroma, sweet, earthy, and pungent.

Ellysetta swayed as dizziness overtook her.

Do not fear, and do not resist. Hawksheart's voice rang in her head like the tolling of a bell, resonant and irresistible. Not Spirit but something else. Something deeper and more powerful. *Grandfather merely shares the scent of his liferings. It will help open your mind to the mirror. Breathe deeply. Take his scent into your lungs.*

Without hesitation, Ellysetta breathed as deeply as her lungs would allow. The dim room took on a hazy cast, as if a mist had crept into the chamber to throw everything out of focus. Beside her, in the depths of the shimmering blue pool, colors began to gather and swirl.

Now hold your hands over the mirror. When I tell you, put your palms upon the surface of the water . . . but be very careful not to submerge them. The mirror is powerful magic, and you are not trained in its use.

Her hands moved of their own volition out over the water. The colors in the pool leaped and twirled towards them as if in greeting. Ellysetta watched with a dazed sense of detachment, as if those hands belonged to someone else.

«Shei'tani?» Rain's thoughts pressed against hers. Some part of her was dimly aware of his concern, but she couldn't seem to summon a response. Her lungs were filled with the overpowering fragrance of the Sentinel, and her mind felt muddled.

She watched with a strange, detached disorientation as her hands lowered, palms down, fingers splayed, until at last the cool water of the mirror touched her skin. Her eyelashes fluttered, and she felt a strange, electric tug, as if the liquid in the pool were pure magic. Perhaps it was—and it was trying to draw her into its blue depths. She leaned forward.

Stop.

Hawksheart's command froze her in place. Her hands barely kissed the still surface of the pool.

You know how to share your essence with a thing. Share it with the mirror now.

She drew a breath, closed her eyes, and summoned the brilliant rainbow-lit darkness of Fey vision. In that darkness the world around her was a bright weave of glowing magic: red Fire, green Earth, gleaming blue Water, silvery Air, and lavender Spirit. Here, in the heart of Grandfather, the colors were so dense the darkness was virtually impossible to see, and the water of the mirror shone a blinding blue-white. Into that dazzling brightness she poured a portion of the potent energy that was her essence, the living magic unique to her alone.

The pool flared. The colors of Grandfather flared as well, and the entire room went so magic-bright Ellysetta cried out and opened her eyes. Fey vision still overlapped natural sight, and what had been a dim, windowless hollow lit only by the glow of the mirror pool was now as bright as the Great Sun. She glanced over her shoulder. Rain and her quintet stood in a protective semicircle directly behind her, and though their silvery Fey luminescence was dazzling to her enhanced vision, each of the Fey appeared as dim shadows against Grandfather's searing light.

Concentrate, Ellysetta Erimea. Find the essence of your Song.

Ellysetta turned towards Galad Hawksheart, but like the Sentinel tree and the mirror pool, the Elf king was so bright he made her eyes hurt. "The light is blinding. I can't see."

You do not need to see. You only need to think of your Song.

"But I don't know my song. Even the tairen could not hear it."

I do not speak of tairen song. You have not yet accepted that part of your soul, so of course you do not hear it. I speak of your life's Song. Everyone has one. It is an individual life's unique pattern, its joys and sorrows, its loves and fears, its memories and dreams. Think of those things. Summon your Song.

Faces flashed across her memory, vignettes of the happiest days of her life. Mama, Papa, the twins. Her fear and awe the day Rain Tairen Soul swooped down from the sky to claim her. Selianne Pyerson, laughing and giggling over some girl-ish fancy. Lillis and Lorelle squealing and dancing in circles, their mink brown curls bobbing against their slender shoulders. Rain gathering her into his arms, his eyes glowing stars that regarded her as if she were the sun around which all his world revolved.

Gradually, other not-so-happy memories emerged as well. Kelissande Minset's sneering superiority. Queen Annoura's scarcely veiled mockery as she assessed Ellysetta during her first appearance at court. The Church of Light priests in Hartslea who'd come to examine her for demon possession. Rain drawing back from her in horror as the black smudge of the Mage's Mark bloomed like a dread flower over her heart.

Bayas. You are doing well. Keep concentrating. Let the memories come.

The memories turned darker still. Nightmares from her childhood. Dreams of blood and death and war. Screaming. The exorcists with their terrible needles. Pain! Oh, dear gods, such pain! Hot tears gathered in her eyes. The tairen dying. The High Mage, with his burning, ember-kissed eyes, laughing in triumph. *You'll kill them, girl. You'll kill them all. It's what you were born for.* Mama dying in her arms. That horrible, unchangeable moment when a *sel'dor* blade had flashed and Mama's head rolled away from her body.

Rage.

She cried out and started to pull her hands from the mirror's surface, hoping that breaking the contact would stop the onslaught.

Anio! Hawksheart barked, his voice a hammer of command. *No. You must continue.*

"I don't want to." She whimpered like a child afraid to set foot into a dark room. Cold shivered down her limbs. She couldn't feel her legs tucked beneath her, but her hands and arms had turned to lumps of ice, freezing and burning all at once.

You must. This is the price for the truth you asked of me.

"I've changed my mind. I don't want it anymore."

The bargain was Elf-struck. It cannot be undone.

The images of her life began to flash faster as the events became more recent. The Massan. Venarra holding the soul of a dying Fey woman to life while other *shei'dalins* worked frantically to heal her broken body. The death of the tairen kitling Forrahl. Ellysetta's descent into the Well of Souls to save the other kitlings. The terrible piercing anguish of two more Mage Marks, and Rain's own daring plunge into the Well to rescue her. The battle of Orest. Rain emerging from Veil Lake, wreathed in blinding magic as he donned the golden war steel of the Feyreisen. Saving Aartys and Truthspeaking the Mage. The dark voices whispering in her mind. The Azrahn-gifted children conceived as a result of her weave. Rain's Rage during the Eld attack. The way Fey'cha fit so comfortably in her hands. The moment she made her bargain with the Elf king.

The images came faster and faster as the scenes they depicted grew closer to the present. When they reached this moment, Ellysetta cried out and her spine went rigid. The flashing images became a blur, yet she could see them with vivid clarity.

War. Armies stretched as far as she could see. Dharsa in smoldering ruins. Rain, in tairen form, roaring in pain as a *sel'dor* bowcannon bolt ripped through his chest and sent him tumbling from the sky. Rain and Ellysetta, captured by the Eld and draped in *sel'dor* chains as black-armored soldiers and a blue-robed Primage prodded them towards a great gaping black maw.

In slow motion, so that each moment seemed to last a lifetime, Ellysetta saw a red Fey'cha plunge into Rain's back, saw Rain's eyes widen in surprise and pain. He fell dead at her feet, his limbs shaking with tremors as the lethal venom from the blade raced through his body. She saw herself standing over his body. Her eyes were black as night, sparkling with malevolent red stars, as she raised the bloody Fey'cha over her head and laughed.

"*No!*" Ellysetta shrieked the denial and tried to pull her hands from the mirror, but something held them in place. She could not free herself, and the visions continued to flash in the bright light of the pool, each more awful than the previous. The worst visions from every nightmare she'd ever harbored. A future so grim she could not bear it.

The world in flames. Millions slaughtered. Celierians, Fey, and Elves in chains. Fey'Bahren a scorched boneyard baking in a merciless sun, while overhead winged monsters that once had been tairen dominated the sky, their hides as bare and scabrous as those of the foul *darrokken*. Acid dripped from their fangs, leaving smoldering pits in the monsters' wakes.

Lillis and Lorelle not dead, but worse: dark-eyed imps of evil, laughing and dancing in showers of blood while they played Stones with the skulls of slaughtered children. And watching them fondly, from a diseased throne of death: herself, the Queen of Darkness.

"Stop!" Ellysetta cried. "Did you bring me here only to torture me? You said there was still hope! Where is the hope in this?" She writhed and yanked at her hands, fighting the unseen power that kept her chained to the mirror pool, but she could not free herself. «*Rain! Help me!*» she called on the bond threads that tied part of his soul to hers.

He didn't answer.

Fear hollowed her out and left her shaking. "Where's Rain? What have you done with him?" She tried to see him but both her Fey vision and her physical sight were now completely blinded by the blazing magic that filled the chamber. All she could see was burning, blinding, dazzling white light.

Calm yourself, Ellysetta Erimea, Hawksheart chided. *Your fears are groundless. Your mate is safe, and exactly where you left him. Be calm.*

Calm? She was blind and trapped and couldn't reach Rain, and this stranger whom Rain didn't trust wanted her to be calm?

"Then why can't I hear him? Why can't I see him? Why are you holding me against my will?"

She heard something that sounded like a sigh. *You cannot leave because our bargain was Elf-struck. Your own magic binds you until the price you agreed to is paid. The harder you struggle, the more powerful the bonds become. You cannot see because the magic that blinds you is a reflection of your own power. The more magic you expend trying to free yourself, the more blinding the light becomes. If you calm yourself and cease your struggle, the light will begin to fade.*

"Why didn't you tell me this before I touched the mirror?"

I had not believed it necessary, but you are much stronger than I Saw. He sounded slightly embarrassed and not quite as sure of himself as he had seemed at their meeting. *And much brighter.*

Ellysetta wasn't sure if he was telling the truth, but as she stopped fighting to free herself, the blinding whiteness around her began to dim. Not much, but once again she could make out the faint shadows of her truemate and her quintet standing nearby.

Her head drooped in relief. Her hands remained touching the cool, motionless surface of the pool, but she was afraid to look again, afraid of what else it would show. "You told us there was still hope, yet every future the mirror has shown me so far is evil. I saw Rain murdered—and I was the one wielding the blade."

Bayas, but you looked into the mirror with fear, and so the mirror reflected the thing you fear most. I looked with a different heart, and I saw other paths . . . several not so bleak. The Elf's voice softened with compassion. *Hope remains, faint though it may be. Look again, child. But this time, let love, not fear, guide your Song.*

If only it were so easy. "I don't think I know how to stop being afraid. It's been such a part of me my whole life."

There are some fears, young Ellysetta, that can never be conquered. Sometimes, all you can do is acknowledge your fear, then act in spite of it. Look again, Ellysetta, but fill your mind with hope.

Hope. The word made her want to weep. When had she ever truly known hope? Her nightmares, her seizures, the fears of demon possession: Evil had haunted her all her life, tainted every happiness with shadow. Most of the few people she'd allowed herself to love had died or been lost because of her: Selianne, Mama, Papa, and the twins. She loved Rain, but all she'd brought him was banishment from the Fading Lands and the threat of certain death.

Somewhere deep inside, some part of her knew their true-mate bond would never be complete. Rain would die because of her. Whether battling the Eld or from bond madness, it made no difference. In the end, she would kill him as surely as she killed him in her nightmares. As surely as she had caused the death of Mama and Selianne.

"He'll die because of me," she wept.

He will most certainly die if you do nothing. But more than that, all the Light of this world will die as well. Is that what you want, Ellysetta?

"No, of course not!"

Then look in the mirror, child. The gods sent you to fight the Dark, Ellysetta Erimea. Do not fear what you were born to do.

If it were only her life at stake, she could not have made herself look in the mirror again to see what other horrors would be revealed. But hers was *not* the only life at risk.

She knew the face of evil. She'd seen it in her dreams, and too often, lately, it had worn her own features. It must be stopped. There was no other option. Because, as Rain had once told her, when evil came calling, you couldn't reason with it. You couldn't bargain with it or strike terms of peace. You couldn't hide behind a locked door and hope that it would go away. Evil had no mercy. Evil didn't value life. It nursed its children on blood and hate. It celebrated death and hailed murder in the name of its Dark God.

She could not fail. No matter the cost to herself. For reasons she would never understand, the gods had apparently chosen her, Ellysetta Baristani, to be the hinge on which the fate of the world turned. And if there was anything in Hawksheart's mirror that would help her defeat the Shadow threatening all she held dear, she needed to find it.

Ellysetta lifted her head and looked back into the mirror.

CHAPTER EIGHTEEN

My love, my mate, my shei'tani
My life in this cage of pain, my soul's other half
I am not free to touch her, to protect her
Though we are one

My love, my child, my daughter
My gift to the world, my gift from the gods
I am not free to hold her, to know her
Though she is the one to save my people
To end my torment

The Torment of Lord Death,
by Shannisorran v'En Celay

"What's wrong?" Rain frowned at Ellysetta as she rose to her feet and stepped away from the blue phosphorescent glow of the mirror pool. "Have you changed your mind about trying to See your Song in the pool after all?"

She stopped in surprise. "But . . . I already did." She looked to Hawksheart, then back at Rain. "We've been at it for bells."

Rain's brows shot up to his hairline. "*Nei*, you knelt at the water's edge, touched the surface for no more than a moment or two, and stood up again." Behind him, her quintet nodded in agreement.

All eyes turned to Hawksheart.

The Elf spread his hands. "You both are correct. Your true-mate and I did, in fact, journey long and far, through a thousand different variations of her Song, though to you, our travels would have passed in the blink of an eye."

"I don't understand."

"The mirror is Elvish magic. Like the Faering Mists, what happens within the mirror exists outside of time. The only difference is that with the mirror, the Seer's body remains in this world and only the Seer's soul takes the journey."

Rain bristled instantly. "You said nothing about Ellysetta's soul leaving her body when she touched the mirror." He knew that was what happened when she entered the Well of Souls to save a life. But he also knew she needed to anchor herself before attempting such a thing, and she had not anchored herself before touching the mirror.

"She was in no danger. I was with her."

Rain kept his gaze pinned on Hawksheart's face, but he sent a tender weave of Spirit to Ellysetta, warm with love and concern. «*Are you all right, shei'tani?*» His hand lifted in silent invitation. She put her fingers in his and he pulled her to the protective safety of his side.

«*I am fine,*» she assured him.

He did not relax until he verified that for himself. His senses stroked hers like a dozen small caresses, probing for signs of distress. When he found none, the tension bristling through him eased a notch. "And did you find what you were looking for, Lord Galad?"

"Many things became clearer," the Elf king hedged. "Which verses of her Song will come to pass, I cannot say."

Rain had no patience for Elvish evasions. "What did you see, *shei'tani?*"

"I . . ." Ellysetta frowned. "I don't remember. A moment ago, I thought I did, but now . . ."

Rain's temper soared. He turned narrowed eyes on the Elf king. "You stole her memories of what she Saw?"

"If I cannot tell you the future for fear of changing it, I certainly couldn't let her See it and remember."

«*I hate the scorching Elves,*» Gil muttered darkly on the Warriors' Path. «*They may See a million futures, but they're flaming useless in the present. They never give a straight answer when a misdirection or evasion will do.*»

Rain shared Gil's sentiments wholeheartedly. The Fey could dance the blade's edge of truth with the best of them, but that didn't mean they liked having the same done to them. Especially not by some two-legged, pointy-eared tree rat.

When buying apples from an Elf, look carefully for the worms. The caution his father had whispered to him more than once now made perfect sense. His mother had always had a soft spot for her Elvish friends, but his father had never viewed them so kindly. *Never trust an Elf, unless you have no choice. And even then don't trust him much.*

Hawksheart spread his hands. "If I could help you more, Tairen Soul, I would, but my hands are tied by the dictates of the Dance. What I Saw in your truemate's Song confirmed that my interference would upset the balance of what must be."

"How about I upset the balance of your scorching head by striking it from your neck," Gil snarled. His hand fell to the hilt of his *meicha* scimitar.

"But the Elves have helped the Fey before," Rain reminded Hawksheart. "You fought as our allies in the Mage Wars."

"And in the Demon Wars before that," Gaelen added.

"And, the Dance willing, we will fight beside you again before our time in this world is done," the Elf king assured them. "But for now, my friends, as daunting as it may be, you must face the Eld without the magic of Elvia to guide or aid you. No matter what the cost, no matter how I'd hoped it would be different, that is how this verse in Ellysetta's Song must play out."

Rain wanted to argue, but he knew it would be pointless. An Elf, once decided upon a course, was impossible to budge—especially when it came to the Dance. Hawksheart and every Elf in his kingdom would rush headlong to their deaths if that was what they believed the Dance demanded.

In that respect, though Rain hated to admit it, Elves were rather like the Fey. The only difference was, the Fey devoted their intensity to the protection of their women, not the dictates of some gods-forsaken prophecy.

"So you will not help us," Rain bit out. "I do not like it, but I do accept it. My *shei'tani* fulfilled her end of your bargain. Now you fulfill yours. Give her the truth of her past, as you vowed to do. And this time, Elf, we will all stand witness so you cannot erase her memories."

Hawksheart closed his eyes briefly, then nodded as if bowing to a fate he would rather avoid. "*Bayas.* The time has indeed come. Please approach the mirror. All of you," he added with a sigh. "Though I had hoped otherwise, you all must witness what the mirror has to show."

Together, the Fey approached the glowing blue pool.

Ellysetta started to kneel beside the mirror pool, but Hawksheart stopped her. "*Anio,* Ellysetta Erimea. This time do not touch the water at all. There is no need, and it could be . . . problematic." The Elf king didn't elucidate. Instead, he closed his eyes, lifted his hands palms up, and began to chant in the fluid, musical tones of the Elven tongue. Once again, the air filled with the intoxicating aroma of the Sentinel's liferings.

This time, however, the surface of the mirror pool did not remain flat. Instead, a mist of shining droplets rose up from the pool to form a shimmering veil that rose and expanded until it touched the ceiling above and stretched from one curved inner wall of the room to the other so that a great screen of water bisected the chamber.

In a voice resonating with power, Hawksheart said, "Behold the circumstances of your birth, Ellysetta Erimea."

The surface of the veil darkened and swirled with color as the mirror had done earlier, but this time the brilliant white light of Ellysetta's power did not turn the room bright as day. The Sentinel's inner chamber remained lit only by the glow of the pool. The images swirling in the veil came into focus, as crisp and clear as if Ellysetta were looking through glass into a scene unfolding in the room next door.

Flickering sconces cast a pale orange-yellow glow around a windowless chamber burrowed out of black stone. A large desk piled high with books, scrolls, and parchments dominated the chamber. Seated behind it was a man, white-haired yet somehow ageless, clad in purple velvet robes that looked almost black in the firelight. His head was bent, and he was scratching a quill across the pages of what looked like a record book of some kind. The man looked up, and Ellysetta's heart froze as familiar, icy silver eyes met hers and seared into her soul.

For a moment, she thought it was real—that the mirror truly was a clear glass portal into that dark room and the High Mage of Eld could see her as clearly as she could see him—but then he bent his head back to his book, dipped his quill in ink, and continued to write.

"That is him? The High Mage?" Rain asked quietly.

She nodded, but didn't pull her eyes off the man in the mirror's shining veil. Though she'd never seen him clearly in her dreams, she recognized him instantly. The invisible Mage Marks that formed a four-pointed ring over her heart went cold, and her stomach tightened with dread. When a knock sounded at the door, and the Mage called, "Enter," her heart slammed in her chest and suspicion hardened to icy certainty.

The man she might never have seen, but his voice was etched eternally in her mind, never to be forgotten. This was the High Mage who had tormented her all her life. The man responsible for her mother's death and all the lives lost on the battlefields of Orest and Teleon.

The man who had stolen the souls and lives of young tairen in the egg and used them for his evil experiments.

Deep within, her tairen begin to growl and rake its claws across her nerves.

Rain's hand slipped into hers, and his broad, warm fingers curled tight, offering protection and reassurance. «*I am with you, shei'tani. And this is just an image from the past. He cannot hurt you.*»

He thought she was afraid of the Mage.

Perhaps she should be. But her only real fear was of the hatred bubbling in her veins like fire. If she were wearing her tairen's true form, her fangs would be dripping venom, ravenous with bloodlust. The urge to kill, to rend and maim—to devour—was so fierce it shook her to her core.

Within the mirror's veil, the scene Hawksheart had summoned continued to play out. The knock on the door was a servant calling the Mage to some appointment. The white-haired High Mage exited his office to walk down a series of dark corridors tunneled out of black rock. Black metal-clad doors lined both sides of the corridor, and muscular guards gripping evil-looking barbed *sel'dor* pikes stood watch beside a number of them.

"Those walls look like they contain *sel'dor* ore," Gil muttered.

"A cave of some kind?" Bel suggested. "Perhaps burrowed into a *sel'dor* mine? It would explain why the Fey never sensed the Mages gathering their power."

"And why the *dahl'reisen* could never track them back to their lair," Gaelen agreed.

"Where are the largest *sel'dor* mines in Eld?" Tajik asked. "If that's where he is, then those are the first places we should start looking."

One of the doors opened, and the Mage entered. Inside was an observation room with a window that looked into an adjoining chamber where a young brunette woman lay chained to a flat table. Her eyes were half-closed, and her head lolled on her shoulders in what appeared to be a drugged stupor.

Another door opened on the far side of the room, and four burly guards, their meaty fists clenched around chains, dragged a snarling, naked man into the room by the *sel'dor* collar clamped around his neck and the manacles that shackled his wrists and ankles. His pale skin shone with a faint luminescence. Dark blond hair hung about his shoulders and face in matted tangles. The moment he caught sight of the woman on the table, his body went still as stone. His head came up sharply, whipping the hair back away from his face to reveal black Azrahn-filled eyes and a scar that tracked from the corner of his mouth to his left ear. His nostrils flared like those of a wolf scenting its prey.

Beside Ellysetta, Gaelen stiffened and drew in a hissing breath.

"You know him?" Rain asked.

"Korren vel Dahn. One of the Brotherhood. Six hundred years ago, I sent him into Eld to find the Mages' lair, but he never returned."

"Well, looks like he found it," Gil muttered.

In the scene unfolding in the mirror's mist, Korren lunged for the woman on the table. His body had reacted to her presence with unmistakable intent. Ellysetta gasped and turned her eyes away as the *dahl'reisen* fell upon the barely conscious woman. Rain's hand tightened on hers, and she felt the disgust and shame roiling through him as he forced himself to watch the creature who had once been an honorable warrior of the Fey commit his unspeakable act.

"May his soul burn in the Seventh Hell for all eternity," Bel whispered in horror.

"Do not judge him so harshly," Hawksheart said quietly. "It took two hundred years to break him, and madness can turn even the best of men into beasts. He wasn't the first and he was far from the last."

Hawksheart's soft-spoken words made Rain flinch and tighten his grip on Ellysetta. With her face pressed to his throat, she could feel his recoiling horror as clearly as her own. *«You could never do such a thing, shei'tan,»* she assured him.

«I could no longer, it's true,» he answered. *«But before your soul called mine? I slaughtered millions without remorse. What would one more foul crime have mattered?»*

«It would have mattered, and you would not have done it.»

His lips touched her brow in a tender caress. *«Korren's deed is done. You can look again.»*

Ellysetta turned back in time to see the woman Korren had raped walking with blank-eyed docility behind several servants. Ellysetta scowled at Hawksheart. "Why are you showing us this? That poor creature is not the woman who gave me birth; nor is Korren vel Dahn my sire." She'd seen the two shadowy figures of her parents in a dream beside the Bay of Flames a month ago, and neither the unconscious woman nor her rapist could have been one of the couple revealed to her.

"*Anio,* they are not. She and vel Dahn were but two of many unfortunate souls imprisoned by the High Mage of Eld."

The scene in the veil of water swirled out of focus. When it cleared again, they saw the same woman strapped to a birthing table, her face flushed with recent exertions, while the white-haired High Mage of Eld held her newborn son in his arms and spun a swirl of Azrahn-laced magic that drew faint sparkles of answering magic to the surface of the baby's eyes.

"We already know he's been trying to breed a Tairen Soul," Rain said.

"Look more closely," Hawksheart advised. The screen shimmered and the woman on the birthing table became a different woman, this one a blond, green-eyed Elf, and the child in the High Mage's hands became a smaller boy crowned with a shock of thick black hair. A moment later, a black-haired woman with deep blue eyes wept as she reached for her son. That mother and child became another, then another and another.

"Not all of the individuals you see are Fey. He's been breeding you, yes, but he's been crossing other magical bloodlines as well. Elvish, Fey, Feraz, Eld."

"Why?"*

"To create something stronger . . . something deadlier than even you, Worldscorcher."

Rain's grip tightened around Ellysetta's fingers. "Ellysetta?"

"She was his first success, though she did not come from his experimental bloodlines."

Tension fell over the room. Unguarded thoughts—mostly from Rain but from the others as well—whispered across her mind. Concern edging on fear pressed against her as the warriors digested Hawksheart's revelations. Rain and Ellysetta were the most powerful creatures they'd ever known. If the Mage had created something even stronger than they . . .

"There are others?" Tajik growled. "Like the Feyreisa?"

"There are others," Hawksheart confirmed. "But none yet who have successfully come into their full power."

"He must be stopped," Bel said.

"*Bayas*," Hawksheart agreed. "He must."

"And yet you and the Elves will not help us," Rain said in a hard, flat voice.

"We cannot."

"Convenient."

The Elf king's eyes flashed. "It is anything but." A muscle jumped in his jaw. "To know a future that you cannot change—that you must merely stand by and witness—to know what must happen and which people you love must suffer or die, and know you must not—you *cannot*—do anything to stop it . . . that is neither convenient nor easy, Worldscorcher. Foreknowledge is the gods' most excruciating form of torture."

"So you say," Gil sneered, "but which of your own loved ones have suffered lately?"

Hawksheart's expression became a mask that seemed carved of smooth, impermeable Sentinel wood: golden, silent, and emotionless. Except for the burning green fire of his eyes. His hand swung gracefully out, and the elegant, tapered fingers gestured. "These."

In the shimmering veil, a new image took shape. A pair of lovers cast in shadow, their skin glowing faintly silver in the darkness. The man tall, broad shouldered, the woman slender and elegant beside him, her hair a mass of gleaming curls that spilled down her back in fiery waves as his powerful arms clutched her tight. Ellysetta's heart skipped a beat as she recognized the couple from her dreams that night by the shores of the Bay of Flames.

Her parents. The tormented souls who had given her birth.

Darkness slashed across the image, and a new, grim picture of the man who was Ellysetta's sire replaced the other. He hung limp and bloodied from thick black metal chains. His head drooped on his chest, and the matted tangle of his black hair draped around his face like a ragged shroud. Slowly, he looked up, paralyzing her with the blazing green gaze that filled her vision . . . pupil-less, radiant green wells of power . . . tairen's eyes.

Rain and every member of Ellysetta's quintet went still, and silence fell over the chamber. The only sound came from the low chant of Elvish words that seemed to rise from the wood of the chamber walls, as if the Grandfather Sentinel tree were alive and speaking in the low murmur of a host of voices.

To the right of the man, another scene took shape. Within a bright, well-lit room, the flame-haired Fey woman lay strapped to a birthing table. She was screaming, her beautiful face creased in anguish as a woman hurried away with a small, swaddled babe. Sensing his mate's grief, the chained man roared and lunged against his bonds in helpless fury.

"Blessed gods." Gaelen's stunned voice—barely more than a whisper—was the first to break the silence.

"But they died," Bel protested. "They were lost in the Wars."

"You know them?" Ellysetta flicked her quintet a quick glance and saw the stunned recognition on their faces. "Who are they?" She turned back to the images of the man and the woman—strangers, yet somehow so familiar—who had given her birth.

"The man is Shannisorran v'En Celay." Gaelen's voice was hoarse. "The fiercest warrior ever to walk the Fading Lands. He was my *chatok* in the Cha Baruk. The woman is his true-mate. Her name is—"

"Elfeya." Tajik sank to his knees. His nails scored bloody lines down his face. "My sister." His hands, his face, his entire body was shaking, and power gathered around him in swirling waves. "The Mage has her? The Mage has my sister?" Slowly, fists clenched, he faced the Elf king. His eyes had turned to blue flame, and magic flared about him in a flash of near-blinding green light. The ground rumbled and shifted as Tajik's Earth magic shook the great Grandfather Sentinel to its deepest roots. "You knew," he snarled.

"*Bayas*," Hawksheart acknowledged without flinching. "I knew."

Tajik snatched two red Fey'cha from their sheaths and whipped his hands back to throw.

"Tajik, *nei!*" Gil cried.

Before the Fey'cha could leave Tajik's hand, Gaelen drove a fist into the side of the Fire master's head. The red-haired Fey dropped like a stone.

Ellysetta cried out and ran to kneel at Tajik's side. After checking to verify that the warrior was unharmed, merely unconscious, she cast Gaelen a reproachful look.

The former *dahl'reisen* met the gazes of his shocked friends with a grim, set jaw and wintry eyes. He snapped a hard glance at Rain. "We should take his memory before he wakes."

"Take his memory?" Bel protested. "This is his sister you're talking about. He has a right to know—"

"To know what?" Gaelen whirled on Bel. "That she's been a captive of the High Mage of Eld for the last thousand years? Tortured, raped, forced to endure and serve gods only know what sort of evil?" His lips curled back. "I know what a powerful Fey can do to avenge his sister. Marikah at least died quick. If she had suffered the same fate as Elfeya, and I knew of it, I would have laid such waste to Eld, not even the gods themselves would have been able to redeem my soul. *Dahl'reisen*? Bah! I would willingly have become the blackest soul of the Mharog and gorged myself on blood and death."

Violence raged just below Gaelen's surface—not hot, as Rain's Rage was, but deadly, icily cold. Only his will kept the power of that Rage from spilling over in a freezing wave.

"Tajik is almost as powerful as I am. If he wakes remembering that the Eld took his sister, all the magic in the world won't keep him from trying to reach her—or seeking his vengeance for what's been done to her. I may not like vel Sibboreh very much, but I've no mind to see him walk the path I tread. Do you?" He looked around. No one could hold his challenging gaze without looking away. "Take his memory. One day, he will thank you for it."

"He is right," Gil said.

Rain's jaw tightened. "*Aiyah.*"

"*Anio.*"

Five warriors whipped their heads around and bared their teeth in a snarl at the Elf king. "Stay out of this, Elf," Rain bit out. "You have done enough."

"This is his verse in the Dance," Hawksheart insisted. "Elfeya is my kin, and more beloved to me than you know, but what has happened—no matter how brutal—was her verse. Her captivity had to happen just as it did. And her brother must have that knowledge."

"Scorch your flaming Dance," Gaelen growled. "For a thousand years, you've watched the torment of your own cousin and done nothing to help her—even knowing her *shei'dalin* powers made her helpless to defend herself. There are not words enough to describe the contempt I feel for you."

Hawksheart lifted his chin. "I understand your feelings."

"Well, I don't understand yours." Bel's voice was colder than Ellysetta had heard it in months. He sounded like the *rasa* he'd been when she'd first met him: dead to emotion, perfectly capable of murdering without a qualm. Perfectly capable of slaughtering Hawksheart right now. "How could any man who claims to be dedicated to Light willingly surrender his own cousin to the Dark as you have done? You let her be taken, and did nothing to save her."

"You think I am a monster, but what happened to Elfeya had to happen."

"*Why?*" Gil snarled.

Hawksheart clamped his lips shut and did not answer. His piercing eyes turned to mirrored stones, hard and aloof. But one betraying flicker in Ellysetta's direction—one fleeting glimpse of searing, all-revealing agony—made her heart rise up in her throat.

And then she knew. She knew why Elfeya and Shannisorran v'En Celay—her birth parents—had been left to suffer the Mage's torments for the last thousand years. She knew why Hawksheart had stood by and let it happen, though he'd internalized his cousin's torment and made it his own, suffering each day as if he were the one imprisoned.

"Because of me," Ellysetta whispered.

"What?" Rain turned to her, outraged. "Do not even suggest such a thing. You have nothing to do with this. You weren't even born!"

"And if my parents had not been captured by the High Mage of Eld, I never would have been. At least, not as I am. Not as the Dance needed me to be." Her voice was soft but sure, her unwavering gaze pinned on Lord Galad's face. The sorrowed closing of his brilliant, haunted eyes confirmed her suspicions. "I wouldn't have been a Tairen Soul. I wouldn't have been your truemate."

Rain drew back in horror and muttered an instinctive *shei'tan*'s denial. "Of course you would have. Our bond was created by the gods, not some Elden Mage."

"But without the Mage, I wouldn't have a tairen's soul tied to mine. That part of my soul wouldn't exist, and that part of your soul would have no mate." She glanced back at Hawksheart.

"What will I do that is so important to the Dance that so many people had to suffer so much?"

"I've already told you. You were born to decide the fate of this world—to secure it for the Light or plunge it into eternal Darkness."

"But if I hadn't been born, I wouldn't be a threat. You could have stopped my birth simply by preventing Shan and Elfeya from being captured and tormented for a thousand years. Why didn't you end it then?"

"You don't understand. You are not the threat, Ellysetta Erimea. You are the gift the gods sent to combat it. A powerful Light born of terrible Darkness. You are the sword that cuts both ways, forged in a crucible of pain and suffering, hammered on the anvil of dark magic, and tempered by the love and sacrifice of both mortal and immortal parents, of your *shei'tan*, and every child of Light offered the chance to serve and protect you. If they prove worthy, you will not fall to Darkness. That is the test of this world—and specifically of the Fey—and that is the price the gods demanded for your birth."

Hawksheart met the hostile gazes of the Fey warriors gathered protectively around her. His eyes burned like green flames in the graven image of his face. "You think I am a monster to have allowed this. Perhaps I am, but I assure you it was no easy thing to stand by and watch one I love suffer as Elfeya has. To know that if I tried to help her, I would condemn the world to Darkness."

"Some things should never be sacrificed, no matter what the risk," Rain interjected. "If you had told us, Elf, every man, woman, and child in the Fading Lands would have fought to the death before allowing a single Fey woman to suffer at the hands of the Mages as Elfeya has done."

"That is exactly why I said nothing." Hawksheart glared at Rain. "If your truemate had never been born, there would have been no hope for this world. That was a truth I Saw plain as the Light of the Great Sun two thousand years ago. The Fey are the gods' chosen champions of Light, yet your race has been in decline much longer than you ever suspected. Ellysetta was born to save the Fey, and by saving them, to save this world."

"She has already saved us," Rain said. "The tairen kitlings are hatched and half a dozen Fey women are with child for the first time in over a thousand years."

"A temporary reprieve only."

"Then what is left to do?" Ellysetta asked. "If saving the tairen and bringing fertility back to the Fey is not enough, what more must I do?"

The Elf's shapely lips compressed. "That, I do not know. No matter how deeply I look, that answer is hidden from me. Even Grandfather—if he knows—will not speak of it. I know only that the future of this world hangs in the balance, and you will tip the scales one way or the other."

In Ellysetta's arms, Tajik began to stir. Instantly solicitous, she bent over his prone form and ran a hand lightly over the bleeding tracks he'd raked in his own cheeks and the swelling lump where Gaelen had hit him. Warm healing magic spilled from her fingertips and sank into his skin, eradicating all signs of the wounds and the blow.

Tajik's eyes fluttered open, hazy at first, then sharpening to full alertness as he focused on her face. Blue as the sky and filled with wonder, those eyes gazed up at her. His hand lifted to her face, but stopped a scant fingerspan from touching her. "*Kem'jita'nessa*. My sister's daughter. How could I not have known?"

Tears gathered at the edges of Ellysetta's lashes and a smile trembled on her lips. She caught his hand and pressed a kiss into the palm before holding it against her cheek. "How are you feeling . . . Uncle?"

Tajik's blue eyes went cloudy, then cold as he rose to his feet and turned a wintry gaze on his cousin, Galad Hawksheart. "I will not rest until I see you dead. This I do swear on—"

"*Parei!*" Ellysetta leapt to her feet and pressed her hand over Tajik's mouth, silencing the vow before he could complete it. "You will not swear vengeance against him. I forbid it."

Tajik gently removed himself from her grip. "*Ajiana*, you are my beloved sister's child and holder of my *lute'asheiva* bond, but this does not concern you."

"If you swear vengeance against him, then you must also swear it against me, for what he did, he did so I could be born."

Tajik's brows plummeted. Scowling, he regarded his brother Fey and found confirmation in their set jaws and brooding gazes.

Ellysetta laid her hand on Tajik's wrist. «*He has suffered,*» she told him privately. «*Every day since before your sister's captivity, he has suffered more than he would ever want anyone to know. He has taken no wife, sired no children, allowed himself no pleasure or joy in his own life since the day he Saw her fate.*» All that had come from the brief moment of unguarded communion when she'd met his Elvish eyes and, intentionally or not, he'd dropped the veil of secrecy he kept wrapped so securely about his private thoughts.

"We will find her, Tajik." Bel stepped forward and laid his hand on his friend's shoulder. "I swear to you, we will find Elfeya, and we will set her free."

"Assuming she and Shan still live," Gil muttered.

Ellysetta turned to Hawksheart. "Do they?"

His lashes fell to shutter the drowning sorrow that filled his eyes. The Elf king was far from the cold, unfeeling observer he appeared. He was simply expert at hiding his emotions. But somehow—perhaps through the communion of their souls when he'd joined her to explore the variations of her Songs—he could no longer hide so well from her.

"*Bayas,*" he admitted. "They still live."

"Show me."

"Child . . ."

Her jaw set. Her chin came up. "Show me," she insisted.

Hawksheart muttered something in Elvish, then closed his eyes briefly and gestured towards the mirror pool with one hand.

The shimmering veil of water rising up from the pool dimmed once more, shadow creeping in from the edges while the center swirled with colors that slowly coalesced into a final, grim vision of Ellysetta's parents, both still alive, but bloodied and broken, their bodies little more than oozing masses of cuts, burns, and mottled bruises.

They lay alone in separate cells carved from black rock, chained like dogs with heavy *sel'dor* manacles clamped around their wrists and ankles and necks. Only a dim glow of light from a flickering sconce lifted the darkness that surrounded them.

A choked moan of denial rattled in Tajik's throat. Elfeya—Ellysetta's birth mother and Tajik's sister—was barely breathing, her face bloodied and swollen, her left arm bent at an unnatural angle. The silvery glow of her Fey essence had been extinguished, and those few bits of skin that were as yet unmarred by blood, burns, or bruises were a pallid, sickly shade. Elfeya wasn't dead, but clearly she wasn't far from it.

Ellysetta clutched Rain's arm in a fierce grip. Horror roiled through her, and on its heels came the other emotion, white-hot and venomous.

Rage.

It raced through her blood like a bolt of lightning, enflaming her senses and igniting a bone-deep fury that threatened to explode into the same raw wildness she'd felt the day she'd watched her adoptive mother die beneath the brutal, decapitating chop of a *sel'dor* blade.

The dim light in her father Shannisorran v'En Celay's cell brightened, and a beam of sickly yellow light fell across his face as the cell door swung inward. A tall, robed figure entered, face hidden by the shadowy folds of the robe's deep hood.

As they had earlier, when Ellysetta had seen the image of the High Mage in Hawksheart's mirror, the Mage Marks over her heart prickled as if a hundred tiny splinters of ice had just jabbed into her skin. The cold of the Marks throbbed painfully against the heat of her Rage. Even without seeing the robed man's face, she recognized the High Mage of Eld.

Her tormentor. The murderer of generations of tairen kitlings.

The torturer of her birth parents. The evil man who'd stolen a tairen kitling's soul and tied it to her own.

Vengeance. Deep inside, the voice of her tairen hissed. *We will have vengeance for what he has done. He will scream as we screamed. He will fear as we feared. We will make him beg for death.*

«*Ellysetta. Shei'tani.*» Rain caught her hand, but the normally soothing peace of his love curled back from her Rage like tinder from flame.

Rip him. Shred him. Tear his flesh. Let his blood shower like rain upon our face. Let his screams be the music of our Song and his dying breath be the wind on which we soar.

Her head snapped back in sudden horror and she yanked her hand from Rain's. That last hate-filled clamor for blood hadn't come from her tairen.

It had come from her.

Before that realization had time to sink in, the High Mage of Eld gestured, and a pair of stocky, muscular guards stepped forward, gripped Shannisorran v'En Celay under his arms, and hauled him to his feet. His head drooped limply on his chest as the men dragged him a short way across the room and hooked the manacles at his wrists to heavy chains dangling from the ceiling.

Eld ~ Boura Fell

Shan's fingers curled around the heavy *sel'dor* chains that held him upright, and though the effort sent bolts of pain screaming through his tormented body, he pulled himself up and raised his head to cast a cold, defiant glare at the hooded face of his ancient tormentor. Every part of his body and soul ached with such pain and weariness it was all he could do to hold on to consciousness, but he would not give Vadim Maur the satisfaction of seeing how close to being broken he truly was. Days ago the countless agonies visited upon his flesh had become one throbbing blur—and with this latest visit, Shan knew his senses would soon be so overwhelmed he wouldn't feel even that anymore.

Elfeya huddled at the back of his mind, her soul taking refuge in his, her own pain no less than his own. They'd spared her nothing this time. She'd suffered so much, he doubted she would ever recover, and the sound of her screams, reverberating in his mind and soul, would haunt him for eternity.

Gently, each brush of his soul a caress of devotion, he detached himself from her and drew the protective barriers around his mind. He poured his strength into making them as strong as he could in the hope that he could buffer her from what was about to befall him. She was so fragile—so close to breaking—that he feared whatever new torment Vadim Maur had in store for him would push her shattered mind into madness. Part of Shan wanted to let that happen, because if she were lost, there would be nothing left to hold him to sanity. And in madness, there was escape. In madness, there existed no grief, no guilt, no shame for the horrors visited upon the mate he could not protect.

But for now, until pain drove him to the haven of unconsciousness or madness claimed him, he would spit defiance at the High Mage of Eld and dare him to do his worst.

"Hello, Maur," he rasped. His throat was swollen and bruised from the strangulating collar the High Mage had tortured him with two days ago. Each word raked through his ruined voice box like knives, but he forced himself to speak all the same. His lip curled. "I'd say you were looking well, but Fey never lie. Has your flesh begun to rot yet?"

He knew he'd scored a hit when the gloved hand peeping out of the robe's wide sleeve curled into a frail, bony fist. Maur's health was failing, and with Elfeya too close to death to heal him, the effects were accelerating.

"Still have some fight in you, Lord Death?" the High Mage sneered. "We'll see how long that lasts." He gestured and the hulking figure standing in the shadows behind him stepped forward.

Despite himself, Shan felt his spirit quail at the sight of the giant's black war hammer glinting dully in the sconce light.

"I see you remember my *umagi* Goram and his hammer." Maur's voice oozed with satisfaction. He nodded his shrouded head in Goram's direction. "You may begin."

Many long centuries had passed since Shan had last prayed to the gods for anything, but when Goram's hammer swung, his mind went completely blank, void of every thought but one.

Gods help me.

Elvia ~ Navahele

Though no sound emerged from Hawksheart's mirror, Shannisorran v'En Celay's scream still rocked the rooted heart of Grandfather Sentinel, and every observing Fey warrior flinched and whispered a prayer for mercy.

Ellysetta's fingernails dug deep enough into Rain's wrist to draw blood.

"*Setah*, Hawksheart!" Rain bit out. "Stop that scorching mirror. Ellysetta has seen enough."

The Elf king nodded, but before he could do as Rain ordered, the Eld hammer swung again, and Shannisorran v'En Celay's head was flung back, his face twisted in a rictus of unimaginable pain.

Ellysetta's body began to shake like it did when one of her seizures began, only this time, she did not fall convulsing to the floor. This time—and far more alarmingly—her power gathered. Her eyes went tairen-bright, the pupils disappearing, and her silvery Fey luminescence became a dazzling light as she called forth the awesome entirety of her magic.

"*Krekk*," Rain muttered. "Ellysetta! Scorch it, Elf, stop that flaming thing!" He sent a blast of Water and Air to do it himself, but instead of obeying his command, the power he summoned spilled out of his body in shining flows . . . and poured into Ellysetta's.

Similar streams of power flowed into her from Gaelen and

Bel and the rest of her quintet. Even Hawksheart's Elvish magic swirled towards her in sparkling golden rivers. She was siphoning their power, drawing it into herself, and as she did, her glow grew brighter and fiercer until Rain's eyes burned from the blinding light.

«*Ellysetta!*» he cried. «*Parei, shei'tani! Stop!*»

But she didn't.

All around the small chamber, the sturdy, smooth grain of Grandfather's heartwood groaned and creaked in protest as the wood bowed inward, towards Ellysetta, as if—not content to drain only Hawksheart and the Fey—she was summoning every scrap of life and power stored in the great tree's ancient form as well.

In the mirror's shimmering veil, Rain saw the Eld hammer strike again, saw Shannisorran v'En Celay's body convulse in agony.

A roar of pure, unfettered Rage shook the Sentinel's heartwood chamber. Power flashed with concussive force, knocking Ellysetta's quintet and the Elf king to the ground. Rain, who was standing closest to her, found himself lifted off his feet and flung across the room to slam hard against the Sentinel's smooth walls. He struggled to raise himself on his elbows, only to fall back again as his head spun and darkness crowded the edges of his vision.

Dimly, he saw Hawksheart crawling towards Ellysetta on hands and knees and heard him screaming, "*Anio!* Do not touch the water!" as Ellysetta—the only one in the room still standing—plunged her hands into the mirror's veil.

Eld ~ Boura Fell

Shan's breath came in shallow pants, and in his pain-dazed mind, set afire by the screaming torment of shattered nerves, he chanted with dogged determination.

Pain is life. Pain is life. Pain is life.

He focused on the words, using them as a shield against the

blinding agony, taking each word and adding it as a mental brick in the wall against his pain. If he built the wall high enough, strong enough, he could endure.

Goram drew back his hammer again. Shan closed his eyes against the oncoming blow, and his chant picked up desperate speed. *Pain is life. Pain is life. Pain is life.*

The hammer landed with a loud crack of shattering bone. Agony exploded in Shan's right knee, and the fragile wall against the pain exploded with it. Shan's scream ripped from his throat.

Please, gods, then let me die.

He nearly wept. Goram had barely begun, and already Shan was breaking. In spirit as well as in body. For months now he'd been tortured on a near-daily basis—these last weeks with a relentless ferocity that made the last thousand years of torment seem a hard day of training at the academy by comparison. Thanks to Elfeya, he'd survived all those previous tortures, but this time, she was not there to steal away the pain or anchor him to Light and life.

The lure to give in, to simply let his life fade was so tempting. But it wasn't what she wanted. And that meant he had to endure. Without her here to help him, he had to be strong enough for them both.

He swung limply from his chains, breathless and dazed, his numbed mind groping for the words to begin again. This time, he whispered them aloud. "Pain is life." *Elfeya, I love you.* The first brick settled in place. "Pain is life." *There is no price I would not pay, no torment I would not suffer for you.* The next locked neatly into place beside the first.

"Pain is life." *You are the sun that shines Light upon my soul.* Another brick joined the rest. "Pain is life." *Because you live, my life has purpose.* And another.

Goram swung his gods-cursed hammer once more.

Shan closed his eyes so he wouldn't see it. "Pain is—"

The bones in his left hip shattered inside his skin. Blinding agony engulfed him. His dazed mind howled and groped for the word. *Pain is . . . is . . . is—*

—Rage.

It came from nowhere and filled him in an instant. Violent fury. Bloodlust. Savage, vengeful ferocity so vast it made the earth tremble.

Goram fell to his knees, and his master staggered back against the rough, carved-out walls of the cell. Maur's hood fell back, revealing the rotting ruins of his face—the skin drooping like melted tallow, patched with oozing sores where his flesh had begun to putrefy.

"You . . . will . . . not . . . touch . . . him!"

The guttural roar of command came from Shan's own throat—but the fierce, rumbling voice was not his.

Concentrated power filled him—searing him from the inside out, all but boiling the blood in his veins. It was as if the Bright Lord himself had poured all the vast energy of the Great Sun into Shan's soul on a bolt of divine lightning.

With the power came a presence—feminine and familiar— and Shan wasn't the only one who sensed it.

Silver eyes fixed on Shan. "You!" he exclaimed, and silver irises darkened to the lurid black of Azrahn.

Shan roared a warning to the daughter he had never seen—the precious, beloved child he and Elfeya had conceived in a world of endless horror. The same child they had risked their lives to save, and now willingly suffered every torment to protect.

The Rage—hers and his combined—exploded, flooding him with fury. *Sel'dor* manacles disintegrated. Agony ripped through him as his body flash-boiled into a cloud of flaming mist and his mind into a fearsome, savage haze.

Burn him! Shred him! Feast on his roasted bones!

The cry howled in his mind, but the fierce battle cry turned to a shriek of pain as the mist he had become resolidified. Limbs formed, but they were twisted and misshapen, half tairen, half Fey, as if man and beast had been fused together in some monstrous amalgamation. Enormous muscles rippled and bulged beneath a patchwork hide, silvery Fey skin covered by broad tracts of black fur. A man's bony hands, larger than serving platters, ripped at the air with a beast's razored claws.

The creature reared back on bulging hind legs and opened its fanged maw. Searing fire spewed forth in an incinerating jet.

Goram screamed as his body turned to lifeless char, and beside him, the hammer he'd wielded with such malevolent enthusiasm melted into a puddle of harmless slag.

The High Mage shifted his initial weave into a powerful shield that withstood the first blast of fire—then he struck. His skeletal arms shoved forward, purple velvet sleeves falling back to reveal clawed hands holding globes of Azrahn that he hurled with a strength far exceeding his frail, wasted appearance.

The dark, corruptive magic splashed against the enormous, furred chest, and the creature that was part Shan, part tairen reared back, roaring with a mix of rage, pain, and fear. Cramped wings beat at the rough rock of the ceiling. Mid-span claws gouged deep furrows into the *sel'dor* ore.

The monster howled as *sel'dor* rubble rained searing acid across its back and the burning ice of the Mage's Azrahn spread across its chest.

Flame exploded from the beast's muzzle.

Vadim Maur dove through the cell door and rolled to the left. His bones bounced painfully across the unyielding stone floor, but neither the jolts nor even the snap of a breaking finger unraveled his concentration.

Pain was the price of great magic, and he had long ago accepted that penalty.

Vast and devastating, his power surged in answer to his call. Blazing, multi-ply threads burst from his hands in dense shield patterns as clouds of intense flame boiled out of the cell to fill the corridor.

The guards by the door—unprotected by similar shields—lit up like matchsticks. They didn't even have time to scream before the ash that had been their living bodies scattered on the searing winds of the maelstrom.

Perspiration broke out on Vadim's skin, then evaporated as the hairs on his arms crackled and his skin turned bright red. He poured more magic into his weaves, but the destructive force of the fire was too great. A six-fold weave—no matter how powerful—had no chance of standing against tairen flame for long. His shields were failing. He was roasting.

Desperate, he arrowed a command to his *umagi* guarding the cell two levels above. «*Go to the shei'dalin Elfeya now. Kill her!*»

Elvia ~ Navahele

Bel groaned and held his hands to his ringing ears. His head felt like that Eld *rultshart* had applied his hammer to Bel's skull. Someone was screaming.

His eyes snapped open and he rolled into a crouch.

Two man lengths away, held captive by some invisible force, Ellysetta stood glued to the shimmering veil of water. Her head was flung back, her spine was arched in visible agony, and she was screaming as if her very soul were being torn asunder.

"Get her away from the mirror!" Hawksheart cried. "She cannot free herself!"

Bel sprang into action. With no hint of his usual devoted care, he launched his body through the air, slammed into Ellysetta's slender form, and tackled her to the ground.

They landed with a teeth-rattling jolt on the floor of the hollow, and Bel's only concession to a *lu'tan's* regard was a last-moment twist of his body so that he—not she—took the brunt of their hard landing.

The instant they hit, Ellysetta went wild. Screaming and roaring, she struck at him with clawed hands, raking burning furrows across his face, ripping through his leathers to score his chest. He tried to block her blows and fend off her attacks without hurting her, but that care was his undoing.

Fast-growing roots shot up from the floor of the Sentinel's hollow and lashed Bel's arms and legs into place, pinning him to the floor. He spun Fire to burn the roots and free himself, but the threads of his magic dissolved the instant they formed, absorbed into the fierce aura of power surrounding Ellysetta.

"Ellysetta!" he protested. Streamers of ice raced through his veins, and a sudden, drugging weakness sapped his strength and left him light-headed.

Ellysetta reared back and Bel got his first glimpse of her face. Her eyes were pure black, lit by lurid red stars, her teeth bared in a snarl of primal savagery. The aura of magic about her was like none he'd ever seen. Like the Great Sun in full eclipse, a dark shadow surrounded her, its edges rimmed by an undulating ring of bright, golden light.

She passed a hand across her leathers, and her palm blazed with green Earth. One of the steel studs in her armor melted and re-formed as a razor-sharp black Fey'cha that she slammed towards him.

Rooted to the ground, his power pouring into her like light feeding the endless hunger of a dark star, he couldn't lift a finger in his defense. He couldn't even move to dodge the blow.

He could only whisper, "Ellysetta, *nei!*" as the knife plunged towards his chest.

Deep in the black heart of Boura Fell, Shan howled as the feel of a knife sinking into an unprotected chest reverberated through his soul.

The connection with his daughter shattered.

CHAPTER NINETEEN

Elvia ~ Navahele

Ellysetta watched Bel's eyes go wide and heard his breath leave his lungs on a stunned gasp.

The face before her had been Vadim Maur's. She was certain of it. Only it had changed at the last moment to Bel's.

She shrieked in horror and denial, feeling the dagger tear through skin and bone to pierce the beating heart beneath as if the blade had ripped through her own chest.

In the same instant, a wall of heat and stone slammed into her side and swept her off her feet. The black Fey'cha flew from her hand and went skittering across the glossy, timeworn surface of the chamber floor. Behind her, the veil of suspended water abruptly splashed back into the mirror pool like a lead curtain suddenly released from its anchors. The spray of chilly droplets spattered across Ellysetta's face.

She was screaming . . . screaming . . . screaming. Death crouched at the periphery of her senses, grinning with malice while voices howled in a savage chorus of fear and agony.

Burn! Destroy! Scorch the world! Flame them all!

Yes! Yes! A terrible, dark, hungry part of Ellysetta's soul howled with dreadful eagerness. She'd killed before. She knew the taste of blood and death, remembered the searing thrill of slaughtering a hated enemy. When Mama died, the ones who'd killed her had paid in blood and screams, and their dying wails had sung through Ellysetta's veins like a visceral symphony.

Ellysetta.

Something held her captive, pinned to the floor. Her arms

flailed, fingers curving into claws. The power rose inside her with wild demand, burning, boiling, tearing at her body with brutal hands until she shrieked with pain and madness.

Ellysetta!

The force inside her was too great for her body to contain. The need to rend and destroy clamored for freedom. Why else had she been born with such power if not to rain death and destruction upon the ones who'd hurt those she loved?

"Ellysetta!" «*Shei'tani!*» In voice and in Spirit and through the powerful bond threads that even now tied so much of her soul to Rain's, the sound of his call broke through her madness.

Those were his arms wrapped around her, his body pressed tight against hers, pinning her to the ground, yes, but covering her with a mate's protective care as well. His hair, smelling like spring rain and shared secrets, fell across her face in warm, silky streamers as his cheek pressed against hers and his lips murmured entreaties of peace and love against her skin.

Sanity returned in a rush. Her eyes flew open and she dragged air into her lungs on a sob.

"Rain?" Shaking hands traced the familiar curve of his head and spine. Fingers dug into the beloved bulwark of strong shoulders, clinging with desperate fear. "Oh, Rain." Tears gathered, hot and burning, and her throat closed up as if clutched in the strangling grip of a tight fist. «*Oh, Rain . . . what have I done? Bel . . .* »

"Shh . . . *las, kem'reisa* . . . he is unharmed."

«*I stabbed him. I stabbed him through the heart. I felt it.*»

«*Nei,*» he soothed. «*I reached you in time. You didn't hurt him. Your blade didn't even break his skin.*»

Her eyes closed and tears of relief spilled down her cheeks. Though the sensation of her knife plunging into Bel's chest and piercing his heart had been so vivid, Rain would never lie. Especially not to her. Bel was unhurt. She hadn't slain him after all.

"*Beylah sallan. Beylah sallan.*" She wept. Her arms curled tight around Rain's neck, and she burrowed close. The frightened, timid Ellie-the-woodcarver's-daughter part of her soul yearned to dive inside his skin and live there, surrounded by him, part of him, kept safe from the world and the world kept safe from her; but after a few moments of comfort, the fiercer instincts of Ellysetta Feyreisa surged to the fore and forced her to pull away from the comfort of Rain's embrace, forced her to make sense of what had just happened.

The moment she lifted her head, Gaelen was there, hand outstretched, to help her to her feet.

Bel, visibly shaken but otherwise unharmed, was half a step behind him.

Ellysetta took one look at Bel, flung her arms around him, and burst into fresh tears. "*Sieks'ta, kem'maresk.* Forgive me. I don't know what happened. I would never hurt you."

He pulled back and met her eyes soberly. "There is nothing to forgive, *kem'falla.* My life is yours. My death is yours, too, should you ever require it."

His simple, unequivocal acceptance nearly broke her heart.

"What happened?" Gaelen interrupted. "When you touched the mirror, what happened to you? To Lord Shan?"

"I . . ." She glanced back at Rain and reached for his hand instinctively. The warm strength of his fingers closed around hers, and fresh vitality infused her flagging courage. "I don't know. I can't explain it. It's as if the moment I touched the mirror, I was suddenly there, with my . . . with Lord v'En Celay . . . as if I were a part of him."

"You were."

The Fey all turned towards Hawksheart.

The Elf king regarded Ellysetta with an inscrutable expression. "The mirror is a viewing portal—but it is also a transport of sorts. You have not been trained in its proper use, so without me to guide you this time, when you touched the water, a part of your soul and your consciousness traveled through the mirror and entered Shan's body."

"Oh, gods." She put a hand to her mouth. "Was it my fault he turned into that . . . thing? Did I do that to him?"

"*Anio*," Hawksheart said instantly. "Don't let such a fear even cross your mind. As I showed you earlier, you were not the first of the High Mage's experiments. In his earliest attempts, he used adult hosts to house the soul of the tairen."

"Blessed gods," Rain breathed. "He tied a tairen's soul to Lord Shan. That's why Shan's eyes were tairen."

"He was one of many captive warriors of the Fey," Hawksheart confirmed, "but the others did not have the anchor of a truemate, as Shan does. When the Mage grafted a tairen's soul to theirs, they all went mad and died. Shan was the only one of those early experiments to survive. And he has thus far been the only one of the High Mage's experiments powerful enough to summon the Change—though, as you witnessed, he has never managed to successfully complete it."

Ellysetta clasped her hands over her mouth. Her stomach roiled as she remembered, with vivid clarity, the horror and pain of the twisted monster Lord Shan had become. "Bright Lord have mercy on him."

"You said adults were the Mage's earliest experiments," Gaelen interrupted.

The Elf nodded. "*Bayas.* The Mage's experiments at merging two unborn souls have been much more successful. Many of those children survived to adulthood, though none have yet been powerful enough to summon the Change."

"Ellysetta will be the first."

"I believe so. More to the point, the High Mage believes it." He glanced at Ellysetta. "Most important, she has not yet fallen prey to the wild savagery that overcame the others when they reached maturity."

"S-savagery?" Ellysetta echoed in a faint voice. Her mouth went dry, and she swayed on her feet. If not for the arm Rain quickly wrapped around her waist, she might have fallen.

"*Bayas.* The others cannot Change even to the extent your father does, but when their *sel'dor* manacles are removed, they still become every bit as wild and vicious as he."

For one horrible moment, she thought she might heave up the contents of her stomach. "You mean I'm turning into some sort of . . . monster? Is that why I've had those seizures and horrible, bloody nightmares all my life?"

"I cannot speak to your nightmares, but most of your seizures come from your father, not from what lives inside you."

"Explain," Rain commanded.

"As best I can tell, when the High Mage performed his soul manipulations on Ellysetta and Shan, he unwittingly created a bridge of sorts between them. A pathway forged by Azrahn and amplified by the biological affinity of father and child . . . perhaps even a bond between the two tairens' souls tied to them. That connection is how you were able to join with him through the mirror a moment ago . . . and how your parents were able to help you in the Well of Souls—both when the Mage tried to claim your soul in the Cathedral of Light and again, more recently, when you saved the tairen kitlings."

Ellysetta's heart skipped a beat. "That was my—" She broke off. Calling the two strangers her parents seemed strangely awkward. Mama and Papa—Lauriana and Sol Baristani—were the only parents she'd ever known. "That was Lord Shan and Lady Elfeya?" she amended.

She remembered the strong, calming presence that had filled her when she'd traveled into the Well of Souls to save the tairen kitlings. Radiant with warmth and love, that presence had helped her spin her weaves with confidence, setting aside the fear and self-doubt that had shadowed her all her life. She'd thought the Bright Lord had been guiding her hands.

"They were with me in the Well?"

"They've always been with you, Ellysetta. Prisoners they may be, but they've always done whatever they could—no matter the cost to themselves—to protect you."

Ellysetta recalled the dream she'd had by the Bay of Flames, of a woman's voice begging forgiveness as a shining veil closed around Ellysetta like a blanket. "They're the ones who bound my magic."

"*Bayas.* They knew what you were before you were born, and they knew what the Mage intended, so they bound your magic to hide it from him and arranged for you to be smuggled out of Eld at the first chance."

"But I don't understand . . . if my parents have used this connection to watch over me and protect me, how can my father be responsible for my seizures?"

"Did you not feel the beginnings of a seizure come upon you when you looked into the mirror and saw the Mage torturing Shan?"

"I . . ." Her brows drew together. She had . . . the feeling had been exactly the same.

"Did you not feel the hammer strike as if it landed upon your own flesh instead of his?"

"Yes, but how did you . . ." Her voice trailed off.

"You think she feels Lord Shan's torture?" Rain asked.

"*Bayas*, that is exactly what I think." Hawksheart turned back to Ellysetta and pinned her with an intense stare from which she could not look away. "Your seizures—and, from what Fanor has told me, apparently even some of the knowledge and skills you possess—come to you from your father through that connection you both share."

"Bright Lord save him," she breathed, remembering with horror how often the seizures had ripped apart her world. Lord v'En Celay—her father—must have suffered agonies beyond reckoning.

"And how would you know that her seizures are a result of Shan's torture?" Tajik interrupted. His blue eyes burned like flames. If looks could kill, Galad Hawksheart would be lying stone dead on the chamber floor. "Unless you were watching them both suffer?"

"I have watched them," Hawksheart replied without ire. "Every day for the last thousand years, I have watched Shan and Elfeya, just as I have watched Ellysetta Erimea every day since she was born."

Tajik lunged for his cousin, and only Rijonn's and Gil's leaping forward to grab his arms and haul him back stopped Tajik's hands from closing around Hawksheart's throat and strangling the life out of him. Tajik swore and struggled against his friends' hold.

"You filthy *rultshart!*" he spat. "You watched them? All this time, you not only knew what was happening to them; you watched it? And you did nothing?"

Fire flamed in his eyes. Five-fold weaves shot from Gaelen's and Bel's fingertips, encasing Tajik in dense shields to keep the Fey general's temper from turning deadly.

Hawksheart withstood his cousin's wrath with impassive calm, and when Bel and Gaelen would have woven similar shields around him, Hawksheart waved them away.

"As I told you, Tajik, helping them was never a choice available to me. *I could not interfere in their verse in the Dance.*" He enunciated each word with deliberate emphasis. "But, yes, I did watch them. Since I could do nothing to save them, the least I could do was bear witness to their bravery and their suffering and their sacrifice. I have been, in effect, their Sentinel, the watcher of their lives. And though I could not reveal myself to them, they have never been alone."

"You think that makes this all right?" Tajik cried. Tears tracked silvery trails down the sides of his face, but he didn't bother to wipe them away.

Hawksheart sighed and looked suddenly weary. "Anio, cousin. Nothing will ever make their suffering all right. But long ago I accepted that this was my Song to sing in the Dance. Just as I accepted that you would never forgive me for it."

"You're right about that." Tajik shook off Bel and Gaelen and glared at them before turning back to the Elf king. "Where are they, *cousin?* And don't pretend you don't know."

For the first time since the Fey had entered Navahele, Hawksheart showed signs of temper. His brows dove together in a scowl. "You just looked into the mirror," he snapped. "Did you see coordinates marked on a map? *Anio*, because the Dance is about the lives we live and the choices we make, not about the space we inhabit. They are somewhere in Eld in a fortress with tunnels carved out of what looks like *sel'dor* ore. There! Now you know as much as I about their location."

The Elf spun on his heel and presented the Fey with his back. He muttered something to Grandfather Sentinel, then swept the long, golden strands of his hair behind his shoulders with a brisk shake of his head and turned back around, his emotions locked once more behind a mask of impenetrable calm. When he spoke again, his voice was cold, each word hard as a stone.

"Even if I did know their exact location, cousin, I would not tell you for fear of upsetting the balance of the Dance with my interference."

"Flame and scorch you to the Seven Hells," Tajik growled. "May the minions of the Dark God visit upon you every torment my sister has suffered and may your screams for mercy be the music that fills their ears as they feast on your body and soul. May you drain every last dreg of bitterness from the cup of death and your heirs curse your name with every breath. May the heartwood of Navahele rot—"

Finally Hawksheart had heard enough and his voice boomed out like a clap of thunder: "Be silent!" The Elf king spat out a tirade of torrential Elvish that turned Tajik's face bright red. What was clearly a scathing rebuke ended in clipped, icy Feyan. "Cousin you may be, but you stand in the heart of Elvia now. And in this land, I am king. You will offer me the courtesy of a civil tongue, Elf-kin, or you will keep your silence. Do I make myself clear?"

Tajik glared, but whatever insults and accusations he still

had to spew remained locked behind gritted teeth and clamped lips. He gave a curt nod.

"A wise choice, cousin." Turning to Rain and Ellysetta, Hawksheart said, "Go now. The night grows late. Enjoy the comforts of Navahele tonight. We will talk again tomorrow."

A dozen Elvian guards were waiting for them at the top of the stair when they reemerged from the bowels of Grandfather Sentinel's heartwood chamber. Rain requested an escort back to their rooms, and with polite bows and distant courtesy, the guards led the way.

Fifteen chimes later, the seven of them ducked into Rain and Ellysetta's cozy bedchamber.

"What are we going to do, Rain?" Ellysetta asked as soon as the door closed behind them. "We can't just leave the v'En Celays in Eld. We've got to find a way to save them."

Rain touched a finger to his lips and shook his head, nodding to the rich wood surrounding them. On a narrow Spirit weave, he warned her, «*This tree, like all the trees in Navahele, is a watcher. Wait for the Fey to spin a privacy weave.*»

Tajik and Gil spun breezy patterns of Earth and Air that swept through every nook and cranny in the chamber, dislodging dust, dirt, insects, and even a small, very disgruntled-looking tree frog. They disposed of their weaves' findings through one of the chamber's small, round windows, then spun swift, dense privacy weaves on every surface in the chamber.

"Do you really think Lord Galad would send frogs and insects to spy on us?" Ellysetta asked.

"Spying is what Elves do, *kem'falla*," Tajik said. "And everything here in Elvia—from the plants and insects, to the animals, to the very soil we walk on—spies for them as well."

"But what could they tell him that he cannot already See?"

Gil grunted. "Probabilities. Despite the destiny that may be mapped out for us, the gods still gave us free will. Hawksheart, for all his power, can never know for certain which verse of their Song a person will choose to sing. Everything the Elves learn, everything they see, everything the sentient creatures of Elvia gather, he uses to interpret the Dance and determine the most likely turns the Songs will take."

"And right now," Tajik said, "he wants to know what we will do to save my sister and her mate and whether or not he needs to stop us."

"Tajik, he isn't as heartless as you think," Ellysetta protested. "Perhaps he doesn't show it, but none of this was easy for him."

"He just admitted he watched my sister suffer for a thousand years because he was determined to see your Song come to fruition." Tajik's blue eyes burned like flame. "He'll do whatever it takes to make sure she stays there if it fits his needs for the Dance."

Gil flung back his long, white-blond hair, and the silvery specks in his black eyes flashed like angry stars. "Well, Hawksheart may be able to stand and watch their suffering without lifting a finger, but we Fey cannot. We must rescue them. Even if Lord Shan and Lady Elfeya were not the Feyreisa's parents—even if they were not two of the greatest truemates born in this Age—we would still be honor-bound to rescue them."

"*Aiyah*," Rijonn agreed, his voice a low, gravelly rumble. "Just say the word and I will grind every vein of *sel'dor* ore in Eld to dust to find them and set them free."

When Rain didn't immediately answer, Ellysetta turned to him. "Rain? You cannot intend to just leave them there."

"Even if we knew where they were being held—which we do not—I cannot see a way to save them that holds hope for any outcome but certain death . . . or worse."

"Since when has risk stopped a Fey from doing what he knows is right?" Bel countered before Ellysetta could speak. His face was as hard as Tajik's, his cobalt eyes as flat and cold as Tajik's flame-blue eyes were fiery. "Now that we know they live—now that we know what they're suffering—we cannot leave them there. You know we cannot. Fey honor isn't just a word. Truemates of the Fey are being held by the High Mage of Eld. They must be saved. There's no other option."

"I know, Bel." Rain thrust a hand through his hair and began to pace. "I know."

Gaelen glanced at the hard, determined expressions of his brother Fey. "Has it not yet occurred to anyone that there may be some specific reason why Hawksheart showed us the truth about Lord Shan and Elfeya? That he wants us to go after them?"

Rain's spine stiffened and his shoulders drew back. "What could Hawksheart possibly hope to gain? If the Fey perish on some hopeless mission into Eld, the Mages win."

"Think about it, Rain. He let Lord Shan and his mate be captured, let them suffer a thousand years of torture, because he believed it necessary to the Dance. And the first time he reveals their fate, to whom does he show it? Their daughter. Their daughter's Tairen Soul truemate. Elfeya's brother. The five bloodsworn warriors who have already pledged their souls to Ellysetta's service. He brought us here. Just us. He let us see what his mirror had to reveal, because he meant us to have that information. He wouldn't let me take Tajik's memory because he *needs* Tajik to remember. What purpose could there be except to use this new knowledge to drive us to action? Not the Fey. Us." He drew a circle with one finger. "We seven."

Ellysetta frowned. "You're suggesting he planned everything that just happened down there? That he manipulated me into demanding the truth about my parents just so we'd go after them because he wants me to confront the High Mage?"

"You are still young, *ajiana*. Still trusting." Sadness and affection softened the ice blue of Gaelen's eyes. "I have been *dahl'reisen*. I learned long ago to trust no one. I also learned long ago that the world holds precious few surprises for an Elf. Do I think he manipulated us? Oh, *aiyah*, I think he did. I think the Lord of Valorian knew precisely what he was doing every step of the way. He wants us to go into Eld."

"Well, he can want all he likes," Rain snapped. "There's no way in the Seven Hells I would ever let Ellysetta set foot in that accursed land. Hawksheart surely knows that." He began to pace again. "*Nei*. No matter what your suspicion tells you, Hawksheart is not such a fool. Besides, you heard him. Ellysetta is the one born to defeat Shadow and secure this world for Light. He would not risk her life so stupidly."

"And how can she defeat Shadow if she never confronts it?" Gaelen countered. "Stop thinking like a Fey, Rain, and start thinking like an Elf. To them, no one life is more important than the outcome of the Dance. Hawksheart said Ellysetta was born to defeat Shadow, but did you even once hear him say she was supposed to survive her fate?"

Rain stopped in his tracks. His expression went blank. "I—"

"*Nei*, you did not." Gaelen supplied the answer himself. "Because he was very careful *not* to say it. Just as he was very careful to block Ellysetta's memories of what she saw, even though he would not let me erase the truth about Elfeya from Tajik's mind."

Silence fell over the chamber. Rain and the rest of Ellysetta's quintet shared troubled glances. They all clearly wanted to refute Gaelen's claims, yet they could not dismiss the former *dahl'reisen's* suspicions.

"Rain was the last Fey to call a Song in the Dance," Gaelen reminded them. "We all know how that turned out. If not for the tairen, he would not have survived."

An uncomfortable silence fell over the room. None of them could dismiss the possibility that Ellysetta's Song would end in devastation. They'd all seen the same dire prognostications in the Eye of Truth.

Bel cleared his throat. "Hawksheart can obfuscate and manipulate all he wants; it will get him nowhere. We may be the seven he chose to hear his revelations, but that doesn't mean we must act on them alone. Once we send word back to the Fading Lands, not even Tenn and his supporters will be able to stop the Fey from demanding that all the force of the Fading Lands be focused on rescuing Lord Shan and his mate."

"Flames scorch that pointy-eared *rultshart*," Rain muttered beneath his breath. He scowled at them. "That's exactly what he was counting on, because he knows it's exactly what I cannot allow to happen." Rain shoved a hand through his hair. "I need the Fey protecting Celieria and the Fading Lands—not rushing into Eld to confront the Mages on their own ground. We're too few—and whatever the Mages used in Teleon and Orest to open those portals, they surely have seeded all over Eld. The moment we march deep enough into their forests, they'll simply surround and slaughter us." He spun on a heel and began to pace.

"*Nei*. We cannot let the truth about Lord Shan and his mate go any farther than the seven of us." His jaw hardened and his eyes went flinty. "And at this point, we must accept there is nothing we can do to save them. For now, they stay where they are."

Eld ~ Boura Fell

"Hurry," Melliandra ordered. She gave the chains that bound the beautiful black-haired woman a hard yank, and the prisoner stumbled forward. "Move your feet!" she snapped without pity. "Lives depend on it—including yours!"

The woman looked at her with dazed eyes, then quickly looked down and shuffled faster. *Sel'dor* chains rattled and clanked on the hard ground beneath the tattered remains of the woman's once beautiful red gown.

Stupid, stupid woman. She'd been too stubborn for her own good, spitting defiance at the High Mage and the *umagi* who served him when a wiser woman would have groveled and begged for mercy to appease them.

Well, they'd taught her. After the beatings and the rapings had reduced her fiery defiance to shattered, dull-eyed submission, they'd bound her in manacles and chains. None of the thin, decorative *sel'dor* bands and earrings for this Fey *shei'dalin*. No. The thick, heavy *sel'dor* shackles usually reserved for *dahl'reisen* prisoners were clamped tight around her ankles and wrists, and the long, sharp spikes fitted along the interior of the shackles drove into the flesh and bone just above her joints to cause her constant, agonizing pain. A matching collar filled with a hundred tiny *sel'dor* needles bound her throat so tightly that every swallow and gasping breath forced the needles deeper into her flesh.

Melliandra hardened her heart. There was nothing to be done. She wasn't about to let those pain-dulled brown eyes draw her in like the tender blue eyes of the now dead Shia. Melliandra's life was already too dangerous and complicated, and if the High Mage ever discovered how she was working against him, death would be the least of her worries.

"Here." She threw a filthy woolen blanket at the woman. "Cover yourself. If the guards get one look at you, it won't go well for either of us."

The woman struggled with the cumbersome scrap of smelly fabric until Melliandra growled a foul curse and yanked the blanket out of the woman's hands and tugged it roughly into place herself. She draped the folds to cover the woman's silky hair, tattered gown, and the telltale shining skin of her manacled arms.

"There," she muttered when she was finished. Melliandra peered at her critically until she was satisfied not one flash of shining Fey skin was revealed. "That will have to do. Now come!" She grabbed a fistful of blanket and hidden chain and gave a yank. "There's not much time."

She dragged the unresisting woman down the corridor. The stench of smoke and scorched flesh hung heavy in the air; and in the refuse pit two levels down, the *darrokken* were howling. Savage screams echoed the creatures' howls, and the sound sent chills up Melliandra's spine.

Death was no stranger to Boura Fell, but today its visit had been like none she'd ever witnessed, coming not at the hands of Mage Fire or Azrahn, nor at the untender hands of torture masters like Goram and his hammer, but instead from tongues of flame, dancing on the lethal music of a magic beast's roar.

Wild, vengeful, hotter than the Seventh Hell, the clouds of boiling flame had blasted up the stairwells and the refuse shaft that ran from the uppermost level of Boura Fell to its darkest depths. The fire seared and scorched everything in its path, catching more than one unwitting Mage and *umagi* in its fiery jaws.

For one sweet, glorious moment of savage joy, she'd thought the Fey Lord had won his victory. She'd actually dared to hope Lord Death had slain the High Mage of Eld.

But abruptly, the Fire had died and the shattered screams of a man gone mad had replaced the roar of the beast and its flames.

And the six icy Marks on Melliandra's chest still remained.

Vadim Maur, father of the Dark bloodline from which she'd sprung, still lived.

Lord Death was the one screaming now.

His mate was the one dying now.

And Melliandra's only hope was to save her.

Elvia ~ Navahele

"We cannot just leave Shan and Elfeya there!" Tajik cried.

"We don't even know where 'there' is," Gaelen pointed out.

"Then we find a way to locate them," Ellysetta announced. "And we put together a plan to rescue them." Her jaw firmed, and her chin lifted as she met Rain's gaze. "I'm sorry, Rain. I know there is far more at stake than just two lives, but we have to do this. I've already lost one mother to the Mages. I'm not about to lose another."

Rain crossed his arms and steeled himself for pain. Refusing to launch a rescue mission to save Shan and Elfeya was one of the hardest decisions he'd ever made. But he knew it was the right choice—the only choice.

"*Shei'tani*, I know you want this—I know you need this—but I cannot allow it. As your *shei'tan*, I would give anything—risk anything—to bring you peace. But I am the Feyreisen, Defender of the Fey, and we are at war. In this matter, I must put the needs of the Fey first."

"My parents are Fey!" she cried. "And they are clearly in need of defending!"

"Please . . . *teska* . . . try to understand. I must make my decision as the Tairen Soul who is their king—and I need you to make your decision as its queen. We must both put what's best for all our people above our own desires and consider *all* the lives at stake, not just these two—no matter who they are."

She flinched and he hated himself for it. His admonition was more than a little unfair. She had always put the needs of others before her own. And now this thing she needed so much, he had to refuse.

An angry, mutinous light sparked in her eyes. "How many does it take, Rain? How many people must suffer for how many years before their lives become important enough to save?"

It was Rain's turn to flinch. "You know that's not what I'm saying."

"Then explain it to me."

Irritation spiked within him. Did she think he liked making this choice? Did she honestly think he would make it if there were any other solution available to him? "Whom should we send, Ellysetta? Your quintet? And leave you unprotected and vulnerable here, outside the Fading Lands, when we all know the High Mage is waiting for just such an opportunity? Should I go myself? The Eld bowcannons nearly killed me in Orest, but I'm sure I could fly straight into the heart of enemy territory undetected, locate your parents in a Mage stronghold, and rescue them without aid."

Color flooded her cheeks and she drew back in affront. "Now who's being ridiculous?"

"Am I?" he countered. "If not me or your quintet, who else should go? Shall I pull warriors off the Celierian borders? The battles have already begun, and we're already seriously out-numbered, but I'm sure Dorian would understand our need to pull back a few of our troops. How many should I withdraw, do you think?"

"I'm not suggesting you pull men off the borders."

"Then whom does that leave, Ellysetta? The *lu'tan*? Their oaths to you supersede any loyalty to me or the Fading Lands. If you ask, they will joyfully die by your command. Are you ready to send them to their deaths? Because, of a certainty, if you direct them to blunder blindly through Eld in the hopes of finding where the Mage is holding your parents, they *will* die."

"Of course I don't mean that!" she exclaimed. "You're twisting my words. You're not being fair."

"*Fair?*" He swooped on the word like a tairen on its prey. "This is life, Ellysetta, a Fey's life. It's almost never *fair*. It's hard. It's thankless. We take what joy we find and treasure it so dearly because we know how rare such blessings are. Every Fey warrior and *shei'dalin* born in the Fading Lands learns very early in life that, like it or not—fair or not—there will be many days when they must decide between a bad choice and a worse one. Today is such a day."

He crossed his arms and leveled a hard look upon his *shei'tani* and her quintet. "I will not send a single blade brother into Eld without some idea of where he's going and what he can expect to find when he gets there. Do you hear me? *I will not issue such a command.* There are too few Fey left in this world to risk a single precious life for such madness."

"So we do nothing?" Tajik cried. "We just leave my sister there to suffer?" His hands were clenched, and his lean, muscular body was trembling with scarcely contained fury.

Gaelen was right, Rain realized. They should have taken Tajik's memories. The warrior was teetering on the brink of full-fledged Rage, and that did not bode well for any of them.

"Calm yourself—and I mean now, Fey," he snapped, hoping a little brisk, plain speaking would pull Taj back from his Rage.

"We're at war, and I need cool heads and clear thinking—not warriors Raging out of control. You're a general of the Fading Lands. Start acting like one."

Tajik's head snapped back as if he'd been slapped.

"Your first duty is your bloodsworn bond to protect Elly-setta, followed by your general's duty to protect the Fading Lands. If we don't defeat the Eld, every *fellana*—every sister, mother, daughter, *shei'tani*, and *e'tani*—*everyone* will suffer the same fate as Elfeya. Do you think for one moment that she and Shan would want that? Do you think they would want you to abandon your *lute'asheiva* bond and leave Elly-setta unprotected while you go after them?"

Tajik's nostrils flared and color rose and fell in his face, but he couldn't hold Rain's gaze. With a bitter, snarled oath, he pivoted on one heel and stalked to the far side of the room.

Jaw set, mouth grim, Rain seared each of the other warriors with a burning look. "We must win this war, no matter the cost. And you must protect Ellysetta with your lives until we do. When we defeat the Mages, we will find Shan and Elfeya and set them free. Until then, this subject is closed." His hand sliced across the air and he leveled a stony, unequivocal glare upon the six warriors. "Is that clear?"

"It's clear, Rain," Bel and Gaelen said simultaneously. The other warriors agreed more slowly—and more grudgingly—but they agreed nonetheless.

That left only Ellysetta.

"*Shei'tani?*" Rain prompted.

Her lips compressed and for a moment he thought she would spit defiance in his face. But then she nodded and looked away.

CHAPTER TWENTY

Melliandra pushed open the door of the cell housing Lord Death's mate and stepped inside.

The red-haired Fey woman lay frail and broken on the black stone of her cell. A large wound gaped grotesquely in the center of her pale, motionless chest, and scarlet blood ran across her ashen skin to gather in a dark, glistening pool beneath her body. Vadim Maur's *umagi* had struck a death blow and left the corpse to be hauled away by the refuse collectors.

Fortunately for the red-hair, Melliandra was the refuse collector for the lower five levels of Boura Fell . . . and she had tended the red-hair's mate enough to know not to come alone.

Beside her, the rag-shrouded Fey gave a gasp and began babbling in her native tongue.

"Hush!" Melliandra hissed. She rushed to close the cell door and spun around to glare at the Fey. "Keep your voice down, dim-skull! They'll hear you!"

But the woman had fallen to her knees beside the red-hair, and she was rocking and weeping and chanting in a broken voice, "*Elfeya falla, Elfeya falla. . . .*" The imprisoned *shei'dalin's* shaking hands hovered over the dying Fey's body. For a moment, Melliandra could have sworn she saw a weak golden glow around the healer's hands, but then the woman cried out and snatched her hands back to her chest.

"Ninnywit. You can't weave with those bands on," Melliandra chided. Not even the red-hair—who was as powerful a healer as any ever seen in Boura Fell—could work the sort of significant healing magic required to snatch a life back from the jaws of death when bound by so much *sel'dor*.

As she hurried to the woman's side, she dug a grimy hand into one of the hidden pockets she'd sewn in the folds of her skirt. Questing fingers brushed across a hard wad of bundled fabric. She pulled the bundle free and quickly unwrapped the layers of cloth to reveal a selection of crudely cut metal keys strung on a strip of braided leather.

The keys were copies of the ones she'd lifted from the *umagi* guards in charge of Master Maur's most important prisoners in the lower levels. A bit of *somulus* powder blown into one of the guards' face while he was sleeping had enabled her to relieve him of his key ring. She'd made an impression of the keys in a small clay tablet and returned the originals to his keeping before he woke from the drug's trance.

For weeks, she'd used every opportunity to scrape and file bits of broken blades and dinner knives into keys that matched the impressions she'd made, taking care to tuck all thoughts and memories of her activity in that part of her mind she'd learned to shield from the Mages. She hadn't finished copying all the keys yet, but she had managed to complete the one used for most of the lockable prisoner restraints.

Luckily for this newest *shei'dalin* prisoner, Master Maur had chained her in a set of those manacles rather than the magic-soldered ones that could not be removed by any means but Mage weaves.

"Let's hope this works," she muttered to herself as she fitted the crudely carved key into the keyhole and twisted.

For one tense moment, the key didn't turn, but after a bit of jiggling, the manacle on the *shei'dalin's* left wrist gave a quiet snick. The *shei'dalin* hissed as long, sharp spikes of *sel'dor* slid out of her wrists, leaving round, ugly boreholes that filled rapidly with blood when Melliandra removed the black metal bands.

The same key worked to release the *shei'dalin's* ankle restraints as well, but none of the ones on the strip of leather fit the collar around the woman's neck.

Melliandra cast a quick, grim glance at the body of Lord Death's mate. She'd seen death before, too many times to count, and she knew the red-hair's soul had already slipped free of her body. A few moments more and only the gods would be able to call her back in anything but demon form. "We're out of time. You'll have to weave with that on."

The dark-haired *shei'dalin* didn't waste time on conversation. She simply dropped to her knees and laid her palms on the dead woman's chest. Her hands began to glow.

Melliandra knew the effect *sel'dor* had on those of Fey blood. There was enough Fey in her own bloodline that she couldn't touch *sel'dor* for long without feeling her skin begin to burn. And she knew that for pureblood Fey, the black metal's touch felt like boiling, corrosive acid poured over their flesh. The sensation was even worse when they spun magic.

Despite the heavy *sel'dor* collar that must have felt like a yoke of fire around her neck, the dark-haired *shei'dalin* merely clenched her jaw and kept weaving until the weak glow Melliandra thought she had seen became a plainly visible orb of warm, shining, golden light.

«*Her mate holds her to the Light, but she is passing through the Veil.*» The *shei'dalin*'s voice tolled in Melliandra's head, powerful, resonant. She was speaking Feyan, but Melliandra had spent enough time around Master Maur's Feyan captives to understand her. «*She has descended too far into the Well for me to follow. I cannot save her.*»

"But you must!" Melliandra protested. "If she dies, he dies. And I need him. He's my only hope."

Desperate, unthinking, she grabbed the *shei'dalin*'s hands and held them against the gaping wound on the dead woman's bloody chest.

"Save her!" she commanded. "You must save her! You *will*!"

Without warning, the world shifted beneath Melliandra's

feet. Energy shot up from her belly and roared through her veins, throwing her so off balance she nearly toppled face-first onto the hard, cold stone floor of the cell. Almost instantly, a familiar sentience turned her way.

"He knows we're here!" Melliandra snatched her hands back from Lord Death's mate, grabbed the other healer by the shoulders, and flung her towards the shadowy corner of the cell. "Don't move! Don't speak!" She threw herself in the opposite direction, turning quickly so that her eyes were focused on the rough, carved surface of the black, *sel'dor*-veined walls. She raced to stuff the memories of her plans and activities behind the invisible barriers in her mind. She barely managed to shove the last thought into hiding before she became aware of the oily darkness, the oppressive pressure of another will bearing down upon her own.

She stared at the black wall and filled her mind with dull, lifeless thoughts of drudgery and subservience.

«What are you up to, umagi?»

The question surprised her. Usually, when the High Mage's mind scoured hers, his will felt like a thousand prying fingers, poking, prodding, ransacking her mind. This time, however, he felt much weaker. Perhaps Lord Death had been more successful than she'd thought.

As quickly as the thought bloomed, she buried it. *«I was sent to collect a corpse, my lord.»*

«Something happened, umagi. Show me.» The press of that icy black mind grew heavier, more insistent. Weaker or not, the Mage was still a powerful force, and she could not resist his will.

She turned slowly, keeping her eyes lowered, and let her gaze drift up the red-hair's body until it came to rest on the faint rise and fall of the woman's bloody chest, where the gaping wound from the executioner's blade was already beginning to close.

«I was sent to collect this woman's body,» Melliandra repeated, *«but she isn't dead, Master Maur.»*

* * *

Eld ~ Boura Fell

"Enough." Vadim Maur gave the healer kneeling at his feet a shove and pushed himself to his feet. Tremors shuddered through his frame. Lord Death's scorching had nearly killed him, and the magic he'd expended to save his own skin had almost finished the job.

A large, loyal brute of an *umagi* stood like an obedient dog beside the chair the High Mage had just vacated. "Lord Death's mate is alive. Take this healer to her now." The words came out garbled. His lips had burned away in Lord Death's fire.

The brute bowed and grabbed the healer's arm in one meaty paw.

When they were gone, he turned to the other four *umagi* in the room, slaves of his since birth, nurtured carefully. Devoid of magic, of course, but utterly, irrevocably his. Standing docilely beside them was a powerfully gifted twenty-year-old novice Mage, one of several Vadim had bred and groomed to be his vessel in the event his plans to incarnate into a Tairen Soul did not come to fruition.

Vadim held out his hands. Hunks of rotting flesh had fallen or burned away, revealing glimpses of the ivory bone beneath. The *umagi* gathered around him and began wrapping perfumed linen around his putrefying flesh. He observed their efforts with detachment.

He could no longer put off the inevitable. Not even his great will could keep life pumping in this ruined body much longer. The end of this incarnation was upon him.

Word would have already raced through the corridors of the Mage halls. Primages with their eyes on the dark throne of Eld would be plotting to steal his chosen vessel and force him to incarnate into some worthless *umagi* devoid of magic so they could plumb his mind for all his vast stores of knowledge and leave him to die in a decaying mortal shell.

But Vadim didn't intend such an ignominious end to his glorious life.

"It is time," he said. He reached for the fresh purple velvet robe his *umagi* had brought to him. "You, ready the incarnation room. You two, take the vessel to be cleansed and prepared. And you"—he turned to the last *umagi*—"you know what to do."

The four *umagi* and the vessel departed. Three of them headed down to the well-guarded, heavily warded incarnation room Vadim Maur had prepared in the bowels of Boura Fell. The fourth *umagi* set out for the laundry with the High Mage's soiled robe. When they were out of earshot of Vadim Maur's chambers, all four *umagi* were stopped, their hoods yanked back to verify their identities. Ten chimes later, the purple-shrouded figure of the High Mage exited the chamber as well, turning down a different tunnel. As Vadim had anticipated, dark figures darted out, clinging to the shadows as they followed.

They waited until their quarry had entered the incarnation chamber to spring. But when they yanked back the purple hood shrouding the High Mage's face, it was not the rotting visage of Vadim Maur they found, but the face of his *umagi* servant.

Deep in the bowels of the earth beneath the forests of Eld, Vadim Maur stepped from the Well of Souls into the doorless chamber he had carved out of solid *sel'dor* ore several weeks ago, when it had become clear to him that his incarnation could no longer be avoided. He tossed the unused *chemar* he'd carried with him on the floor and, with a grunt of disgust, shed the scratchy woolen folds of the *umagi* robe he'd donned after his first transport through the Well from his chambers to the laundry. There, he'd exchanged places with the *umagi* carrying his soiled robe, and used a second *chemar* to bring himself here, to his true incarnation chamber.

The room was lit only by a dim illumination weave. Fingers

of light fell upon the ashen face of the barely conscious man bound to the *sel'dor* table. Vadim's most trusted *umagi* stood beside the table, cutting away the remains of the bound man's once-elegant Celierian garb. He cleansed the man's body with herbal soap, then anointed it with fragrant oil.

Vadim's examined his vessel. There wasn't a single mark on the man's youthful, well-tended body. His torture—though agonizing enough to drive its victim quite mad—had been achieved completely through the use of Spirit weaves and Azrahn, destroying the mind, but leaving the body—and all its powers—completely intact.

"I expected such great things from you, Nour. Your bloodlines were impeccable, your gifts exceptional. But you didn't have the wit to use your talents to their best advantage. You've been a terrible disappointment to me." He leaned over the Primage's limp body and gripped his jaw with one bandaged hand. Bloody drool from his lipless mouth dropped onto Nour's cheek. "At last, I've found the perfect use for you."

Elvia ~ Navahele

Strangely compelling music woke Ellysetta from sleep, a melody she'd never heard before yet somehow recognized.

She sat up and turned her head to gaze down upon Rain sleeping beside her. He lay tangled in the silken sheets, his limbs shining silver in the dimly lit confines of their bower. Love swelled in her heart, but she was aware of it in an oddly detached way, as if the emotion belonged to someone else.

The music in her mind grew louder, more insistent. She rose from the bed. The sheets slid from her body without a sound. She reached for an Elvish robe draped across the back of a chair and pulled it on as her feet moved soundlessly across the cool wooden floor.

The door to the small bower opened, and she passed through, stepping into the chill enchantment of the autumn night. The air was redolent with the aromas of night-blooming flowers, crisp fall dew, the earthy scents of the forest, and the unmistakable tang of magic.

Her bare feet skimmed down the steps that circled the Sentinel trunk. Around her the world was silent except for the sound of the song. The melody called to her, beckoned her, and she followed it with a strange, detached sense of purpose, a surety devoid of doubt or fear or even curiosity. Some part of her knew exactly where she was going and why.

The song led her through the heart of Navahele, past the moon-silvered stillness of its ponds, across the latticed bridges formed from blossoming vines and woven Sentinel roots. All around her the great trees of Navahele seemed to bend towards her as she passed. She made her way with swift but unhurried steps and passed through the opening in Grandfather Sentinel's smooth, arching golden trunk to the soaring hollow of Galad Hawksheart's throne room within.

The throne room was empty, the guards absent from their posts. The door at the back of the throne swung open as she approached, and she descended down the long, circling stair into the deep, glowing blue heart of Grandfather Sentinel.

Galad Hawksheart stood beside the mirror pool, waiting for her.

The notes of the melody that had drawn her here faded, still audible but muted, playing softly in the background, the only sound in the silence until she spoke.

"Is this a dream?" Her voice flowed out like ripples on a pond, each word echoing as if multiple Ellysettas had asked the question.

Lord Galad's green eyes glowed in the dim chamber, mesmerizing and full of secrets. "The lucid dream of a Seer, Ellysetta Erimea, but it is nothing to fear. You drank *elethea* and took your rest in the boughs of a Sentinel. Your Elvish blood awakens."

"I'm not afraid." And strangely, she wasn't. She was utterly at peace—even the Rage of her tairen lay still and silent. "Did you summon me?"

"I did not. If anything, you summoned me. You still have questions in need of answers?"

"Yes." She had not known the questions were there until he mentioned them, but once he did, they rose like bubbles of air floating to the surface of a pond. With them came the rebirth of emotion. "My Fey parents . . ." she began.

"—would not want you to sacrifice yourself to save them," Hawksheart interrupted. "You have considered using your connection to your father to find them." The Elf leaned forward, his green eyes burning into hers. "*You must not do this. The High Mage will be waiting, and all will be lost.*"

"You're telling me there's nothing I can do to save them?"

"On the contrary, you are the only one who can. But what price will you pay to do so? How many people will you condemn to death to set them free? Because if you rush to their aid now, many will die. Many times many."

"So I must leave them there to suffer?" The very thought of standing by and doing nothing while her family suffered went against everything she believed. She'd never met Shan and Elfeya v'En Celay, but it didn't matter. She'd felt their torment. She'd shared her father's mind . . . part of his soul.

"Unless you would plunge the world into the abyss, *bayas*. Your fierce defense of those you love is one of your greatest strengths, child, but the High Mage will use those feelings against you. You must think with your head, not your heart. Just as I have done all these thousand years."

She'd felt Lord Galad's torment over that decision. He'd shared it with her on purpose, she now realized—not so she would feel sympathy for him, but so she would understand his choice and realize why she must make the same one. Just as Rain had done, even though she'd railed at him and pushed him into vowing he would rescue her parents once their location was known.

Hawksheart moved closer. "But this is not the real reason you came to me tonight, alone. This question you could have asked in the presence of others."

She stepped back, retreating from his approach. His gaze held hers captive, the relentless power of his Elvish eyes piercing her barriers and delving deep into the secrets she held within. "Your truemate's madness begins. The incompletion of your bond begins to unravel his mind, and you wish to know how much time he has before the madness consumes him."

Her body trembled, but his power dragged the answer from her lips. "Yes." She told herself she had not broken her vow to Rain by confirming the question. Hawksheart had already Seen in her mind.

"Too much Shadow lies upon him," Hawksheart replied. "Though he offers you hope, he already knows the end will come quickly."

Her mouth went dry. She met Hawksheart's piercing gaze and this time asked directly, all pretense gone, "How quickly?" When he hesitated, her brows drew together. "You already owe a debt to my family so great you will never be able to repay it—you can give me this much, at least."

Lord Galad's jaw clenched at her accusation, but after a moment, he nodded. "Very well. For the love I bear your mother, I will answer." The Elf king closed his eyes and held a hand over the mirror pool. A spout of shining blue water arose to bathe his palm. His fingers tapped against the water. "A month. No more than that. The war will accelerate your *shei'tan's* decline."

She bit back a muted cry as a rush of desperate denial filled her. So little time.

"Can I not heal his soul to give him more time?" Even though Rain had already given her an answer, she thought perhaps Hawksheart might know something her *shei'tan* did not.

Hawksheart shook his head. "There is only one way for you to heal what ails him now. You must complete your bond, or Rain will die before the last day of Seledos. No matter what else happens, that much is certain."

She drew a breath. The muted cry of denial grew louder. "Yet still you will not tell me how to do it?"

"The key already exists within you, Ellysetta. When the time comes, you will either do what you must or you will let your mate die. The choice will be yours."

She gave a humorless laugh. "Choice? Since when have I had that?" It seemed to Ellie that most of her life, she'd been swept along by the powerful currents of forces greater than she.

A knowing light shone from Lord Galad's green eyes. "You think because you face situations not of your making that you exercise no choice? That you are helpless? To the contrary, child. Your whole life has been full of choices. Hiding from a hard truth is a choice. Surrender—even to the inevitable—is a choice. Even in death there is choice. You may have no control over the time or manner of your death, but you can choose how you face it."

"Is death how my Song ends?"

He smiled, and his eyes were filled with a mix of sadness, understanding, and unexpected affection. "All living things die, Ellysetta. Even Elves and Fey . . . though we usually take longer to do it than most. But the Light that exists within us"—he laid his hand over her heart—"that spark of divine power we call our souls—the only way for that to truly perish is for us to surrender our Light to the Dark. So even if this body you now inhabit does not survive your Song, so long as you hold fast to the Light, the soul that is Ellysetta Erimea will live on. Let that bring you what comfort it may."

"But if I die, then Rain dies. . . ." Her own death she could accept, but not Rain's. Never Rain's. "Please, you've got to tell me—"

"*Anio.*" Hawksheart held up a hand for silence. "I have already said more than I should. I vowed to hold my silence . . . but you are so very like her." His lips compressed and he turned away. "Go now, cousin. Sleep without dreams. I will speak with you on the morrow."

She took a half step towards him; but he clapped his hands, and her vision dissolved in a shower of gold and green sparks. Consciousness faded, and she knew no more.

The Faering Mists

Lillis and Eiliss had reached the valley floor. The trail led through a dense copse of towering evergreens and into a clearing where a small village nestled amidst the trees. Shining Fey, tall, slender, and beautiful, turned with serene calm to watch Eiliss and Lillis emerge from the woods.

"Lillis!" One figure, much smaller than the rest, came pelting out of a nearby building and raced across the clearing. "Lillis! You're here!"

"Lorelle!" With a shout of delight, Lillis raced to meet her twin. The girls met in the center of the clearing and twirled in each other's arms, hugging and laughing.

"I'm so glad you're safe," Lillis exclaimed. "I was afraid something terrible had happened to you."

"And me you," Lorelle agreed. "Lady Eiliss found me and Papa and brought us here."

"Papa?" Lillis grabbed Lorelle's hands tightly. "Where is he?"

Lorelle pointed to the building she'd come from. "In there. Wait! Lillis, there's something else you should—"

But Lillis was already racing across the ground into the building Lorelle had indicated. "Papa! Papa! I'm here!" She smelled the familiar, beloved scent of pipe smoke long before she saw her father and followed the aroma through the airy rooms towards a private courtyard at the center of the house. "It's Lillis, Papa! I'm here! I'm all right! Lady Eiliss found me just like she found you and Lorelle!"

Lillis burst into the courtyard. Her father was standing beside a pretty fountain near a copse of small, flowering trees. "Papa!" She raced towards him, only to stop, frozen in her tracks, when he turned to face her.

Only then did she realize what Lorelle had been trying to tell her.

Papa wasn't alone. He was with someone else, a person he'd been standing so near, Lillis hadn't seen her until Papa turned.

Lillis felt her body shake. Tears filled her eyes, blurring her vision and spilling down her cheeks. She took one shaky step, then another and another. Then she was running.

She crossed the small courtyard in a flash and threw herself into the waiting arms of the woman standing beside Sol Baristani. And when the familiar arms, so strong, so loving, closed around her, and the familiar scent of rosewater filled her nose, Lillis sobbed brokenly.

"Mama. Oh, Mama, I've missed you so much."

CHAPTER TWENTY-ONE

I am born a thousand times
When I see you,
I live a thousand lives
When I am with you,
And I die a thousand deaths
When you leave.

Born, Live, Die, a courtship poem from
Adrial vel Arquinas to his truemate

Elvia ~ Navahele

Ellysetta woke to the ethereal beauty of Elvish dawn song rising through the trees and the joy of Rain's warm body wrapped around hers. For a moment, she lay there, hugging the arm draped over her. She ran her fingers lightly over his and carried his hand to her lips. Such strength, such power, and yet ultimately so fragile.

The memory of Hawksheart's dire prediction of Rain's fate made her eyes close in grief. She had only one month to bind her soul to Rain's or lose him to the bond madness. Just the thought of it made panic tighten her chest and robbed her lungs of breath.

She couldn't lose him. Not to bond madness. Not to war. Not to the High Mage.

«*Shei'tani?*» A sleepy thread of Spirit brushed across her senses. Rain's fingers flexed against her lips. The body that had been relaxed against her in sleep now shifted and his arms tightened around her. «*Arast sha de?*» What is it?

She turned towards him. His eyes were still closed. He was still half-asleep, and it was only her distress that had roused him. She stroked his brow. «*Neitha, shei'tan. It's nothing. Go back to sleep.*» She accompanied the reassurance with a light weave of compulsion and peace.

But as he began to sink back into weary sleep, a staccato rap upon the door shattered the silence.

Rain's eyes flashed open. Before she could take another breath, he'd leapt from the bed and crossed the room in a blur of speed. His *meicha* scimitar flew out of its sheath and into his hand as he went, and he flung open the door, razored steel in one hand, magic blazing in the other.

An Elf stood on the landing outside the bower door.

"Forgive the intrusion," he said calmly, as if confronting naked, sword- and magic-wielding Tairen Souls were an everyday occurrence. "Lord Galad sends his apologies but says you must depart immediately. Please gather your things and join him on Grandfather's island."

Half a bell later, clad once more in her studded red leathers and bloodsworn blades, Ellysetta stood by Rain's side at the base of Grandfather Sentinel. Early morning light filtered through the cool, dew-drenched leaves, and curling clouds of mist rose from the silvery ponds at the city's center, lending a dreamlike feel to the peaceful enchantment of Navahele.

Galad Hawksheart stood at the base of the ancient Sentinel tree, garbed in flowing, silver-shot robes of sage green. "I had invited the leaders of the Danae to join us in Elvia so you could meet with them. Unfortunately, there is no longer time. You must depart for the Celierian-Eld border immediately."

"Why?" Rain asked. "What has happened?"

"A verse I'd long hoped would remain silent has begun to play." Hawksheart's face was etched in grim lines. "The next battle begins in six days' time, not the two weeks you were expecting. And without you, defeat is certain."

"Where?" Rain asked instantly. "Kreppes?"

Hawksheart bowed his head. "Lord Barrial's Elf blood has long made his family a target of interest for this High Mage."

Beside Ellysetta, a sudden bloom of heat burned through the morning mist as Tajik's Fire magic flared. "Barrial as well?" His hands bunched into fists. "You stand here and tell us another of your kin is in mortal danger—and no doubt you Saw it centuries ago—yet still you will not lift a finger to save him?"

The Elf king's eyes flashed with ire. "Have I not just revealed a truth you did not know? Am I not sending you to Lord Barrial's aid? As I have explained, I cannot do more without causing great harm. You Fey look for patterns in the gods' weaves. We Elves See them. We help where we can, Tajik, but some weaves must be spun. Some Songs must be sung."

"So you always say. No matter who pays the price." Tajik spat a curse and stalked off.

"Tajik is overset by the news of his sister," Rijonn said. "I'm sure when his emotions calm, he will regret his harsh words."

"No, he won't." Hawksheart gave a thin smile. "I know my cousin. He's a hothead. Always has been. But he's a strong blade, and a fierce and tireless champion of the Light. You'll need both before this Song is done. Here." He thrust a long, cloth-wrapped bundle into Rain's hands with none of his usual Elvish grace. "This is my gift to you."

Rain frowned and unwrapped the bundle. His brows climbed to his hairline when the soft cloth fell away to reveal a spiraling silver horn. "Shadar horn?"

"War is a perilous venture. Take it. One day, you may find use for it."

The Elf king turned to Ellysetta and held out a woven circlet of slender branches covered with tiny golden flowers that looked like sunbursts against a backdrop of broad, glossy green leaves. "Sentinel blooms," he said. "A gift from Grandfather. Place them beneath your head when you sleep, to keep evil from invading your dreams. Once you leave Elvia's borders, do not sleep without them. And do not leave your mate's side. His presence offers more protection even than the Sentinel blooms . . . and yours offers him the same. You shield each other, and you hold each other to the Light. Only together can you walk the Path the gods have set before you."

She reached out to take his hand, and for the first time saw Hawksheart startled. He had isolated himself so completely over the centuries that even the simple touch of a hand was a shock. "*Beylah vo*, Lord Galad. I am grateful for your aid and guidance. I still do not know why the gods chose me for this task, but I pray I can fulfill it."

"Whom else would they send to defeat the Darkness, if not their brightest Light?" The Elf king lifted his free hand and, after a brief hesitation, laid his palm atop their clasped hands. His eyes softened and he regarded her with something near affection. "Do not be afraid, Ellysetta Erimea. The gods did not set you on this path alone." His gaze traveled around the ring of warriors surrounding her. "Rain, your *lu'tan*, your birth parents, even your Celierian father and mother, all came into your life for a reason. Each was chosen to guide and guard you, to teach you what they could and keep you safe from Shadow's harm. Remember that, Ellysetta. Trust in those you love, and let them teach you to trust in yourself."

He looked deeply into her eyes, and his voice tolled in her mind. *Find your strength, cousin. You have much more than you know. And heed your dreams. Elf blood runs in your veins. What your soul Sees when your mind sleeps does not all come from the Mage.*

He stepped back and offered a final nod. "Fare thee well, my friends. May the gods shine their Light upon your Path and keep you safe from harm."

Fanor led the Fey away from the soaring golden tower of Grandfather Sentinel and towards a small green meadow where a dozen saddled Aquilines stood waiting, their snowy wings tucked against their sides and their reins held by a trio of beautiful Elves.

Gil stopped in his tracks. "We're riding *those?*"

"They have agreed to allow it," Fanor said, "and they can carry you out of Elvia and across the mountains much faster than any other Elvish steed."

The winged steeds nickered and snorted as the Fey grew near. Like most horses, they smelled the scent of predator on the Fey, and they were not as placidly unconcerned as the great *ba'houda* behemoths that had carried the Fey to Navahele.

"*Esa,*" Fanor soothed in a crooning voice. "*Esa,* my friends." He gestured to the Fey. "Come. Approach slowly and offer them your hands. They will settle once they become accustomed to your scent."

Following Fanor's directions, the Fey mounted the Aquilines. As the snowy chargers leapt into the sky, their flight swift and graceful, Ellysetta glanced over her shoulder towards Grandfather Sentinel.

The lone figure of Galad Hawksheart stood at the base of the giant tree. His voice sounded in her head, deep and rich and melodic, with all the power of a great river carving a path through solid stone. *Remember, cousin, trust in yourself. And when it seems all Paths lead to Shadow, let love, not fear, be your guide.*

The Aquilines flew from Navahele to southern Celieria faster than *ba'houda* or even Fey could have run, carrying their riders across the vast forests of Elvia, over the soaring, snowcapped peaks of the Valorian Mountains and the deep plunge of Braveheart Chasm. They galloped northwest across the sky, following the Valorians to the scythe-shaped curve of Celieria's Tivali Range, where they dove and turned through the ice- and snowbound peaks, startling iridescent pink and blue kolitou from their frozen aeries.

At sunrise, three days after leaving Navahele, they reached the northernmost apex of the Tivali curve. The Aquilines alit on the steep mountain slopes, and Fanor Farsight and the Elves took their leave of the Fey.

"This is where our paths part," Fanor said as they made their farewells. "Aquilines will not fly over open land outside of Elvia."

"*Beylah vo*, Fanor," Rain said. "For everything."

"*Anio*, it is I who thank you," the Elf replied. "What you did at the Lake of Glass . . . you gave me a way to make peace with a sorrow that has pained me all my life. For that, I will always be grateful."

"Will we ever meet again?" Ellysetta asked.

"I hope so." He took her hands and gazed into her eyes—not the deep, piercing stare of an Elf, but the warm gaze of a friend—and a faint smile softened his normally austere features. "And hope is a rare emotion for a race accustomed to knowing what the future holds."

Fanor's Aquiline, Stormsinger, had grown impatient. He snorted and pawed the ground, and his strong white teeth closed around the hem of the Elf's cloak, giving it a hard yank.

"We must go," Fanor said. "Stormsinger and his herd are uncomfortable in the mortal world." With an apologetic look, the Elf stepped back. "Farewell, my friends. May the Light guide you and grant you strength." His green cloak swirled behind him, and the copper leaves of his scale mail chimed as he swung back into the saddle behind Stormsinger's great white wings.

Rain, Ellysetta, and her bloodsworn quintet watched in silence as the Aquilines galloped towards the cliff's edge and leapt into the sky, broad wings spread wide to scoop the air and propel them upwards. Within a few chimes, they were tiny birdlike specks in the sky that dove into a cloud bank and disappeared.

"Secure your steel and gather your magic, my brothers," Rain said. "We have three days to reach Kreppes before the battle Hawksheart predicted begins." He Changed and took to the sky, while the warriors leapt off the cliffs and slid down great flowing currents of Air to the base of the mountain where Ellysetta's *lu'tan* were already waiting. Together, with Rain and Ellysetta flying overhead, they raced north.

Celieria ~ Greatwood ~ Three days later

Pale morning sunlight pushed back the dark of night. Softly, the autumn hues of Celieria's Greatwood Forest emerged from shadowed gloom. Talisa Barrial diSebourne stared up at the lightening sky, and her fingers clenched in tight fists.

She'd never hated dawn until this week, and never hated it more than now.

"*Shei'tani. Teska.*" The voice of the man she loved more than her own life pleaded softly in her ear. "Come away with me. We can go to the Fading Lands."

Talisa closed her eyes as Adrial's hands gripped her shoulders and his body pressed close. The strength of his presence overwhelmed her. Like a sorceror's spell, his voice sapped her resistance. Longing pressed against her will, thinning it to the point of surrender. She could. She could leave with him right now . . . run away. . . . She could just . . . not go back. Adrial would take her to the Fading Lands. They would live out the rest of their lives together in perfect love and happiness . . .

. . . while her family shouldered the burden of her shame, two of Celieria's great Houses became bitter enemies, and the

Eld used their dissension to rip the country apart and conquer it piece by disharmonious piece.

Talisa bit her lip and forced herself to step back away from him when all she wanted to do was lean into his body and let his arms close tight around her. Adrial's simplest touch roused in her more passion, more love, more *need*, than the deepest intimacies she'd shared with Colum, her husband.

Her hand clenched in a fist. "Please, Adrial. Don't do this. You agreed we would part when the army reached Kreppes. We'll be there tonight." That was how she'd justified her adultery. She would love Adrial in secret with every ounce of passion in her soul until they reached Kreppes, and then they would part and she would return to live out her life with Colum.

She'd thought she could gorge herself on Adrial and live on the memories of their time together. But Adrial had showered her with such tenderness and glorious, dazzling ardor, that every touch, every kiss, every word and caress only bound her to him more securely than before. Gods help her, she didn't even want to think of the night when the wife sleeping in Colum's bed would be her instead of some Fey-spun illusion. How was she ever going to find the strength to let him touch her after Adrial?

"I know," Adrial agreed raggedly. "I know I agreed we would part; it's just—" His voice broke. "I didn't think it would be this hard."

She turned to him and her breath caught on a sob. So beautiful. Ah, gods, he was so beautiful. Skin as pale and luminous as crushed pearls, shining with the silvery glow of the Fey. Eyes brown as a fawn's, golden near the edge of the irises, deepening to rich dark chocolate at the center. Those eyes had haunted her dreams as long as she could remember. The pain in them now struck her like a blow.

She laid one hand on his chest and the other on his smooth jaw. "It's just one mortal lifetime, *shei'tan*. Barely more than a chime in a Fey's life. Then I will come to you in the Fading Lands and we will be together forever after."

When he'd finally accepted that she could not leave her husband and realized his continued presence would only cause her greater pain, he'd told her about the Feyreisa's idea. About the sleeping weave that would suspend him in time until she came to awaken him. There was no certainty it would work, but she was desperate enough for even the smallest glimmer of hope that she'd latched onto the idea.

Thirty . . . perhaps fifty years in a loveless marriage. That was a small enough price to pay for a love that would last throughout eternity.

He bowed his head. *"Doreh shabeila de, shei'tani."* So shall it be. He held out a small, capped scroll box. "This is for you, *kem'san*. My last courtship gift to you until we meet again and our souls can at last live as one."

He'd given her many tiny treasures since their first night together. Little gifts that symbolized some aspect of his love for her, his hopes for them. But this . . . She uncapped the scroll box, then extracted and uncurled the small parchment stored inside—this brought tears to her eyes and made her throat clench tight with unshed tears.

"I made it last night while you slept," he said. "The words are my own, written from my heart."

"It's beautiful." He'd written her a poem and carefully executed each aching, mournful word in flowing, calligraphic script embellished with fanciful curls and richly illuminated with tiny images so perfectly drawn and painted they seemed to leap and move on the page. Flowers bloomed, tairen soared, and other magical creatures danced amongst the flowing lines of Adrial's script. And everywhere, tiny sketches of her and him together, walking, embracing, adoring each other.

In the last stanza, separated by the swooping curls of the final words, a somber Adrial reached out for the departing figure of Talisa, who stood, looking back over her shoulder at him, both their faces filled with longing and sorrow.

I die a thousand deaths when you leave.

Her fingers trembled as she caressed the words and traced

the painted lines of his face. He was right: Each parting was an inexpressible agony, as if her heart were being ripped from her chest time and time again.

Her fingertips brushed across the final image on the page, Adrial's hope for them: a shining city of white and gold rising from forested hills, and two tiny figures embracing before they entered the verdant paradise.

"Oh, Adrial." She flung herself into his arms and fused her lips to his, pouring every desperate ounce of the love and longing she felt into her kiss. How was she ever going to live a single day—let alone a whole lifetime—without the taste of him on her lips, the feel of his arms holding her close, the rush of emotion that shot through her when his skin pressed against hers?

"I love you," she sobbed against his lips, pulling back to feather desperate kisses across his face, the hard curve of his jaw, his cheek, his ear. "Dear gods, I love you so much."

His arms wrapped tight around her, and for one last chime, they shared a final, passionate embrace that would have to last a lifetime. When at last she pulled away, she cast a tearful glance at the silent, stone-faced shadow of Adrial's brother, Rowan. "Take care of him for me," she begged. "Keep him safe." And to Adrial, "I will come for you, beloved. No matter how long it takes, no matter how many years I must wait to be free, I will come to you. I swear it."

Unable to bear the agony of their parting a moment longer, she spun away. Her quintet wove invisibility to hide their presence, and they hurried out of the forest towards the shadowy outline of tents that dotted the farmlands just beyond the northern border of Greatwood.

The Great Sun was breaking over the horizon, and soldiers were just beginning to stir as Talisa ducked into the still-dark interior of the tent she shared with Colum.

A cool breeze wafted over her, making her skin prickle. The sound of a match being struck broke the silence, and a dim light flared as the match burst into flame.

Colum was sitting in the corner of the tent, his gray eyes pinned on her, his expression colder than she'd ever seen as he calmly lit the small candle lamp on the camp table beside him.

"Welcome back, my dear," he said. "And how is your lover today?"

Celieria ~ Norban

Rain, Ellysetta, and the *lu'tan* had stopped just south of the woodland hamelet of Norban to rest and eat. They'd been running since before dawn, trying to reach Kreppes by midday. As they rested, Gaelen and the rest of the quintet worked with Ellysetta to improve her battle skills and adjust her aim to fit her own body's reach and height rather than her father's.

At her side, Bel's body went taut and his eyes turned hazy as someone directed a Spirit weave his way. A moment later, he blinked and his eyes turned back to their usual pure, clear cobalt. They were filled with concern like nothing Ellysetta had ever seen before.

"Bel?" she asked, straightening from her throwing crouch, Fey'cha gripped loosely in her hand. "What is it?"

But he had already pivoted on one heel and was marching across the short distance to Rain. A moment later, Rain called, "Fey! Prepare to depart!" and his tone was so clipped and grim, Ellysetta knew something was very, very wrong.

At once, she spoke the word that returned her steel to its sheaths, and ran to his side. All around the small clearing, her *lu'tan* did the same. Within moments, she was soaring over Greatwood Forest on Rain's back while the dark shadow of her Fey warriors raced across the ground below. Only then did she ask, "What is it, Rain?"

With bleak, blunt honesty, he told her. "Adrial's presence has been discovered by Talisa's husband. The Sebournes are calling for his execution."

* * *

Celieria ~ North of Greatwood

"Have you gone mad, Talisa? Have you lost all sense? Do you comprehend even the tiniest fraction of the gravity of your situation?"

Talisa clenched her hands at her waist as her father paced the confines of the king's tent like a caged wolf and railed against her stupidity.

A small *sel'dor* ring had been her downfall. Lord Sebourne, who had been growing increasingly suspicious of the Fey as they neared the borders, had given the ring to his son as a protection against Fey magic. When Colum had caressed what he thought was his sleeping wife, the ring had passed through her shoulder, revealing her to be a Spirit weave.

Her quintet was now bound in *sel'dor* and under heavy guard. Two score King's Guard had ridden into Greatwood in search of Adrial and his brother. Colum had tried to drag Talisa off to his family's estate at Dunbarrow—insisting that only on Sebourne land would he and his family be safe from the threat of Fey retaliation—but her father had put a stop to that by going to the king. She'd been taken out of Colum's custody and caged here, under guard, until Adrial was found and brought to the king for inquisition.

"Da . . . I—"

"No." He cut her off with a slash of his hand. "Don't say anything. Just listen. You are not some farmer's wench who can tumble half the stable lads in her village without harm to any reputation but her own. You are the daughter of the great House Barrial. Wed to the heir of another great House. Third in rank to a princess of Celieria. When you commit adultery, it's a matter of consequence! When you commit adultery with an envoy from another nation, it's a matter of state! And when you compound your adultery with the manipulation of your husband's mind in direct violation of the Fey-Celierian alliance, you turn your lust into a crime punishable by death. Colum and Sebourne have already demanded the heads of vel Arquinas and every warrior involved in his deception. And I can't say I disagree."

All the blood leached from her face. "Da!" She gaped at her father in genuine shock. She couldn't believe her ears. He'd always been a friend of the Fey—always! "How can you say that? *I* made the choice to go with Adrial. I'm the one who betrayed Colum. Adrial's not to blame for what I've done."

Cann bared his teeth in a snarl. "*Is he not?* He brought dishonor to my House and House Sebourne. He lured my daughter from her marriage vows. He used his magic to trick and manipulate mortals incapable of seeing through his illusions. I am not blind to your fault in this, Talisa, but you are a love-drunk twenty-five-year-old mortal. He is an immortal who has walked the earth for gods know how many centuries. He has long been man enough to know the difference between right and wrong and to discipline his passions and avoid the misuse of his magic."

"I'm not some innocent victim, Da, and I won't let you pretend that I am. I went because I *love* him, Da. I've loved him all my life. How can you not understand that?"

"What about your duty? What about honoring your vows? Did you think of anyone besides yourself? Your family? Your brothers? Your country, for the Haven's sake!"

Her spine stiffened. "How dare you accuse me of that? What do you think brought me back?" She flung up her hands in outrage. "If I hadn't honored my vows, I would have run away with Adrial months ago. If not for my *duty*"—she spat the word like a curse—"I never would have married Colum in the first place! I don't love him—I never have and never will. So don't talk to me about duty! If I hadn't wed out of duty to my family, I would have been free when Adrial came! I would have had a chance to be happy. You remember what happiness is, don't you, Da? It's what you had with Mum. That's what I wanted to have. It's all I've ever wanted."

Her father's cheeks went ruddy, and with a muffled curse he spun away and thrust a large hand through his hair. "Flames scorch it," he swore. He cast an agonized look over his shoulder. "Do you think I ever wanted anything less than happiness for you? But some things, once done, can't be undone. Oaths, once given, can't be rescinded. Honor is all we have, Talisa. Without it, we're nothing."

Tears shimmered in his eyes. "Do you think you're the only person ever to be trapped in a loveless marriage? Your mum was the sun, moons, and stars to me. When she died, it was like I'd lost half my soul. Every day I fought just to keep the blade from my own throat. I forced myself to go on because my children deserved a father. Now there's a woman in Celieria City carrying my child in her belly because the Feyreisa spun a weave I couldn't protect myself against. And though I don't love her and never shall, we wed by proxy two days ago so my child would have my name and all the protection that goes with it. And I will honor her as my wife, and be faithful to my oath, even though I'll never love her. And I will keep the blade from my throat still, every day, because she deserves a husband and the child we made deserves a father. Honor is what makes us worthy of love, Tallie. In that, I agree with the Fey. And every day I live with honor is a day I honor your mother and the love we shared."

Talisa's face crumpled and the tears she'd been battling all morning spilled over. "Oh, Da."

At the sight of her tears, all of her father's anger melted. The hard-eyed stranger disappeared and he became once more the warm, loving father she'd always turned to in times of trouble. His arms opened, and she rushed into them.

"Oh, Da, what am I going to do?"

He tilted his head against hers. "I don't know, Tallie. I just don't know."

A sound at the entrance of the tent made them turn. The tent flaps parted and Luce, one of Talisa's brothers, ducked inside. "They've found vel Arquinas and his brother. The King's Guard are bringing them in now."

"Adrial vel Arquinas, you stand accused of violating the king's justice, manipulating mortal minds by magic, violating the Fey-Celierian treaty, adultery against a lord of the realm, conspiracy to commit adultery against a lord of the realm, spying upon a lord of the realm by means of magic, defrauding a lord of the realm by means of magic, controlling the actions of a lord of the realm by means of magic, unlawful theft by means of magic. . . ."

The litany of the charges against Adrial continued on for nearly three chimes. In their determination to see him executed, the Sebournes had charged him, his brother, and Talisa's quintet with every possible crime and variation of a crime they could think of.

At Talisa's urging, her father had done everything he could to delay the inquisition. The Feyreisen and his mate were on their way, and he had insisted that the judgment of Adrial wait until the Feyreisa arrived to Truthspeak him. Lord Sebourne flew into a rage at the mere suggestion.

"Out of the question, Sire!" Colum's father railed. "How can we possibly trust anything they say ever again? The Tairen Soul had to have known vel Arquinas never left Celieria. He was in collusion with Talisa's lover to steal my son's wife—in direct violation of your earlier judgment! There's no other credible explanation! The Fey have been lying to you and manipulating you all along, Sire!"

In a bleak, toneless voice, the king had agreed with Lord Sebourne. "Given the circumstances, Lord Sebourne is right. Vel Arquinas will hear the charges against him and have an opportunity to make a response. We will not wait for the Feyreisa or any other *shei'dalin* of the Fey."

Now Talisa waited at her father's side as Adrial, Rowan, and her quintet stood before the king to face their accusers.

At Talisa's left, Colum and his father watched the proceedings with curled lips and smug satisfaction.

Adrial held his head proudly erect, never taking his eyes from her as the charges were read. And though he was bound in so much *sel'dor* she could almost feel it burning her own skin, still he spoke to her in Spirit.

«*Ke vo san, shei'tani. Throughout this life and every life that follows, I shall always love you. Forgive me for causing you such pain. I should have put your happiness before my own, and I did not.*»

The sorrowful acceptance in his Spirit voice should have warned her, but it still came as a shock when the king's steward finished reading the charges, and Adrial turned to the king, his clear voice ringing out as he said, "I do confess to all charges against me and ask that all similar charges against my brother and the warriors of my *shei'tani's* quintet be dismissed. I alone am responsible for every Celierian law that was broken."

King Dorian sat up, and his brows drew together. "You confess? Just like that?"

"I am Fey, Your Majesty. Despite my recent actions, I am a warrior of honor. I confess that I used magic to manipulate the thoughts, actions, and memories of Colum diSebourne. He is wed by Celierian custom to my *shei'tani*, my soul's other half. By your laws, she belongs to him, but her soul was created by the gods to complete my own, as mine was created to complete hers. After Your Majesty's judgment this summer, I believed that Celieria's refusal to recognize the will of the gods justified the breaking of your mortal laws. I was wrong."

Now he turned his gaze back to Talisa, and continued in a softer, more penitent tone. "My actions have subjected my mate to shame and condemnation and thus I have dishonored myself. I have brought shame to my line, my *shei'tani*, my king, and my brother Fey."

Her vision blurred as tears filled her eyes. «*Adrial . . . no. Oh, no, beloved, you haven't shamed me. What I did, I did by my own choice, because I loved you and I always will.*»

His lips trembled before he clamped them together and turned his attention swiftly back to the king. "King Dorian of Celieria, this Fey does most humbly beg your forgiveness. He has acted without honor and proven himself unworthy of the great gift the gods bestowed upon him."

«*Adrial!*»

King Dorian leaned forward. "Ser vel Arquinas, you understand what you're saying? You understand that the price of your transgressions is death?"

Adrial's jaw clenched. "This Fey understands the penalty Celierian law demands and he accepts it. This Fey's only request is that he be afforded the opportunity to expunge the stain upon his honor. If Your Majesty will permit it, this Fey requests the right to *sheisan'dahlein*, the honor death."

"What? Adrial, no!" Talisa surged forward, but her father caught her and held her back. "No! You can't! You can't!" «*Shei'tan, you can't do this! Run! Go back to the Fading Lands. Wait for me, as we agreed. I can bear anything if I know you are alive and that one day I will be with you again.*» Tears filled her eyes and spilled down her cheeks.

He didn't look at her, but a gentle, sweet breeze of Air caressed her face. «*It's too late for that, shei'tani. This is the only way now. We will be together again, I promise you. But not in this life. May I prove more worthy in the next.*»

«*You're worthy now! Please don't do this. The Feyreisen and Feyreisa are coming. Wait for them. Perhaps they can find some other solution. Adrial!*»

"Your Majesty can't be considering it?" Colum huffed when King Dorian did not immediately reply. "This jaffing wife thief deserves nothing more than a common criminal's execution. To be hanged by the neck until dead, his body left for the carrion birds to feast upon."

"As do the other criminals who aided him!" his father agreed. "Including the Tairen Soul, who knew this was going on and turned a blind eye to it!"

Dorian flashed a hot look at father and son. "And how

many immortal lives will it take to assuage bruised Sebourne pride? Your son was cuckolded. The Fey-Celierian treaty was broken, but for no purpose more calamitous than that. I will not demand the execution of a Fey king because your son's wife jaffed another man. You are mad to even suggest it."

"But—"

"Be silent." Dorian rose to his feet. "Adrial vel Arquinas, you have been charged and have confessed to crimes punishable by death. You have agreed to accept the king's justice."

Adrial gave a curt nod. Behind him, his brother, Rowan, stood like a warrior carved from stone, unmoving, unflinching, his face pale as death but otherwise wiped clean of all expression.

"Very well then." The king drew a breath. "Adrial vel Arquinas, as you have confessed to all abuses of magic and crimes charged against you and claimed sole responsibility for the same, I do hereby find you guilty of the charges in their entirety. As punishment for all crimes committed by you and on your behalf, I sentence you to death. In deference to the centuries of alliance and kinship between our two nations, I commute the sentence of death by hanging to *sheisan'dahlein*, the Fey honor death, and order that it shall be be carried out within the bell. You may use that time to say your good-byes and make your peace. May the gods have mercy on your soul."

As King Dorian turned and walked towards his tent, Talisa broke into tortured sobs. She would have fallen to her knees except for the strong hands of her father and brother Luce holding her up.

"Adrial . . . Adrial . . ." Weeping, she stumbled towards him and fell into his arms.

Colum stepped towards her, an ugly look on his face, but Luce bared his teeth. "Back off, diSebourne. You've done more than enough for one day."

Colum feigned affront. "Me? I am the injured party here!"

"If that were true, you'd be the one crying like your heart was being ripped from your chest." Luce stood back and swept a cold gaze over his sister's husband. "You're a selfish, self-serving *rultshart*, and I'm sorry we ever thought any better of you. You knew she didn't love you. If you'd loved her even the least little bit, you would have let her go when the Fey came. This is all your fault. Because you're a greedy, grasping, controlling little turd pretending to be a man."

"Luce!" Cann snapped. "That's enough." To Colum he said, "But Luce is right: You've done enough for one day. So now I suggest you and your father get the Hells out and leave Talisa in peace to share this last bell with the man she loves." His other two sons, Parsis and Severn, joined Luce and Cann to form a barrier between Talisa and the Sebournes.

Colum snarled and spat a foul curse, but the two of them were no match for four Barrials, and they knew it. Together, puffed up with arrogance and self-righteous indignation, Lord Sebourne and his son stalked away.

"Adrial, I love you. I love you so much." Talisa cupped his beloved face in her hands and showered him with tears and kisses. "I don't want to live without you. I can't bear to lose you. Not like this."

"Shh." Adrial smiled into her eyes. His heart was breaking. Each tear that spilled from her eyes burned his soul the way the *sel'dor* chains burned his flesh. He'd done this to her. He'd brought this sorrow to her door. Because in his own way, he was as selfish as diSebourne. Both of them fighting over her like dogs over a bone. "*Sieks'ta, shei'tani.* I did not do right by you in this life, but I swear to you, I will be everything you deserve in the next." He took her hand and carried it to his lips. "This isn't the end, *shei'tani.* No matter how many years or lifetimes it takes, I will find you again. And we will be happy. You have my oath on it."

Weeping, she curled in his lap and laid her head on his shoulder. "Tell me what it will be like, *shei'tan,* when we're together."

He pressed his face to her hair and closed his eyes as his

own tears fell. His throat was too tight to speak, so he wove Spirit, not just words but pictures, bringing the images from his last courtship gift to life. Dharsa in full bloom, and the two of them, together, forever. For each chime of the next bell, he spun his hopes for them, his dreams of their future, their love, the children they would have in another lifetime when joy, bright as sunlight, would suffuse their united souls.

And when they came for him, though she wept and clung to him until they pulled him away, the first of their bond threads had formed, and light like the warmth of a thousand suns shone on both their souls.

They gathered outside King Dorian's tent.

Her tearstained face proudly unveiled, her spine straight and unyielding, Talisa stood at her father's side. It would kill a part of her soul to watch Adrial's death, but since she could not stop it, she wanted the last thing he saw to be her face, and the last thing he felt to be her love.

A shadow moved across the corner of her eye and she glanced to her right to find Colum standing there. "We will get through this, Talisa. It is hard for me to forgive you your transgressions, but you are my wife, and I am determined we will build a good life together."

She drew a breath, her hands curling tight together. "Heir to a great House you may be, but you are a despicable *rultshart*, Colum diSebourne. And you're a fool if you think you'll ever be anything to me but the monster who killed the man I love. I will give you nothing—not a touch, not a smile, not a kind word." She looked at him then, to make sure he saw the utter loathing in her eyes. "Your name is a curse to me."

His brows drew together in a dark scowl. "You dare—"

He started to grab her, but she swiftly sidestepped his grip and bared her teeth in a snarl every bit as dangerous as her father's. "Lay a finger on me, and I'll kill you myself." And the pure hatred that vibrated in her voice was enough to make him stop in shock.

She swept her skirts away and moved to the other side of her father and brothers.

Silence fell over the gathering as King Dorian emerged from his tent. He took his place between Colum and Talisa's father, then nodded, and the king's guard led Rowan and the other Fey—still shackled—to one side of the circle, where they stood, under guard. A moment later, four more guards marched Adrial to the center of the circle.

He'd changed his black leathers for red. His dark hair hung loose about his shoulders and his face was pale but calm, almost serene. *Sel'dor* shackles still encased his wrists and ankles.

She forced her lips into a trembling smile. *«I am here, shei'tan. I will always be here.»*

He didn't smile back, but his love poured over her in waves, and the sweet promises he'd spun for her in Spirit filled her mind once more. *«Ver reisa ku'chae, Talisa. Kem surah shei'tani. In this life and every life to come.»*

The king's drummers began to play as one of the king's guard stepped forward in between Colum and the king, holding one of Adrial's Fey'cha harnesses draped across his two hands. A second guard withdrew one of the red Fey'cha, but before he could carry it across the short distance to Adrial, a roar rumbled through the sky like thunder.

They all glanced up to see the Tairen Soul soaring in the skies to the south. From this distance, which must have been twenty or thirty miles at the very least, he looked more like a great bird than a tairen. He winged with purpose across the sky, heading straight for the encampment.

"Adrial! The Tairen Soul is here!" Hope bloomed in Talisa's breast. If anyone in Celieria could stop this travesty of justice, it was the Fey king and his mate.

Colum must have had the same thought, because while all eyes were on the Tairen Soul, he lunged forward, snatching one of the remaining red Fey'cha from the harness held by the guard in front of him and pulling back his arm to throw it.

Talisa didn't think. She just leapt forward, calling a warning to her truemate. "Adrial! Watch out!" And she threw her body between Adrial and Colum.

The dagger struck her between the shoulders. It didn't hurt much. Just a tiny explosion of pain. A single searing stab, gone almost in an instant. But the blow robbed her of breath and strength, and she fell forward into Adrial's arms.

"Adrial." She blinked in dazed surprise. "Adrial, I . . ." Her thoughts tangled. Her vision began to blur, and her words slurred. "Adri . . . al . . ."

The last thing she saw was his beloved face, and the last thing she felt was his love, tinged by desperate horror as tairen venom raced through her veins and death dimmed her vision.

Adrial clutched Talisa's body to his chest, her chestnut hair spilling over his arms. "Talisa . . . *shei'tani* . . . *nei* . . . *nei*. *Nei va*. Don't go! *Ster eva ku*. Stay with me. *Teska. Teska*." His shoulders quaked with racking sobs and tears poured freely down his face as her eyes glazed over. Her limbs gave a final, weak twitch, then went limp. "Ah, *nei, nei. Teska sallan. Ku'ruveli, shei'tani*. Come back to me." He knew the instant her soul slipped free of her slender body. Her passing ripped him apart from the inside out, leaving a gaping hole where her brightness had taken root.

He flung back his head and howled as the agony of her death shredded his soul.

In the skies over Celieria, Adrial's pain seared Ellysetta's empathic senses like a bolt of lightning. Her fingers clenched around the pommel of the saddle and her body shuddered with the force of his devastation. Then another emotion chased after the first, every bit as jolting, and infinitely more alarming.

«*Rain!*» She leaned forward, grasping thick handfuls of the fur at his neck in her urgency. «*Hurry. Hurry!*»

Without a word, Rain put on a burst of magic-powered speed, and his tairen form raced across the sky, leaving the *lu'tan* far behind.

Adrial's head snapped down. His eyes flashed open, glaring from beneath dark brows, pinning Colum diSebourne with the deadly force of the Rage in his blazing gaze. Setting Talisa's body on the ground, he rose to his feet. White sparks of Air whirled around him, flashing with red sparks of Fire. Green Earth flowed out from his body like wild, ravenous tendrils of some carnivorous plant. They dove into the soil, and the ground began to tremble and shake. The wind began to howl and spin, gathering force and speed.

Adrial vel Arquinas was a master of Air and Earth, and in his Rage, not even the *sel'dor* shackles that bound him could suppress his great magic.

"Adrial!" Rowan called his brother in desperation. He tried to summon his own command of Fire and Earth, hoping to counteract Adrial's weaves, but without the Rage to feed his power, the *sel'dor* shackles blunted his efforts.

Fearful for the king's life, archers fired arrows at Adrial, but the cyclones whirling about him snatched the arrows in mid-flight and tossed them to the ground like matchsticks. His shining Fey skin grew brighter and brighter as he drew deep from the source of his power, gathering the magic, absorbing the energy into his own flesh, and holding it there until he glowed star-bright and looked more like an avenging Light Warrior of Adelis than a Fey.

The ground trembled, and everyone but Adrial stumbled and nearly fell. Weaves of green Earth erupted like vines from the grass at Colum's feet, twining up his legs, imprisoning him in curling shackles of solid stone. The vortexes spinning around Adrial expanded and joined together, forming a single, large cyclone of air that encompassed Adrial and diSebourne, isolating them in the center of a whirlwind.

"She was returning to you." Magic vibrated in Adrial's

voice, each word filled with palpable energy that reverberated like the deep tolling of a giant bell. "We had agreed I would go back to the Fading Lands and she would live out her life with you. But you would not even give us that. You would rather shatter her heart and destroy her hope than live knowing that any part of her belonged to another."

Adrial raised his shackled hands. His palms, like his eyes, now radiated blinding light. Colum began to choke and gasp for air. His eyes bulged. The skin at his temples rippled and his head tossed from side to side. His mouth opened in a wordless, gurgling scream, and his body swelled like a grotesque balloon.

"For your crimes against my *shei'tani*, mortal, I sentence you to death. May your soul rot forever in the Seven Hells."

Adrial brought his hands together in a thunderous clap. Magic shot from his fingertips like a geyser of fiery light, shooting not up into the sky but horizontally across the distance and into Colum's chest. DiSebourne's body lit up like a candleshade.

For one instant, Talisa's husband stood there, bulging eyes rolling back in his head, body convulsing in violent seizures. But then Adrial's magic ignited the flammable gases he'd expanded inside Colum's body, and diSebourne exploded in a fiery blast of light and magic.

When the blast faded, diSebourne was gone, the vortex around them had died, and Adrial fell heavily to his knees. The captain of the king's guard cried out a command, and a volley of arrows darkened the sky. Adrial's body jerked as dozens of the missiles pierced his chest and back, but the arrows only finished the job Talisa's death had already begun.

"*Shei'tani*," he breathed on the last gasp of air in his lungs. His body toppled across hers and he gave himself willingly to the waiting darkness of the Well.

With his *shei'tani's* body in his arms and her name emblazoned on his soul forever, Adrial vel Arquinas passed through the Veil and was no more.

* * *

The Fey sang bittersweet songs of lost love and second chances and the promise of future joy as they prepared to send the bodies of their brother Adrial and his *shei'tani* back to the elements.

Once Rain had shared Hawksheart's warning that the battle would begin on the morrow, the king and his army had broken camp and continued their northward trek. A bitter Lord Sebourne had gathered his men and ridden off towards Moreland. Only Cannevar Barrial and his sons remained with the Fey to tend the bodies of Adrial and Talisa.

They garbed the pair in snowy white as a symbol of their ascent into the Light and laid the couple side by side on a crystal bier fashioned by the Earth masters. When all the songs were sung, and Cannevar and his sons had said their last good-byes, the Fey gathered around the truemates' bier and summoned a dense weave of magic that settled over the bodies like a blanket of light. The weave flared bright and when it faded, nothing remained of Adrial and Talisa except a single, sparkling cabochon crystal. Adrial's *sorreisu kiyr*.

"Three lives needlessly lost." Anger mixed with the terrible grief in Ellysetta's heart. Her hands clenched in fists at her sides. "I failed them. I should have been able to save them."

Standing beside her, Rain shook his head. "It was too late, *shei'tani*. There was nothing you could have done. Nothing anyone could have done. They had already passed beyond the Veil."

"But—"

"*Nei.* No buts." He brushed silencing fingers across her lips. "Not all battles can be won. Not all lives can be saved. And no matter how we wish it, not all songs end in joy."

She frowned and tilted her head back to look up at him. "Will ours?"

"I pray so." Somber acceptance darkened his eyes, and he stroked her cheek in a light caress. "But even if we do not find joy in this lifetime, we will be born again to love once more. That much, I believe without question. In this lifetime, or the next, or even the lifetime after that, our souls will be one . . . as will Adrial's and Talisa's."

She nodded and leaned her head against his shoulder, letting the tumultuous roil of anger and grief drain from her. In its wake bloomed a small bud of infant hope that no matter what happened in this life, joy would ultimately be theirs, as it would for Adrial and Talisa.

"Come, my friends," Rain said a few chimes later. "When the battle begins, King Dorian will need us." Together, the Barrials and the Fey left the scene of their tragic loss and travelled the remaining distance to Kreppes.

By the time they reached the fortified stone keep perched on a mountain overlooking the Heras River, night had fallen. As the quiet whoosh of Rain's wings carried them forward, Ellysetta swept her gaze across the darkened horizon. A small light, noticeable for its surprising brightness, sparkled low on the horizon. The sight made her heart skip a beat.

Erimea—or as the Celierians called her, Selena, Shadow's Light—was shining in the sky over Eld.

Celierian Language / Terms

bell—hour

chime—minute

dorn—a furry, round somnolent rodent. Eaten in stews. A "soggy *dorn*" is an idiom for someone who is spoiling someone else's fun. A party pooper.

Lord Adelis—god of light. While Celierians worship a pantheon of gods and goddesses (thirteen in all), The Church of Light worships Adelis, Lord of Light, above all others. He is considered the supreme god, with dominion over the other twelve.

Lord Seledorn—god of darkness, Lord of Shadows.

rultshart—a vile, smelly, boarlike animal. The term is often used as an insult.

Elden Language / Terms

Primage—master mage

Sulimage—journeyman mage

umagi—a mage-claimed individual, subordinate to the will of his/her master.

Fey Language / Terms

In Feyan, apostrophes are used in the following ways:

• Meaning "of." *Kem'falla*…my lady, literally "lady of mine." *E'tani*, literally "mate of the heart." *Shei'tani*, literally "mate of the truth/soul."

• In lieu of hyphen, and to indicate emphasis for words combined of multiple root words.

• Sometimes used to replace missing letters/vowels. *Ni v'al'ta!* (literally *Ni ve al'ta.*)

aiyah—yes

ajiana—sweet one

Azrahn—common name of Azreisenahn, the soul magic

bas'ka—all right

beylah vo—thank you (literally "thanks to you")

bote cha!—blades ready! (weapons at the ready!)

Cha Baruk—Dance of Knives

cha'kor—literal translation is five knives. Fey word for "quintet."

chadin—little knife; literally "small fang"; a student in the Dance of Knives. Each student is paired with a mentor who guides their progress through four hundred years of training in the school. It is an apprenticeship of sorts, though many teachers will contribute to the actual education.

chakai—First Knife or First Blade. Champion.

chatok—Big Knife (mentor, leader, also teacher in the dance of knives.)

chatokkai—First General (leader of all Fey armies, 2nd in command to the Tairen Soul). Belliard vel Jelani is the *chatokkai* of the Fading Lands

chervil—a Fey expletive. Bastard, as in, "You smug *chervil*."

dahl'reisen—Literally "lost soul." Name given to unmated Fey warriors who are banished from the Fading Lands. They either seek *sheisan'dahlein* or serve as mercenaries/assassins to mortal races.

deskor—bad

doreh shabeila de—so be it (so shall it be)

e'tan—beloved / husband / mate (of the heart, not the truemate of the soul)

e'tani—beloved / wife / mate (of the heart, not the truemate of the soul)

e'tanitsa—a chosen bond of the heart, not a truemate bond

faer—magic

falla—lady

Felah Baruk—Dance of Joy

Fey'cha—a Fey throwing dagger. Fey'cha have either black handles or red handles. Red Fey'cha are deadly poison. Fey warriors carry dozens of each kind of Fey'cha in leather straps crisscrossed across their chests.

Feyreisa—Tairen Soul's mate; Queen

Feyreisen—Tairen Soul; King

jaffed—a Fey expletive. Used as in, "We'd be jaffed if that happened."

jita'nos—sister's son

kabei—good

ke vo san—I love you

kem'falla—my lady

kem'san—my love/ my heart

krekk—a Fey expletive

ku'shalah aiyah to nei—bid me yes or no

las—peace, hush, calm

liss—light

lute—red (also blood)

Massan—the council of five powerful Fey statesmen who oversee the domestic governance of the Fading Lands. They do not convene without the *Shei'dalin* and the Feyreisen except in times of extreme need.

Mei felani. Bei santi. Nehtah, bas desrali—Live well, love deep. Tomorrow, we (will) die.

meicha—a curving, scimitarlike blade. Each fey warrior carries two *meicha*, one at each hip.

miora felah ti'Feyreisan—joy to the Feyreisa (literally "Joyful life to the Feyreisa")

nei—no

parei—stop

sel'dor—literally "black pain." A rare black metal that painfully disrupts Fey magic.

selkahr—black crystals used by Mages. Made from Azrahn-corrupted Tairen's Eye crystal.

setah!—enough!

seyani—a Fey warrior's longsword. Each Fey warrior carries two *seyani* swords strapped to his back.

sha vel'mei—you're welcome

shei'dalin—Fey healer and Truthspeaker; capped when referring to their leader.

sheisan'dahlein—Fey honor death. Ceremonial suicide for the good of the Fey.

shei'tan—beloved / husband / truemate

shei'tani—beloved / wife / truemate

shei'tanitsa—the truemate bond

sieks'ta—I have shame (I'm sorry; I beg your pardon)

sorreisu kiyr—Soul Quest crystal

Spirit—lavender color, the mystic magic of consciousness, thought, and illusion

Tairen—flying catlike creatures that live in the Fading Lands. The Fey are the Tairenfolk, magical because of their close kinship with the Tairen.

Tairen Soul—also known as Feyreisen; they are rare Fey who can transform into tairen. Masters of all five Fey magics, they are feared and revered for their power. The oldest Tairen Soul becomes the Feyreisen, the Fey King.

teska—please

Ver reisa ku'chae. Kem surah, shei'tani—Your soul calls out. Mine answers, beloved.

Naming Syntax

Truemated men go from vel to v'En. Mated men go from vel to vel'En.

Truemated women go from vol to v'En. Mated women go from vol to vol'En.

For example:

• Marissya and Dax v'En Solande are truemates.

• Rain vel'En Daris and Sariel vol'En Daris were mates (*e'tanitsa* mates).

THE BATTLE SYLPH

Welcome to his world.

(CHECK OUT A SAMPLE:
www.ljmcdonald.ca/Battle_preview.html.com)